9/88

F
VAN   Van Wormer, Laura,
        1955-

        Riverside Drive
                081344

$18.95

DATE			

RIVERSIDE DRIVE

RIVERSIDE DRIVE

LAURA VAN WORMER

Doubleday

NEW YORK   LONDON   TORONTO   SYDNEY

_18.95_

Published by Doubleday, a division of Bantam Doubleday Dell Publishing Group, Inc., 666 Fifth Avenue, New York, New York 10103.

Doubleday and the portrayal of an anchor with a dolphin are trademarks of Doubleday, a division of Bantam Doubleday Dell Publishing Group, Inc.

_89 B17286_

Library of Congress Cataloging-in-Publication Data
Van Wormer, Laura, 1955–
Riverside Drive.
I. Title.
PS3572.A42285R58   1988   813'.54   87-36413
ISBN 0-385-24467-3

Copyright © 1988 by Laura Van Wormer

BG

In Memory of My Mother
Margaret Garner Van Wormer

And for My Father
Benjamin Francis Van Wormer

And My "New" Mother of 18 Years
Marjorie Law Ault Van Wormer

An Acknowledgment

I would still be talking rather than writing had it not been for two extraordinary individuals named Loretta Barrett and Ann Douglas. Their wisdom, generosity and powers of reassurance are awe-inspiring. Their spirit is too. I can only wonder at my good fortune for having met them in this life and say, from the bottom of my heart, thank you for all you have taught me.

PART I

1

THE COCHRANS HAVE A PARTY

Cassy Cochran was upset.

Michael, her husband, had gone to pick up ice four hours ago and hadn't been seen since; Henry, her son, was supposed to be back from Shea Stadium but wasn't; and Rosanne, the cleaning woman, was currently threatening the new bartender in the kitchen with deportation proceedings if he didn't see her way of doing things.

Not a terrific beginning for a party that Cassy absolutely did not want to have.

"Hey, Mrs. C?" It was Rosanne, standing in the doorway to the living room.

Cassy turned.

"If Mr. C comes back, he's gonna be pretty upset about how this guy's settin' up the bar. Could you—" She frowned suddenly and leaned her head back into the kitchen. "What?" she said. "Well, it's about time." Rosanne swung back around the doorway, waving her hand. "Never mind, Mrs. C, Mr. Moscow here suddenly understands English."

Cassy smiled, shaking her head slightly, and then surveyed the living room. It was a very large, very airy room that, in truth, almost anything would look marvelous in. And Cassy's taste for antiques (or "early attic," as Michael described her preference) was especially fitting, seeing as every floorboard in the apartment creaked. But then, the apartment was really much more like a house, a big old country farmhouse, only with high ceilings. And windows. The three largest rooms—the living room, the master bedroom and Henry's room—all had huge windows facing out on the Hudson River.

The windows had been washed this week. Before, shrouded in a misty gray, the view from the twelfth floor had been eerily reminiscent of London on what Henry called a Sherlock Holmes kind of day. But no, this was New York; and the winter's soot had all been washed away and the late afternoon April sun, setting across the river in New Jersey, was, at this moment, flooding the living room with gentle light.

For a woman from the Midwest, the view from the Cochrans' apartment never failed to slightly astonish Cassy. This was New York City? That steely, horrid, ugly place that her mother had warned her about? No, no . . . Mother had been wrong. Hmmm. Mother had been right about many things, but no, not about New York. Not here. Not the place the Cochrans had made their home.

Sometimes the view made Cassy long to cry. The feeling—whatever it was —would start deep in her chest, slowly rise to her throat and then catch there, hurting her, Cassy unable to bring it up or to press it back down from where it had come. She was feeling that now, holding onto the sash of the middle window, looking out, her forehead resting against the glass.

The Cochrans lived at 162 Riverside Drive, on the north corner of 88th Street. Looking down from the window, Cassy's eyes crossed over the Drive to the promenade that marked the edge of Riverside Park. The promenade was arbored by maple, oak and elm trees, underneath which, across from the Cochrans', were a line of cannons from the Revolutionary War, still aimed out toward unseen enemy ships. To the right, up a block, was the gigantic stone terrace around the Soldiers' and Sailors' Monument, a circular, pillared tower patterned after the monument of Lysicrates in Athens. But this part of Riverside Drive was built on a major bluff, and it was beneath it that lay the heart of the park's glory.

Acre upon acre of the park was coming alive under the touch of spring, the trees bursting with new leaves, the dogwoods and magnolias flowering their most precious best. From here, too, Cassy could look down and see the community garden; in a month it would be one long sea of flowers, flowing down through a valley of green.

Traveling down the slope of the park, Cassy's eyes, out of habit, skipped over the West Side Highway and down to the walkway by the river's edge. It was green there, too. And then, down there, the Hudson River. Lord, she was beautiful.

It was the river that always played with Cassy's heart. There were days when Cassy looked out and thought to herself, *How does she know?* She would be as dark and gray and cold as Cassy felt inside. But then there were those days when the river was as blue and as dazzling as Cassy's own eyes were. Oh, how awful it was on those days when Cassy's heart was cold and dark, and the river was so beautiful. Like now. *How does she do it?* Cassy wondered. The river had all of these crazy New Yorkers on one side of her, and all of these crazy New Jerseyites on the other, forever throwing rocks and trash at her, dumping things in her, and, sometimes, even throwing themselves into her in an effort to get this thing called life over with. And yet . . . her tides continued to ebb and flow, and the winds continued to blow across her, and her rhythms of regeneration went on, pulling, pulling downward, her glorious expanse gracing the urban landscape, pulling, pulling downward, spending herself, finally, totally, into the relentless mouth of New York Harbor.

Cassy sighed.

"You okay?"

Cassy pressed the bridge of her nose for a moment and then turned around. "I'm fine," she said. And then she smiled at Rosanne. And then she laughed.

"What?" Rosanne said.

"Well," Cassy began, pausing, touching at her earring.

Rosanne's eyes narrowed slightly.

Cassy glanced at her watch and then back to Rosanne. Back to the "Cooperstown Baseball Hall of Fame" bandanna that was slipping down over Rosanne's eyes. Back to Rosanne's blue denim shirt, whose shirttail was hanging down to her knees. Back to her jeans, whose hem lay in folds around the top of her Adidases. Back to thin little Rosanne, all five feet of her, standing there, just waiting for Cassy to say it.

Cassy moved forward toward her. "It's time for you to change," she said, smiling.

Rosanne looked to the ceiling. "Here we go," she said. "Ya know, Mrs.

C," she continued, as Cassy took her by the elbow and steered her toward the kitchen, "you never said nothin' about me havin' to play dress-up."

They were in the kitchen now, and Cassy stopped, looking back at Rosanne. She smiled, yanked the bandanna down over Rosanne's eyes and turned to the bartender. "Have everything you need, Ivor?"

"Yes, Madame Coch-ah-ren," he replied, bowing slightly.

"Good," she said, pulling Rosanne along through the kitchen to the back hall. Rosanne scooped up her bag from the counter along the way.

"And I never said I was a caterer," Rosanne reminded her.

"Right," Cassy said.

"So I don't know why you get so picky about what I wear—it's not as if you like any of these guys."

They were in the master bedroom now, and Cassy headed toward her closet. "I think you're going to like it," she said, opening the doors.

"Mrs. C," Rosanne said, throwing her bag on the bed, "ya know, if you'd just tell me, I'd bring one of the ones you already got me."

"Well, I was in Macy's and there it was, just hanging there, calling, 'Rosanne, Rosanne, I was made for Rosanne.' "

Rosanne sighed, pulled off her bandanna and shook out her hair. Cassy turned around, holding a pretty blue and black print dress. "Hair," she said, "good Lord, Rosanne, you have hair."

"Come on, Mrs. C," Rosanne said, turning away.

Cassy walked over and laid the dress out on the bed. She looked at Rosanne a moment and then smiled, gently. "Tell me the truth—do you really hate doing this?"

Rosanne shrugged and proceeded to pull some things out of her bag: a slip, some panty hose and a pair of shoes.

The doorbell rang.

"Uh-oh," Cassy said, looking at her watch, "somebody's here already. No, let Ivor get it, Rosanne. You go ahead and get changed."

Rosanne shrugged again and started undoing the buttons of her shirt while Cassy walked back to stand in front of the closet door mirror. She scanned it. A few wisps of blond hair were already falling out of the clip. But her eyes were still blue. Her nose was still perfect. Her mouth still had lipstick. Body was still tall and slim. Bracelets, check. Earrings, check.

Cassy was still beautiful. Cassy was still forty-one. She would not stand closer to the mirror than she was; she would not care to see the reminders of her age showing around her eyes, mouth and neck.

"Don't know how good Mr. Moscow's gonna be at greetin' guests," Rosanne said.

"Hmmm," Cassy said, raising her chin slightly, still looking at herself in the mirror.

"And you don't want to scare him right off the bat," Rosanne continued. Cassy laughed.

"They said he was the last bartender they'd send us," she reminded her.

"Oh, Lord, that's right." Cassy closed the closet door and sailed out of the bedroom, down the hall and through the kitchen to the front hall, where she found Ivor standing in front of the open door. "Who is it, Ivor?" When he gave her a vacant look, she stepped forward to peer around his shoulder. "Oh, Amos. Hi."

"Hi," Amos Franklin said. Both Ivor's and Cassy's eyes were fixed on the stuffed head of an unidentifiable animal that was snarling on top of Amos' head.

"It's okay, Ivor," Cassy said, patting the arm with which Ivor was blocking the door.

Ivor did not seem convinced.

"He's a guest," Cassy told him. "We're supposed to let him in." Ivor's eyes shifted to her. She nodded, smiling encouragement. He took one more look out the door, frowned, and slipped behind Cassy to return to the kitchen. "Sorry about that," Cassy said, waving Amos in. "I have no idea what I've done to earn his protection.

"Any man would want to protect you," Amos whispered.

Here we go, Cassy thought. Amos was forever whispering little things like that—that is, when his wife wasn't around. "Nice hat," she said, snarling fangs sweeping in past her eyes.

"Michael gave it to me for my birthday," Amos said. He reached up, groped around, and patted the animal on the nose. "I don't think it's real, though."

Cassy led Amos into the living room, explaining that Michael was out getting some ice.

"Good," Amos said, sitting on the couch and patting the seat next to him, "it will give me a chance to talk to you."

Cassy sat down in one of the chairs.

"You're beautiful."

"What?"

"You're beautiful," Amos repeated.

"Ivor!" Cassy called out. He was there like a shot. "Ivor," Cassy directed, "ask Mr. Franklin what he would like to drink."

Ivor stared at him.

"Scotch on the rocks," Amos said.

Ivor moved over to Cassy. Bowing, "Madame?"

"A Perrier with lime, please. Thank you, Ivor."

Ivor took one more look at Amos and departed.

"So, Amos, tell me how you are."

Amos was not good. As the head writer for Michael's newsroom at WWKK, he never made a secret of his keen dislike for Michael Cochran. After a mini-lecture on the abuse and misuse of Amos Franklin at work, he would invariably end up with a pitch for Cassy to hire him at her station, WST. Cassy's mind wandered, and as Amos progressed with his story about how "a certain egomaniac who will go unnamed" took credit for a job done by "a certain unsung hero who will go unnamed", Cassy—not for the first time—thought about Michael's parties.

Once a month Cassy's husband wanted to have a party. Cassy had never, ever wanted any of these parties, but it wasn't because she was antisocial. It was because Michael had this thing about only inviting people who seemed to despise him. And too, they—these people who despised Michael—were all professionally dependent on him. And so, whether it was Amos, or a technical director, or a character generator operator, they all came to Michael's parties and drank with him and laughed with him and despised him. If Cassy made the mistake of trying to talk Michael out of one of these parties he would go ahead and invite the people anyway and then spring it on her the morning of the day it was being held. This was not the case this Sunday evening, however; this party had been announced Friday night. ("Cocktails." "For how many?" "Ten, fifty maybe.")

"Have you met the Kansas Kitten yet?" Amos was asking her, taking his drink from Ivor.

Cassy tried to think. "Oh, the new anchor. No, I haven't. Thanks, Ivor." He bowed again.

"Alexandra Waring—that *wearing* woman, we all call her," Amos said, stirring his drink with his finger. He put the finger in his mouth for several moments and sent a meaningful look to Cassy—who chose to ignore it. Slightly annoyed, Amos continued. "But you know all about Michael's private coaching lessons." When she didn't say anything, he laughed sharply, adding, "Day and night lessons."

"If Michael brought Alexandra Waring here from Kansas," Cassy said, rising out of her chair, "then she must be extraordinarily talented. Excuse me, Amos, I have to check on things in the kitchen."

"Extraordinarily talented," she heard Amos say. "Too bad we're not talking about the newsroom."

In the kitchen, Cassy told Ivor to listen for the doorbell. "And let whoever it is, Ivor, *in*. All right? Oh—" She retraced her steps. "Take that tray of hors d'oeuvres in, please. And if that animal tries to bite you, you have my permission to kill it."

Cassy walked back to the bedroom, knocked, and let herself in. Rosanne was standing in front of the mirror—in the dress. She looked terrific and Cassy told her so, moving over to check the fit from a closer view.

"Did Mr. C lose his keys again?"

"No," Cassy said, turning Rosanne and looking at the hem, "that was Amos."

"The guy I threw the sponge at last time?"

"Yes. Rosanne, come here." Cassy pulled her over to the dressing table and sat her down. She picked up her own brush and paused. To Rosanne's reflection in the mirror she said, "I want to try something with your hair." Rosanne shrugged. Cassy took it as consent and started to brush out Rosanne's long hair.

"Too bad you didn't have a daughter," Rosanne said into the mirror.

"Hmmm." Cassy had hairpins in her mouth. She was bringing the sides of Rosanne's hair back up off her face. The doorbell rang; Rosanne started to rise; Cassy pushed her back down into the chair. "Not yet."

Rosanne watched her work for a while and then said, "Who did you play dress-up with before me? Not the kid, I hope." The kid was Henry, Cassy's sixteen-year-old son.

"No one," Cassy said. She looked down into the mirror, turning Rosanne's head slightly. She considered their progress and then met Rosanne's eyes. "You know, Rosanne," she said, "the only reason I do this is because you'll need it one day." She paused, letting her hand fall on Rosanne's shoulder. (The doorbell rang again.) "You're not going to be cleaning houses forever." Rosanne's eyes lowered. "Maybe you don't think so," Cassy said, resuming brushing, "but I know so. And I want you to be ready."

Silence.

It wasn't a lie, what Cassy had said. But it certainly wasn't the whole truth behind "playin' dress-up." The first time Cassy had coaxed Rosanne out of her usual cleaning garb and into a dress, Cassy had been quite taken aback. For some reason Cassy couldn't understand, Rosanne seemed determined to conceal from the world not only her body but the basic truth of an attractive face. Here, right now, in the mirror, was a nice-looking young woman with long, wavy brown hair, large brown eyes (with lashes to die for) and a slightly Roman nose. And her skin! Twenty-six years of a difficult life, and yet not a mark was to be found on Rosanne's complexion.

And so the whole truth had a lot to do with Cassy's pleasure at performing a miracle make-over. And it did seem miraculous to Cassy, this transformation of Rosanne, because she herself always looked the same—at her best. And Cassy longed for a startling transformation for herself, but there was no transformation to be had. No, that was not true. There was one long, painful, startling transformation left to Cassy now—to lose her beauty to age. Others might not have noticed yet but, boy, she had. Every day. Every single day.

"I want you to enjoy what you have while you've got it," Cassy murmured, picking up an eyeliner pencil.

Rosanne made a face in the mirror (decidedly on the demonic side) and then sighed. "Well, if I'm gonna lose it, maybe I don't wanna get used to havin' whatever it is you keep sayin' I got."

"Youth," Cassy said, smiling slightly, tilting Rosanne's face up. "Close your eyes, please."

"Youth?" Rosanne said, complying with Cassy's request. "Man, if this is youth, then middle age'll kill me for sure."

"I know what you mean," Cassy said.

The doorbell rang again.

"So you're on strike, or what?"

"Maybe," Cassy said. "Hold still."

Ten minutes later the doorbell rang again and Cassy hurried to reassess and touch up her work. There was a great deal of noise coming from the front of the apartment now, and Cassy hoped that Ivor hadn't quit yet. "Okay," she said, stepping back, "that's it. If I do say so myself, you look wonderful. Here," she added, handing Rosanne some earrings, "put those on and then come out and make your debut. I better get out there."

As Cassy reached the door, Rosanne said, "Hey—Mrs. C."

"Yes?"

Rosanne was admiring herself in the mirror. "Thanks."

Cassy smiled. "The pleasure's all mine." She turned around and nearly collided with a young woman in the hall. Cassy stepped back, profusely excusing herself. The young woman merely laughed.

Who was this?

C," she continued, as Cassy took her by the elbow and steered her toward the kitchen, "you never said nothin' about me havin' to play dress-up."

They were in the kitchen now, and Cassy stopped, looking back at Rosanne. She smiled, yanked the bandanna down over Rosanne's eyes and turned to the bartender. "Have everything you need, Ivor?"

"Yes, Madame Coch-ah-ren," he replied, bowing slightly.

"Good," she said, pulling Rosanne along through the kitchen to the back hall. Rosanne scooped up her bag from the counter along the way.

"And I never said I was a caterer," Rosanne reminded her.

"Right," Cassy said.

"So I don't know why you get so picky about what I wear—it's not as if you like any of these guys."

They were in the master bedroom now, and Cassy headed toward her closet. "I think you're going to like it," she said, opening the doors.

"Mrs. C," Rosanne said, throwing her bag on the bed, "ya know, if you'd just tell me, I'd bring one of the ones you already got me."

"Well, I was in Macy's and there it was, just hanging there, calling, 'Rosanne, Rosanne, I was made for Rosanne.' "

Rosanne sighed, pulled off her bandanna and shook out her hair. Cassy turned around, holding a pretty blue and black print dress. "Hair," she said, "good Lord, Rosanne, you have hair."

"Come on, Mrs. C," Rosanne said, turning away.

Cassy walked over and laid the dress out on the bed. She looked at Rosanne a moment and then smiled, gently. "Tell me the truth—do you really hate doing this?"

Rosanne shrugged and proceeded to pull some things out of her bag: a slip, some panty hose and a pair of shoes.

The doorbell rang.

"Uh-oh," Cassy said, looking at her watch, "somebody's here already. No, let Ivor get it, Rosanne. You go ahead and get changed."

Rosanne shrugged again and started undoing the buttons of her shirt while Cassy walked back to stand in front of the closet door mirror. She scanned it. A few wisps of blond hair were already falling out of the clip. But her eyes were still blue. Her nose was still perfect. Her mouth still had lipstick. Body was still tall and slim. Bracelets, check. Earrings, check.

Cassy was still beautiful. Cassy was still forty-one. She would not stand closer to the mirror than she was; she would not care to see the reminders of her age showing around her eyes, mouth and neck.

"Don't know how good Mr. Moscow's gonna be at greetin' guests," Rosanne said.

"Hmmm," Cassy said, raising her chin slightly, still looking at herself in the mirror.

"And you don't want to scare him right off the bat," Rosanne continued.

Cassy laughed.

"They said he was the last bartender they'd send us," she reminded her.

"Oh, Lord, that's right." Cassy closed the closet door and sailed out of the bedroom, down the hall and through the kitchen to the front hall, where she found Ivor standing in front of the open door. "Who is it, Ivor?" When he gave her a vacant look, she stepped forward to peer around his shoulder. "Oh, Amos. Hi."

"Hi," Amos Franklin said. Both Ivor's and Cassy's eyes were fixed on the stuffed head of an unidentifiable animal that was snarling on top of Amos' head.

"It's okay, Ivor," Cassy said, patting the arm with which Ivor was blocking the door.

Ivor did not seem convinced.

"He's a guest," Cassy told him. "We're supposed to let him in." Ivor's eyes shifted to her. She nodded, smiling encouragement. He took one more look out the door, frowned, and slipped behind Cassy to return to the kitchen. "Sorry about that," Cassy said, waving Amos in. "I have no idea what I've done to earn his protection."

"Any man would want to protect you," Amos whispered.

Here we go, Cassy thought. Amos was forever whispering little things like that—that is, when his wife wasn't around. "Nice hat," she said, snarling fangs sweeping in past her eyes.

"Michael gave it to me for my birthday," Amos said. He reached up, groped around, and patted the animal on the nose. "I don't think it's real, though."

Cassy led Amos into the living room, explaining that Michael was out getting some ice.

"Good," Amos said, sitting on the couch and patting the seat next to him, "it will give me a chance to talk to you."

Cassy sat down in one of the chairs.

"You're beautiful."

"What?"

"You're beautiful," Amos repeated.

Looking at Cassy was the most exquisite set of blue-gray eyes she had ever seen. And the eyes were not alone—great eyebrows, good cheekbones, a wide, lovely mouth. And her hair . . . This wonderfully dark, wildly attractive hair about the woman's face.

How young you are, Cassy thought.

"You must be Cassy," the girl said. Her voice was deep, her diction perfect.

Cassy realized the girl was offering her hand to be shaken and so she took it, and did it, still fascinated with her eyes. "Yes," she said, "and you're . . . ?"

"Alexandra Waring," she said, baring a splendid smile.

Cassy apparently jerked her hand away, for the girl took hold of her arm and said, "I'm sorry, did I startle you?"

Oh, Lord, Cassy thought, *you may be the one Michael will want to marry.* "How old are you?" Cassy said, cringing inside at how ridiculous the question sounded.

"Twenty-eight," Alexandra said, laughing.

"Well," Cassy said, clasping her hands together in front of her and composing herself slightly, "Michael has told me a great deal about you." When the girl merely continued to smile at her, Cassy shrugged and said, "So—don't you want to ask me how old I am?"

The girl's smile turned to confusion on that one, and the moment was saved by Rosanne's head appearing over Cassy's shoulder. "I saw you in the *Daily News,*" she said. "Liz Smith says they're gonna can Boxby to make room for ya."

"I really don't know," Alexandra said vaguely.

"Better read Liz Smith then," Rosanne suggested.

"Oh, brother!" cried a booming voice. It was Michael, his six-foot-two frame looming from the other end of the hallway. Cassy could already tell that he was three—no, maybe only two—sheets to the wind. "What are you doing, Cassy, introducing Alexandra to the maid?"

"I was just about to." Cassy made the appropriate gestures. "Rosanne, this is Alexandra Waring. Alexandra, Rosanne DiSantos."

Michael laughed, lumbering down to the group. "Who is this?" he cried, reaching around Cassy to pull Rosanne out into view. "Wooo-weee, look at you! How did you get so gorgeous?"

"Hey, watch the merchandise," Rosanne warned him.

Alexandra turned to Cassy, smiling slightly. "Has she worked for you long?"

Cassy glanced at her. "Three years." Her eyes swung back to Michael. "Not to be nosy, but where have you been?"

"Out," Michael said, yanking the skirt of Rosanne's dress.

"Yeah," Rosanne said, yanking her dress back. "Five hours gettin' ice. *Gettin'* iced is more like it."

"Big bad Rosanne, huh?" Michael said, putting up his dukes.

"You two—" Cassy began.

"Hey, Mr. C," Rosanne said, sparring as best she could in the confined space, "listen, we gotta go easy on Mr. Moscow tonight. He's the last guy they'll send over."

"Mr. Moscow?" Alexandra asked.

"The bartender," Cassy said, catching the sleeve of Michael's sweat shirt. "You better get changed."

He stopped sparring and looked at her. "I stopped by the station," he said.

"May I throw my things in there?" Alexandra asked, nodding toward the bedroom. "Cassy?"

"What?"

"My things—may I put them in there?"

"Stop lookin' at me like that," Rosanne said, swatting Michael's arm. "I'm not gonna be a cleanin' houses forever, ya know."

"Rosanne," Cassy said, "will you please get out there and pass hors d'oeuvres? And be forewarned that Amos has an animal on his head."

"Amos," Michael sighed, leaning heavily into the wall. "What an asshole."

"He claims you gave him that thing for his birthday."

"Yeah," Michael sighed. "It's a hyena. Looks like him, doesn't it?"

"I'm takin' the sponge with me then," Rosanne said, moving down the hall, "just so ya know."

"Cassy—" Alexandra tried again.

"Yes?"

"My things?"

"Yes. In there. On the bed."

"And I'll help you," Michael said, brightening.

Cassy snatched his arm and turned him around. "You, in the kitchen—now."

"Wait," Michael said, turning around. Cassy pushed him backward down the hall by his stomach. "No, wait, Cass, I just want to know what Alexandra wants to drink—*ALEXANDRA. WHAT DO YOU WANT TO DRINK?*"

"Good Lord," Cassy sighed.

"Perrier!" came the reply.

This did not make him happy. Cranky, *"WHAT?"*

"Michael," Cassy said.

"I'd like a Perrier," Alexandra said, emerging from the bedroom.

"Oh, man," Michael whined, turning around and walking to the kitchen of his own volition. "What is it with you guys? Get within ten feet of Cassy and suddenly everybody's drinking Perrier. Shit."

Cassy waited to escort Alexandra out of the hall. "What do you usually drink?" she asked, letting Alexandra pass in front of her.

"Perrier," Alexandra said.

A nice figure, too. This is not good. "Really?"

Alexandra turned and smiled. Ratings were made on smiles like these. "Really," she said.

Cassy's father, Henry Littlefield, had always told her that she was the most beautiful girl in the world. Cassy's mother, Catherine, yelled every time he said it. "If you keep telling her that, you're going to make her a very unhappy woman!"

Cassy was twelve when her father died. Afterward, Catherine—over and over again, year in, year out—strongly advised Cassy to forget everything her father had ever told her. Her explanation ran something like this:

Catherine had been quite a beauty herself, although you couldn't tell that now. Years of slaving on Cassy's behalf had destroyed her looks. But the point was, you see, Catherine had been a beauty. Everyone had always told her so and Catherine had believed them. She had also believed everyone when they said that her beauty would win her the best man alive and she would marry him and live happily ever after.

But instead of going for the Miss Iowa title in 1939 (which she won hands down, don't you know), she should have gone to college and learned something. But she didn't and she didn't win the Miss America title, but she did win Henry Littlefield and life went steadily downhill after that.

It wasn't that Henry had exactly been a bad man. No, no, far from it. It was just that he was so unlucky. Catherine had never seen anyone so unlucky. His career never got off the ground and they never did manage to move out of their starter house (or pay for it) and then Cassy came along and Catherine had to stay home all the time to take care of her and then Henry went off and died on her and Catherine had to work as a receptionist at Thompson Electronics to support Cassy and—

Sigh.

"You know, sweetie, life is tough and then you're dead and if only they hadn't all kept telling me how beautiful I was."

But you'll be different, honey lamb. I won't let that happen to you. You're going to make something of yourself and not end up like your poor old mother.

And Cassy was different, and she did listen to her mother. She was a good girl; she did graduate at the top of her class; she did receive a full scholarship to Northwestern. She didn't keep bad company (she didn't really keep any company at all, frankly) and she didn't fill her head with silly notions about boys.

That is, until Michael Cochran. Oh, but he was handsome in those days. So darkly, devastatingly handsome. (He still was, with a suntan.) And Cassy fell in love with him, despite the fact that she did not *want* to fall in love with him. He was too wild, too untrustworthy. (She was never quite sure, but over the years Cassy had come to suspect that her falling in love with him may have had something to do with the fact that he had never openly appeared to be in love with her—unlike almost every other man.) But Michael was always laughing, always on top of the world, and was such a good-natured, warm, fun-loving bear of a man—much like Cassy's father had been. And Michael was so worldly! After six years of working at his hometown paper in Indiana, twenty-four-year-old Michael Cochran was an awesome entity in the journalism school. (Cassy was the second.)

They dated throughout college and Cassy agreed to marry him shortly after graduation. Catherine was horrified and refused to have anything to do with the wedding. If Cassy wanted to marry that "good-time Charlie" and throw her life away, she could go ahead and consider herself an orphan. Cassy and Michael went ahead and got married.

The Cochrans were hired as a team in the news department at a network affiliate in Chicago, Michael as a writer and Cassy as some glorified term for a secretary. They both worked very hard and Michael also played very hard. The guys in management, big drinkers themselves, loved having Michael along on their city jaunts. Michael was a kick; Michael was smart; Michael Cochran was going places.

And so was Cassy—on his coattails. When Michael was offered a producer slot in documentary, he demanded and got Cassy as his assistant producer. They worked extremely well together, Michael with his grand visions and good writing, and Cassy with her sharp technical eye and awesome organizational skills. In short, Michael would get a great idea and

Cassy would see that it was carried through to completion. Michael *hated* details and follow-through ("DETAILS!" he would roar. "FUCK 'EM—LET'S JUST DO IT!").

Cassy got pregnant in 1968 and miscarried in her third month. But then in 1969 she conceived again and everyone (even her mother, who had deigned to speak to her again) was thrilled when Cassy's term progressed without any problems. She continued working up to the week Henry was born, and did not return to work full time until two years later, when the biggest documentary of Michael's life was falling apart—all because of those insidious DETAILS. She had not stopped working since.

They made the move to New York City in 1973 when Michael was offered the job of news director at WWKK. Cassy was hired as a feature segment producer in the news department at rival independent station WST. Both did very well, Michael earning more and more money, and Cassy, in 1976, becoming managing director of news operations at WST. But then, in 1978, Cassy started doing better-well than Michael. She was made managing director of news operations *and* coprogramming director for the station. But since Michael was a vice-president and she wasn't, it was okay for a while. But then in 1980 she was made vice-president and managing director, news and programming, and the situation became sticky. And then in 1982, when Cassy was promoted to vice-president and general station manager, the Cochran marriage began to rock. As some sort of unspoken compromise— in terms of work—they spoke of news and only of news, and Michael was to remain the indisputable authority.

So here were the Cochrans of 1986, ensconced in the large West Side apartment on Riverside Drive they had owned for seven years now, both with careers they adored (most of the time) and a son they always adored. They were so lucky in that department, with Henry.

So why did Michael and she have so many problems? Cassy wondered. Problems that were never out in the open, problems that were tied into everything else in such nebulous ways that it was near impossible to even isolate them as such.

Fact (or Fact?): Michael may or may not have had anywhere between fourteen and thirty-seven affairs in the last ten years. (Cassy was always sure, but never really sure, and never wanted to know for sure.)

Fact: Their relationship as husband and wife had evolved into something suspiciously similar to that between an errant student and teacher.

Fact: Cassy and Michael rarely agreed on anything anymore, except a desire not to openly fight. Even on the subject of their son, their viewpoints were so far apart that it was amazing to think they had even known each other for twenty years, much less been married to each other. Michael cast his son as a jock and booming ladies' man; Cassy knew him as a quiet, shy, gentle young man who was perhaps a bit too smart and too sensitive for his own good. As for the ladies' man part of Michael's perception, that only came up when Michael was drinking—when he would attribute all of his own sexual exploits and conquests to his son, going on and on in front of other people, daring to see how far he could go before Cassy showed visible signs of distress.

Looking in the powder-room mirror, tracing the hairs slipping from the clip with her fingers, Cassy considered the amount of gray she could distinguish from the ash blond. She was an expert at this by now. Would she . . . ? No, not yet.

She leaned over the sink and sighed, slowly. She raised her head and again looked at her face. She touched her cheek, her chin, her mouth. Yes, she was still quite beautiful, but she looked like someone else now. Maybe she was a Catherine now, like her mother, too old to be a Cassy.

Good Lord, she was *fading*. That was it. Just fading. From radiance to glow. Like her eyesight, her face was fading. Reading glasses she had almost resigned herself to, but when it's your face—what do you do, wear a mask?

Yes. But you call it makeup.

Was it worth it, this life? In love with Henry in the odd moment he expressed a need for her, in love with her television station, in love with her schedules, DETAILS, in love with ignoring the passing days of her life. When, exactly, was it that she had stopped insisting they drive out every weekend to the house in Connecticut? When was it she had decided to let the garden go, and not care if the house was painted or not? When had she stopped wishing they had a dog?

When had Cassy Cochran stopped wishing for anything?

Someone was knocking on the door. "Just a minute," she called out. And *what* was this singsong in her voice? Why didn't she just gently cast flowers from a basket as she walked?

It was Rosanne, balancing a tray of hors d'oeuvres on her hip. "Henry's on the phone. The kid sounds funny so I thought I better get you."

Cassy's heart skipped a beat, for Henry never sounded "funny." "I'll take it in the study." Cassy walked down the hall and opened the door to the study. It was off limits at parties because it was here that the Cochrans harbored what they did best—sift and sort through work and projects. There were three television sets, two VCRs, tons of scripts, computer printouts and magazines. There were two solid walls of video tapes; the other two walls were covered with photographs of the Cochrans with various television greats over the years and, too, there were a number of awards: Emmys, Peabodys, a Christopher, a Silver Gavel, two Duponts, and even a Clio from a free-lance job of Michael's years ago. What a lovely mess. Pictures and papers. What they both understood completely. His chair, his desk; her chair, her desk; the old sofa they couldn't part with, where Henry had been conceived so many years before.

"Henry?"

"Hi, Mom."

He does sound funny.

"What's wrong?"

Pause. "Well, Mom, I'm sort of in a situation where I'm not really sure what to do." Pause. "Mom?"

"Yes?"

He sighed and sounded old. "I'm over at Skipper's and the Marshalls aren't home yet." Pause.

Let him explain.

"Skipper was drinking beer at Shea and then here . . . Mom, he's kind of getting sick all over the place and I don't know what to do." He hurried on. "I tried to get him to go to bed but he threw up all over the place and then started running around." Little voice. "He just got sick in the dining room. Mom—"

"Listen, sweetheart, don't panic, I'm coming right over. But listen to me carefully. Stay with Skipper and make sure he doesn't hurt himself."

"He's sort of out of it."

"If he starts to get sick again, make sure he's sitting up. Don't let him choke. Okay, sweetheart? Just hang on, I'll be right there."

Cassy grabbed her coat and purse and went back into the party to find Michael. Easier said than done. Where had all these people come from anyway? Some woman was playing "Hey, Look Me Over" on the piano, while Elvis was belting "Blue Suede Shoes" on the stereo.

Where the hell is Michael?

Where the hell is Alexandra Waring?

Well, at least Cassy knew who was with whom.

The Marshalls lived on Park Avenue at 84th Street. Skipper was a classmate of Henry's, a friendship sanctioned by Michael since Roderick Marshall was the longtime president of the Mainwright Club, of which Michael yearned to be a member. (He was turned down year after year.) As for

Cassy, she thought the Marshalls were stupid people. Period. And because she felt that way, she had become rather fond of Skipper for openly airing all of the family secrets (his mother had had *two* face lifts; his father went away on weekends with his mistress; they had paid two hundred and fifty thousand dollars to marry off Skipper's hopeless sister . . .).

While Cassy wouldn't have chosen Skipper as Henry's buddy, she did appreciate one of Skipper's attributes—he absolutely worshiped the ground Henry walked on. And he was bright; he understood all of Henry's complicated interests; and he was loyal, not only to Henry, but to all of the Cochrans. (Whenever Cassy told the boys it was time to go to bed, Skipper always made a point of thanking her for letting him stay over. "I really *like* it here," he would declare. "I would really like it if you liked my liking it— do you, Mrs. C?" "Yes, Skipper, I do," Cassy would say, making him grin.)

The poor kids. Cassy found Henry sitting shell-shocked on the lid of the toilet seat in the front powder room while Skipper snored on the tile floor, his arm curled around the base of the john. Lord, what a mess. Henry held Skipper up so that Cassy could at least wash the vomit off his face and take off his shirt. They took him to his room, changed him into pajamas, and then put him to bed in one of the guest rooms since his own was such a mess. With Henry's help she found the number of the maid and Cassy called. Would she come over since no one knew where the Marshalls were, or when they could come home? She would.

Cassy stripped the sheets in Skipper's room and, with Henry, cleaned up the worst from the carpets around the house. Aside from answering her questions about where things were, Henry hadn't volunteered anything. Cassy checked on Skipper again; he was long gone, in a peaceful sleep now.

They sat in the kitchen and shared a Coke.

"Are you sure the Marshalls didn't leave a number?"

Glum. "Yes."

"Henry," Cassy asked after a moment, "do you like to drink?"

He glared at her. *"Mom."*

"No, sweetheart, it's okay. I mean, I know all kids experiment sometime. I just wondered about you. About how you felt about alcohol."

He shook his head and looked down at the table, restlessly moving his glass.

"Henry—"

"I hate it." His voice was so low, so hostile, Cassy wasn't sure she'd heard it right.

"What, sweetheart?"

He looked up briefly, let go of his glass, and leaned back on the legs of the chair. He caught his mother's look and came back down on the floor with a thump. Back to the old tried and true position. "I hate the stuff. It makes me sick." A short pause. "Why do people have to drink that stuff? It just makes them act like jerks and it's not good for your body, so what's the point?"

Cassy's mind raced with that one. After a moment she asked, "Does Skipper drink a lot?"

Henry gave her a does-he-look-like-he-does-silly-old-Mom look. "He tries to."

"Has he ever said why?"

Another look, not dissimilar to the last. "No. He just does it whenever he's pissed at his parents."

"Angry."

"What?"

"Angry at his parents."

"Yeah, anyway—today his mother told him he couldn't go to Colorado."

"Why not?"

Henry shrugged. "Bad mood, probably. She's like that."

By the time the maid arrived, Cassy had changed her mind about what to do. She apologized to Angie for bringing her over, and explained that she had second thoughts about sticking her with the situation. Cassy would take Skipper home with her. She left a note by the front door:

> Deidre,
>   Skipper is safe and sound at our house. He is not feeling very well and since I didn't know where to reach you, I thought it best to bring him home with me. Call me when you get home and I'll explain.
>
>   Cassy Cochran

Michael was bellowing "My Wild Irish Rose" down the hall for the benefit of departing guests. Cassy sighed, Henry's back snapped to attention and Skipper, bless his heart, did his best to move along between them without letting his eyes roll back into his head.

"Hey, kid, nice to see you! Didn't want to miss the fun with your old man, huh?" Michael said, holding his glass high. "Hey, Skip!"

"Skipper's ill," Cassy said, ushering Skipper by him. "I'm putting him to bed in the guest room."

"Too bad, Skipperino," Michael said. He got hold of Henry's arm. "Come on," he urged, pulling him along. "Kiddo, I want you to meet one hot cookie. Our new star." He halted suddenly, pretending to whisper. "Kid, she's so beautiful—I can't tell you how beautiful she is, so hold onto your hat . . ."

Cassy was reluctant to leave Henry, but Skipper was fading fast. Rosanne, in the kitchen, took one look at him and followed them back to the guest room. While Cassy stripped Skipper down to the pajamas he was wearing under his clothes, Rosanne turned down the bed and set out a pail beside it. Cassy sat for a minute or two with Skipper, reassuring him that he would be feeling better after he slept, stroking his forehead all the while. She left the hall light on and the door open.

When Cassy went into the living room, she found Michael practically shoving Henry into Alexandra's lap on the couch. When Henry saw his mother it apparently gave him courage, for he slapped his father's hand away, excused himself to Alexandra, shot past Cassy without a word and headed for his room.

There were only six guests left—the die-hards, five of whom were in worse shape than Michael. Alexandra was stone cold sober and looked as though she wished she could go to her room too.

Hmmm.

Cassy went into the kitchen, where Ivor asked her what she would like to drink. She asked for a Perrier, changed her mind, and asked for a glass of white wine.

"That Waring chick is a strange one," Rosanne said, rinsing a tray in the sink. Clang, clatter, into the rack.

Cassy accepted her glass of wine, sipped it, and moved across the kitchen to lean back against the counter. "Why, what did she do?"

Rosanne pulled off her rubber gloves, untied her apron and threw it on the dish rack. "She comes in here like the Queen of Sheba and so I look at her, and like Mr. C's standin' over there by the bar."

"And?"

"And so she stands there," Rosanne continued, pointing at the very spot on the floor, "and says"—Rosanne stood on her tiptoes to accurately re-enact the scene—" 'Where is Mrs. Cochran?' So I said"—dropping down to her heels, plunking a hand on her hip—" 'If she's got any sense, she's hidin' from the likes of you.' "

"Oh, Rosanne," Cassy groaned, covering her face.

"Naw, naw," Rosanne said, shaking her head. "I didn't say that. I said,

'She's out.' So she says"—back on her toes—" 'When is she coming back?'
So then Mr. C says"—holding her arms out to the side, implying largesse—
" 'What do ya want Cassy for?' And she says, 'I'd like to know her better,'
and so then Mr. C starts gettin' upset, and she says—cheez it, the cops."

Cassy was about to say, "Alexandra Waring said, 'Cheez it, the cops'?"
when she realized that Michael and Alexandra had come into the kitchen. A
look back at Rosanne found her busy at the sink, minding her own business
of course.

"So what's with Henry?" Michael said, shoving his glass into Ivor's hand
and then grunting.

"He's had a rough afternoon." Cassy glanced at Alexandra and added,
"We'll talk about it later."

"Brooding kid sometimes," Michael said to Alexandra. "Oh, thanks,
Igor."

"Ivor, Michael—the man's name is Ivor," Cassy sighed, sitting down on a
stool.

"Igor, Ivor, you don't care as long as you get paid, right?" he said,
slapping Igor-Ivor on the arm.

Cassy noticed that Amos' hat was leering down from on top of the refrigerator, a cigarette dangling from its jaws.

Michael turned to Alexandra. "You know where the kid gets it from?" He
swallowed almost his entire drink and laughed. "We made the kid on the
couch I showed you in the den—" He started cracking up.

"Michael—" Cassy said.

"And the whole time, Cass kept oooing and ahhhing and then all of a
sudden she starts yelping about a spring stabbing her in the rear end—"

Cassy slumped over the counter.

"And the kid inherited it! He gets this look like—*Jesus, something's stabbing me in the rear end.*" Michael fell back against the doorway, hysterical.
"You saw him, Alexandra! Isn't that what he looks like?"

Rosanne hurled a handful of clean silverware into the sink; Ivor examined
the wallpaper; Michael continued laughing and Cassy left the room. She was
halfway down the hall when she heard her name being called. It was Alexandra. Cassy turned around and stood there, waiting.

"I'm sorry," she said.

"Why," Cassy said, "what have you done?"

"No, that's not what I meant, I—"

Cassy silenced her by raising her hand. "Look," she said, "do me a favor,
will you? Just please get out of here and take those drunken idiots with you.

Michael included. All right?" And then she fled to the guest room, slamming the door behind her. Having awakened poor Skipper, Cassy stayed with him for a while until he fell back to sleep. When she emerged from the room, she found that Alexandra had granted her her favor; the party had departed for dinner at Caramba's.

They didn't say much while cleaning up and were done by ten-thirty. When Cassy paid Ivor and tipped him well (in the far-flung hope he might give the agency a favorable report), Rosanne whispered to offer him Amos' hat. Cassy stared at her. She nodded. And so she did, and Ivor took Amos' hat home with him in a Zabar's bag.

"I had a hunch he liked it," Rosanne said after he left. "He kept lookin' at it."

Cassy asked Rosanne if she wanted some hot chocolate; she was making some for Henry and herself. Rosanne declined, saying she had to get going —had to be at Howie and the Bitch's early the next morning.

"Do you know how I cringe, Rosanne, when I think of how you must describe us to your other clients?" Cassy said, stirring Ovaltine into a saucepan of milk.

"I call ya the C's, that's all," Rosanne said. "Honest."

Cassy smiled slightly.

"Well," Rosanne reconsidered, slipping on her coat, "maybe *once* I said that Mr. C stood for Mr. Crazy."

Cassy wanted to say something but didn't. She just stirred and stirred until the handle of the stainless steel spoon was too hot to hold. She put it down on the stove top. What was this? Tears? Yes, a tear, spilling down her cheek. And she wasn't even crying. At least she didn't feel as though she was crying. She wiped at her face with the back of her hand, sniffed, and said, "I'm sorry, I'm just so tired . . ."

"Mrs. C," Rosanne said, moving to the doorway. Cassy didn't look up. "Like it's never easy, ya know?"

"No," Cassy finally said, "I don't suppose it is."

Silence.

"Thanks a lot for the dress. I really like it."

Quietly, "You're welcome."

And Rosanne left.

Henry accepted his hot chocolate and put an issue of the *Backpacker* aside.

"I think Skipper will be fine," Cassy reported, sipping from her mug. "When do you suppose the Marshalls will get home?"

"They won't call, Mom, so don't wait up for them."

After a moment Cassy patted Henry's knee and he scooted over so she could sit next to him on the twin bed. It was a tight fit, but a well-practiced maneuver. They drank their hot chocolate, both looking across the room at the window.

"Tug?" Cassy asked.

"Police boat," he said. Henry knew all the boats on the river at night.

"Oh, yes."

Silence.

"Mom," Henry said, "do you ever get scared for no particular reason?"

She swallowed. "Sometimes. Usually when I'm wondering what's going to happen. Life always seems like an unlikely proposition when I try to figure out how everything's going to turn out."

Pause.

"What are you going to do, Mom?"

"Talk to Mrs. Marshall."

Long pause. "I meant about Dad. He's really getting—you know, like that summer in Newport."

Cassy looked at her son. How much did he know? "What do you mean?"

Henry was uncomfortable. "You know, that woman. He's acting like that again."

So he did know. Probably more than Cassy herself knew. If she hadn't wanted to know for sure about Michael's affairs, she supposed she was about to find out.

"Mom—why don't you *do* something?" This was delivered in a whisper.

Where the energy came from she wasn't sure. But it came. She put her cup down on the night table and put her arm around Henry. She sighed. "Sweetheart, Henry, your father and I, no matter what our troubles—we both love you more than anything else in the world."

Silence.

"Mom, he humiliates you. He humiliates me. Is he sleeping with that woman who was here tonight? If he is, why doesn't he do like other guys and at least hide it?"

Cassy felt nauseous.

"He just throws it in your face. Rosanne knows it, I know it, half the station knows it. Why don't you do something?"

Cassy vowed not to cry. Quietly, "What do you think I should do?"

"I don't know. Talk to him." And then, blurting it out, "Make him love you again."

"Oh, sweetheart." Cassy was close to breaking down. *What to say, God, what to say?* Did her son not think she had tried?

The pain was centered right there, right on that. *I have not tried and we both know it.*

Cassy raised her head and saw that Henry was not angry with her; he was trying to comfort her. Tell her he was on her side.

When did he start needing to shave? was her next thought. *When did that happen?*

The doorbell was ringing. Cassy kissed Henry on the cheek, got up and slipped on her shoes. The doorbell was persistent. She leaned over and kissed Henry again. "It's probably Mrs. Marshall," she said.

Cassy was hardly in any shape to deal with Deidre Marshall, but, she thought, anything was an improvement over continuing that talk with Henry. She swung open the front door just as she thought she should have peered through the peephole first.

It was Alexandra Waring.

Rubbing her eye, Cassy had to laugh to herself.

Alexandra shifted her stance slightly. "I told them I was tired," she said.

"You came to the right place, then," Cassy said. "We always are here."

The brilliant eyes were asking for mercy and it threw Cassy. What was up?

"May I come in for five minutes? There was something I wanted to say to you."

"To me?"

Alexandra nodded.

"Well," Cassy said, stepping back and waving her in, "I suppose you'd better come in and say it then. Let's go in the living room."

It fascinated Cassy how nervous the girl was. Offered a chair, she declined, choosing instead to pace the floor with her hands jammed into the pockets of her raincoat. Cassy sat down on the couch and watched her. Alexandra looked over at her once or twice but continued to pace.

This was to be the woman to launch a thousand broadcasts? Tell of earthquakes? Assassinations? Terrorism? Fatal diseases? This was Michael's Wonder Woman? Well, Cassy would be kind. She would assume that Alexandra could do better sitting behind a desk.

The girl finally said, "I want to apologize and I'm not exactly sure what I'm apologizing for, since I haven't done anything wrong."

Cassy lofted her eyebrows.

The girl started to pace again, stopped, and suddenly threw herself down on the end of the couch, to which Cassy reacted by crossing her legs in the opposite direction.

"There's no other way to say it, so I'll just say it. I'm terrified of your husband, of offending him, because I desperately want this assignment to work." She ran her hand through her hair and dropped it in her lap. "Tonight was a nightmare and I couldn't stand watching what was happening, but I couldn't do anything either—can you understand that?"

Somewhere, perhaps between the words "terrified" and "desperately," a gray veil had dropped over Cassy's head, shielding her from any sense that this conversation was actually taking place.

Alexandra sighed, lowering her head for a moment. Cassy noted how gorgeous her hair was. No gray. Nothing but black, thick, wonderful young hair. *How crazy it must make Michael.*

"Are you having an affair with my husband?"

Alexandra's head kicked up. "God, no," she whispered. "Never. I wouldn't do that—"

Cassy shrugged. "Thought I might as well ask."

"I'm very fond of your husband," the girl said. "I'm also very loyal to him. You of all people must realize the enormity of the opportunity he's giving me."

Cassy nodded. "Yes, I do."

"So you can understand how difficult my situation is."

Cassy sighed, looking past her to the window. A barge was making its way down the river.

"Tonight, when I saw you—" Alexandra said, voice hesitant. "I've heard about you, your career—people told me how beautiful you are—"

Cassy winced slightly. *If you think I'm beautiful now, you should have seen me before.*

"So when I saw you tonight," Alexandra rushed on, "I knew at once that something had to be terribly wrong if he—" She cut herself off. "Oh, God, I'm sorry—this is coming out all wrong—"

Cassy held a hand up for her to stop. "Look, Alexandra, I appreciate what it is you're trying to do—"

"But I can't do anything, that's the point—"

"Please, listen to me for a minute, will you?" The girl leaned back against the arm of the couch. It was a good move, Cassy noted, the way she had posed herself. The way Alexandra looked at this moment was enough to make Cassy want to slash her wrists to put an end to this curse of middle age once and for all. "In my day, if you got anywhere in news—really, anywhere in almost any profession, women were always accused of sleeping their way there." She laughed slightly. "And I did—I was married to Michael and he was my boss. Did you know that?"

"He's told me everything about you," Alexandra said, faint smile emerging. "He talks about you a lot."

Cassy nodded. "Okay. Well, the only point I want to make is that all women, particularly beautiful women, sooner or later have a Michael making their lives difficult. The fact that it is my husband, I can't—I won't—"

"Of course not. I can handle him—it—that," Alexandra said. "What's difficult is just what you said—about being accused of sleeping . . ." She sighed, running her hand through her hair again. She looked at Cassy. "Everyone thinks I'm sleeping with him—and that's why he brought me to New York."

Cassy rubbed her face, thinking, *Lord, what must I look like?* "If I were you," she said, lowering her hands, "I would just go on doing what you're doing and let them think whatever they want. Alexandra—they're going to think whatever they want to think anyway. No matter what you do. I think you know that."

Alexandra lowered her eyes. "I care what you think," she said. "That's why I came back."

Michael, you'd be crazy not to want to marry this girl. Either she was a first-rate liar, or she was a nice girl from Kansas. "I think—" Cassy began, starting to smile.

Alexandra met her eyes.

"If you're half the person on air that you are right now, you're going to be just fine."

"Thank you." It was scarcely a whisper. They were still looking at each other and Alexandra suddenly pulled her eyes away.

"Alexandra—"

The girl started.

Either Cassy was seeing things, or the nice girl from Kansas was blushing.

"I was just going to say that a friend of my son's is here, who's sick, and I'm rather tired and I think you are too . . ."

"Yes, of course," Alexandra said, rising.

In the kitchen they found Henry with his head in the refrigerator. He jerked back, first looking at Alexandra and then to his mother.

"It's okay, sweetheart," Cassy said.

"Henry," Alexandra said, going over and shaking his hand, "I hope I see you again one day soon. When it's a little less rowdy." Pause. A gesture to Cassy. "Your mom and I were just talking—well, she'll tell you."

Henry looked to his mother and Cassy nodded, smiling.

"I'm just going to see Alexandra to the door." Cassy led the way through the front hall. "Well, it's been quite a day," she said, opening the door.

"Yes," Alexandra sighed, stepping outside the door and turning around.

Cassy held out her hand and Alexandra shook it. "Thank you, Alexandra. You're a very courageous young lady."

Alexandra smiled.

The ratings have just soared in the tri-state area.

"Thank you for being so nice," Alexandra said. She let go of Cassy's hand, walked down to the elevator and pressed the button. "Will I see you again soon, do you think?"

"Well," Cassy said, hanging on the door, "I'll be seeing a lot of you. We tend to watch a lot of news around here."

"Great," Alexandra said.

"Good night," Cassy said, closing the door.

"Good night."

Cassy locked the door and leaned against it. And then, after hesitating a moment, she ventured a look out the peephole.

He won't give up on this one, she thought.

2

THE STEWARTS

Howard heard the front door of the apartment slam. "Hi, Rosanne," he called, pouring the rest of the water into the coffee maker.

"Hi." Swish, swish, swish; the familiar sound of Rosanne's jeans.

Silence.

Howard looked over his shoulder and saw her leaning against the doorway. "You look very tired," he said, moving over to the butcher-block table.

"You got it." She let her bag slide down off her shoulder to thump on the floor. "Party at the C's last night."

"Okay," Howard said, picking up a piece of paper and examining it, "I'll strike 'windows' off of Melissa's list." He leaned over the table to pencil in "next week."

Rosanne tossed her bag up onto the counter and adjusted her bandanna to a more pirate-y angle. "Been on the list for three years," she said, "you'd think she'd catch on."

Howard smiled, pushing his glasses up higher on his nose. "Melissa doesn't like to admit defeat."

Rosanne gave him a look and moved on to the refrigerator. "You oughtta get a medal or somethin'," she said, opening the door.

Howard let the comment pass. "I got some half-and-half—it's in the door."

"Great, thanks."

"And there're some bran muffins in the breadbox."

Rosanne closed the refrigerator door and walked over to the coffee maker. Tapping her fingers on it, trying to hurry it along, she said, "So how are ya?"

Howard tossed the pencil down on the table. "Good, I guess."

"I brought that book back," Rosanne said, reaching for her bag.

"What did you think?"

Rosanne pulled it out and handed it to him. "I liked it. I liked it a lot, only—"

Howard was looking down at the jacket of the hard-cover volume of a Reader's Digest Condensed Books. "Only what?"

"I don't know, Howie," she sighed, swinging her weight to one leg. "Like I don't know if it's so good for me to be readin' romances. Kinda gets me depressed after—it's not like it's like real life or nothin'."

"Well," Howard said, considering this.

"But I liked it okay," she finished. "And I read another one in there about the family movin' out West—gettin' shot at and attacked and all." She moved over to the sink. "Weird how it was like now back then."

Howard laughed. "I'll give you something a little different this week," he promised.

Rosanne opened the cabinets under the sink and squatted down. "Yeah, okay," she said, pulling out various cleaning agents and plunking them down on the floor. She shook the bathroom cleanser container. "We need some Comet, Howie," she said. Howard wrote this down. "And you better tell her highness," Rosanne added, whipping her head around in his direction, "that we don't want any of that el cheapo cleaner she always gets. Brother," she muttered, standing up and slamming the cabinets shut, "you'd think if she wanted a clean house she'd get some decent cleanin' stuff."

"I'll get it," Howard said, dropping the pencil.

Rosanne turned around to look at him.

"What?"

Her mouth twitched one way and then the other. "Nothin'," she finally said, waving him away. "Go do your work. I wanna listen to the radio."

As Howard walked through the living room he heard Rosanne whirling the radio dial. In a few minutes, he knew, every radio and television in the apartment, save in the master bedroom, would be on (9 A.M., Radios: Howard Stern (WXRK), John Gambling (WOR), Don Imus (WNBC); TVs: Leonard Philbin and "The Munsters." 10 A.M., Radios: K-Rock, Sherre Henry (WOR) and WPLJ; TVs: Oprah Winfrey and Phil Donahue). At eleven, while Rosanne cleaned their bedroom to Joan Hamburg (WOR), Howard would move to the living room for a half hour and either turn off the TV or give in and watch "Father Knows Best."

In the beginning, Howard had stayed home on Monday mornings to read manuscripts as an accommodation to Melissa to have someone home while Rosanne was there. Melissa was still under the impression—kept there, quite deliberately—that these mornings were of enormous inconvenience to Howard when, in fact, they were often the best times of his week.

Howard settled down into Melissa's pink chaise longue and picked up the remaining unread part of a manuscript that had been submitted to him at the office. It was not holding his attention, however, and in a moment he was staring out the window at the Hudson River.

Howard Mills Stewart was thirty-three years old and in perfect health. He had been married for eight years, was living in a fabulous three-bedroom apartment, was an esteemed editor at Gardiner & Grayson, one of the most famous publishing houses in the world, and yet—

And yet . . .

Why, he wondered, did he feel so terribly unhappy? So lonely. So utterly lost.

When twenty-two-year-old Howard Stewart joined the training program at Gardiner & Grayson Publishers, Inc., in 1975, to say that he was unprepared for the world of book publishing is putting it mildly. Nothing he had studied at Duke, nothing he had imagined as a teenager in Columbus, Ohio, had seemed to be of use to him. No, that was not quite correct. There was one thing he had brought along with him that was of enormous value: to so love reading, to so love books, that not even book publishing could scare him into seeking another means of employment.

When he had arrived in New York City—at the Chelsea apartment he shared with no less than five other recent college graduates—Howard had no doubts that he would discover great writers and nurture them to stagger-

ing heights of critical success. It would take him about a year, he thought.
He even had a list—in his head—of the kind of writers they would be: a
Charles Dickens; an Edith Wharton; an F. Scott Fitzgerald; a John Cheever;
and a John Updike. And so, when he arrived at Gardiner & Grayson for his
first day of "training," he was rather taken aback by being asked to type
some three hundred mailing labels to send out review copies of books.

When the publisher, Harrison Dreiden, recruited Howard to work as an
assistant in his office, everyone told Howard how lucky he was. Howard
wondered. Could book publishing really be like this? As far as he could
make out from the vantage point of his desk, no one in the office ever read
or ever edited. All that seemed to go on were phone calls, typing and meetings, meetings, meetings and more meetings.

"What exactly is it that you do all day?" Howard once asked a senior
editor. She had thrown her head back and laughed. "Okay, Howard," she
said, checking her watch, "I will give you a one-minute summary of an
editor's job. Ready?"

Howard nodded.

"The editor represents the house to the author, and the author to the
house, right? Okay then, lesson number one: the editor is responsible for
absolutely everything to absolutely everybody."

"Got it," Howard said, a trifle annoyed with this simplicity.

"And it means that the editor has to make sure that everyone working on
the book in house does his or her job, even though the editor might be the
only one who's read it."

Howard frowned.

"So the editor is in contact with everybody who is working on the book:
the author, of course, and the agent on the outside, and on the inside, well"
—a deep breath—"the managing editor, the business manager, production
coordinator, design, copy editing, the art director, sub rights—reprint, book
clubs, serial and foreign rights—marketing, publicity, advertising, the flap
copy writer, the sales manager, royalty department, the sales reps"—breath
—"and that's when everything's going smoothly. Otherwise there's the legal
department—"

"So you talk to them all the time?"

"That or we memo each other to death." Pause. "And that's only one
book—I'm usually working on six to eight books at the same time, with a
new list starting every six months. But I won't have anything to work on
unless I get out there"—a wide, sweeping gesture to the window—"and find
good books to sign up."

"Oh," Howard said, his frown deepening. "So when do you edit? I mean, do you?"

Another burst of laughter. "Of course I do. Oh, Howard," she said, patting his shoulder, "you'll find out. Publishing isn't a career, you know, it's a calling. In this house it is, at any rate. But don't worry—either you'll get it or it will get you."

Howard's phone calls and letters back to Columbus did not paint an accurate picture of his life in New York. The truth, he felt, would only upset those who had taken an interest in him early in his life, who had done great favors for him, believed in him, and expected great things of him.

Howard's dad, Raymond, was born the year the Stewarts lost the two-thousand-acre plantation in North Carolina that had been in the family for over a hundred and fifty years. The Depression was on, and the Stewarts moved to Ohio in search of work. When Ray was nineteen, working as a fence builder, he enticed a freshman at Ohio State by name of Allyson Mills to elope with him. Allyson was the daughter of a prominent Shaker Heights attorney. At her urging, Ray worked for his father-in-law as "the highest-paid filing clerk in the world" until he couldn't stand it anymore, quit, and took his bride to the outskirts of Columbus to start a landscaping business. Howard's dad was sort of, well—yes, he was at home with a shovel, but no, not with a necktie. And Howard's mom, devoted to Ray, decided she was happy if he was happy and, since he seemed to be, learned how to function in the capacities of the servants she had grown up with.

This was not to say that Ray Stewart did not have high hopes for his eldest son. The trick was how to give Howard every opportunity without accepting any help from his father-in-law (Allyson, too, was eager to do this). The Stewarts had a lot to work with. People liked Howard, they always had. He was acutely bright, good-looking, athletic, and just—just such a great guy. The kind of guy who fit in anywhere, never claiming to be any better or worse than who he was with.

Ray's friends were local small business owners like himself, forever involved in—and rallying together to protect their interests in—the Chamber of Commerce and the Rotary Club. And all of Ray's friends seemed to see something in Howard they wished to help along. When Howard proved to be good in Little League, he was given a job sweeping out a sporting goods store and got his pick of the best equipment available for any sport that interested him. When Howard was twelve, he was slipped in with the union caddies at a country club. When he was fourteen he earned high wages (under the table) building tennis courts. When he was sixteen, he bought himself a red Camaro (at cost, from yet another friend of his father's) to drive himself around to the suburban estates where he gave private tennis lessons to wealthy ladies bemoaning their backhands. The ladies adored him. ("You are so kind, Howard," Mrs. Lane said once, handing him a twenty-dollar tip. "You make me feel as though everything's going to be all right, even my tennis.") And the husbands trusted him. ("She hasn't had a martini before five all summer," Mr. Lane said, handing him a two-hundred-dollar bonus.) When one of his dad's friends built an indoor tennis complex, Howard was hired part time and his summer clientele followed him.

When Howard won a partial scholarship to Duke, the Rotary Club bestowed another on him. That, with what money Ray could throw in, with the good deal of money Howard already had (and would continue to make over the summers), enabled Howard to arrive at Duke with no worries save academic and social success. And he achieved both, making the folks back home terribly, terribly proud—of his honors, of his editing the newspaper, of his fraternity, of how Ray could still take Howard down to Leo's Bar for a "couple of cold ones" and show the boys how their investment was taking shape. (His first summer home, Howard's parents had promptly sent him up to see Allyson's family in Shaker Heights. "Make sure Father knows that Ray's given you money so you don't have to work at school," his mother whispered to him. "And if he starts in about your cousin Alfred at Harvard, you tell him to go to hell and come straight home.")

No, during those first two years in New York, Howard did not want to tell his parents that he made seven-thousand dollars a year, spent his days answering other people's phones and typing their memos and letters, and spent his nights with cotton in his ears, trying to read manuscripts while his roommates partied around him. And no, not to this day had he ever told his parents that he had sold his car to support his courtship of Melissa.

Ah, yes, Melissa.

It's important, at this point, to visualize the kind of figure Howard cut in those days. He was nearly six feet, had a strong, outdoorsy kind of build, and yet had this bookish air about him, fostered by the tweed jackets, baggy corduroy pants and horn-rimmed glasses he always wore. He had marvelously wavy, unruly brown hair. His face was imbued with serious lines—a strong nose and jaw—but was almost always seen in varying degrees of good humor. His blue eyes twinkled in any mood; his premature crow's-feet invited trust; and his mouth held a kind of mysterious promise for many of the women at Gardiner & Grayson. "This mouth is wonderful in any romantic scenario you may care to imagine," they thought it said.

Harrison Dreiden regularly took Howard to the Century Club for drinks. Harrison—in a way that reminded Howard very much of his dad's friends in Rotary—had set his sights on Howard as a protégé. Which was fine with Howard, since he thought Harrison might well be God's twin brother. After Howard started working on Harrison's long list of bestselling authors, the two of them would have long talks that began with Howard's quest for Dickens, Wharton, Fitzgerald & Gang, and ended with Harrison's strong recommendation that Howard lower his sights and expand his horizons for the sake of some kind of future in the business.

Even though Howard was the captain of the company softball and squash teams, even though there wasn't an employee at Gardiner & Grayson who did not like Howard, there was still a bit of a row when Harrison promoted him to associate editor. Apparently some of his colleagues did not seem to think Howard had done much to deserve it, and thus, at the age of twenty-four, Howard acquired a nickname around the house: Prince Charming. ("This is our head publicist, Harriet Wyatt," one editor had said to an author at a cocktail party, "and this is Mr. Charming, who works in editorial.")

The Friday night after his promotion, Howard had gone to Crawdaddy's to meet an old college roommate for a drink. He did so with the first genuine enthusiasm he had felt since arriving in New York. Okay, so what if Teddy was making exactly twenty-three thousand dollars more than Howard at Manchester Hannonford Bank? *Howard was an editor at the finest trade publishing house in the world.* And so, over a million Heinekens (it seemed), Howard reveled in the feeling of having regained his place in the world.

Enter Melissa.

The noise in Crawdaddy's was so loud, Howard did not hear her name when Teddy introduced them, and yet Howard felt as though he knew exactly who she was—his. It is true; it happened like that. Howard looked up and instantly felt that he would never find a finer woman to be his wife than the one standing before him. She was perfect. Everything about Melissa was slim, elegant, cool and classy. And it was in that moment, that very first moment, that Howard vowed he would try to win her as his own.

But first there was the overgrown preppy with her to contend with. "Stephen Manischell, Manchester Hannonford," he said to Howard, shaking his hand. The four of them sat down together at a table, where Howard learned that Melissa Collins also worked at "Manny Hanny" and was currently seriously involved with the creep next to her. But Melissa was not immune to Howard's intense fascination with her. In fact, within an hour she had moved her chair over to Howard and, with their heads looming closer and closer to each other, told him all about the important aspects of her training program at Manny Hanny (pausing only to tell Stephen to please be quiet, couldn't he see that she was talking), and what it was like commuting every day from New Canaan, Connecticut. She told him about her parents' guest house that she lived in. She told him that her mother had cancer and that her father, "Daddy," imported more cocktail napkins, plastic toothpicks and swizzle sticks than anyone in the world. (She didn't describe it like that, but even through the haze of alcohol and his fantasies of what her breasts might be like, Howard had figured out what "cocktail accouterments" were.)

Then it was Howard's turn. Howard was an editor at Gardiner & Grayson, the youngest, he added, that they had ever had. Duke. Yes. Phi Beta Kappa. Columbus, Ohio. "Uh, well, Mom is a housewife. . . . Dad? Oh, Dad's in real estate."

Miracle upon miracle, Melissa whispered to Howard that if he left now she would meet him outside in five minutes and he could walk her to the train. If he wanted to, that is. Whether it was his heart or the Heinekens talking, Howard was never sure, but Melissa to this day swore that he said, "Want to? God, I would crawl if only to see you."

And so Melissa had given Stephen the slip that night and Howard had walked her through Grand Central to her train. At the door of the train Melissa kissed Howard on the cheek and he tried to kiss her on the mouth and she stopped him. Her hand placed lightly over his mouth, she laughed (looking so beautiful, so right, so utterly glorious in a *Town and Country* kind of way) and said, "It would be so wonderful if you turned out to be the man I want to give myself to."

And then Howard went slightly mad. He had never met a girl like Melissa before. There was something about her that drove him wild inside, a kind of craving, a kind of nameless longing that he had never experienced before. Oh yeah, there had been Debbie, at seventeen, with whom he had launched his sexual career in the back of his mother's station wagon. ("Heh-heh," his father had said, winking, when Howard requested to drive it instead of his Camaro one night. "Make sure you take a raincoat—it might rain, heh-heh.") And there had been Susie the Senior his freshman year, and then Cornelia Fordyce the next three. And one or two quickies in New

York, and always something with Debbie whenever he was home, and all of them, *all* of them, were very smart, very attractive women. But they weren't anything like Melissa. God, Melissa. Walk into a room with her on your arm and, well—everything that could be said was said just by looking at her.

But then, as it has been said, Howard had gone slightly mad.

Melissa explained to him that while she knew it was terribly old-fashioned of her, she really couldn't even *think* of engaging in *any* sexual activity until she was married to the man she loved.

Did that—did that mean Melissa was a . . .

"Oh, Howard," she would whisper, shyly touching his hand, "wonder if you turn out to be the man I love? Wouldn't you want me to be able to say to you, 'Everything I have belongs to you and to you alone? Always and forever?' "

Oh, yes, but Howard wanted that, and Howard sold his car after Melissa dumped Stephen once and for all in favor of giving Howard his chance to win her heart. He learned to relish chaste kisses; he learned to meet her train in the morning and walk her to work. He took her to expensive restaurants for dinner, to the theater, the ballet, and he went out to New Canaan on Sundays to spend the day with the Collinses.

He hated "Daddy" Collins from the beginning, but—since Melissa was utterly devoted to him—Howard learned to let him beat him at golf, lecture him on the swizzle-stick business, and suffer his observations about publishing. ("Kind of a faggy way to make a living, if you ask me.") Mr. Collins hated him too, Howard quickly realized, but things between them improved once Daddy found out that Howard—as a doubles partner—meant that he could finally "beat the shit out of those assholes at the club."

Mrs. Collins, on the other hand, was wonderful. And it was from her that Melissa had inherited her regal looks. But Mrs. Collins was very quiet, very, very gentle, and by the time Howard met her, was bedridden with the cancer that was slowly killing her. She never complained of the constant pain she was in, and her eyes always lit up when Howard came in to see her. They spent a great deal of time together, actually. And once Howard started bringing her Anthony Trollope novels to read, even Melissa found it difficult to lure Howard away from their talks about them. ("Always see the mother before you commit," Ray Stewart had told his son, "so you can see what you're getting into." Cancer or no cancer, Howard often wondered if he hadn't fallen a bit in love with Mrs. Collins.)

It was clear to everyone in that mausoleum of a house that things were getting serious. Daddy Collins was getting ruder and ruder, Melissa started talking about how grand it was going to be when she was the president of Manchester Hannonford and Howard was the president of Gardiner & Grayson, and Mrs. Collins, well . . .

One Sunday afternoon Mrs. Collins took his hand (which she often did) and asked Howard if he was in love with her daughter. Howard said yes. And then Mrs. Collins had closed her eyes, thinking, and when she opened them again she said she hoped she would not offend Howard but . . .

But?

Did Howard realize that Melissa was—was rather special?

Yes, yes, he certainly did.

She had smiled, though her eyes had not smiled. Slowly, carefully, she said that Melissa was her only child, that she loved Melissa very, very much, but . . .

But?

Howard could see how spoiled Melissa was, yes?

Spoiled, nonsense!

A chuckle from the invalid lady. "Oh, Howard, she's dreadfully spoiled, and she always will be. Her father has seen to that."

Silence.

"My husband, and please, do understand, Howard—it is out of his love for Melissa that he did it—"

"Did—"

"Looked into your background. Your parents, your father's—real estate business . . ."

Sigh. "Mrs. Collins, my father's not in real estate, he's in the landscaping business."

"Yes. I know. Howard—listen to me, Howard."

Silence.

"You must sit down and explain to Melissa. She—and I'm sure you did not misrepresent it to her—but Melissa led my husband to believe that your father owns half of Columbus."

Oh, boy.

"And you must set my husband straight—*now*, Howard, before he . . ."

Mrs. Collins had started to cry.

"It's okay, Mrs. Collins, it's okay."

"She so needs a man who understands her. She's fragile in ways . . . Oh, Howard, promise me that you'll help Melissa leave this house. She won't be able to do it on her own and I'm too ill . . ."

Howard explained everything to Melissa that afternoon, prompting her to moan, "Oh, my God, what will I tell Daddy?" and flee to the guest house. And then Howard found Mr. Collins in the playroom and set him straight about the exact state of his finances and those of his family. Though he had readied himself for a fight, Howard was frankly a little scared when Mr. Collins grabbed the wrong end of a cue stick and smashed the sliding glass door with it. "Goddam carpetbagger!" he screamed, face turning purple. (Mr. Collins was from the South.) He broke the cue stick on the corner of the billiard table and slammed the remaining portion down on it, again and again, ruining the mahogany. "A fraud, a goddam fraud, strutting around here like the King of England!"

(Years later, Howard realized that it was not the state of his finances that had so enraged Mr. Collins, but that he—having volunteered the information before proposing to Melissa—had disarmed Mr. Collins of the weapon he had been planning to use to get rid of him with. Ill as she was, Mrs. Collins had been quite on the ball.)

Howard did not hear from Melissa for five days, and then she had called him at work. Could he come to New Canaan? Please, could he? Right now? They needed him, Daddy and she did, desperately. "Oh, Howard, Mother died this morning."

Harrison gave him some time off and Howard went out to New Canaan. (Poor Harrison. It had been some time since he had got any real work out of Howard, what with this time-consuming business of courtship.) Mr. Collins didn't say a word to him, but he did seem relieved that there was someone to look after Melissa as he went through the ordeal of funeral services. And then, after the burial, Mr. Collins disappeared to have some time to himself and Melissa became so hysterical that a doctor had to be called to sedate her.

"Why did he leave? Why?" she kept crying, Valium seeming to do very little but confuse her and slur her words. But after a few days she started to come around and soon she was not hysterical but furious with her father. She started cursing Daddy and endearing Howard. She started discounting Daddy ("He has no imagination, *none*") and overpricing Howard ("No one is smarter than you, Howard, I'm sure of it"). And then she started tearing Daddy apart ("He is heartless and cruel and selfish") and building Howard up to ever increasing heights ("You are the finest, greatest man I have ever known").

(Howard didn't know what the hell was going on, but he knew he liked it a good deal better than Melissa locking herself in the guest house and Mr. Collins calling him a carpetbagger.)

And then—and then, the night Howard came upstairs to check on Melissa and found her on her knees, crying next to her mother's bed. Howard had knelt down beside her, held her close, and told her he loved her. He was not good enough for her, he knew, but he would do everything in his power to make her happy. He loved her, God, how he loved her, and he would take care of her. He would never ever leave her. No, never, and they would have each other, forever and ever and always. "Oh, Melissa, please let me take care of you so you'll never be hurt again."

"Hey, Howie?" Rosanne called from the hall.

"Yeah?"

"I want ya to come see Mrs. C on TV. She's doin' an editorial or somethin' and I told her I'd watch."

"Yeah, okay." Mrs. C? What was her name? "Fridays" was how Rosanne usually referred to her.

Howard wrapped a thick elastic around the manuscript he had (not) been reading and dropped it to the floor. He certainly wasn't getting much done this morning. But then, even when he was working full throttle these days, he still felt like he was spinning his wheels.

Howard went into the living room and sat down on the couch. "Turn to Channel 8, would 'cha?" Rosanne said, coming in from the kitchen with a toasted bran muffin on a plate. He picked up the remote control from the coffee table and pushed 8. "Oh," Rosanne said, sitting down cross-legged on the floor, "I found that envelope in the couch. It belongs to her highness." Howard saw the envelope on the arm of the couch and picked it up while Rosanne hummed along with the theme song of the McDonald's commercial.

"138 East 77th Street" the return address said in thin black type

Jackass, Howard thought, turning the envelope over.

"Melissa Collins"

Melissa Collins Stewart, jackass.

"Oh, Howard," Melissa had said to him when the first one arrived. "Stephen's just lonely. The divorce really hit him hard."

Yeah, right, Howard had thought. So hard that Stephen Manischell felt free to call and write his wife whenever he felt like it.

"Oh, Howard," Melissa had said later, "it was entirely accidental. Stephen used to summer on Fishers Island and he rented the house this year not even knowing we'd be there."

Yeah, right, Howard had thought.

"I thought you'd be pleased, Howard," Melissa had wisely added. "You won't have to play gin with Daddy." (Daddy owned a house down the road.) "Stephen loves playing gin with Daddy."

Hmmm, Howard had thought, brightening a little.

What the hell do I care anyway? Howard thought, tossing the envelope on the table. *If he gets her in bed, I'll pay him for the secret of how he did it.*

"She's on! She's on!" Rosanne cried, pointing to the screen.

"Hey—I know her," Howard said. "What's her name again?"

"Mrs. C—now shut up, Howie."

Mrs. C was the stunning blonde who lived on the other side of 88th, in 162. Howard had been watching her in passing for years. From the way Rosanne talked about her, Howard had always visualized "Mrs. C" as looking something like his mother (slightly plump, graying, matronly). Melissa knew her from the Block Association but had never introduced him to her. ("Oh, I suppose Cassy's all right," Melissa would say, "but not for us.")

"How old is she?" Howard asked.

Rosanne held her hand out to shut him up and so he did.

"Using the Oval Office as his pulpit, President Reagan recently compared abortion rights to the institution of slavery," Cassy was saying into the camera. "He also said that we cannot survive as a free nation until the constitutional right to abortion is overturned. Mr. Reagan did not, however, bother to explain that the views he expressed are his own personal opinions, and not the shared belief of the majority of Americans, to say nothing of the highest court in the land."

I bet she has fun in bed, Howard thought.

Abusing the powers of the executive office . . . Injecting religious doctrine into the political process . . . Defiance of the Constitution . . . WST does not condone or condemn abortion policy . . . WST vehemently opposes the merging of church and state . . .

"Hi, I'm Howard Stewart. I saw you today on television. If I may say so, you were wonderful."

The editorial was over and Cassy smiled in a way that made Howard smile back. *Nice.* "I'm Catherine Cochran, vice-president and general station manager of WST. Thank you."

"Wowee kazow and go gettum, baby!" Rosanne cried, rolling backward into a somersault.

With their engagement official and documented in the New York *Times,* Howard took Melissa to Columbus to meet his family. It was not a great trip. The nice middle-class home in the nice middle-class neighborhood was not to Melissa's liking. Nor was Howard's father. Oh, Melissa was polite, but Howard knew her withdrawal into silence was a condemnation. And Howard noticed that his dad's undershirts showed in the top of his open shirts, that he brought his beer bottle to the table, and that he did not notice Melissa swooning at the suggestion that she and Howard attend the dance at the VFW Hall. And then Howard's younger brother had clomped in, bare-chested, from his construction job, and his sister announced she had to get ready for her date, which was fine, until her date arrived and explained to Melissa that he was an undertaker's assistant.

On the plane, flying back, Howard had dared only to ask Melissa's opinion of his mother. "I liked her," she said. And then, gazing out the window, she added, "But it must be very difficult for her."

"What do you mean?"

Melissa sighed slightly, turning to look at Howard. "Well, it's rather like being stranded for her, isn't it? Didn't you tell me her parents were well off?"

Melissa had not gone over very well with the Stewarts, either. And it wasn't her money, his father claimed over the phone in the kitchen. She was, well, kinda uppity, wasn't she? "We mean, Howard," his mother had said from the extension in the bedroom, "do you have fun with her? Do you —laugh?"

Howard and Melissa were married in a huge wedding outside on the grounds of the Collins house. It was the most god-awful wedding Howard had ever attended, though everyone said they had had the best time of their lives. Melissa's mother's family, the Hastingses, adored the Millses of Shaker Heights, and they had a grand time of it at the tables by the dance floor which Melissa had designated for them. The Al Capones who comprised Mr. Collins' business associates had a ball in the house, filling the playroom with cigar smoke, playing billiards ("stupidest pool table I ever saw") and making phone calls to Hong Kong about missing shipments of swizzle sticks. Ray and his friends were lured away to the swimming pool by a keg of ale and a box of fireworks that Melissa thoughtfully told them about. The Stewart contingents from Maleanderville, North Carolina, Vandergrift, Pennsylvania, and Teaneck, New Jersey, conducted their family reunion under the tent Melissa had set up for them by the gardens at the bottom of the hill. As for Mr. Collins' family, apparently he had none (or, perhaps, had none he cared to acknowledge).

And then there had been the legion of Melissa's "friends." Hundreds and hundreds (it seemed) of perfectly coiffeured dainties—selected and collected at Ethel Walker, Bryn Mawr, Yale, God only knew where—escorted by an army of vaguely good-looking men, all appearing to be wearing the same suit. ("Harvard," one said to Howard, flapping his school tie at him. "Princeton," said the one next to him, flapping his. "Manchester Hannonford," Stephen Manischell joked. "Merrill Lynch," said the one with the Princeton tie. "House of Morgan," Harvard said, stopping the other two dead in their tracks. "Bragging, dear?" Harvard's wife then asked, coming up behind him. "Stephanie told me that Wiley made over four hundred thousand at Salomon Brothers last year.")

Had they intimidated Howard? No. They had terrified him. Round and round the floor they had danced, talking of mergers and acquisitions and what stocks would give the Stewarts a brighter future. "The publisher of my life," Melissa kept introducing him as. "His family is over there," she said, pointing to the Millses of Shaker Heights. "Oh, Daddy? He gave us a beautiful apartment in the city, didn't he, Howard? Howard's just crazy about it. On Riverside Drive. Oh, I know, but Daddy didn't know that and he spent a great deal of money on it and I just couldn't hurt him that way. I mean, what would I say? No, Daddy'd never believe Howard wanted to live on the East Side. Daddy says Howard would be happiest in a log cabin."

"I'm gonna put this letter on her highness' dresser," Rosanne said, placing it there.

"Oh, fine."

"And here's some coffee," she added, walking over and handing him a cup.

"Thanks."

Rosanne walked toward the door, stopped and turned around. "Mrs. C's over twenty-nine," she announced.

"Oh, yeah?" Howard said, smiling.

"Go back to work," she said. "But remind me, Howie, before I leave I wanna talk to you about Tuesdays."

Howard swallowed some coffee. "You want to switch days?"

"Naw," she said. "I wanna talk to ya about Amanda, but I gotta finish the oven first."

Howard leafed through the pile of short proposals in his lap, sighed, and let them fall back in his lap. His eyes were on Melissa's dresser now. He rubbed his chin, thinking. It would be a low thing to do. And yet, knowing how meticulous Melissa was, he was sure the letter had been left in the couch for him to find. "Rosanne?" he called.

One second, two, three . . .

"Better make it short if you want an oven left!"

"Where was that envelope?" he called, rising from the chaise longue.

"The couch!" In a moment, she appeared at the door, wiping her forehead with the back of a rubber glove that was brown with gook.

"In it or on it?" Howard asked her.

"Sort of stickin' up between the cushions." She blew a strand of hair away from her eye. "Finished, Mr. Mason?"

Howard offered a half smile and slid his hands into his pockets. "Yes." When Rosanne returned to the kitchen, he went over and read the letter.

> Dear Melissa,
>
> I don't know what I would do without you these past months. No one told us it would be like this, did they? Forgive me when I say that I can't help wondering what would have happened if we hadn't met Howard that night. We'd both be a lot happier, I know. You told me Barbara wasn't clever enough for me, and I told you that Howard would disappoint you—so I guess we both got what we deserved for not listening to each other.
>
> I just wanted to thank you for listening to me the other day. My success at Beacon Dunlap would mean nothing without someone to share it with and, as always, you understand the importance of everything.
>
> Not long until Fishers Island! (I'm seeing your father next week for lunch.)
>
> Melissa, dear friend, you are all that is keeping me going.
>
> > Love,
> > Stephen

The first night of their honeymoon, spent at the Plaza, Howard had accepted that Melissa was too exhausted to have sex. So exhausted, in fact, he excused her when she pushed him away when he wanted to hold her as they fell asleep. Her excuses the next night, in London, and the next and the next and the next, were all quite reasonable. Melissa was of course shy; it would take time.

As it turned out, they did not consummate their marriage until they moved into the Riverside Drive apartment. Melissa had lain there, eyes closed, chin up, enduring Howard's touch as though it were a prelude to being shot. When it came to actual penetration, Melissa cried and pleaded and begged Howard not to do it because it was *killing* her. Howard stopped, but then he thought of Mrs. Collins and Daddy Collins and the wedding and somehow he knew that if he didn't just push ahead and do it, *it* might never happen. After he—ever so gently—managed to come inside of her, Melissa jumped out of bed, locked herself in the bathroom, and stayed in the bathtub for nearly an hour. Afterward, robe firmly knotted around her waist, she curled up with the telephone on the living-room couch and called, of course, Daddy. "Everything's fine," Howard overheard from the hallway. "Remember how you used to wake me up when you couldn't sleep? It's like that, Daddy."

Howard racked his brain about how to help Melissa. (God, how to help himself.) When therapy was dismissed as ridiculous, Howard pledged his faith in time and gentle reassurance. The only problem was that Melissa seemed to hate reassurance more than she hated sex. ("Just please stop talking about it!" she would wail, clapping her hands over her ears.) But time did bring a change, a compromise, they had lived with since: Melissa used sex (a loose term, considering what it was like) to force Howard into doing whatever horrible thing she had her heart set on. If they spent the weekend in New Canaan with Daddy, if they went to Daddy's reunion at Schnickle State College in Tennessee, or if Daddy came in and spent the weekend with them, then Howard could look forward to sex the first night after the ordeal was over. And summers! That was an interesting game, renting down the road from Daddy. The three or four weekends a summer that Daddy was not there were the weekends Melissa gave the signal, "I'll be ready for you in twenty-five minutes, Howard."

Howard had never cheated on Melissa. Amazing, but true. But then, life with Melissa was not all bad. No, far from it. The Stewarts enjoyed a way of life for which Howard never ceased to be grateful. They had this wonderful apartment (where Howard had the large library/study he had always dreamed of); they had their tennis and squash club memberships; they had their BMW (replaced biannually by Daddy); they had their annual three-week trip to Europe; they had their ballet and theater tickets and they had their big old rambling house in the summer (subsidized in part by Daddy).

Did anyone know what it was like for Howard to walk into Shakespeare & Company or Endicott Booksellers and buy four, five, eight hard-cover books? Did anyone know what it was like for Ray's son to be greeted by name in Brooks Brothers? To give his family a VCR for Christmas? To quietly send his sister a thousand dollars when she got "in trouble" and tell

her she never had to pay him back? Did anyone know how Howard had felt
when he told Melissa of his mother's admission of the terrible year Ray was
having, and Melissa wrote out a check for ten thousand dollars, telling
Howard exactly how to "invest" it in Stewart Landscaping in a way that his
father could accept? Did anyone know what it was like to live like this and
be an editor in trade book publishing?

Melissa was generous. The strings were long and complicated, but yes,
Melissa was generous. "Just work on becoming publisher, Howard, and I'll
take care of the rest." And she was. Melissa was now, in 1986, a junior vice-
president at First Steel Citizen, pulling down some seventy-five thousand
dollars a year (not counting bonuses, which, last year, had come to almost
thirty thousand dollars—two thousand less than Howard's entire salary).

Melissa's energies and abilities—in Howard's and everyone else's eyes—
bordered on the supernatural. ("It's the Daddy in me," she would say.)
Dinner party for twenty—tonight? Billion-dollar loan to Madrid? Fifty
pairs of tickets to the Cancer Ball? "I'd be delighted to handle it," she would
say without hesitation. And she *would* be delighted, moving and managing
people, money and events in discreet euphoria.

But Melissa had a temper, too. And some nights Howard literally barricaded himself in his study against the sound of her tirades. "Layton Sinclair
has been promoted past you!" she had recently screamed, pounding on the
door. "He can't even speak and he smells and he's been promoted past you!
God damn it, Howard, what is wrong with you?"

Nothing was wrong with him, he thought, except that he couldn't bring
himself to be the kind of editor Layton Sinclair was. Because, you see, after
his marriage, Howard had truly become a good editor. No one, after 1980,
after Gertrude Bristol, had ever called Howard Prince Charming again.

Gertrude Bristol had been writing bestselling romance suspense novels for
thirty-five years. Her editor at G & G retired and Harrison, at an editorial
meeting, queried the group as to who was interested in taking Gertrude on.
To be more specific, Harrison was looking directly at his new young woman
protégé, sending the kind of signal that Howard used to get from him (and
foolishly ignore): *Trust me, this is an author you should take on.*

Howard—who had been floundering in terms of acquisitions—found himself cutting Harrison's protégé off at the pass. "Harrison—I'd like to work
with Gertrude Bristol." The whole group had stared at him in amazement.
*Howard? Romance suspense? It's-Not-as-Good-as-Cheever-So-It's-Not-Good-
Enough-for-Me Howard?* "Uh," Howard had added, "that is, if she wants to
work with me."

And so Howard had taken home ten of Gertrude's books to read ("Halle-lujah," Melissa had said, picking one up, "someone I've finally heard of") and received the first of many pleasant surprises to come. Since Howard had never read a romance suspense novel, he had always assumed they must be . . . well, not serious and certainly not literary. But Gertrude was both.

He flew up to Boston to meet the great lady and did so with great humil-ity. Gertrude needed his editorial expertise about as much as Jessica Tandy needed acting lessons, and Howard was not foolish enough to make any promises to her other than that he would do his best to make sure she continued to be happily published by Gardiner & Grayson. Gertrude seemed rather bored by all this and was much more interested in whether Howard could stay over another day and speak to one of her classes at Radcliffe.

Howard stayed over another day and the single most important event of his career occurred—he listened to Gertrude's fifteen-minute introduction to her class, in which she explained what editors do. "People working in the editorial process of book publishing today," she said, "generally fall into two camps—the agents, who 'discover' new talent, and the editors, who introduce that talent in the best light possible." But, she went on to say, the truly great editors would go mad if they did not, on occasion, make personal discoveries of their own. "How do they do this? Every newspaper they read, every magazine, every film they see, every person they meet, every short story, every poem, letter, billboard they read—*everything* an editor experi-ences in his or her life is unconsciously or quite consciously judged in terms of a possible book. Isn't that right, Howard?"

Howard, pale, nodded.

"Editors looking for fiction attend writers' conferences, read literary mag-azines, journals and short-story collections—or, if they are in the upper ranks of editorial, they make sure someone on their staff is. Editors looking for nonfiction habitually shoot off telegrams and letters in response to news stories. Editors often choose a particular city or part of the country to concentrate on, making themselves known there, getting to know the liter-ary community. Some editors concentrate on the academic community, or the religious community, or the business community, professional sports or the recording industry . . ."

(Howard's head was spinning.)

"It is the great editor's job," Gertrude had finished with, "to be on the cutting edge of contemporary culture, and to be on the cutting edge of discovering our past. It is an impossible job, but, as they say, someone's got to do it, and with us today is someone who does. Class, Mr. Howard Stewart of Gardiner & Grayson."

Oh, God. Howard had got up and fumbled and stumbled through a recitation of anything and everything he could remember Harrison having ever said to him. Gertrude's little talk had completely thrown him; he had never done any of things that she had talked about. Not *one.*

He returned to New York as Gertrude Bristol's editor. And something clicked into place as he reported his trip to Harrison. A connection was made—as he stood there, watching Harrison's smile grow wider and wider —between his old scorn for certain kinds of books and the fact that he had never read those kinds of books to find out what they were like in the first place. And so he started reading differently. And at lunch, with agents, he stopped saying he was looking for F. Scott Fitzgerald and started saying that he was looking for a new talent, someone with promise, someone whom he could work with, build with, over a period of years.

His first endeavor at "discovering" resulted in a bestseller. Driving home alone one night from Fishers Island, Howard was listening to a radio sex therapist, Dr. Ruth Hutchins. The topic was sexual dysfunction within a marriage, and Howard was (of course) listening with a great deal of interest. And then it hit him: *If the radio show is so popular, and if I'm even interested in it . . .*

He fired off a letter to Dr. Hutchins and learned that he was only one of many editors around town who had had the same idea. When Dr. Hutchins and her agent said it was not so much a question of money but which publisher best comprehended the nature of her professional goals, Howard sat down and wrote the table of contents of the book he himself would want to read. And so, on the strength of a good advance, a great marketing plan from Harriet Wyatt and the outline of *Sex: How to Get What You Want and Need* (with the jacket line: *Without Hurting Anyone, Including Yourself),* Dr. Hutchins chose Gardiner & Grayson. *Sex* climbed onto the *Times* bestseller list and stayed there for thirty-four weeks.

Howard started to experience joy. One morning he literally tore a page out of the *Times* and bolted from the breakfast table. "What's wrong?" Melissa asked, running after him to the front door. "The MacArthur Foundation winners!" Howard yelled, taking the stairs down because it was faster. What fun it was writing "discovery" letters! What elation to receive to receive a letter that said, "You have no idea what your letter meant to me. As a matter of fact, I'm in the process of expanding that short story into a novel now." Howard was even thrilled when he got a phone call from Los

Angeles that said, "Miss Margaret does not wish to write her memoirs at this time. However, she asked me to thank you for your kind letter, and to tell you that, should she decide to do so, she will certainly keep Gardiner & Grayson in mind."

First novel! Literary biography! Collected short stories! Spy thriller! Victorian anthology! Investigative reporting! Editing Saturday and Sundays! Reading from seven until midnight! Gertrude breaks 100,000-copy mark! *Sex* sells for $600,000 reprint! Editorial meetings! Marketing meetings! Sales conferences! ABA! Howard was on cloud nine (exhausted, thin, bleary-eyed, but up there all the same).

And then the winds suddenly shifted at Gardiner & Grayson, marked by the arrival of a man named Mack Sperry in the business department, and the subsequent hiring of several MBAs. The old sails of power started to rend, and it was soon clear that Harrison, at sixty, was losing control of the ship. Memorandums started appearing:

7 OUT OF 10 BOOKS LOSE MONEY AT GARDINER & GRAYSON. PROFIT AND LOSS STATEMENTS ARE BEING RUN ON EACH BOOK AND EACH EDITOR.

Two editors were fired and two editors resigned. They were not replaced.

ALL EDITORS ARE TO SUPPLY THE BUSINESS DEPARTMENT WITH DATA FOR THE FORECAST.

The MBAs flew into editorial waving yellow legal pads. "Data for the forecast, data for the forecast!" The editors looked up the answers to their questions in their files and in a few weeks a bound report was circulated. THE FORECAST, it said, emblazoned in bold display type on the cover. Inside were pages and pages of graphs plotting the intricate lives of factors "Y" and "X" in "000's." The editors looked at it and then at each other, wondering who (or what) on earth "Y" and "X" were. And then a bulletin was hand-delivered—DISREGARD FORECAST—and all the MBAs were fired and twice as many were hired and back into editorial they flew, rousing the now familiar cry, "Data for the forecast!"

PUBLISHING PROPOSALS APPROVED BY HARRISON DREIDEN WILL BE FORWARDED TO THE BUSINESS DEPARTMENT. *No editor can make an offer until he receives written approval from the Business Department.*

Seven out of ten projects approved by Harrison were killed in the business department. ("Rejected," the business department said about Howard's proposal to publish a biography of William Carlos Williams. "William Carlos is not famous enough.")

EDITORS ARE TO REPORT TO CONFERENCE ROOM 2 FOR GUIDELINES ON ACQUISITIONS. ATTENDANCE IS MANDATORY.

The guidelines issued by the business department were based on a simple premise: Gardiner & Grayson would become cost conscious and commercially aware. (In plain English, they wanted editors to do thinly disguised rip-offs of everything on the bestseller lists—for cheap.)

Layton Sinclair adapted beautifully to the new guidelines. When the business department expressed the urgent desire that someone "put together" an *Iacocca* pronto, Layton raced out of the gate. Now, the book the business department was referring to was a brilliantly conceived and executed business autobiography published by Bantam Books in 1985. The idea for the book had been "born" within Bantam, and they teamed the hero of Chrysler with a marvelous writer named William Novak, and so carefully orchestrated the book's debut and afterlife that, to date, it was threatening to break the two-*million* hard-cover sales mark. *Iacocca* was precisely the kind of original, breakthrough publishing Howard longed to do.

So one can imagine Howard's disgust when Layton—sensing a powerful ally for his career in Mack Sperry of the business department—claimed that, if promoted right, the illiterate manuscript of a man who had inherited a chain of motels could be the next *Iacocca*. "Layton," Harrison said at the editorial meeting, "you are an editor, not an android. This, this, this—" "*Lefty,*" Layton said (referring to the title, taken from the author's name of Lefty Lucerne). "*Thing,*" Harrison continued, "isn't a book. *Iacocca* is a book, Layton. A good book. And a book is a body of work that reflects original human thought and experience. This," he said, pushing the manuscript away from him, "is the most horrifying thing I've ever seen let in the doors of Gardiner & Grayson."

At the next marketing meeting, members of the business department asked how Layton's version of *Iacocca* was coming and, on the strength of Layton's verbal description, approved it on the spot. "It's for the readers of *Iacocca* and *The Search for Excellence.*" (The latter had been a business blockbluster of a different sort.) The business department was elated and told Layton to "make the jacket look like *Iacocca,* but use the colors of *The Search for Excellence* in the background." Harrison slammed his fist down on the table and said, "Not only is it unreadable, but I hasten to remind you that Lefty Lucerne was once imprisoned on racketeering charges, a fact that he neglects to mention in this so-called memoir." (A murmur from the MBAs that this sounded like a good promotion angle.) And then, when Layton added that the author's company would guarantee to buy fifty thousand copies of the book and that Gardiner & Grayson didn't have to pay an advance if they didn't want to, talk turned to making *Lefty* the lead book on the fall list.

"Promote him!" Harriet Wyatt angrily exclaimed at the next marketing meeting. "The man is brain-dead!" It was then explained that the author was so pleased to be published that he was giving a hundred thousand dollars to Gardiner & Grayson to promote the book. "Wonderful," Harriet said, "I'll find the best cart and coffin money can buy and launch him at Forest Lawn. Mr. Sperry," she then said, rising from her chair, "I will be fired before I make my people work on a vanity press project. You'll have to buy an outside publicist."

The matter of *Lefty* then raged all the way to the office of G & G's chairman of the board. There it was decided that Harriet would not be fired but an outside agency would be hired; that the book in question would not bear the Gardiner & Grayson name but would be distributed by them under a new imprint called Sperry Books; and that Layton Sinclair would receive the title of executive editor of the imprint but would remain a part of the G & G editorial staff.

And so Layton Sinclair had been promoted and Melissa was furious with Howard and Howard was sick at what was happening at Gardiner & Grayson. Oh, they were still putting up a valiant fight—encouraging one another, conspiring like members of the underground—but it was exhausting. ("Look, gang, we've got to get that first novel of Patricia's through," Harrison recently said in a closed-door meeting in his office, "so I want each of you to write a report that swears the author is the next Jacqueline Susann." Fortunately no one in the business department liked to read. "Patricia, call it *Valley of Desire,* but once you get the contract signed, keep changing the title on the pub list so they'll forget what it was supposed to have been.")

Sigh.

It was all coming apart now for Howard. In the old days, he really had wanted to work toward becoming publisher of Gardiner & Grayson, to be on the "cutting edge" of the publishing frontier, and he had wanted to do it with the colleagues he had grown up with. The ones who had called him Prince Charming and then had rewarded him with camaraderie when he started being an editor. The people who had listened to his ideas and to his problems, and who had shared their ideas and their problems with him. The people who—over the course of ten-hour days, five days a week for eleven years—had become his family. But now, now . . .

"Then *leave,* Howard," Melissa screamed, "find another job and leave!"

But Melissa didn't understand and Howard didn't think he could explain it to her. What would he say? "Melissa, you don't seem to understand. My colleagues at Gardiner & Grayson have been filling the void of our marriage for years. If I leave them, then I have no one."

No. Howard could not tell Melissa that.

"Amanda," Rosanne was saying to Howard, "you know, Tuesdays."

"And she's writing a book?"

"Is she? It's in *boxes* all over the apartment."

Howard chuckled to himself, picking up a book from the window sill in his study.

"But like she's really smart, Howie," Rosanne said. But then she paused, debating a minute, and then admitted, "Well, sometimes she does get kinda loony—sort of like Esmeralda on 'Bewitched' or somethin'."

Howard handed Rosanne the book. "Here. I haven't even read it yet. A friend just sent it to me."

Rosanne took it from him and looked at the cover. "Mickey Mantle! Oh, man, this is great, Howie. Frank's gonna love this too." She slid the jacket off and handed it back to him. "Better keep that to keep it lookin' nice. Wow," she sighed, smiling, putting the book in her bag.

Howard grinned, touching at his glasses. "So what's Tuesdays' book about, do you know?"

"Oh, it's about that queen—you know, the one that everybody says screwed horses."

"Catherine the Great?"

"Yeah—"

"She didn't, Rosanne."

"Well, that's a relief," Rosanne declared, hefting her bag onto her shoulder, " 'cause Amanda kinda thinks she *is* Catherine the Great. The way she talks—sometimes I don't know what the heck she's sayin'. I mean, like she's never mad or nothin'—she's always 'vexed' or some numbnuts thing."

Howard laughed.

"*You'd* love the way she talks," Rosanne added, pointing a finger at him. "So, anyway," she continued, backing out of the room, "the way I figure it, you're just the guy to help her."

"Help her?" Howard said.

3

TEA AT AMANDA MILLER'S

"**D**arling heart," Mrs. Goldblum said, "all women go a bit mad in their thirties. That's why it's so terribly important to marry well."

The younger woman blinked.

"You see, dear," Mrs. Goldblum continued, "in her twenties, every girl believes she knows what she wants out of life, and she settles into the life she is convinced will bring it to her. And no one can tell her differently." She smiled into her teacup and took a discreet sip. "And then the thirties arrive and she suddenly realizes the world can say no to her, and she becomes convinced she has made all the wrong choices . . . and," Mrs. Goldblum sighed, "she realizes that, instead of knowing everything, she knows very little." Mrs. Goldblum smiled. "It is not an easy time."

The younger woman nodded, thinking.

Mrs. Goldblum took a delicate bite from the small pepper jelly and cream cheese sandwich on her plate. The women were sitting across from each other at a round table in front of the largest of the living-room windows. The four corners of a white linen tablecloth hung nearly to the floor; the silver tea service sparkled in the afternoon sunlight; across the room a fire was burning in the fireplace, the brass fender set gleaming in the contrast of lights.

Both women wore black, but it was not in melancholy. Instead, it was fitting. The room in which they sat had furniture from an earlier century— dark, massive, gleaming products of English workmanship, settees and chairs covered in deep burgundy velvet. There was an enormous oriental rug, and the fringed edges highlighted the dark wood floors that were exposed around it. Old paintings of every size adorned the walls; the high ceiling was an intricate work of white panels and carved plaster. And there was clutter in the room. On every surface—table tops, shelves, even along the enormous mahogany mantel—there were bits and pieces of brass and hand-colored glass, and there were antique frames with pressed flowers and porcelain vases with dried flowers, and little leather Shakespeares and ivory elephants and all kinds of other small distractions.

The older woman sat perfectly erect. The black dress—whose era was anyone's guess—though faded slightly, still draped from her shoulders in flattering folds. A small gold brooch rested on the left of her chest; a gold charm bracelet on one wrist occasionally made small tinkling sounds. Her breath was gentle and slow; her hands moved gracefully, unobtrusively, often finding rest in each other's company on her lap. Her hair was pure white, the complexion beneath pale and sweet, and her face conveyed enduring strength of some seventy-seven years.

Her glasses were the only thing out of place. The lenses being thick, they distorted the woman's languid brown eyes into something almost comical. But they weren't comical. They were searching the face of her companion, looking for clues as to the younger woman's thoughts.

"I never liked him, you know," Mrs. Goldblum said.

The younger woman laughed. "You certainly deceived me there."

"Of course I had to be polite. You seemed so keen on the young man, I vowed I would come to like him in time. I never did, however."

The younger woman shook her head, looking down to her lap. Mrs. Goldblum reached across the table to cover her hand with her own. "Drink your tea, dear. You'll feel better."

The young lady raised her head. Her eyes, usually bright, were rather tired. A smile was pressed into use and her face changed considerably. It was a fascinating, striking face. But it was not beautiful. Every feature, though brilliantly conceived on an independent basis, was in contrast to the next. The large, hazel eyes competed with the strong, perfectly chiseled nose (that decidedly linked her to the portraits on the walls). The high cheekbones did not know the wide, full mouth, and the olive of her complexion was at odds with the light brown of her hair. And her hair, long and straight, parted in the middle and spilling down over her shoulders, certainly did not know what to make of the black dress and pearls. And the contrasts did not end there. Her ample breasts made no sense of her thinness; her hands, whose fingers were long but large, hinted at a line of heritage that once knew the fields—or service under the people from whom her nose had come.

Mrs. Goldblum watched Amanda Miller take her suggestion regarding the tea. She smiled, nodding slightly. "Better now?"

"Yes, thank you," Amanda said. She cleared her throat. "I must apologize—I'm not quite myself today."

On that note, Rosanne came in, wafting her arms in the air as though she were a loon in descent toward water. She came to a rest at Mrs. Goldblum's side—with Mrs. Goldblum none the wiser as to how she had traveled there —and pulled down on the crisp black uniform dress she was wearing. Every Tuesday, Rosanne cleaned Amanda Miller's apartment until early afternoon and then changed for the ritual of serving high tea at three. ("You gotta be kiddin'," Rosanne had said when Amanda first suggested it. "Well, maybe," she had reconsidered, once a generous offer of financial compensation for such an ordeal was discreetly tendered. "Ah, geez!" she had cried during her first "tea etiquette" lesson. "You make me do that [a curtsy] and I'm gonna go down like a house of cards.") All in all, the arrangement had worked out fairly well. As for Rosanne's etiquette, once she had latched onto Glinda the Good Witch in *The Wizard of Oz* as a model for her demeanor, she had gained a rather peculiar but nonetheless pleasant form of grace.

"Would you care for some more sandwiches, Lady Goldblum?" Rosanne said.

"Lady," Mrs. Goldblum chuckled, looking over at Amanda. "Oh, my, my." She turned back to Rosanne, softly touching her wrist. "No, thank you, dear."

"Very good," Rosanne said, curtsying. She raised herself onto her tiptoes and teetered over to Amanda, waving her imaginary wand once in her face. "And you, Empress?" she asked.

"No, thank you, Rosanne," Amanda said, laughing, covering her mouth with her napkin.

"Very good, ladies," Rosanne said, curtsying. Once she was safely behind Mrs. Goldblum, she raised her wings and glided back into the kitchen.

Mrs. Goldblum turned to make sure that Rosanne had left the room, looked back to Amanda and said, softly, "There is a lesson to be learned, Amanda dear. She married the man she thought she wanted—and she will waste her life waiting for him to be the man she wants him to be."

Something crashed in the kitchen.

"I realize it is difficult to understand, Mrs. Goldblum," Amanda said, "but I never wanted him—" Her eyes settled on a silver napkin ring. "I was not, am not, in love with him."

Mrs. Goldblum apparently did not hear the crash or Amanda. "To love and be loved in return is the greatest gift life has to offer. To love those who don't love themselves is—" Mrs. Goldblum refolded her napkin in her lap and then smoothed it with the palm of her hand, over and over. "I was very fortunate," she finally said. "Mr. Goldblum and I had a wonderful marriage."

"Why?"

Mrs. Goldblum looked surprised. "Why, compromise. Every good marriage is one of compromise. Of acceptance. The pleasure and satisfaction of knowing that you both are willing to give up certain things in exchange for receiving much more than you could have alone."

Amanda touched at her pearls. "What kind of compromises did you make?"

"Oh, gracious," Mrs. Goldblum said, looking past Amanda to the window. Her voice grew faint. "It's been so many years, I can hardly remember what I cared about before Mr. Goldblum. Dances, friends, pretty ribbons, I suppose. Isn't it odd," she said, bringing her eyes back to Amanda, "I can't seem to remember anything of importance before I was married."

Or afterward, Amanda thought.

"And once the children arrived"—she chuckled to herself, shaking her head—"there was no time to miss anything."

Mrs. Goldblum's attention seemed to have drifted to her charm bracelet. Amanda patiently waited for her to continue.

"And, of course, there was Mr. Goldblum to look after. He worked so very hard." She looked up, smiling. "I used to bathe the children at five. With the children's nanny, Muerta—a Swiss girl. We had help in those days. And when Mr. Goldblum came home, the children and I would be lined up at the door, as neat as tacks, waiting to welcome him home."

"And after the children grew up?"

"Oh, gracious," Mrs. Goldblum laughed, "I missed them terribly. So did Mr. Goldblum. We always believed Sarah would be with us for a few years longer, but then, Ben was such a catch!" A long pause. "Can it be twelve years?" she wondered aloud. "It must be. She died in 1974."

After a moment, Amanda said, "When the children left home . . ."

Mrs. Goldblum smiled again. She drew out a white hankie that was discreetly tucked in the underside of one sleeve, patted her nose with it and replaced it. "Mr. Goldblum and I didn't know quite what to do with each other." She laughed quietly. "Sometimes," she said, leaning forward, "I would look at him across the dinner table and think, *Who is this man?* It was as if I had never seen him before. The man I married had black hair. The man sitting across from me had gray hair." She eased back in her chair. "But then," she sighed, "there were still those moments when I felt as though he and I shared the same body, the same life, the very same thoughts. And in those moments I was the happiest woman on earth."

The clock on the mantel struck the half hour.

"Dear me, I've overstayed my welcome," Mrs. Goldblum said.

"Nonsense," Amanda said, rising from the table. "I would be deeply offended if you left so soon." She lifted the teapot. "We will have some freshly made tea, perhaps by the fire."

"No, I'm fine, thank you, right where I am," Mrs. Goldblum said. She looked at the teapot. "I do so love a cup of good hot tea."

"And good and hot it shall be," Amanda said. "Excuse me." She carried the teapot out to the kitchen. Rosanne was banging candlesticks in the sink, apparently in some effort meant to clean them. "Rosanne," Amanda began.

"It's not fair," Rosanne said, throwing down the sponge.

"What's not fair?"

Rosanne rested the back of one rubber glove against her forehead for a moment and then whipped around to face Amanda. "She shouldn't talk about Frank behind my back," she said, clearly upset.

"Oh, Rosanne," Amanda said softly, putting the teapot down on the counter. "Rosanne, no, no. It was not meant as a criticism—"

"I heard what she said." Rosanne's eyes fell, and she swallowed. "She just shouldn't talk about him, that's all."

Amanda considered this, absently toying with her pearls. "No," she finally said, "you're right. But you know, Rosanne, Mrs. Goldblum is getting on in years . . . She would never intentionally say or do anything to hurt you. She was only trying to comfort me."

Amanda. There they were—when the sun came out—strolling, sometimes inching their way, on the sidewalk, sometimes arm in arm, sometimes on a walker, almost always with a fiercely determined expression that said to the world, "Nope! I'm not dead yet!" It made Amanda want to scream, "Please! Why can't we give them whatever they want?"

When Amanda left the store, she had found Mrs. Goldblum sitting on the fire hydrant that came out of the side of the building. Her pocketbook and precious purchases were lying on the ground at her feet. She was a little dizzy, she said. It would pass in a minute. Wasn't Amanda kind to pick up her belongings?

Amanda had ended up walking Mrs. Goldblum back to her apartment on Riverside Drive at the south corner of 91st Street. Mrs. Goldblum described to her how all the doormen up and down the Drive, in the old days, had polished the brass buttons on their uniforms and had taken pride in the white gloves they had worn.

Mrs. Goldblum's apartment was enormous but vacuous. And rather dusty. Amanda had stayed for tea and a tour of the apartment, receiving a history of the remaining furniture and a description of all the pieces that had since been shipped to her son in Chicago. Amanda learned that Mrs. Goldblum had been a widow for sixteen years, that her daughter had died of leukemia. That Mrs. Goldblum used the one bedroom, that the other two were empty. That she didn't live alone—she had her cat, Missy, whom she had recently adopted from the ASPCA. And that, before Missy, her cat's name had been Abigail.

Amanda had learned that Mrs. Goldblum was one wonderful older lady whose friendship meant the world to her. While Amanda fought the urge to shower money on her—an urge that, if Mrs. Goldblum ever suspected, would undoubtedly raise her wrath—she did manage to hatch two plots that did much to cheer her older friend's life: a cleaning woman (Rosanne) who would come once a week for twenty-five dollars (supplemented in secret by a twenty-five-dollar increase on Amanda's tab); and a formal tea served at Amanda's every Tuesday afternoon.

"Don't drop it, Rosanne," Mrs. Goldblum was saying, "*place* it on the table."

Rosanne was looking dangerous. She yanked on the hem of her uniform but said nothing.

"I'm sure the tea is lovely," Mrs. Goldblum added. "You always make it perfectly."

Rosanne's mouth twitched. "Thanks," she finally said.

Rosanne sighed, pulling off the rubber gloves. "Yeah, I know," she
tered, reaching for the teapot. "You want another?"

"I'll make it," Amanda offered.

Rosanne looked at her. "Ah, geez, don't start playin' Mother of Mercy
me. Go back and play the-good-ol'-days with Mrs. G."

"All right," Amanda said, walking to the door. She turned around the
hand resting on the doorway. "Are you all right?"

"Yeah, yeah," Rosanne said, moving to the stove.

When Amanda returned to the living room, Mrs. Goldblum asked if she
had told her that Daniel called.

"Oh?" Amanda walked over to take a small log out of the woodbox and
place it on the fire.

"Yes. He said he'll be coming for a visit soon."

"That's nice." Poke, poke, sparks fly.

Pause. "He has suffered a minor reversal in business recently," Mrs.
Goldblum said slowly.

Amanda remained silent. Her frank opinion of Mrs. Goldblum's only
living child was less than complimentary; she thought he was a self-centered, worthless rogue. For the life of her, Amanda could not understand
how Daniel could shut his mother out of his life—that is, when Daniel did
not require money. Mrs. Goldblum was a fine, amazing lady. How could he
ignore her? She was loving, warm, cheerful . . . and very, very lonely.

The first time Amanda ever laid eyes on Mrs. Goldblum was in line at the
Food Emporium in 1983. Amanda had sailed up behind her with a shopping
cart of liquid staples: a case of seltzer, coffee, milk, tea, Tab, and cranberry,
apple, orange, grape and grapefruit juice. After loading them on the
counter, Amanda had reached ahead for the delivery pad. Mrs. Goldblum
had smiled at her; Amanda had smiled back; and then Amanda noticed
Mrs. Goldblum's purchases: two potatoes in a plastic bag, one orange, a can
of tuna fish, a pint of milk, a box of butter biscuits and six cans of cat food.
For some reason the nice old lady's purchases hurt Amanda. (For some
reason, all nice old ladies' purchases hurt Amanda.)

After filling out the delivery slip, Amanda had yanked a copy of the
Enquirer out of the rack to look at it. Over the top of the page—over a
picture of Hepburn caught walking on the streets of New York—Amanda
watched Mrs. Goldblum's change purse come out. Inwardly, Amanda had
drawn a sigh of relief at the sight of two twenties in it. *Good,* she had
thought at the time, *I don't have to worry about her.*

The older women on the West Side of New York always unnerved

Amanda walked back to the table from the fireplace. "I quite agree with Mrs. Goldblum," she said, smiling. "You know, Rosanne, we are very, very fortunate to have you."

"I couldn't agree more," Mrs. Goldblum said, taking Rosanne's hand. "You know, dear," she said, "I often wish you could have been with us when the children were small."

Rosanne squinted at this declaration.

Mrs. Goldblum looked at Amanda. "I'm quite sure Mr. Goldblum would have been every bit as fond of her as I am. And," she said, eyes turning up toward Rosanne, "we had all of our lovely things then, things I would have liked very much for you to see."

"What, like the bone china?" Rosanne asked her.

A small, wistful sigh. "Yes," she said, eyes moving down to her bracelet, "my lovely china."

"Well, you still got that plate," Rosanne said. To Amanda: "You should see it. It's really nice. Sort of pink, with flowers."

"Painted by hand," Mrs. Goldblum said.

Rosanne gave Mrs. Goldblum's hand a little shake. "I can just see how it looked at Sunday dinner, Mrs. G. All I have to do is look at that plate and I can see the whole thing."

Mrs. Goldblum smiled.

The doorbell rang.

"I'll get it," Rosanne said, gently disengaging her hand from Mrs. Goldblum's and heading for the double doors that opened on to the hall.

"Thank you, Rosanne," Amanda said. "I can't imagine who that might be," she added, frowning slightly.

"Perhaps it is a neighbor," Mrs. Goldblum suggested.

But Amanda didn't have any neighbors on this floor of the building. That is, unless Mrs. Goldblum was taking into consideration the ghost who was said to be living in the south tower.

"No!" they heard from the foyer. "You wait right *there*. Don't move an inch until I find out what Ms. Miller has to say—*if* she's at home." Silence. "Hey! I told you not to move and I mean, *don't move.*"

Amanda and Mrs. Goldblum looked at each other.

Rosanne came in and closed the double doors behind her. "Oh, boy," she sighed, slumping against the doors, "it's Mr. Computer Head and he's got flowers."

Amanda's back went ramrod straight.

"Yeah," Rosanne confirmed, "and I don't think they're for your word processor."

"Is it your young man?" Mrs. Goldblum asked Amanda.

"Yeah," Rosanne said, "the guy we just finished trashin'."

Amanda seemed disoriented. Mrs. Goldblum didn't say a word; she merely looked down at her napkin.

"I—" Amanda started, and then stopped.

Mrs. Goldblum placed her napkin on the table. "Of course you must see him, dear," Mrs. Goldblum said. "It's time for me to leave on any account."

"Take him into the writing room and tell him I'll be with him momentarily," Amanda told Rosanne.

Rosanne sighed and did as she was told, closing the doors behind her. "Ms. Miller has guests," they heard her say, "but she'll see ya for a minute. Follow me."

Amanda saw Mrs. Goldblum to the front door, where she assisted her with the pinning of her hat in place, with her coat and with her walking stick. "It was lovely, darling Amanda, and I so enjoyed myself," Mrs. Goldblum said. She turned her face to allow Amanda to kiss her cheek, adding, "Just remember, dear, if you feel pain, it's because you've left the road for a thicket."

Amanda smiled and kissed her again. Closing the door, she paused there a moment. *Straighten* UP; *shoulders* BACK; WALK.

Roger was sifting through a pile of discs by her word processor when she walked in. He looked up and smiled. "Hi," he said.

"Hello," Amanda said, standing there.

Rosanne pushed past Amanda in the doorway to plunk down a vase of white roses on the table. On her way out, she said loudly, "I'll offer Mr. Smith some more tea."

"The flowers are lovely, thank you," Amanda said, closing the door.

Roger sighed and ran his hand through his hair. He was a good-looking man in his early forties. Well, Amanda reconsidered, pleasant-looking, but it was never for his looks that she had got involved with him.

He gestured to the word processor. "I see you've been working on Catherine." He laughed to himself, hitting one of the keys. "If nothing else, at least you can run this baby by yourself now."

"Yes," Amanda said.

That was how Amanda had met Roger. He had sold her the machine and delivered it himself. And then he had tried to teach her how to work it. And

then he had tried to teach her how to work him. Amanda had been emi-
nently more successful at her first attempt at one than the other.

Grinning at her, he plunged his hand in his pants pocket and furiously
jingled the change in it.

"Roger," Amanda said, moving to sit in the easy chair, "what do you
want?"

He cocked his head. "I'm not sure, exactly." His eyes trailed down, to
there. To Amanda's breasts.

She must be flat-chested, Amanda thought, crossing her legs.

He moved closer to her, coins still jingling. "Maybe I thought I was
making a mistake," he said. Amanda didn't say anything. "Maybe I thought
I had to be sure."

Amanda sighed, looking down at the armrest. "I don't think so," she said
finally, looking up. "There was never any pretense between us. That there
was any more to it than . . ."

"Yeah," he said, eyes narrowing. *Jingle. Jingle. Jingle.*

"Good grief," Amanda said, shaking her head. She was surprised—was
she really?—at the erection apparent in his pants. It was coming closer into
view. *Jingle. Jingle. Jingle.* Amanda lunged out of the chair. "Roger—" she
said again, whirling around, "what on earth do you think you're doing?"
She walked to the window, held onto the cross pane, and looked out at the
river. "What about your girl? The one who adores you?"

"Cooking dinner, probably," came the answer.

Amanda turned around and leaned back against the sill. "But she's not
enough for you, I presume."

Jingle, jingle, jingle. He was on the move again.

"I was under the impression that you were going to marry this girl."

"I might," he said, smiling, moving toward her.

"This is a marvelous start for a marriage," Amanda observed, folding her
arms across her chest.

"Hmmm," he said, placing his hands on her shoulders. Amanda dropped
her head. He kissed the top of it. "What do you care?" he murmured. "You
never pretended to care for me." He lifted the hair away and pressed his lips
against her neck.

Amanda's mind raced. It was undeniable, what she felt. What she felt like
doing. What she always felt like doing with Roger, and it wasn't conversing.
This unbearable, insufferable computer salesman also possessed an unbearable, insufferable member that was, at this moment, pressing against her.

Only the words weren't really "unbearable" and "insufferable"; they were "unbelievable" and "insatiable." Like the compatible parts of her own body.

He had his hand on her breast and in a few moments Amanda was reaching down to feel the length and breadth of his excitement. He moaned into her neck, dropping his hand to press between her legs. "I am aching to get inside you," he whispered in her ear.

The phone started ringing. Both of them froze. It rang and rang and rang. "Rosanne will get it," Amanda whispered, their palms still pressed against each other.

But she didn't. On the eighth ring, Amanda sighed, pulled away from Roger and smoothed her hair. "Hello?"

"I just wanted to remind you that Mr. Smith's out here," Rosanne's voice said.

Amanda closed her eyes.

"You know, like he's out here if you need him," Rosanne was saying. Amanda also heard the sound of a zipper. She opened her eyes to see Roger lifting himself out of his pants. "I can knock on the door—" Roger moved in close and pulled Amanda's hand down to hold him. She did. "Or maybe Mr. Smith could even yell for ya, ya never know. Or maybe he could break somethin' in the kitchen 'cause he's jealous or somethin'." Roger slid Amanda's dress up to her waist and managed to work her panty hose down. And her underwear. "Too bad there's no gun around. A coupla shots would do the trick." Roger parted her legs with one hand, eased himself out of Amanda's hand, and moved behind her. "How 'bout a light bulb? Sounds just like a gun sometimes." He pushed her forward over the desk. "Amanda," she finally said, "if you need some help you're gonna have to say somethin'." Roger felt for, and found, the right place and brought himself up into position.

And then Amanda cried, "No!" and tried to twist away.

And then Rosanne started pounding on the door.

She had been divorced for six years. Six *years.* Could it be? Six years since she had been Mrs. Christopher Gain? It was hard to believe.

If it had been six years since her marriage, then Catherine the Great had been living in her head for ten years, and existing on paper for—let's see . . . five years. Could that be right?

That was right.

Amanda Miller was thirty-two years old. Thirty-*two?* That would make her mother—fifty-eight, her father . . . *seventy?*

Yes.

Yes, that was right.

In 1946 a WASP-y rich girl from Baltimore entered Syracuse University as a freshman. Tinker Fowles was her name. Tinker Fowles fell head over heels with her dreamy-eyed English teacher, and scandal ensued. Not only was this Associate Professor Reuben Miller twelve years older, but he was Jewish as well. ("His mother does not even speak English!" Nana Fowles had shrieked in Baltimore, pulling her hair out.) The Fowleses filed an official protest with the university, but to no avail. Tinker went ahead and married Reuben and, to her parents' fury, Tinker transferred the million-dollar trust fund left to her from her grandmother to a Syracuse bank.

The year 1950 brought Tinker a degree in English; 1952 brought a master's degree; 1954 brought baby Amanda; 1955 brought a doctorate in English literature; and 1957 found Professor and Associate Professor Miller both working in the English department. They were, as everyone on campus noted, the most ridiculously romantic couple ever seen in this century. The Professors Miller left poetry in each other's office mailboxes; La Professora (as Reuben often called his wife) received flowers often; My Darling Own (as Tinker often called her husband) found silk ties and handkerchiefs hidden in his office; and every evening at six the two could be seen strolling out of the Hall of Languages, crossing the lawn, listening to the music students play the bells of Crouse Tower. They would stand there, hand in hand, smiling at each other. My Darling Own would, as he would describe, "dare to slip his hand around his dearest's waist."

Amanda, everyone agreed, was adorable, but certainly the oddest child around. To begin with, she was forever floating about in costume. One afternoon it would be as a princess, the next as a prince. Fridays usually found her streaking around the campus, laughing to herself, trailing multicolored layers of capes and scarves. She was reading by four and, by special arrangement, received her education at the hands of the students in the School of Education.

The Millers lived in a hundred-year-old Victorian house in Jamesville. Amanda had the entire third floor as her own. She spent hours up there by herself, reading and writing, playing music on her record player, and acting out plays that had no beginnings and no endings. She sang too (though terribly off key), and had a passion for what she considered dramatic dance (anything between ballet and the twist, or combinations thereof).

Adults were fascinated (and ultimately won over) by Amanda; children were decidedly leery of her. Upon introduction, Amanda was prone to break into merry song of her own composition and do a little dance—taking little leaps this way and that—to the usual response of her new acquaintances skedaddling but quick. But Amanda did not seem to mind; it was the attention of adults that made her happiest.

By age fifteen Amanda—strange as ever—took her SATs. And there was a bit of a problem. She scored a perfect 800 on the English part and 200 in the math (the 200 one receives for merely signing one's name). Nana Fowles (now the widow dowager of Baltimore) pleaded with Tinker to give Amanda to her for a year—to get Amanda "stabilized," to get this math problem straightened away and to prepare Amanda for something other than reciting poetry at the top of her lungs in the stairwells of the Hall of Languages.

Amanda begged to go. By this time Nana had made her year-round residence the Fowles Farm, a source of wonder and enchantment to Amanda all of her young life. And so Amanda traveled to Baltimore in Nana's limousine to get stabilized.

While Nana was otherwise rather forbidding in nature, she was helpless against the charms of her granddaughter. For the next fourteen months Amanda could be seen daily riding across the expanse of Fowles Farm, scarves trailing in the wind behind her. It had not been Nana's intention to put Amanda's fantasy world on four legs, but the girl was growing so quickly, so alarmingly, that even Nana had to admit that adulthood and labors of the heart would be arriving soon enough.

However, every afternoon at four, Monday through Friday, poor old Mr. Hammer would arrive, shouldering the burden of trying to teach Amanda mathematics. Amanda was cheerful, amiable, and even stopped touching Mr. Hammer's ears when he asked her to ("They are ever so remarkably red," Amanda would say), but she seemed to go into some kind of autistic trance when his lesson began. She watched as hard as she could but heard nothing. It was a language that her brain did not understand.

"Amanda," Mr. Hammer would say, marking a big red X by every question on the test sheet, "you have outdone yourself. Now, not only can you not do algebra, but you appear to have lost the ability to add."

Amanda would slide down in her chair and examine her hair at close range. "Nana will be most grievously vexed," she would sigh.

Poor Nana was also suffering grievous vexation over the bodily changes that had descended on her granddaughter. The slight girl who had arrived was blossoming in ways that Fowles women did not. "You must do something," Nana would direct the seamstress, "about that—about her—" The movement of her hand would indicate that the seamstress was to do something about concealing Amanda's ever expanding chest.

Amanda, Nana noted, was the only one oblivious to her new body. The gardener had taken to trailing around after her; the groom smiled in a most inappropriate way when he insisted on giving Amanda a leg up on her horse; even Randolph, the butler—who was at least as old as Nana—could be seen gazing elsewhere than at the gravy he was supposed to be serving.

If Amanda gained any permanent knowledge from her "stabilization" at Fowles Farm, it was Nana's opinion of the saving graces and potential downfalls of her heritage. Amanda loved Fowles Farm because, Nana said, her Fowles blood responded to it. Amanda's thinness, her five-eight height, her light brown hair (and its straightness), her nose, her straight white teeth, her strong jaw line and her long arms and legs were all Fowles. As for the shape of her eyes, their strange shade of hazel, those long lashes, that mouth, and the "overendowment" (referring to her chest), they all—sigh—clearly came from the Millers (said with the same emphasis as *murderers).*

Mr. Hammer pounded enough mathematics into Amanda's head—right up to the door of the examination room in Baltimore—for her to score a 560 on the SAT. As for the English part, if the examiners had taken her essay on "What George Orwell Would Think of the Design of This Test" into consideration, surely Amanda would have scored higher than her 800.

Amanda went to Amherst on the strength of her desire to attend school with Emily Dickinson's ghost. She enjoyed school very much and felt at home around the English department. She also made great friends with the curator of the Dickinson house. As for her contemporaries, everyone liked her—and some even admired her—but always from a distance. She was, in their words, "just sooo weird."

In her senior year Nana died. It became campus news that Amanda had inherited some four million dollars. And it was right around then that Christopher Gain appeared on her doorstep—literally. She was dressed in billowing white, just departing from her cottage to visit the curator. Christopher was dressed like Zorro. He bowed, deeply, his hat in hand, swept his cape to the side and offered her his hand. The girls roared from the windows above, but after Amanda smiled pleasantly at them, she turned to Christopher and took his hand.

Christopher had graduated some years before from Dartmouth. Since that time he had been hanging out at Amherst, discussing his future as a brilliant writer with various gorgeous coeds. He himself had gorgeous blond looks, tremendous charm and appeal, and a three-hundred-year-old pedigree.

Amanda found Christopher slightly magical. Sitting on the grass outside Emily's house, in the dark of the night, he cited poem after poem that the great lady had written. While Amanda noticed that he kept bending the emphasis to imply that Emily had been writing to some lover hiding beneath her bed, rather than to her universal lover in the heavens above, she enjoyed the performance immensely. And then, offering his hand to her again, he had led her behind some trees. He spread his cloak, gently helped her down, and then gracefully, gently, lay himself down on top of her.

Amanda marveled aloud at the way Christopher touched her. What he was doing, what it felt like—what she did not know it felt like. But it felt wonderful, she said, over and over. Amanda said a lot of things. In fact, she rendered a verbal narrative description of everything Christopher was doing to her—as he did it to her—as if it would help her to remember it all.

Amanda had never been touched that way before. Amanda had never been so much as kissed on the mouth before. Amanda was introduced to earthly delights beyond her comprehension. It wasn't like Mr. Hammer's mathematics—but it was very much like reading, she thought. It was taking her somewhere quite far away, somewhere quite different from the places she had been—inside of her? outside of her? where?—and she had the feeling that, yes, like reading, she would not fully understand it until she reached the end of what Christopher had to share with her.

They married three weeks after her graduation and moved to Florence. For two years Amanda and Christopher read and played and talked and dressed and drifted and reveled in Italy. They also spent hours making love.

At night, Christopher would go off alone to the cafés to think about his novel. Amanda preferred to stay home, reading and writing, playing records on the stereo, and acting out plays that had no beginnings and no endings. . . .

Amanda's first brush with reality struck when Christopher said he couldn't have sex with her because he had herpes. Had what? Christopher took her to the doctor with him, where it was carefully explained to her that she was lucky not to have caught it. But what was it? How did one catch such a dreadful thing? Did it have something to do with the water here?

The doctor explained.

Christopher said it happened one night, late, when he was so drunk he didn't know what he was doing. It would never happen again. And soon he would be well, he was sure, and then— "oh, darling, do you know what I'm going to do to you?"

On Christopher's inspiration, the couple moved to New York City in 1978, renting an apartment on 73rd Street between Fifth and Madison avenues. Two weeks after they arrived, Amanda came home from registration at Columbia University to find a young man named Marco wandering around in her kitchen with a towel around his waist.

It took almost six months for it to penetrate, but Reality Part II visited Amanda. Christopher, by his own admission, was bisexual. For Amanda, this information did seem like Mr. Hammer's mathematics. Not until Christopher persistently pounded it into her head was she able to glean what it was he was talking about. ("But I don't understand, how can this be?" "It just is, Amanda." "Is *what?*" "Like it is between you and me." "But he's *not* like me—how *could* it be like us?")

Amanda took her furrowed brow to Columbia to concentrate on an MFA in their creative writing program. It didn't work. With each passing day she and Christopher were splitting apart. Their sex life broke down completely and Amanda, for the first time in her life, felt terribly lonely. She stopped writing, she could scarcely read, she could not act out plays of any kind. After a while, not even the huge mirror of the wardrobe could evoke a line from her. Her costumes hung in the closets; her attire died into jeans, the denim growing looser, her blouses growing baggier. She dropped out of graduate school.

In 1979, Tinker and Reuben surprised the Gainses by arriving in New York to see them. (It was the first time they had actually made it.) The Millers were frightened by the change in their daughter. They were also stunned by Christopher, who, last time they had seen him, had not being sailing in and out of the house in silk pajamas. And there was something else—something Tinker had to talk about in private with Amanda.

Tinker didn't mean to pry, but Nana's lawyer, Mr. Osborne—did Amanda remember Mr. Osborne at the reading of the will? Amanda did— told her that the Gainses had spent some four hundred thousand dollars in the last eight months. Mr. Osborne—who only had Amanda's best interests at heart—said three hundred and forty thousand of that money had flowed through Christopher. Did Amanda know that? Was, perhaps, Christopher starting a business?

When Amanda sank down in her chair and started playing with her hair, Tinker had called her husband in. Together, standing before her, holding hands, the Millers gently suggested to their daughter that she might want to see a doctor . . . perhaps she and Christopher together.

Christopher, no . . . but yes, Amanda would see the doctor.

Amanda had been in therapy for five months when she flew up to Syracuse for a visit. Her parents were encouraged by the change in her. (Though, they sighed in secret, she was not *their* Amanda anymore, was she?) There were papers to be signed with Mr. Osborne, money matters to be rearranged. Amanda wasn't sure what all the papers meant (a Mr. Osborne was not of much value without a Mr. Hammer), but she agreed that it would be a good idea to curtail Christopher's access to her money.

When Amanda came home—on that fateful Saturday evening—she found her home in a full-swing party, the majority of the guests being what are sometimes described as "screaming queens." Her husband, Christopher, was the loudest. Wearing a little fig leaf. And in the dining room, among the bottles of booze and piles of joints, Amanda saw an array of pills and powders and needles and razors and a mirror, and a burner was scorching the finish off of Nana's table and—

Amanda moved into the Plaza Hotel—where, she remembered, her earliest literary heroine, Eloise, lived—and asked Mr. Osborne to handle her divorce.

Amanda settled fifty thousand dollars on Christopher, though Mr. Osborne told her she certainly didn't owe him a thing. Amanda thought she did though.

She bought the apartment on Riverside Drive at once. From the ground looking up, she thought her building looked like a castle. And her apartment, on the top floor, came complete with a tower room. She flew down to Baltimore, tagged furniture that was in storage from Fowles Farm, and had it shipped to her new home. In time, Amanda started riding in Central Park, and then her reading resumed, and her writing resumed, and then her talking to herself resumed. But the plays never came back, nor did her costumes ever leave the closet.

The idea of writing a novel from the perspective of Catherine the Great had originated in Florence. After having read and digested some three hundred tomes of Russian and European history over the years, in the fall of 1981 Amanda finally sat down and wrote the first line of the book. "I, Catherine, Imperial Empress of Russia, answer to no man."

* * *

"He's gone," Rosanne said, coming back into the writing room. She stared at Amanda for a moment and then abruptly turned away. "Uh, ya better . . ."

Amanda was confused. But then she looked down at herself and saw the state of her dress, of her undress, of her half undress. She pulled the dress down over her thighs and smoothed it. She brushed back her hair with her hands and felt the absence of an earring. Amanda rubbed her face, dropped her hands and sat back against the window. She sighed. "I am utterly at a loss as to what to say to you—except, thank you."

Exhibiting caution, Rosanne slowly brought her eyes back around. "Don't worry about it," she said. She swung her weight onto one leg and brought up her hand to the opposite hip. "Look, Amanda," she said, looking down at the floor, "it's none of my business—and it's not none of Mrs. G's either—" She looked up.

Amanda covered her mouth and coughed.

"Don't get mad—"

Amanda crossed her arms over her chest, sighing.

"I think you're great," Rosanne said.

Amanda was looking confused again.

"And Mrs. G thinks so too, and we just kinda worry about ya. I mean, it's not like we think anything's wrong with that guy or nothin'," she rushed on, "it's just we wish you were a little happier."

Amanda nodded slightly, lowering her eyes. "Thank you for your concern, Rosanne," she murmured.

"You're not mad or nothin'—*vexed,* are ya?"

Amanda raised her eyes, shaking her head. "Of course not," she said.

"Okay then. Well, I better be goin'," Rosanne said, moving toward the door. "Oh, man, I almost forgot to tell ya." She spun around. "Amanda, I think Howie wants to read your book."

Amanda blinked.

"Howie—you know, Mondays, Howard Stewart. The editor." Rosanne waved her arm in the air to make sure Amanda was paying attention. "Listen, okay?"

"I'm listening," Amanda said.

"Now don't go gettin' freaky, but he was really interested in your book. I told him it wasn't finished or nothin', and I told him it was kinda long—"

"Long," Amanda repeated, looking at the shelves that were Catherine.

"So is it okay if he calls you or somethin'?"

Amanda looked at her, hesitating.

"He's really the greatest guy," Rosanne said. "Just talk to him, will ya? You know, like he's an editor. And he won't push ya about it, he isn't pushy at all." She nodded her head vigorously. "Just say yes, Amanda."

Amanda lowered her arms to her side, sighed and said, "Yes."

"Great!" Rosanne said, leaving the room. "See ya next week!"

Amanda covered her face with her hands. *I nearly had sex in front of the cleaning woman,* she imagined herself saying to Dr. Vanderkeaton.

It had started with the apartment on Riverside Drive. This sex thing had. One man on Mondays and never one that she could even remotely like. For the last eight months it had been Roger, and Rosanne and Mrs. Goldblum had known about him only because Roger had forever been stopping in to try his luck. ("Mondays," Amanda would hiss at the door, with Rosanne lurking dangerously close by, "I have told you repeatedly. Every other Monday at one o'clock." "*Yes*terday was Monday," Roger would hiss back, trying to grab hold of her, "and I came back to finish up." "Mrs. G told me to tell ya," Rosanne would say, coming out into the foyer, "that she hopes you'll invite your visitor to join you guys for tea." And the confounded dolt had said, "Love to!" no less than six times.)

In the beginning, five years ago, it had worked. Sex had pushed something back into place for Amanda. After one of those Monday afternoons something would temporarily subside inside of her—that awful, gnawing sensation that her moorings were fraying to the snapping point. But, over time, it had stopped working that way, leaving Amanda only to agonize over what seemed like some sort of curse on her body. On her.

She still ran into Christopher on occasion. Once at F.A.O. Schwarz, once at Lincoln Center, twice on the terrace outside the Stanhope and, most recently, in the Whitney Museum. She had been alone; Christopher was never alone.

Each time she saw him—and most strongly this last time—Amanda felt weak at the sight of how unattractive he had become. His hair was thinning almost too fast to be normal; he had lost far too much weight; his muscle tone was gone; and his teeth showed nicotine stains when he smiled at her. His eyes, too, had lost their luster. And Christopher was losing his—his *maleness,* too.

Looking at him made Amanda feel queasy and disoriented. This was the man who had commanded such love and desire from her? This was her Christopher?

Amanda lowered her hands from her face and looked at the shelves of

Catherine that made up one wall of the writing room. There was her work, yes. There was that. And maybe . . . maybe it was time to do something about it. What had Rosanne said? Something about an editor wanting to read it?

The thought made her feel cold and scared and so she banished it.

She walked over to the desk, sat down, and pulled the telephone toward her. She looked at it a moment, lifted the receiver, and pushed the button marked "in house." "Yes, Peter, is that you? It is Amanda Miller calling. . . .Fine, thank you, and you? . . . I'm very glad to hear it. Peter, the reason why I am calling is to say that under no circumstances is Mr. Slats to be granted entry into this building. . . . That is correct—don't let him in. . . . Exactly. Not now, not ever."

4

THE WYATTS

"**Y**ou *are* different, Althea, and I'll tell you how," Sam Wyatt said to his daughter, voice rising. "You've got a nice home, a family that loves you and the best damn education money can buy. The question is, are you going to do anything with it?"

"Mom," Althea said, looking to her mother.

Sam slammed the *Times* down on the breakfast table.

"Don't," his wife said softly, placing a hand on his arm.

"You talk to her," Sam said, jerking the paper back up.

Harriet lowered her head slightly, took a long breath, and then looked at her daughter. Althea was standing there, arms rigid with anger. "Honey," she said, "if you had the money to go on your own, it would be a different matter. But you don't, and since your father doesn't agree with you that it's a good trip to make, you can hardly be furious with him for not giving you the money."

"I'm eighteen," Althea began.

The *Times* came crashing down. "Yeah," her father said, "so maybe if you're old enough to want to go palling around with Muffy, Scruffy and Whupsie—the Honky Sisters—you're old enough to support yourself."

"Oh, Dad," Althea said, storming into the kitchen.

The *Times* was thrown to the floor. "What is it with that girl?" he said, yanking first one shirt cuff down over his wrist and then the other.

Harriet was eating her scrambled eggs.

"If I had the advantages she has—"

"You didn't," Harriet said.

"You better believe it."

"I know, Sam."

It was even odds whether the man named Sam Wyatt would explode or deflate at this point. His wife, sitting next to him, chewing, watched to see which it would be. When he fell back into his chair with a sigh, a faint smile passed over her lips and she moved on to her English muffin.

Sam took a deep breath, straightened his tie and then paid serious attention to his tie clip. "I don't want her to get hurt," he said quietly.

"I know, honey," his wife said.

He let go of his tie clip, plunked his arms down on the arms of the chair, and looked at himself in the dining-room mirror. He straightened his tie again.

At fifty, Sam Wyatt possessed a handsomeness that was not easily defined. He was one of those men whose looks came alive with expression, animation, and since he was forever—as his eldest daughter would say— "intense," he was most often rather striking. He was tall, nearly six foot one, and squarely made across the shoulders. His skin was a deep, ebony black, and his closely cut hair had gray coming in fast at the sides. His mouth— perfectly fine when still—had a curious habit of lifting to the right side when in use. (Four years ago, when Sam brought home a publicity photograph of himself from the office, three-year-old Samantha had burst into tears. "That's not Daddy!" The Wyatts had finally pieced together that what was scaring Samantha was the absence of "Daddy's cook-ked smile.") Sam's nose was long and a tad sharp ("Where do you suppose *that* came from?" Althea would ask, pulling on it). And his eyes were large and bright, veiled by long lashes.

"Sam," his wife said, lowering her English muffin, "is there something else? Something other than Althea, I mean."

Sam thought for a moment and then sat back up to the table. "Would you want to go to Southampton with a bunch of white girls?"

"Not particularly," Harriet said, pulling the bit of muffin into small pieces on her plate, "but then, I'm not Althea. And they're nice girls, Sam, and I know she wouldn't have been invited unless they really wanted her to go. And it's preseason—" She frowned as Sam started humming "The Battle Hymn of the Republic"; she picked up a piece of the muffin and bounced it off his nose. "You're worse than a weather vane," she said. "Make up your mind, are you in a good mood or a bad mood?"

"Yeah, I'd like that—weather reports," Rosanne said, swinging in from the kitchen with a coffeepot. "Nobody told me hurricane Althea was gonna tear up the kitchen this mornin'."

"What is she doing?" Harriet asked.

"Aw, nothin'," Rosanne said, putting the coffee down on the table, "she's okay. Killed the last muffin, though. I think it's behind the refrigerator."

Harriet giggled and the sound of it made both Sam and Rosanne smile. Harriet Wyatt was one of those lucky women who in her forties had gained ten pounds and a rather astonishing new voluptuousness. But her black hair —straightened and coiffed in a stunning sleek cut around her neck—her spring suit and silk blouse and her gold hoop earrings and bracelets did nothing by way of indicating that she could be a woman who giggled. But that was Harriet, forever coming forth with warm and happy surprises. That is, unless she thought one was wrong, and then she would grow ten feet tall (it would seem to Sam) and everything about Harriet would turn hard with the warning, "Just try and mess with me."

"Can't imagine where she gets her temper from," Harriet said.

"Yeah," Rosanne said, going around Sam's chair to pick up the newspaper from the floor. "Here, Mr. W, let's set an example," she said, refolding it and placing it at his side.

Sam gave her a look out of the corner of his eye (with the side of his mouth rising accordingly) and then reached for the coffee.

"I wanted to ask ya somethin', Mrs. W," Rosanne said, moving back around the table.

"Coffee, Harriet?" Sam asked.

She nodded and turned to Rosanne. "Shoot."

"Like, well," Rosanne said, rolling up her sleeves, "Howie's a good editor, isn't he?"

Both Harriet and Sam burst out laughing.

"What? What?" Rosanne wanted to know, looking at one and then the other.

"I knew it!" Sam cried. "Harriet, I told you she's going to write a book about us. Remember?"

"I'm not writin' a book," Rosanne declared, stamping her foot. "But let me tell ya, if I was"—she poked Sam in the shoulder—"I wouldn't waste it on the likes of you. I got a lot more interestin' things to write about than you two spoonies."

"Hear that, Harriet?" Sam said. "She says we're too boring."

"Then thank God for boring," Harriet said to the skies above. She looked back at Rosanne, smiling. "Howard is a very good editor."

"I thought so," Rosanne said, starting to clear the dishes. "He's gonna read a friend of mine's book."

Sam's eyebrows rose, but he didn't say anything.

"Sam," Harriet said, sipping her coffee, "I'm supposed to have a meeting this morning with Harrison."

He nodded, but then, after hesitating a moment, said, "I wanted to talk some more about that job offer."

"Aw, no," Rosanne said, balancing the pile of dirty dishes, "you're not gonna leave, are ya?"

Harriet reached out to touch Rosanne's arm. "I'm only thinking about it, Rosanne, so please don't mention it to Howard."

"Naw, I won't," Rosanne promised, going out to the kitchen. "He's down in the dumps enough as it is."

"We all are," Harriet sighed. "The place is a battlefield."

Sam was sitting there, stirring his coffee. "How long do you have before you have to give them a decision?"

"Oh, I don't know. A couple of weeks, I guess." She looked at him. "Why?"

"Well," Sam said, slowly putting his spoon down on the saucer, "I wish you could put it off for a little while."

"Why?" she said again, clearly puzzled.

"Well, with summer coming—I don't know," he mumbled, shaking his head.

Harriet was frowning. "I don't understand. On Sunday you were all for it. As I recall, your exact words were, 'It's time one of us took a risk—go for it.'"

He sighed, sitting back in his chair. "I've been thinking about it, and I'm not so sure you want to leave—"

"What are you talking about, Sam? Haven't you heard anything I've said to you for the last year? It's—"

Seven-year-old Samantha chose that moment to come in and announce a crisis concerning a missing blue sock.

"I'll help you, honey," Harriet said, rising from her chair. "Sam," she added on her way by him, "I want to talk about this some more tonight."

"We don't have to talk about it," Sam mumbled.

Harriet stopped in her tracks and turned around. Finally, her husband looked at her. She started to say something, stopped, squinted slightly, and then said, "We do have to talk, Sam. We do."

"I don't know where it is!" Samantha wailed from the hall.

"Did you hear me, Sam?"

He nodded, tossing his napkin on the table.

"Honey," Harriet said, coming back to him.

"I know, I know," he said, lifting the jacket of his suit from the back of the chair. "We'll talk tonight."

As Harriet went in one direction, Althea came in from the other. She avoided her father's eyes, intending to pass him by, but he caught hold of her arm. "Hey," he said, pulling her back to face him.

Althea was not going to cooperate.

"Look," he said, tilting her chin up, "Althea, in a couple of years, you're going to be able to do whatever you want. You can run for *mayor* of Southampton if you want to, and I won't care. But for right now, while you're in school, while you're living here with us, I'm afraid you're just going to have to pacify your old man."

Althea rolled her eyes.

Very slowly, very deliberately, he said, "I love you, you know. And I don't want to see you get hurt."

"I don't see how going to Southampton is going to hurt me," Althea sulked.

Sam slid his arm around his daughter and made her walk him to the front door. "Look, I think it's nice that your friends invited you, but I don't think they understand—"

"Understand what?" Althea persisted, twisting away.

"That I don't want anyone looking at my daughter like she's a second-class citizen and, Althea, that's what you'll get out there." He shook his head. "You know, you act as though your mother and I don't know anything about how this world works. Well, let me tell you something, we didn't get where we are by hanging out—" He raised his hand and then dropped it, shaking his head again. "Did it ever occur to you that there was a reason why we decided to raise you kids here and not in the suburbs?"

" 'Cause you work here."

Sam closed his eyes and then, slowly, reopened them.

"You're so uptight, Daddy," Althea said, turning away. "You're so uptight about everything."

Sam looked at his daughter's back and sighed. And then he left for work.

Sam regretted almost every decision they had made concerning how to bring up Althea. For one, they never should have enrolled her in the Gregory School. Yes, it was true, at the time Sam had been extremely proud that Althea had been accepted at one of the best private schools in the city. And yes, he had been very proud that he and Harriet had been able to send her there at a cost of nearly five thousand dollars a year.

And, actually, the Gregory School had been fine until Althea hit her teens. Looking back, Sam and Harriet wondered at their naiveté. After putting their daughter in a nearly all-white school, how had they expected Althea to maintain many black friends? The one black boy in her class Althea didn't even like. ("He's a jerk!" Althea had exclaimed, when her parents asked why she wasn't going to the dance with him instead of John Schwartz. "Just because his father plays for the Jets, he thinks he's God's gift.") And when they talked about pulling her out of Gregory, Althea's counselor had made a very good point: Althea was happy there, and her grades and popularity showed it. And so the Wyatts had tried to compensate by pushing Althea into extracurricular activities—a plan that failed as well. ("I don't *want* to go out for the team at the Y—I want to swim for Gregory!")

Althea graduated from Gregory with a 3.8 average and the Wyatts were relieved when she expressed a desire to stay in New York and attend Columbia. ("Smith!" Sam had yelled during Althea's time of uncertainty. "Harriet! Your daughter wants to go to Smith with a friend named Poo!") And again, Sam had been very, very proud of Althea. And of him and Harriet. How many blacks, he wondered, how many kids *any*where, were smart enough to get into an Ivy League school and had parents who could afford to send them there? ("The way I figure it," Sam had said to Harriet as they sat down to plan out Althea's tuition for the next four years, "we can send Althea through school, or we can buy Mexico.")

Althea, thus far in her freshman year, had done extremely well, but Sam was still nervous about her. Of all the different students, Althea still undeniably gravitated toward those affluent whites she had grown up with at Gregory. She did have some black friends, and her last boyfriend too (thank God) had been black, but still . . .

It wasn't that Althea disregarded her heritage. On the contrary, Althea

made being black seem like an asset in the world. An asset because to know
Althea Wyatt was to associate a young black woman with all the things all
people everywhere coveted: brains, beauty and the brightest of futures. Did
that bother Sam? No, not really. What gnawed at him was how self-centered
Althea seemed to be. That everything Althea sought was for her own benefit, hers alone, with apparently no thought of rechanneling some of her good
fortune back into the black community.

Harriet did not worry about it as much as he did. But then, Harriet was
forever clouding the issue (for Sam) by claiming that Althea, as a black
woman, couldn't afford to give anything away until she reached that almost
nonexistent place called power. "For *you* it's a white man's world," Harriet
would storm on occasion. "But for me, Sam, for Althea, and for our little
Samantha in there, it's a *man's* world first, Sam, and *then* it's a white man's
world." And then Harriet would burst into tears and Sam would feel terrible as Harriet would say, "You make me so furious sometimes. You always
say you understand and you never have. You just don't know, Sam, you just
don't." Sniff. "And I'll tell you something else, Sam Wyatt, why should our
daughter do a darn thing for all those groups of yours? Look at them, Sam
—they're all men. And who do you men help? Young men. You have two
daughters, Sam—don't you think you could give *one* scholarship to *one*
woman? Can't you guys even pretend that women matter?" (Sam, incidentally, no longer participated in any group that did not include women.)

But the issue of race and of sex and of Althea's upbringing had another
all-encompassing issue attached to it. It was the issue of addiction. From the
day she was born, Althea had clearly been her father's daughter. She looked
like him, she talked like him, and her attitudes were just like his—in the old
days, that is. Would Althea inherit *it?* they wondered. Had Althea been
given *it* when she was little? What does one do when scared of the onslaught
of *it? It* that has raged through half of your child's heritage, *it* that is waiting
out there, on every street corner, in every schoolyard, in every place where
people are—what could the Wyatts do about *it?* They could—and did—
watch over their baby, try to safeguard her in ways that caused these other
problems. Like the Gregory School. Had they really sent Althea there to
educate her, or had they sent her there to keep her safe?

Hmmm . . .

No, it was true. They had sent her there to keep her safe.

And Columbia? Living at home?

They had kept her there to keep her safe.

Safe from *it?*
Yes, safe from getting sick like her father.

Sam Wyatt was the youngest of six children. His father had been an "army man," which sounded a good deal better than "a cook." Private Wyatt and his family moved from camp to camp in the United States, living in the colored housing where all the other indentured servants in the guise of privates had lived in the late 1930s and early '40s.

Sam was seven when his father went off on a drunken spree from which he never returned. They had been living in Texas then, at a camp that was frantically processing young men for shipment to the South Pacific. The army lost the trail of AWOL Private Wyatt in Nogales, Mexico, where he had apparently taken up with a barmaid named Juanita. Penniless, Sam's mother Clowie had no choice but to parcel her children out to her siblings. Sam landed in Philadelphia at his aunt Jessima's.

Aunt Jessima had the fear of God in her and she did her best to instil it in Sam. Sam's childhood and teen-age years seemed like one long prayer meeting, with Aunt Jessima's particular friend, Reverend Hope, officiating. Sam behaved, he did as he was told, and vowed that when he grew up he would never enter a church again.

By the time Sam enlisted in the army in 1956 the Wyatt family was sadly depleted. His mother had died of pneumonia in Milwaukee; his brother John had died in a car crash in Arizona; his brother Matthew, in the army, had shot himself through the mouth in Germany; and Sam's sister Bernice, only two years older than he, had been stabbed to death by her boyfriend in Los Angeles. His eldest sister, Ruth, had not been heard from in years; and his brother Isiah was preaching the gospel somewhere in the Everglades of Florida.

Sam spent four years in the army, was honorably discharged as a sergeant and went to Howard University on the GI Bill. He was smart, he was cocky and he was known for his way with women and having a good time. With his business degree in hand, he landed in New York City in 1965 and was hired in the personnel department of Electronika International. He was very well paid to assist a Mr. Pratt in all phases of personnel operations, and since Mr. Pratt did nothing Sam assisted him in all phases of nothing and enjoyed a pretty footloose and fancy-free time of it.

And then he met Penn graduate Harriet Morris, another Philadelphia expatriate, who was working as a secretary in the publicity department of Turner Lyman Publishers. Harriet was the first woman Sam had ever felt inclined to be faithful to. She was very pretty and very smart, and was the product of a middle-class Methodist family that was so happy it used to make Sam sick. In fact, if it had been anyone but Harriet, Sam wouldn't have gone within ten miles of a person like her. Harriet was a devout churchgoer. Harriet read the Bible every night before going to sleep (she still did). Harriet didn't drink. Harriet was forever saying things like, "Look on the bright side." And Harriet was very critical, very hard on anyone she didn't think was living up to his potential—namely, Sam.

On their fifth date Harriet ventured to tell Sam that he was a fool to be in personnel. Sam, drinking a martini, dressed in a very expensive suit, asked her how much she made at Turner Lyman and, when she told him, he pointed out that he made five times what she did. So what the hell did she know?

"Did you major in personnel at Howard?" Harriet asked him, smiling over her Coke.

Of course he hadn't.

"Did you interview with Electronika to work in personnel?" she asked.

No. He had interviewed for their training program.

"And they offered you more money to go into personnel, didn't they?"

Well, yes, they had.

"And you never wondered why?" she asked him.

"Well—"

"Sam," she said, tapping a swizzle stick against her lower lip, "show me in the *Wall Street Journal* where it announces power changes in personnel."

"What?"

"They're putting you in the ghetto," she said.

Now just what the hell was she—

"The government says, 'Hire blacks.' Okay, they say, we will. And where is the safest place to put them? Think, Sam. Where can they pay a good salary, call blacks executives, and never ever have to worry about them getting any power?"

Well, needless to say, had Harriet not been quite as attractive as she had been that night, had she not followed her criticism of Sam's career by an utterly disarming seduction of him emotionally, he never would have seen her again.

Instead, six months later, he married her. Right after he took a pay cut to move into the marketing department at Electronika.

Sam worked like a demon—mostly because he loved his work and loved what he was learning (including that he was very good at it), and partly because he wanted to leave the sea of white faces around him back in the wash. He was under enormous pressure—real and self-induced—and a twelve-hour day was nothing unusual for him. When Harriet got pregnant in 1967, he worked even harder—pushing, pushing, pushing himself—and by the time Althea was born (the day after Martin Luther King was shot), Sam was supervising a department of ten in the new-product division.

Although Harriet did not drink at all, Sam customarily had two scotches before dinner and a beer with. In the few years following Althea's birth Sam and Harriet joined a group of other black professional couples who met once a week for dinner. It was more of an encounter group on the state of black America than it was a social event, and they usually talked into the wee hours of the morning, sitting around on the living-room floor, with Sam and a few of the others drinking throughout. Something happened to the group after a while—around 1972—and the dynamics of it began to shift. The wives grew reluctant to come; Sam and two other men were drinking more and more and once even a fistfight broke out. The women stopped participating altogether and the talk of the men started to change, and suddenly it was no longer about "them, the white establishment, but about *"them,"* the wives and children who chained them to jobs they hated and to a lifestyle that was smothering them.

The men moved to bars and Sam went with them. And then it was just Sam in the bars, with whoever was around. And then there were terrible fights between Sam and Harriet, always around the issue of his drinking. And then there were terrible fights over Sam's drinking and Sam's women.

Harriet went to work in the publicity department of Gardiner & Grayson at the end of 1972. In 1973 she started warning Sam that if he did not do something about his drinking she was going to leave him. And then, in November, Sam passed out in his chair and his lighted cigarette started a small fire. Harriet told him he was on his last chance. The very next night Sam did not come home at all, and Harriet took Althea and moved in with her aunt in Harlem.

Sam cried and pleaded and did everything he could to get Harriet back— except stop drinking. Then he said to hell with her and started hitting the bars straight after work, finding sympathetic women to tell his sad story to, to buy drinks for, and to sleep with that night. It was amazing how much he was still able to function at work in those days—particularly since he had taken to martinis at lunchtime—but word began to get around the office about the caution needed to make sure Wyatt was in the right "mood" when he made a decision.

By 1975 it was anyone's guess whom Sam might wake up with in the morning. His blackouts were unpredictable, coming anywhere after two to ten drinks. At his company physical, he was told his liver was enlarged, his blood pressure was far too high and that he was running the risk of becoming diabetic. As for Harriet, she was so sick of Sam's middle-of-the-night assaults on her aunt's apartment (that he never remembered), she started calling the police and having Sam hauled away to the precinct.

And then Sam's boss called him in one day, sat him down, and gently, quietly offered Sam a choice: take a leave of absence and sign himself in for treatment or be fired.

To this day Sam does not know why he agreed to go to a rehab. At the time he didn't think he had a drinking problem. He thought he had a lousy wife and a lousy job problem. But somewhere, somewhere very deep inside of him, a little voice told him that maybe . . . maybe he would be better off if he stopped drinking for a while. And so, very quietly, very confidentially, Electronika flew him out to Minnesota for treatment.

Two months free of drinking, Sam went back to work. Four months free of drinking, Althea stopped hiding when he came to visit. Eight months free of drinking, Sam and Harriet went out on a date. Fifteen months free of drinking, Harriet and Althea came home to live with Sam. Thirty-nine months free of drinking, the Wyatts gave birth to a second daughter, Samantha, and Sam quit smoking. Sixty-two months free of drinking, Sam was made a vice-president of Electronika. Sixty-four months free of drinking, Harriet was made director of promotion, publicity and advertising at Gardiner & Grayson. Seventy months free of drinking, the Wyatts were profiled in the New York *Times Magazine* as examples of Manhattan's black upper middle class. Seventy-eight months free of drinking, the Wyatts bought a four-bedroom apartment on Riverside Drive.

Sam and his family were now one hundred and thirty-five months free of drinking. Of *it.*

Samuel J. Wyatt, Vice-President, New Product Development, sat in his office on the forty-seventh floor and wondered what the hell to do.

He sighed, turning his chair away from the window and back around to his desk. He looked up at his wall, covered with plaques and certificates of recognition, and of pictures of him at various functions. Sam, it should be said, was a doer. He didn't just talk the talk, he walked the walk. The Urban League, the United Negro College Fund, the Howard University Trustees Board, Junior Achievement . . . Sam sat on so many boards he had lost count, but he had never lost his energy or his willingness to do what he could for any organization he thought was effective.

But now . . .

Sam had recently pulled off a coup at Electronika. He had swung the deal for Electronika to take over a small British company called Trinity Electronics, which had developed a gem of a copying machine that no one had ever seen the likes of. The ZT 5000 could be used to reproduce originals; it could be hooked up to computer systems; it could be hooked up to wire services; and it could copy images of any size—from a postage stamp to the center fold of a city newspaper—and automatically cut the paper to size. In seconds. And at a cost that was leaving the competition agape.

Trial machines had been placed in key accounts across the country, and when the ZT started shipping five months from now, in October, it was already guaranteed some forty thousand placements and promised to move into every good library, telecommunications center and computer graphics room in the country before the end of the decade. On the strength of the machine's early reviews, Electronika's stock had climbed eleven points on the New York Stock Exchange.

Sam had been dancing in the aisles. With a hit like this, with Electronika miles ahead (in a product line they had always been sorely lagging in), it meant a huge promotion for him, vaulting him out of the divisional and into the corporate vice-presidential ranks.

But now there was a problem.

Oh, *man,* was there a problem.

And Sam was hoping against hope that today it would turn out that it had all been some terrible misunderstanding.

It has to be, he thought, pressing his temples.

Yesterday afternoon the new president of Electronika had summoned Sam to his office. There had not been any of the pleasantries that Sam had been accustomed to for the last six months from Walter Brennan. Brennan had scarcely greeted him, pointed to a chair and then had let him have it. "We're in one hell of a mess with the ZT 5000."

Immediately Sam's stomach had lurched. *I knew it was too good to be true,* he had thought.

"And I'm not very happy about it," Brennan had continued, pacing back and forth behind his desk. "Now, technically speaking, you're not responsible for the production end of the machines—"

"No," Sam had said, "Chet Canley handled that part of it." Chet Canley was the senior executive vice-president who had come to Electronika with Walter Brennan.

"But you are responsible for Electronika acquiring Trinity Electronics in the first place."

"Yes," Sam had conceded, "that's true."

"So I thought you might be able to shed some light on the problem we've discovered," Brennan said. Pause. He laughed suddenly, kicking his head back. "Christ!" he cried, looking at Sam. "The irony of it."

"Of what?"

"Asking my black executive if he can shed some light on why we're assembling machines in Pretoria, South Africa."

"*What?*" Sam was up and out of his chair. "What?" he repeated, leaning over Brennan's desk.

"Yeah," Brennan said, nodding his head. "You got it. Chet has informed me that the ZT is being assembled in a plant in Pretoria."

"That's impossible," Sam said, dropping back in his chair. "It's just impossible. The components ship from Tokyo, San Francisco and London for assembly in Nairobi, Kenya."

Brennan scratched his ear. "So you don't know anything about the Pretoria plant?"

Sam snorted, jerking his head to the side. He looked back at Brennan. "I know I don't do business with South Africa, I can tell you that. And I can tell you that nobody I dealt with at Trinity does either."

"Well, somebody sure as hell does," Brennan observed.

And so Sam had not slept very well last night. The whole thing had kept spinning around in his head and in his stomach. On the first level, he was furious. On the second level, he was furious because he didn't know who to be furious at—Trinity Electronics or—or . . . himself. Could it be possible that he had prompted Electronika to take over a company producing in South Africa? *South* Africa? Sam Wyatt's ZT 5000 was being assembled in South Africa? His big coup was with the inventors of apartheid?

Oh, God, his stomach hurt.

No, he had decided, he was not at fault. And Brennan knew that; he had only been looking for answers to a problem. But man, oh, man, if word got out on this—that Electronika was selling to institutional accounts machines that were being produced in South Africa—the ZT 5000 would be killed. It was just the year before that Sam had applauded the student demonstration at Columbia to protest the school's stockholdings in companies doing business in South Africa. And Columbia had divested itself of those stocks—and

Columbia was a major institutional account for the ZT 5000! (Suddenly, visions of Althea conducting a sit-in in front of the Wyatts' apartment building swam past Sam's eyes. Suddenly, visions of protests across the country against Electronika swam past Sam's eyes. Suddenly, visions of his own photograph accompanied by the headline BLACK EXEC BREAKS BOYCOTT IN SOUTH AFRICA swam past Sam's eyes.)

Would he be fired? Sam had wondered. What was Electronika going to do? Sam had wondered. What was *he* going to do? he had wondered. Sit back, let them handle it, or try to find out more about what had happened, how it had happened?

He had decided not to panic, and he had decided to makes some calls to Trinity in London to find out what or how this had happened. Sam looked at his watch. His secretary had been on the phone to London for over fifteen minutes. Was no one in? He looked at his watch again. It was only three-thirty in the afternoon there.

Finally his secretary, Mabel, appeared in the doorway of Sam's office. Sam looked at his phone, saw no lights on, and frowned. "Didn't you get Lane Smith?"

Mabel shook her head.

"Well, did you try George?"

"Yes, but he's not—"

"Well then, get Alice on the phone," Sam said.

"Mr. Wyatt," Mabel said, gesturing futility with her hands, "there's no one there."

"What is it, a holiday or something?"

Mabel looked down at the paper in her hand. "I tried every single name in the Trinity file—Lane Smith, George O'Shea, Alice Tilly, Ian Claremont, John Sawyer—"

"How about that guy in manufacturing," Sam said, "Peter, Peter—"

"Johnson. I tried him too." Pause. "Mr. Wyatt, none of them work there anymore."

"What?" Sam sat back in his chair, thinking a moment. "Were they fired or did they quit?"

"They wouldn't tell me," Mabel said, "they just said, 'He is no longer with the company.'"

5

MRS. GOLDBLUM AT HOME

Dear Mrs. Goldblum [the letter said],

After repeated telephone conversations with you regarding your late husband's employment with Horowitz & Sons, I am forced to reiterate the facts in letter form in the hope that the matter can be put to rest.

You informed us that from the time of your husband's death in 1970, until February of 1984, Bernard Horowitz issued certain sums of money to you. You informed us that these payments were from your late husband's pension plan.

If Mr. Horowitz did indeed make these payments, he did so out of his personal funds. Nowhere—and I have personally gone through every file—is there any record of a pension fund being set up for your husband. In fact, no employee at Horowitz & Sons had a pension fund with the company.

In conclusion, Charger Industries has absolutely no obligation to the estate of the late Robert Goldblum.

I hope this answers your questions.

Sincerely,
Phillip S. Robin

"Hey, Mrs. G," Rosanne said, coming into the kitchen, "Amanda gave me—Mrs. G, are you okay?"

Mrs. Goldblum lowered the letter onto the table. "I'm quite fine, thank you."

"You don't look so hot." Rosanne edged closer. "Bad news?" she asked, nodding toward the letter.

"No," Mrs. Goldblum said softly, slipping the letter back into the envelope it arrived in. "There is some lovely chicken salad for your luncheon. It's in the refrigerator."

"Thanks," Rosanne said. She looked at Mrs. Goldblum a moment longer and then went over to the refrigerator. "Are you gonna wants yours on lettuce or in a sandwich?"

"No, thank you, dear. I've already eaten."

Rosanne frowned slightly. "Well, you sure eat fast then, since I've been here all morning."

"No, thank you, dear." Mrs. Goldblum rose from her chair and, taking the letter with her, made her way toward the living room. Her hip was quite stiff today and she wondered if she shouldn't be using her cane. And she wondered if she shouldn't get over her keen dislike of having such a thing in the house.

Carefully, she sat herself down at her secretary.

Now then. The letter.

Mr. Robin is wrong, Mrs. Goldblum thought. She pulled out the tissue in her sleeve and dabbed at her nose. *Oh, why do one's friends have to die? If dear Bernie was still alive, none of this confusion would have ever taken place.*

No pension plan—indeed!

Does this Mr. Robin think Robert hadn't planned for his retirement? Of course he had! Bernie told me that he had—right in this very room. Why, every month like clockwork, a check arrived from Horowitz & Sons for $416. And right on the check it said, "Pension Benefit—Estate of Robert Goldblum." What is wrong with this Mr. Robin?

What was she going to do now? Should she go to a lawyer? But how to find one? How to *pay* for one? Right now she had a little over $600 left in the bank. The rent would be due in two weeks. That would leave $320. There was the doctor's bill that was overdue and Mrs. Goldblum was supposed to go back to see him this week. Well, that was out of the question. How could she face him with an overdue bill? And the dentist. Oh, dear. Such a jumble; how much was it she owed him? Eighteen hundred dollars?

She would have to call Daniel. If she could locate him. The last time she had tried to call him, a recording said that the number had been changed. Did he give her his number last weekend?

No, he hadn't.

Mrs. Goldblum's cat, Missy, came sauntering in. Missy purred, arched her back and rubbed against Mrs. Goldblum's leg. "Hello, Miss-Miss," Mrs. Goldblum said, dropping her hand beneath the desk of the secretary. Missy rubbed her face in Mrs. Goldblum's hand. "Yes, you are my good girl."

There was no point in calling Daniel, Mrs. Goldblum realized. Her son wouldn't be able to help her. But *maybe* he could. Maybe he could come and straighten all of this out—

She didn't even have enough money to send him a ticket.

Well.

She would go to the bank and look in the safety deposit box again. There must be some bond or stock certificates left. Just to tide her over until this pension business was cleared up.

"Oh, my," Mrs. Goldblum sighed out loud. It seemed impossible that there was no money left. Where could it have gone?

Oh, dear. This was a painful question she really hadn't meant to raise.

—$50,000 for Daniel's video business.

—$25,000 for Daniel's video business to stay afloat.

—$10,000 for Daniel after the business failed.

—$16,000 for Daniel's credit card problem.

—$20,000 for Daniel's late child-support payments.

—$ 4,000 for Mrs. Goldblum's lower plate.

—$ 5,000 after Daniel's ex-wife's and children's pleas for help.

And that was only the last year and a half.

Mrs. Goldblum closed her eyes, choosing not to think back any further than that.

Mrs. Goldblum flexed her hands. It was becoming a little more difficult to ignore these days, the arthritis. Particularly on humid days. It made one think in different terms. *That is when they want you to go into a home,* Mrs. Goldblum thought. *When you speak of it taking sixteen and a half twists to open a six-ounce can of cat food.*

"What are you talking about, Mother?" Daniel had yelled on the phone.

"About using the can opener, dear. About feeding Missy."

"Do you think I called all the way from Chicago to talk about a cat?"

"I am simply answering your question, Daniel. You asked me how I am and I'm telling you how I am."

"You're talking about can openers and cats!" he had cried.

Rosanne breezed into the living room, breaking Mrs. Goldblum's train of thought. "Before I forget again," she said, holding out a large Saks Fifth Avenue shopping bag, "Amanda bought the wrong kind of shower curtain and can't return it and wondered if you'd like it." She pulled it out of the bag for Mrs. Goldblum to see.

It was a pale pink. Mrs. Goldblum liked it very much indeed and reached out to touch it. "Wasn't that thoughtful of her."

"Well, I don't know, Mrs. G. Seems to me if Amanda was thoughtful she wouldn't always be buyin' the wrong stuff. 'Member when she gave me the watch? 'Member?"

"I'm not sure that I do," Mrs. Goldblum said.

"Aw, sure ya do, Mrs. G," Rosanne said. "When I told her to get some Windex and she came back with a watch? This one?" She held up her wrist.

"Oh, my, yes, now I recall," Mrs. Goldblum chuckled.

Rosanne listened to her watch for a moment and then shrugged. "So, ya want me to hang this up?"

"Would you, dear? Is that too much to ask? I do think it would look lovely in the bathroom. Don't you agree?"

Rosanne smiled at her. "Yeah, Mrs. G, I agree."

When Rosanne left, Mrs. Goldblum returned her attention to the desk. After a few moments of consideration she decided to file the letter in one of the pigeonholes and look at it again tomorrow.

She heard soft purring. Missy was back, looking up into the eyes of her mistress with all the charm she possessed. It worked. Mrs. Goldblum picked her up, sat Missy in the lap of her dress and petted her. Within seconds, white hairs from Missy's chest jumped to Mrs. Goldblum's navy-blue dress. But not to worry, Mrs. Goldblum still had the Miracle Brush she had purchased at Woolworth's some twenty years before.

"Mrs. G, come see!" Rosanne was calling from the bathroom.

"I have to go see Rosanne," Mrs. Goldblum said, giving Missy a little shove. The cat jumped down and Mrs. Goldblum slowly, stiffly got up from the chair.

"Mrs. G?"

"I'm coming," Mrs. Goldblum said, walking down the hall. She reached the bathroom door, held onto the molding and peeked in. "Oh, my goodness, isn't it lovely."

"Yeah," Rosanne said. In her hand she was holding the old shower curtain and liner.

"But," Mrs. Goldblum said, gesturing to the floor, "where did this rug come from?"

"Oh, that," Rosanne said, looking down under her feet. "It came with the shower curtain. You know, like it's a set." Pause. "It does kinda look good in here—made Amanda's bathroom look like a whorehouse."

"Rosanne!"

"House of ill repute."

Mrs. Goldblum looked concerned and touched at her glasses. "You don't think . . ."

"Aw, no, Mrs. G. It looks great. Very feminine, Mrs. G. Very you," she said with additional emphasis. "And did you see here? These little towels that match? And there's a soap dish."

Mrs. Goldblum stepped in to feel one of the hand towels. "They are very pretty."

"Well," Rosanne said, moving around Mrs. Goldblum, "I'm gonna chuck this thing."

Mrs. Goldblum caught her arm. "Oh, must we? Couldn't we use it—"

"Ya can't use this thing for nothin', Mrs. G," Rosanne said, pulling the old shower curtain away from her. "It's gonna walk on its own legs in a minute."

"Oh," Mrs. Goldblum said. She let go of Rosanne and refocused on the new shower curtain. "I must reimburse Amanda for these things."

"She said you'd say that," Rosanne said. "So I'm supposed to tell ya that if you won't just take 'em, then she'll just give 'em away to somebody else."

"Well then, I suppose I must accept them as a gift."

"I would if I were you," Rosanne said, moving down the hall.

"I shall write her a thank-you note," Mrs. Goldblum decided, turning off the light in the bathroom. She walked slowly down the hall to the living room.

"Hey, Mrs. G," Rosanne called from the kitchen, "you oughtta come see this—the cat's laughin'."

Mrs. Goldblum frowned slightly. "No, dear," she said, "I believe it may be fur balls."

"Be what?"

One second, two, three . . .

"Oh, yuck!"

Mrs. Goldblum smiled as Missy came bounding into the living room, feeling much better now and quite ready to play.

6

THE KRANDELL ARMS HOTEL

The Krandell Arms Hotel was on the city's endangered species list. As a result, no matter how many millions of dollars the landlord could make—by converting the 104 "box" rooms, 16 communal bathrooms and 8 communal kitchens into 24 coop apartments—Mayor Koch wouldn't let him. The Krandell Arms was a single-room-occupancy hotel, an SRO, and since it was located on 94th Street between Riverside Drive and West End Avenue, it had earned the protection of the mayor by being in an SRO safety zone. The ban on SRO conversions in safety zones was temporary, but nonetheless a godsend, seeing as the only alternative for Manhattan's poor was to move into the street or into an abandoned building—which was, incidentally, exactly how several thousands of people were living in Manhattan.

In any event, it was a very confusing neighborhood that had sprung up around the Krandell Arms over the years. While the residents of the hotel paid between sixty and ninety dollars a week for a room, if they went outside, turned right and walked sixty feet, they would be standing in front of a building whose last one-bedroom apartment had been sold for two hundred thousand dollars. Or they could turn left and walk two blocks east to Broadway and look at the high-rise "luxury housing" that was being thrown up. Everywhere on Broadway, down was coming the granite, the genuine brick, the beautifully sculpted detail of the old buildings, and up, up, up—way up into the air—were going cinder blocks, brick veneer sheeting and brown metal windows in soul-sick repetition. Taken together, these skyscrapers of prefab horror were introducing a new community to the Upper West Side: HIGH-RISE LEVITTOWN.

Dunkin' Donuts, McDonald's, The Gap, Pathmark—this was the scenic landscape of Broadway at 96th Street. And the high-rise Levittownians were paying upward of a hundred and seventy-five thousand dollars for the pleasure of viewing it.

But then it had been years since the residents of the Krandell Arms had fully understood the ways of civilization.

Rosanne arrived at the door of the Krandell Arms Hotel with two bags of groceries in her arms. As usual on a nice day, there were people hanging out in front, pulling on pint bottles of Thunderbird, smoking cigarettes and reefer, milling around, waiting for something to happen. And, as usual, nothing was happening, and some nameless creep was standing in Rosanne's way, his hand outstretched, mumbling, "Canyousparesomechangenicelady?"

"Shove off," Rosanne said. When he failed to move (he was barely cognizant), Rosanne used her groceries as a shield to push her way past him.

"Bless ya," the creep said.

The inner doors of the hotel were wide open, and Buzzy and Creature were hanging out in the hallway. They were high, Rosanne spotted right away, and so she knew to use Attitude B on them. (Attitude A was reserved for those times when they were straight—when Rosanne would treat them like the friends of her husband's that they were.)

"Hey, sistah," Buzzy said, touching his leather hat. He was too wrecked to successfully execute the bow he wished to offer and staggered against the wall. He slapped the arm of his companion, who was already parked against the wall. "Man, Creatcha, did ya ever see such a fine piece of ass?"

"Mess with me and I'll kick your ass to New Jersey," Rosanne said, craning her neck to see through the glass partition of the front desk.

"Who-whooo!" the boys hooted, falling against each other.

"Where the hell is Ernesto?" Rosanne demanded.

"Man, I'd love to get my ass kicked by you, babe," Buzzy said.

A little black boy, about six, came skidding around the corner. He shot past the three, making for the front door, and he almost made it before Rosanne yelled, "James! Stop right there!"

The boy stopped in his tracks. With his shoulders hunched, he slowly raised his hands over his head and turned around. "Got me," he said.

Buzzy and Creature thought this was great and started slapping their legs and "Who-whooo"-ing again.

"Come here," Rosanne demanded.

James dropped his head and shuffled back in her direction. Rosanne sighed and kneeled to put the bags of groceries down. Still kneeling, she reached for James and pulled him close. James let his hand be held and, after a moment, looked up at Rosanne. "Why aren't you at school?" Rosanne asked, her voice decidedly more gentle.

James looked past Rosanne to the wall. "I'm sick. I got a fever."

Rosanne felt the little boy's forehead. "Well, you don't anymore." She started tucking his shirt into his jeans. "Is your mother home?"

James shook his head.

Buzzy and Creature started pitching pennies.

Rosanne licked her thumb and wiped at the unidentifiable food stain on the corner of James's mouth. "Who's staying with you?"

"Nobody," James said, looking at the wall again.

"Where's your mommy?"

"Work."

Rosanne stroked the top of James's head once, sighed and gathered her bags. "Why don't you come upstairs with me and I'll fix you a nice sandwich. Would you like that?"

"Okay," James said.

Rosanne led James down the corridor to the elevator. The elevator took forever to come. But at least it came, which was more than yesterday. They got off on the seventh floor, where the smell of garlic assaulted them. The seventh-floor hall ran square, and the noise from the rooms echoed along the bare walls and linoleum floors—around and around and around—until they blended together into one garbled torrent of sound.

Most of the doors on the hallway were open, and residents could be seen sitting around inside. Rosanne and James passed the kitchen where someone's unattended endeavor was spilling liquid all over the stove top. Rosanne shifted her groceries and turned the burner off.

The DiSantos door was open too, which meant that Frank was home. Rosanne pushed it open with her foot and went inside. Frank was lying on the bed, watching TV. Beside him, on the floor, were two crushed Old English cans.

"I brought a guest," Rosanne said, dropping the bags on the table. "You know James, Frank."

Frank, eyes still on the TV, said, "Hi, kid."

James ran over and hung on Rosanne's leg. "Here," Rosanne said, prying him loose, "you sit here." She pulled out a chair from the table. "I thought you were workin' today," she said, moving back to close the door.

"They didn't have nothin' for me today. Tomorrow, they said." His eyes didn't leave the screen.

Rosanne went over and kissed him on the forehead. "What are you watchin'?"

"Some shit," he said.

Rosanne moved back to the table and started unloading groceries. To James, "How about a nice ham sandwich?"

He nodded vigorously.

To Frank, as she made the sandwich for James, "I thought we'd have a steak tonight."

"I'm going out."

"You have to eat—"

"I'm eatin' out."

"Okay," Rosanne said, cutting James's sandwich into fours on a plate and pushing it in front of him. When James reached for it, Rosanne caught him by the wrist. She nodded toward the sink. "Wash your hands first, okay?" While James made a halfhearted attempt at fulfilling this request, Rosanne poured him a glass of milk. Under Rosanne's direction, Frank had built an intricate system of shelves on one wall, the bottom part of which was made up of locked cabinets. It was in these cabinets that the refrigerator, the microwave and other illegal appliances were kept concealed.

When James was well into his sandwich, Rosanne moved toward the door. "Frank, keep an eye on James, will you? I'll be back in a minute."

At this, Frank tore his eyes away from the set to glance at the kid. "Yeah, okay," he said.

Rosanne walked down the corridor and around the corner to Ceily's room. Although the door was closed, Rosanne could hear darn well what was going on behind it.

"Oh, baby, oh, baby, oh, baby," Ceily was saying. (Ceily said that her act for her clients was patterned after Sophia Loren's portrayal of grief in some movie she once saw—"Oh, not my baby, not my baby, please, not my baby.")

"I've got James at my place!" Rosanne shouted through the door.

Back in the DiSantoses' room, James was now sitting on the floor, watching TV with Frank.

"I saw Sissy on the corner this morning," Rosanne said to her husband, carefully stepping over James to get to the closet. "Did you see her?" Rosanne reached up to the shelf of the closet and brought down a plastic action-doll of the Hulk. "Frank?"

"Yeah, I saw her. She looks like shit."

"James," Rosanne said. The little boy looked up. "This belongs to Jason, but you can play with it while you're here." His eyes widened and Rosanne smiled. She handed it to him.

"I thought she was in Veritas Villa," Rosanne said, moving back to the table.

No response. Rosanne opened a bottle of Slice and poured herself a glass.

Of course it was pointless to pursue the topic of Sissy. Sissy, when on the up-and-up, was Frank's most generous source of drugs.

Rosanne sat down at the table and for a few minutes watched James play with the Hulk. Then she looked at her husband. Frank was still a good-looking man—if he dressed, if he shaved, if he showered, if he was straight.

Rosanne Minero had been fifteen years old when her family was invited to a welcome-home party for their next door neighbors' son. Any excuse for getting out of the house in those days was good enough for Rosanne, and she went to the party, holding her latest baby brother in her arms and leading four more of her younger siblings.

The second Rosanne saw Frank DiSantos, she was in love. He was just home from Vietnam, still in uniform, and was wearing several medals. He was handsome and he was proud, and he flashed a smile in Rosanne's direction and nodded, as if to tip her off that he found her attractive. And she was—though no one, at first meeting, would have thought she was any younger than, say, twenty-three or so. A young life spent cleaning and cooking and changing diapers and mothering had already robbed Rosanne of the gifts of childhood. ("Lean and mean," Frank would say.)

Later, when the throng of DiSantos relatives had touched and kissed Frank enough, when the toasts of the best Detroit homemade wine had tapered off, Frank had taken Rosanne aside to tell her of his plans. Of the car dealership he would open with two of his buddies from the war. Of the car he himself would own (a Porsche), of the house he would buy, of his (after living a little) intention of marrying and raising children, at least one of whom would grow up to be the President of the United States. And then he told her, in a hoarse whisper of blatant sexuality (which he offered in such a way as not to sully the ears of the four-month-old in Rosanne's arms), of his need, right now, *right this moment,* for a "good" woman to welcome him home from the war.

Fifteen-year-old Rosanne Minero and twenty-three-year-old Frank Di-Santos were married three months later. They moved to New York, into a nice apartment in the Bronx, and they were extremely happy—until the night Rosanne discovered that her husband had brought another friend home from the war with him. The friend's name was Heroin. When his addiction seemed to be as harmless as Frank said it was, when Frank opened his car dealership with his buddies, when Frank continued to be the sweetest, nicest guy in the world, Rosanne learned to accommodate it.

Two years later, in 1977, Frank sold his interest in the dealership to support the DiSantoses'—and the DiSantoses' friend. In 1978, Frank went into the VA Hospital in Manhattan and entered their methadone treatment. In 1979, he kicked methadone and got a job as a mechanic in a West Side garage in Manhattan. He did very well, and Rosanne, who had been employed as a housekeeper in the Windercolt mansion on Gracie Square, also had money coming in. In 1980 the DiSantoses lucked into a lovely Manhattan apartment in the West 70s. Shortly thereafter, appearing as a miracle to Frank, Rosanne announced she was pregnant. (It was no miracle to Rosanne—she had simply stopped using the birth control pills she had been taking during the "bad" years.)

Jason was born on April 19, 1981. On May 1, 1981, Frank was fired from the garage for stealing and Rosanne knew in her heart that he was on drugs again. He lost a series of jobs thereafter and, in 1983, Frank was admitted to the VA again for heroin. Rosanne, with Jason in her arms, four months' back rent to pay, no income and a pride that kept her from going to her family, applied for, and received, residence in the Krandell Arms Hotel.

It was temporary, Rosanne assured Frank when he got out of the VA, and they would move as soon as he was back on his feet. Why she had assured him of this—when she herself was sick and horrified at the environment to which she had brought her child—she never quite understood.

Frank never did get back on his feet. Instead of his old drive and energy and dreams, he seemed to grow more depressed and listless by the day. So Rosanne did the only thing she could think of. She found a young mother on West End Avenue who would look after Jason for a few hours a day, five days a week, leaving Rosanne free to clean apartments on Riverside Drive. (She wanted a view of the river.) It not only brought in the cash the DiSantoses were desperate for, but it also allowed Rosanne to stay near Jason—and near to Frank, who, at this point, needed someone close by when he "got in trouble." It also gave Rosanne a few hours' respite from a life that felt like it was choking her to death.

"We didn't hire Rosanne," Cassy Cochran would laugh. "She hired *us.*" And it was true. Rosanne conducted a "trial day" in eighteen households before she selected the four original clients she wished to work for: the Cochrans—on the strength of Mrs. C and Henry (Mr. C always made such a mess); the Wyatts—Rosanne liked all of them, particularly Althea, and when she spotted an Alcoholics Anonymous meeting book on Mr. W's dresser she figured it might come in handy to know somebody on the other side of the fence; Amanda Miller—a shoo-in from the start since, (a) she was so nice, and (b) Rosanne could paint the house with mud for all Amanda would notice; and the Stewarts—well, like Mrs. W had forewarned her, the Bitch was impossible, but Howie was so wonderful that Rosanne had accepted the job on the condition that she would never have to deal directly with *her.* And then later good ol' Mrs. G had been added—that had been Amanda's doing and, besides, Rosanne had loved how Mrs. G kept calling her "dear."

Financially speaking, Rosanne knew she was very lucky. Not once—not once in three years—had a single client failed to leave her the full cash amount for her day's work. Everywhere else Rosanne had worked, the client was forever "forgetting" about her, leaving partial payments, or, worse yet, writing checks that took days to clear (if they cleared at all). And then Mrs. C had her thing about coming across clothes that "had Rosanne written all over them"; Mr. W had his about needing to "get something for a boy once in a while"; Amanda had hers about needing to feel that "someone, somewhere, could turn to me if they needed help" (which Rosanne had once, when Frank had been arrested); Howie had his about "when it's harder work than usual, you should get paid more than usual"; and Mrs. G—man, that Mrs. G—had her thing about wanting Rosanne to have some of her personal possessions—a pin, a plate, a fine piece of linen—offers that Rosanne never accepted, but scored very high with her all the same.

But it was the generosity of her clients' hearts that most affected Rosanne. One time—and Rosanne would never forget it—during one of Mr. C's infamous parties, Rosanne had walked in on him while he was giving it to one of the video kittens in the guest room. She had shut the door and was standing there, in shock, when Mrs. C came down the hall. Mrs. C wanted to know what was going on and Rosanne wouldn't tell her, but neither would she let her past. And then all of a sudden Mrs. C had dragged her down the hall by the hand, stopped her in the doorway, held her by the shoulders, and said, "Rosanne, I love you. Do you understand? I love you for trying to protect me. As far as I'm concerned, you have just joined the family."

And there was the time the Wyatts took her to Samantha's Christmas pageant. ("Anyone who baby-sits for her deserves to see her act like an angel once," Sam explained.) And the time Amanda took her and Jason to the Museum of Natural History. And the first time Howie had given her a book to read, encouraging her, pushing her, to "get into the habit." And the time Mrs. G gave her a copy of *The Amy Vanderbilt Book of Etiquette* so that Rosanne would "know exactly what to do at all the wonderful places I'm sure life will take you one day."

Yeah, right. Wonderful places.

One night, in the summer of 1984, Rosanne asked Frank and Creature to keep an eye on Jason while she took a shower. When she emerged from the west bathroom, toweling her hair, she saw some hulking crazy dragging Jason down the hall by his three-year-old hand—heading for the open window at the end of the floor. Rosanne silently tore down the hall, grabbed her child in her arms, and when the crazy turned on her—bantering about the Devil—she kicked him as hard as she could in the crotch and started screaming.

Frank and Creature came running (having been busy doing something other than watching Jason) and, without asking questions, beat the hell out of the crazy. Rosanne ran back to her room, clutching Jason against her chest, rocking him and sobbing hysterically for hours.

The next day Rosanne had Jason placed in a foster home. Temporarily. Just until the DiSantoses got on their feet again.

Rosanne visited with her son as often as she could. He had not been back to the Krandell Arms, not even for a visit. And Rosanne vowed he never would. Not ever again.

"Who're you going out with tonight?" Rosanne asked her husband.

"Zigs, Carson."

"Where?"

"Uptown. Shoot some pool." Silence. Then Frank sat up, the first time all evening. "I need some money."

"I gave you twenty this morning—James, don't touch the wire." When James didn't pay any heed, Rosanne leaped up and went over to him.

"Sweetie," she said, pulling his hand back, "you should never, never touch wires. They'll hurt you and make you cry." She picked James up from under his arms and swung him and the Hulk up onto the bed.

Frank was slipping on a shirt over the undershirt he had been featuring. "Come on, I need some more."

Rosanne sighed, moving back toward the table. "How much more?"

"Another twenty," Frank said, following her.

Rosanne spun around, hands on hips. "So what if I don't have another twenty?"

"We'll just find out," he said, lunging for her pocketbook. Rosanne was quicker though, and reached it first, whirling around and bringing it up against her chest. "Don't fuck with me, Rosanne," Frank warned her.

"If you want to blow money on pool, blow yours," she said.

She didn't stand a chance. Five feet versus six. Frank pinned her against the shelves with one hand and yanked the pocketbook from her with the other. Rosanne reached for it and he roughly pushed her back against the shelves, making everything on them rattle.

Rosanne rubbed her shoulder, glaring at him. "Son of a bitch," she said, taking a step forward. "Go ahead, take it. Take it all." She yanked the pocketbook back from him, tore it open, took her wallet out, and threw it at him. She missed and the wallet went sailing clear across the room. James dove under the pillows. Frank laughed and went after the wallet.

"There's fifty bucks in there!" Rosanne screamed. "Every cent we have, you fool. But take it! Go ahead! What do you care?"

He was taking it. He stuffed the bills in his jeans pocket, slung his black leather jacket over his shoulder, popped on one of his hats, and waltzed out the door. " 'Bye, baby," he said.

"Don't you come back here tonight!" Rosanne yelled after him. She ran over to the door and shouted. "I'm sick of you lying around here like a bum! You can go to hell for all I care!" She slammed the door and it bounced back open. So she kicked it.

Ceily waved a hand in the doorway and made sounds of admiration. Rosanne backed away slightly. "So the girl's got a temper after all," Ceily said. " 'Bout time." James's head flew up from the pillows at the sound of her voice. In a moment he was at her side, hanging on her hand. "Hi, sugar," Ceily cooed. "Hey," she said, looking back up, "Rosanne, thanks."

Rosanne shrugged it off. "I don't mind. Listen, I gave him a sandwich."

Ceily retied the satin robe she was wearing. "Thanks." She pulled her son out into the hall and then swung her head back into the doorway. "You okay?"

"Oh, I'm fine," Rosanne said. "Business as usual."

Ceily laughed, a long, bitter affair. "Yeah, don't I know it."

By midnight, Rosanne's familiar terror had set in.
Frank with fifty dollars—
He'd—
He's—
He might be—
What if—
And she went out to search in the neon of Broadway.

7

ALEXANDRA WARING IS A HIT

On the first Monday of May, Susan Boxby called in sick and Alexandra Waring made her debut as a coanchor on WWKK's six o'clock news. Fifteen minutes into the broadcast the switchboard jammed with calls. Who Alexandra was, where she had come from, was not the concern of the men, women and children who called; their message was very simple: *"We love her."* Michael quickly slotted her into the eleven o'clock broadcast that night and the switchboard jammed *again*.

"Cass," Michael shouted over the telephone at 11:07 P.M., "you've got to see this!"

"I'm watching, Michael," Cassy said, sipping Perrier on the couch.

"Is the kid watching?"

"The kid has a trigonometry final in the morning."

There was nothing run-of-the-mill about Alexandra, Cassy had to admit. In fact, Alexandra's broadcast was the most impressive debut she had seen in years. First of all, the girl had dressed down, appearing in a simple navy-blue dress and pearls. But the effect of her eyes against the navy was electrifying. Cassy distinctly remembered thinking—when she had first met Alexandra—how much her eyes were like a stormy Atlantic, possessing those same hypnotic blue/gray depths. But here her eyes were blue . . . No, looking again, Cassy could see that it was only an illusion, but—good Lord —what an illusion. "Go ahead," Alexandra's eyes were daring. "Just try and look anywhere else while I'm on camera."

Whatever color her eyes were, Cassy was also acutely aware of the fact that Alexandra had her listening to every word she was saying. It had nothing to do with her eyes (and was, perhaps, in spite of them); it was through a superb, seemingly effortless delivery of what was just darn good copy. And since WWKK wouldn't know a hard fact or figure if they tripped over it, Cassy knew Alexandra must have written the copy herself. Cassy's final observation was that Alexandra Waring had just changed the course of WWKK's newsroom forever. She was that good.

There was no city in the world that had more television news being broadcast from it than New York; and as America's number one market for television, New York City was also America's number one consumer of local television news. The network flagship affiliates, WABC, WCBS and WNBC, traditionally had the six and eleven o'clock time periods to themselves to battle it out in the ratings, while the independents, WNYW, WOR, WPIX, WST and WWKK, shifted their newscasts to either before or after the network affiliates and national network news. (Cassy's own WST ran its "News Update & Tri-State Report" at seven-thirty.) The fierce competition in town drove news in one direction or the other—to be the best, or to be the most sensational.

Michael Cochran's "WWKK News" had been moved around to so many time slots over the years that the industry called it "The Sonja Henie Show." Two years ago, when at long last it seemed WWKK had found its home at five o'clock, another network affiliate expanded its evening news to begin at five and WWKK was blown out of the water. Michael had thrown a fit like no one had ever seen (he put his foot through a monitor) and declared that the time had come to stop running, take a stand, and fight the network affiliates.

Michael moved "WWKK News" to the six and eleven o'clock time periods and gave the flagships a minor but very real run for their money—in other words, he dented their ratings. Against the tremendous money and resources behind "Channel 2 News," "News Center 4" and "Channel 7 Eyewitness News," Michael used the strongest weapons in any TV arsenal

—sex, violence and gambling. His secret was that he loathed doing it; his pride was that his news show survived where other independents' could not.

WWKK's coanchors were Mike True and Susan Boxby. According to his PR sheet, Mike was formerly a radio announcer in Georgia and the spokesperson for a machine that enlarged biceps. However, for anyone "in the know," Mike True had also been Tad Long, the heavily endowed star of many a porno feature. (When the *Post* broke that story, WWKK gained an entire rating point.) As for Susan Boxby, she was the former Chapped Lips Stix Girl. Susan was quite cheery and laughed a lot on the air (throwing her head back and shaking it from side to side, showing her long blond hair to advantage). To maintain their ratings, WWKK had two mandatory parts to their broadcast: (1) that at some point they got a shot of Mike standing up and (2) that each show close with a close-up of Susan obscenely licking her lips.

Other members of the WWKK news team included:

Mack Truck Thompson, the former professional wrestler whose career in that capacity abruptly ended when Dark Dog Dahoney accidentally broke his back. Mack Truck covered sports. On Fridays, Mack Truck would run a tape of all the injuries suffered in professional sports that week. "Now watch right here . . . Bam! YEAH!" (Every New Year's Eve, as a special treat, Mack Truck would run the tape showing his back being broken.)

Zippy Stevens, a spritely lost soul of unknown origins, covered the weather. If the forecast was rain, Zippy would come out soaking wet. If it was sunny, she would come out in a gauzy robe over a bathing suit and sunglasses. If it was cold, a fur coat with apparently nothing underneath. (Fans longed for the preciously few hail forecasts, when Zippy would come out in a costume of one hundred Formica ice cubes sewn together.)

And last but not least . . . infamous friend to the Hollywood stars, Slicker MacCoy, the celebrity gossip. Now, in actuality, no one in his or her right mind would ever go near Slicker, much less talk to him, but celebrity gossip was not really the reason he was on the air. It was because Slicker MacCoy betting syndicates had sprung up all over the city. People were placing two-dollar bets on the exact day and time that Slicker would next knock his toupee askew on the air. Sometimes—when Slicker was particularly intoxicated and riled—he would knock it askew as many as three times in one week, and so the syndicate pots would be small. But then sometimes a week would go by and the pot would build and—whoops!—the winner would take home a bundle.

These were the colleagues of Alexandra Waring.

Cassy had to hand it to Alexandra, she sure handled her first broadcast well. She had faced off with her clowny colleagues in the only way that had a chance of winning—Alexandra had ignored them. Cassy played back the tape of the six o'clock newscast to watch one segment again.

Mike True gets up from behind the desk for his mandatory standing shot. (He is wearing pants that look suspiciously close to sweat pants.) He is pointing to a map of the country. Taped to it are winning lottery numbers in the states that hold them. Mike reads these numbers aloud. (He is allowed to turn from the waist up, but never, *never* is he allowed to turn the lower portion of his body away from the camera.)

"Alexandra," Mike True ad-libs from the script, "why don't you just sachet on over here and show our viewers your beautiful *Kan*sas."

Camera cuts to Alexandra for reaction shot. She looks straight into it and says, "U.S. officials are calling the accident at the Soviet nuclear power plant at Chernobyl—quote—a disaster. The explosion nine days ago . . ."

Mike True was stranded off screen. (Cassy clapped.)

Susan Boxby's "illness" continued for the rest of the week, and by Friday, Mike True was suddenly stricken ill too, and Alexandra was slated to fly solo through the following week. By Wednesday WWKK's ratings had risen one point, while two network affiliates lost half a rating point each. An article in *Newsday* said that Alexandra Waring possessed, in its opinion, the highest TV-Q of any anchor in town.

The Cochran household was transformed into the Alexandra Waring Media Center. Michael had tapes playing all night: Alexandra's special report on crack; Alexandra's interview with the governor; Alexandra's . . .

"Look at her, Cass," Michael would say near two in the morning. "Just look at her. *Listen* to her. They are *crazy* about her. Did I tell you she got a call from ABC already?

"I'm revamping the whole show around her, from top to bottom. I'm bringing in Walter Darden as coanchor. Alexandra's taking Zippy to Lord & Taylor's for some clothes. I'm talking to Ripton, the old Mets pitcher. We're going to keep old Slicker for a while yet. Cass, it's gonna be great!"

"Michael," Cassy said at one point, "don't you think you need some sleep? You haven't—"

"You go on," Michael urged.

In the bedroom, night after night, Cassy fell asleep to the sound of Alexandra's voice. There was no reprieve at the office, either. Everyone around town was buzzing about "Miss TV-Q" on WWKK.

Michael's hours became increasingly wild. He was running on Alexandra, scotch and the smell of victory. When he was home, he was raving, plotting and planning. When he was at the newsroom he called Cassy every two hours to bounce an idea off her.

Cassy, in the meantime, was trying to uphold her part in Henry's end-of-the-school-year activities, get him organized for his approaching departure for Camp Survival in Colorado, and—heaven help her—orchestrate the block party coming up on June 7. (At a meeting she hadn't attended, the neighborhood had unanimously elected her president of the Block Association.)

Within eighteen days of Alexandra's debut, Michael had completely overhauled the weeknight news, and WWKK had come up with a media campaign to launch it. By this point, Cassy and Henry—even Rosanne—could barely stand the mention of Alexandra's name. And then Michael really did it.

Michael brought home a subway station billboard of Alexandra's face:

WHAT DID KANSAS EVER GIVE NEW YORK?
ONLY THEIR GREATEST NATURAL RESOURCE.

ALEXANDRA WARING AT SIX O'CLOCK—WWKK CHANNEL 6

It was framed and sealed in nonreflecting glass. Getting up Friday morning, Cassy had unsuspectingly walked into the living room and screamed. Henry stumbled on it next, claiming it was worse than "The Attack of the Fifty-Foot Woman." Rosanne didn't say a word about it, but by the time she left there was a black comb Scotch-taped under Alexandra's nose.

When Michael saw the comb he got upset. When Michael hinted that the billboard was going up in their bedroom Cassy got upset.

"What on earth would make you think I want to wake up to that!"

Michael was further dismayed when Henry rejected his offer to hang Alexandra in his room. "No, thanks, Dad. I don't think it's very polite. I mean, like I know her."

Alexandra was currently leaning against a bed in the guest room.

It was strange enough to watch her husband fall desperately in love with this young woman, but what made it more confusing to Cassy was Michael's insistence on sharing his obsession with her. More than once Michael had awakened Cassy in the middle of the night to ask, "Just tell me what you think of Alexandra, Cass. Am I crazy or am I right there's no one like her?"

A question like that was unclear to Cassy. Was Michael asking if Alexandra was his ticket to professional glory, or was Michael asking her if she would understand if he left her for Alexandra? Or was he simply asking for Cassy to put his massive insecurities to rest? Or could it be that Michael wished to use Alexandra as a new bond between them?

Cassy didn't have the slightest idea. But it sure made her edgy. If nothing else, Alexandra's arrival had prompted some of the heaviest drinking Michael had done in years. But then Cassy had to admit that it was not the drinking of despair, but rather the drinking of excitement, dreams and ambition that had marked the early years of their marriage. It was as if the drinking was the only thing stopping Michael from running around the clock in jubilant euphoria. And there was something else this wild time had kicked up in Michael—sexual desire.

Cassy was pretty sure Michael's sudden sexual interest in her meant that Alexandra was still only in his head and never in his arms. On the other hand, there was the nagging voice of experience that reminded Cassy that Michael's affairs usually began with sexual reattention to Cassy, as if giving Cassy what he was giving to another woman somehow lifted the guilt.

The last week of May, Michael announced at breakfast that the Cochrans were going to have dinner with Alexandra and a friend of hers on Saturday night.

"Saturday?" Cassy asked.

"Yeah. It's okay, isn't it? There's nothing on the calendar."

"No, no, that will be fine," Cassy said, placing a bowl of fresh fruit salad in front of Michael and Henry.

"I don't have to go, do I?" Henry asked.

"No, hotshot. Just your mom and me."

Cassy sat down at the table and sipped her grapefruit juice. "We're going to Alexandra's house?"

"No, 21. We'll be editing all day."

"Oh," Cassy said.

"It was Alexandra's idea," Michael said. "Said she'd like to see you again." Michael ate some fruit and waited for a response from Cassy, which did not come. "She liked you, Cass."

"Maybe she thinks Mom'll hire her," Henry suggested.

Michael booed at his son. "Bad idea, kid."

"What are you working on?" Cassy asked.

Michael ate another spoonful of fruit before answering. "Bombings on family planning centers around town."

Cassy nodded her approval. "From the angle—"

"Can I have your orange juice?" Henry interrupted to ask his father, reaching for the glass.

Michael grabbed the glass and pulled it closer to him. "Get your own, lazy."

Henry looked at his mother, frowned, and got up. Cassy looked at Michael. Michael raised the orange glass, said, "I want it," and drank it all down.

Silence.

It was one of Henry's oldest ploys to find out which way the wind was blowing with his father. What just transpired had told son and mother that father's orange juice was spiked with vodka this morning.

"Alexandra maintains that bombings are normally classified as terrorist activities in the U.S.," Michael said. "So if Macy's or something got bombed, the FBI would be called in like a shot. But because of the abortion issue, the Feds are reclassifying the bombings as arson so they can forbid the FBI's involvement."

"She's got guts," Cassy said. "She'll have the Right to Lifers at her doorstep within hours, to say nothing of the mad bombers."

"Yeah," Michael said, sighing, "that's what I told her. But," he continued, eyes lighting up, "you know what, Cass?"

"What?"

"The other day I was trying to think who it is that Alexandra reminds me so much of. And you know who it is?" He smiled, dangling his spoon.

"Who?"

"You." He nodded, his smile expanding. "Yeah. She reminds of you in the old days."

Cassy arrived at the 21 Club bar promptly at seven. A good-looking young man came up to her and introduced himself as Gordon Strenn, reminding Cassy that they had met at the Peabody Awards three years before. Cassy remembered him—ah yes, wasn't he with KSBH in Los Angeles? *Was,* now producing independently for public television. They were standing there talking for ten minutes before Cassy realized that Gordon was Alexandra's date.

Gordon and Cassy had just sat down to order a drink at a table when Michael and Alexandra arrived. Cassy was struck by how old Michael looked, and how terribly young Alexandra looked; and how Alexandra almost looked as if she could be his daughter. Michael kissed her hello (smelling of scotch). Alexandra kissed Gordon hello and, ignoring Michael's direction, sat down next to Cassy.

"I hope this was a good idea," Alexandra said to her. "I'm so tired I might fall asleep on you."

Well, yes, there were small traces of fatigue around Alexandra's eyes, but they did little to making Cassy feel sympathetic. When she was Alexandra's age, she could go two nights running with no sleep and still look sensational. Not anymore though. One all-nighter these days showed on her face like a misplaced tent pole.

While Michael was politely talking with Gordon, Cassy took the opportunity to find out if there was any reason to hate Alexandra. Resting her chin on her hand, Cassy leaned close to her and said, "I've got a bone to pick with you."

Alexandra's forehead furrowed immediately. "With me?"

"Yes. I've got a billboard of your face sitting in my house and a husband who's determined to hang it somewhere."

Alexandra, clearly surprised, pulled back. When Cassy didn't say anything, Alexandra smiled and leaned forward to whisper, "If I wanted him to have a remembrance of me, don't you think I'd be a little more discreet? A wallet-size photo perhaps?"

Cassy burst out laughing, bringing the men's conversation to a halt. Michael cleared his throat. Cassy looked over at him and knew that he was displeased about something.

Michael started discussing Alexandra's special report on the bombings and received Alexandra's full attention. As they talked, Cassy watched Alexandra and contrasted her now against her TV persona. There was a difference, all right. On air, Alexandra was rock-still, relying almost exclusively on her eyes for establishing the mood of the story she was relating. She was at her best on stories of villainy, when her eyes would sear through the screen with an intensity that accomplished the goal of every television personality—to so absorb the viewers as to make them oblivious to the fact that it is a television set they are watching, not a live person. But here, sitting next to Cassy, Alexandra was relaxed, and her otherwise terrific posture was continually interrupted by unconscious (Cassy was sure) dramatic body movements:

Alexandra Laughing: falling back hard against her chair, making it rock.

Alexandra Fascinated: hands pressing down so hard on the table in front of her that fingertips turned white.

Alexandra Caught up in Making a Point: hands jammed into her hair on top of her head.

Alexandra in Agreement: head bobbing emphatically, earrings swinging.

Alexandra Waiting to Disagree: hands clasped under her chair, arms trying to lift it from the floor.

She is like me in the old days.

Entranced by her observations, Cassy was only half aware that Alexandra had pulled her into the conversation.

"Chester's always written his own copy," Cassy heard herself saying. "The old school usually does. It's the new talent we have problems with. But then, of course," she added, "we're just about the only newsroom left in town that still insists the anchors write their own copy."

"You have to understand, Alexandra," Michael said, voice rising, "Cassy still caters to liberal creeps."

"Then I must be a liberal creep," Alexandra said. "I like WST's newscast."

Cassy thought Michael might blow up, but then, smart girl that Alexandra was, she treated Michael to a glorious smile meant only for him. The anger in his eyes vanished.

"So, Gordon," Cassy said, "tell me about this South African film that has Walter Annenberg so upset."

Michael managed to down three scotches before they went upstairs to dinner. He had another before ordering. With each one, a layer of courtesy was stripped. Michael eventually ignored Cassy and Gordon entirely. To her credit, Alexandra repeatedly tried to say something to Gordon and Cassy, or listen to what they were saying, but Michael would, if he had to, start shaking Alexandra's shoulder until she paid attention to him again. If Gordon hadn't had such a good sense of humor about it, Cassy would have forcibly dragged Michael out of the restaurant. But a compromise of sorts was silently worked out at the table. Cassy would entertain Gordon and Alexandra would baby-sit Michael.

After Cassy realized that Alexandra was amazingly good at saving Michael from embarrassing them all (somehow she got him to lower his voice; somehow she stopped him from snapping his fingers at the waiter; somehow she kept track of his silverware before it was swept to the floor), Cassy actually began to enjoy herself. She was intrigued with Gordon's series under production for public television, an adaptation of F. Scott Fitzgerald's *This Side of Paradise.*

Michael dropped his glass of wine in his dinner plate. He got upset. Alexandra gave him what was left on her plate to eat and he was happy again. Other than that near crisis, they got through to coffee and dessert (and brandy for Michael) without incident. Cassy excused herself to visit the ladies' room and Alexandra followed.

They did not speak until they were washing their hands. Looking at Cassy in the mirror, Alexandra asked her if she would ever consider having lunch with her.

"What an odd way of putting it," Cassy said, accepting a towel from the attendant. "Thank you." To Alexandra, "Why wouldn't I want to have lunch with you?"

Alexandra merely smiled and accepted a towel from the attendant.

"I'd like to have lunch with you. Particularly after a night like this." She withdrew a dollar from her purse and placed it in the dish. Alexandra followed suit. "The only problem though," Cassy said, "is that I'm a little overwhelmed the next couple of weeks. But let's talk this week—when I've got my calendar in front me."

"Great," Alexandra said, handing the towel back to the attendant.

A woman was standing in the doorway. Cassy glanced at her and saw that she was staring at Alexandra. Alexandra followed Cassy's eyes and smiled at the woman. "Hello."

"Aren't you the new girl—Alexandria?"

"No," Alexandra said, "that's a city in Egypt."

The woman looked as though she might die on the spot. Alexandra laughed and touched the woman's arm. "That's okay, my grandmother used to make the same mistake."

The woman followed them out to the lounge and stammered out a request for Alexandra's autograph. Cassy came up with paper and pen, and Alexandra sat down on the settee, using her pocketbook as a lapboard.

"S-M-I-T-H," the woman spelled, hanging over Alexandra's shoulder.

"That's her first name?"

"Yes. It was my maiden name."

Alexandra scribbled away, signed her name and handed the paper to the woman.

"For Smith, with best wishes for good news and happiness, Alexandra Waring." The woman looked up. "That's so nice."

"You're welcome."

When the woman left them, Alexandra joined Cassy at the mirror to brush her hair.

"What are you doing next Saturday?" Cassy asked her.

Alexandra sighed, looking at herself in the mirror. "Working, no doubt— but why?"

"You couldn't come to our block party for an hour or two, could you? I'd love to stick you in a booth and have you sign some autographs—we'd make a fortune off you."

Alexandra shrugged, turning to view the side of her hair. "Why not? I'd love to."

"Really?"

"Sure." Alexandra put her brush away and turned toward Cassy. "I could really use a change of pace—for a day."

"That would be great," Cassy said. "And then maybe afterward you'd stay for dinner and we'd have a chance to talk."

Alexandra looked into her eyes and smiled. "I'd like that," she said. She dropped her eyes. "I, um—"

Um? Alexandra says um?

"I don't really know anyone in New York," Alexandra finished.

Cassy looked at her face closely. Was Alexandra about to cry? "Are you all right?" she asked quietly.

Alexandra closed her eyes and touched her forehead. After a moment she nodded and opened her eyes. "I'm fine, I think I'm just—"

"Here," Cassy said, leading her to the settee, "sit down a minute and let me get you a glass of water."

"No, no water." But she did sit down.

Cassy sat down beside her. "Are you dizzy?"

"No," Alexandra said. It did not sound convincing. "I think I'm just exhausted."

"Undoubtedly," Cassy said.

The woman cruised back through the lounge with her piece of paper. "Thank you again," she said to Alexandra.

"You're very welcome." The door closed.

"You forget you're human, don't you?" Cassy asked, smiling.

Alexandra offered a weak smile.

Cassy patted her back and rubbed it briefly. "Well, old Mother Cochran says no work tomorrow. You need twenty-four hours' bed rest, old movies and the New York *Times.*"

"Sounds wonderful," Alexandra murmured.

Cassy stood up. "If you're not dizzy, I think the best thing to do is to get you home straight away." No response. She moved in front of Alexandra. "One great thing about being old and a mother is that no one can argue with me when I'm feeling old and want to give motherly advice."

Alexandra looked up at her.

Cassy held out her hand.

"You're very beautiful," Alexandra said.

Cassy felt her face redden. "We better get you home," she said, "your eyes are failing."

Alexandra stood up. "I can't bear to hear you talk about yourself that way. You did the other night too, after the party."

Cassy's mouth parted, but nothing came out.

"You're not old," Alexandra declared. "You're one of the most beautiful women I've ever seen in my life." Then she grinned—grinned the way Cassy imagined a twelve-year-old Kansas farm girl would, posing by a fence post for a picture on a sunny day. And then it was gone, and the familiar Alexandra reappeared. "We'd better go back," she said, swinging the door open.

"Yes," Cassy said, standing there. "Yes, of course," she said, sweeping her purse up from the settee.

Their reappearance at the table was not without drama. Michael had tucked the corner of the tablecloth in with his shirttail, so when he stood up, everyone had to dive to catch something. Michael just stood there and roared. The maître d' hovered, anxious for a conclusion to this act. Gordon and Alexandra, propping Michael up between them as discreetly as possible, ushered him downstairs while Cassy signed for the check.

When Cassy joined them under the awning outside, Michael, his arm around Gordon's neck, said, "Hey, Cass, Alexshzandra's comin' to the block party!"

"I know, Mike," she said. Turning to Alexandra, "How do you feel?"

"Fine. The fresh air—" She breathed deeply to illustrate its regenerative effect.

"Would you mind then if we took the first cab?"

"I have my car just around the corner," Gordon said.

"Do you want a ride?" Alexandra asked.

"No—a cab will be fine."

The attendant flagged down the cab in question.

"Alexshzandra's gonna sell kisses at the block party."

"No, dear, Alexandra's going to sign autographs."

The attendant held the door as Gordon rolled Michael into the cab. "Maybe—" Gordon started.

"No, that's all right. We'll be fine," Cassy said, pressing some money on the attendant. She held out her hand to Gordon. "It was lovely to see you again."

"I wanna say good night to Alexshzandra!" Michael demanded, trying to crawl out of the cab.

Cassy grabbed hold of his coat to keep him in place while Alexandra leaned in and kissed him on the cheek. "Good night, Michael, I'll see you on Monday."

Cassy pushed herself against Michael to get into the cab. "Phew!" she said as Gordon closed the door. She rolled down the window. "Thanks." She held her hand out to Alexandra. "I'll talk to you next—Michael!" Michael's hand was up her dress. Cassy yanked his hand away and made a face for the benefit of their audience. "Riverside and 88th," she said to the driver. "Good night!"

"Good night!" Alexandra and Gordon and the attendant called.

Cassy thanked God that Henry was staying overnight at a classmate's.

The doorman helped her get Michael upstairs. Once they got him to the bed, Michael was out cold. Cassy saw the doorman out, gave him a five, and returned to the bedroom to proceed with the routine that had become second nature to her:

Take off Michael's shoes, then his socks, then his tie; unbutton shirt, undo belt, unzip his pants; roll on left side and slip off right arm of jacket and shirt, tug at pants; roll on right side and slip off left arm of jacket and shirt, tug at pants; roll on stomach, move to end of bed, pull off pants. There. Put clothes away; wipe Michael's face with washcloth; leave glass of water on nightstand; undress self and take hot bath.

Lying there, the hot water lapping against her neck, Cassy thought of Alexandra and decided she did not want to think about Alexandra. It was painful, this proximity to youth. It made her wonder what it was like to be young and beautiful and unmarried. What it would be like to be taken home by a Gordon. What it would be like to have more beginnings in front of her instead of so many endings, or worse—to have so many things the same, day after day after day. . . .

But not all was the same, Cassy found out after her bath. Michael had done something new. Michael had wet the bed.

8

HOWARD AT WORK

Howard came out of the editorial meeting with Patricia MacMannis. Before the War with the business department began, Harrison had lured Patricia away from the Robinson Press to bolster their roster of "up-and-coming" writers. (Patricia had produced three bestsellers in two years, all of them first novels by writers under thirty years of age.) Thus far, Patricia had the best batting average for acquisitions in the war, largely due to what Harrison fondly described as her "divine sense of duplicity." Simply put, the business department thought she was an angel, when, in fact, she really was the Devil when it came to a book she wanted to buy.

A case in point: Patricia had a collection of short stories she wished to publish. Short-story anthologies had been one of the first targets of the business department, so Patricia had a lot of work to do. She conspired with her colleagues to get the reader's reports she wanted and then had lunch with Mack Sperry. (The duplicitous angel was not without powers of innuendo, either, and Mack Sperry seemed slightly mesmerized by Patricia's long gazes and slightly parted mouth.) She nearly cried at the lunch table, bemoaning to Sperry that Harrison was making her sign up the "most lurid short stories. Mack, what will my mother say when she finds out that I edited a book that has metaphors for deep-throat oral sex on every other page?" And so Mack Sperry asked to read the stories, and since every reader's report talked about the lurid sexual metaphors that ran throughout the book, one can only assume that Mack Sperry actually saw lurid sexual metaphors in the short stories since the book sailed through with his approval.

Six months ago, Howard had almost started an affair with Patricia. It had been Patricia's birthday. Howard had come into her office in the evening to talk to her about a problem with one of his books. They had ended up sitting on her office floor, in the dark, until nine o'clock at night, drinking two bottles of champagne that she had received, solving all of the problems of the world. But then Howard had kissed her—and Patricia had kissed him back—and then she had started to cry. Patricia, it turned out, was already having an affair with Tom West, another senior editor at G & G. And Tom was, on her birthday, at home with his wife and kids. And so they had sat there until eleven o'clock, sharing the tormenting truths of their lives. (Which neither quite remembered.)

They had been great friends since.

"I hear Sperry's going to be coming to the editorial meeting," Patricia said to him, coming out of the conference room.

"Who did you hear that from?" Howard said, frowning, loosening his tie.

Patricia batted her eyes. "Why, Mr. Sperry himself."

"I'm telling you, Patricia," Howard said, walking with her, "you better be careful of that guy."

"Howard," Carol Roundtree called from behind them.

He stopped and turned.

"I need to talk to you for a second." Carol was the crafts and cookbook editor.

"Sure," Howard said.

"I'll stop by your office later," Patricia said, walking on.

Carol was juggling a couple of manuscripts. Carol was always juggling a couple of manuscripts (that usually turned out to be only one). The production people always ran when they saw her. Eight hundred pages of recipes almost always did them in. "Take this one—on the top—will you?"

Howard lifted it from the stack in her arms and squinted at the top page. *"Flying Made Easy?"*

Carol looked around and, lowering her voice, said, "It's Greg's." She looked up and down the hall again before continuing. "I'm sorry, but you said you'd take the next one and this is it. It's due into production next week."

"Flying?" Howard said, pushing his glasses up. "Carol, what do I know about flying?"

"As much as the people who'll buy it, I suspect," she said.

"Yeah, right," Howard said, thumbing through the top pages. "And what about the art? There must be illustrations to this."

"Office services is bringing them up on the cart," Carol said, quickly moving toward the door of the stairwell.

"On the cart?" Howard said, staring at her departing figure. "You can't *move* the illustrations without a cart?"

Holding the door, Carol turned and whispered, "There isn't anyone else who can do it, Howard. I've got the whole Elementary Photography Series in my lap." Her eyes shifted past Howard, making him turn to look.

Harrison Dreiden, Tom West and Layton Sinclair were coming down the hall. Tom and Layton were arguing; Carol and Howard nodded to Harrison.

"Layton, I swear to God, if you *ever* tamper with one of my books again," Tom was saying, "I'll take a horsewhip to you." (Layton had tried to annex one of Tom's books for the Sperry imprint.)

"Howard," Harrison said, touching Howard's elbow, "I'd like to see you in my office for a minute."

"The material should be up soon," Carol said, disappearing into the stairwell.

Harrison led Howard to his office, motioned him in, and closed the door behind him. "Sit down," he said.

Howard sat in one of the chairs and waited for Harrison to be seated.

"Howard," Harrison began, leaning forward on his desk, "I wanted to tell you the news myself—before you heard it elsewhere."

This was not going to be good.

Harrison looked down at his folded hands. "Mack Sperry is being named president and publisher tomorrow."

In a split second Howard had slammed *Flying Made Easy* on Harrison's desk and was on his feet. "They can't do that! Sperry? The guy used to sell hardware, for God's sake!"

Harrison motioned him back down into his chair. "It's done. The announcement will come out tomorrow." Pause, leaning back in his chair. "I'm to remain as editor-in-chief."

"Unbelievable," Howard muttered, dropping his head. "They're mad."

"They believe Sperry can turn the house around financially, and maybe they're right."

Howard raised his eyes to meet Harrison's. He saw the pain in the older man's eyes and realized how excruciating this must be for him. "Is there anything I can do?"

"Yes," Harrison said, smiling slightly and leaning forward again. "You can show that jerk how good you are."

Howard laughed. "Oh, boy," he sighed a moment later, "this place." He shook his head. Looking back at Harrison, Howard saw that his eyes were on the manuscript.

"Taking up flying?" Harrison said, a trace of his usual sparkle in his eye.

"Oh, that."

Harrison smiled for real. "It's Greg's book, isn't it?" When Howard didn't say anything, Harrison rose from his chair. He turned and rested his hands on the windowsill, looking out at the view of the East River. "I know all about it," he said. He glanced back at Howard. "I think you kids are terrific for doing what you're doing." Looking back out the window, "It's the kind of thing that always makes me proud of Gardiner & Grayson. It *is* like a family. We look after our own." Harrison turned to look at Howard. "Tell me the truth—how is he?"

"I'm not sure," Howard said. "He's getting blood transfusions and afterward he always feels better, has more energy . . ." He hesitated.

"It's been ten weeks," Harrison said.

"He came in last Friday—I saw him."

"So did I." Harrison frowned slightly. "I don't know how long we're going to be able to keep this from Sperry," he said. "He's bound to catch on, sooner or later." He rubbed his ear. "It's a horrible thing."

"Yes, sir. And Sperry's a horrible thing too."

Silence.

Harrison pushed himself off the windowsill. "You know," he said, moving over to the couch and sitting down, "when I started here, we didn't know who was going to come back alive from the war. Now we don't know who's going to come back alive from a one-night stand." He sifted through the magazines on the coffee table. He sighed. "Why does it always take a tragedy to make us stop and think about what is really important in this world?" He paused, looking over to Howard. "It makes everything— Sperry, these idiotic meetings, this whole charade—seem so . . . stupid. So utterly pointless." He sat back against the couch, holding his knee up in his hands. "AIDS . . . Now cancer, that sounds like what it is. But AIDS

. . . Kool-Aid. First aid. Children. Help. No . . ." He shook his head and sighed. "You know what I did Friday night, after I saw Greg?"

"No," Howard said.

"I called my daughter—at three in the morning—to say hello to her." He swallowed, staring off into space. "It's probably the first time I ever called her just to say hello."

Howard left Harrison Dreiden's office feeling very sad.

Dutifully stationed at the desk outside Howard's office was Bob, his assistant. Howard's office was one of six along this side of the building, and Bob's desk was one of the six lined up outside of them. "Hi."

"I've got a ton of messages for you," Bob said, reaching for his log. Very efficient, Bob was. Not only did he make Howard call the people he didn't want to call, he also had a safeguard system against Howard "accidentally" losing the phone messages. Each and every call was entered in the spiral-bound book—the date, time of the call, the message, and the phone number—and while the top sheet could be torn off and handed to Howard, the carbon copy remained in Bob's permanent safekeeping.

Reading from the log, Bob said, "Lucinda Ryan wants to know if the Mason contract was sent via Cape Horn. If not, where is it? You promised it last week. Roger Sneed called from Chicago to scream there aren't any books in the bookstores. He wants to know what is the point of him promoting a book people can't buy. Sidney from sub rights wants to discuss the floor on *Lost Love, New Love*. He says Avon's biting at the bit." Breath. "Some guy named Peter Pretzie from Alabama called to see if you want to read his book about the role of mules in World War I. He says he met you at ABA last year—don't know how well you know him though, since he kept calling you Harold." Turn page. "John Pratt is meeting with Arnold Stevens this afternoon at three and wonders if you can stop in. Clark Bryson says twelve-thirty is fine and he'll see you at the Barclay. Reverend Holland says he's got the green light for the Reading in the Prisons committee and he said to thank you for your letter and that it did the trick." Pause, squint. "I didn't take this message, Holly did. I think it says your wife called. That or 'Yorfee' called."

Howard started to move into his office.

"Wait—" Bob said, rising out of his chair, reading as fast as he could. "Don Casey said you wanted to know where the Clarie Munson book went. He said to tell you that it went to Crown."

"Did he say who's the editor?"

"Betty Prashker."

"Ten to one she makes it a bestseller," Howard said, giving the door to his office a kick. "Damn it," he muttered, "when are we going to buy some good books again around here?"

"Yeah, well, seems to me you've got too many books for this office to handle as it is," Bob said. (A snicker from the girl at the next desk.) "Amanda Miller called and said she got your letter. She said you could stop by any time, just let her know when, or she'll come into the office to see you. Oh—and Susan Kelly will be sending you the Norm Ericson manuscript next week."

Bob handed him a neat stack of messages.

"Did you call contracts about the Mason contract?"

"Not yet, I haven't had a chance."

"Well, call now, will you? Tell them we must have it today."

"I'll try."

"And tell John I'll drop by for that meeting."

"You've got a marketing meeting at three-thirty."

"Tell him that and say I'll swing by at about three-ten."

In his office, Howard took off his jacket before sitting down. God, his desk looked like a bomb had hit it. All this paper, where to begin? The phone rang and Bob picked it up outside. Howard waited a minute, was satisfied that his attention wasn't required, and then called his wife.

"Melissa Stewart," she said. She wasted no time, no breath. If her secretary wasn't on top of the phone, Melissa got right to it.

"Hi, I had a message that Yurfee called and Bob and I figure that must be you."

"Howard, we've been robbed."

He had a chill. "What?"

"The Barneses saw a man coming out of our apartment with a TV set. They called downstairs and Ernie stopped him in the lobby and the guy dropped it and took off."

"Did they catch him?"

"Not yet. The police are there now and need one of us to tell them what's missing. Can you go?"

"Well—when?"

"Now."

"Can't they come back tonight?"

"Howard, all I know is that they called me and asked if one of us could go."

"I'm not sure I'd even know what was missing."

"Damn it, Howard."

"Look, Melissa, why don't I call Rosanne? I really can't get out of here. Rosanne knows the apartment inside and out."

Silence.

"I think Rosanne has something to do with it," Melissa said.

"What? Are you out of your mind?"

"Common sense," Melissa hissed into the phone. "Don't you think it's the slightest bit strange that we're robbed the day after her drug addict husband visits our apartment?"

"Melissa, *you're* strange. And you sure as hell better not make any accusations to the police."

"Since I'm the one going home, I feel free to tell them whatever I want." She hung up.

Howard slammed the phone down.

The intercom on the phone buzzed and Howard had to pick up again.

"I've got contracts on the phone," Bob told him, "and they say the Mason contract's been sitting on Sperry's desk."

"Who are you talking to?"

"Beth."

"I'll talk to her." Push button. "Beth, hi, it's Howard. Why won't Sperry countersign the contract?"

"Rumor has it he wants it renegotiated."

"Renegotiated *how?"* Howard yelled. He then composed himself, thanked Beth for telling him, hung up the phone—and threw an eraser across his office as hard as he could. It ricocheted off a photograph of Gertrude and disappeared behind a pile of manuscripts in the corner.

With each phone call he returned he got more depressed. And after Lucinda Ryan got through screaming at him that if she didn't get the countersigned contract and advance check within twenty-four hours she was going to yank the book out of Gardiner & Grayson, Howard pushed all the messages to the side save the one that had the possibility of being friendly. Amanda Miller.

He was glad he called. If nothing else, this Amanda Miller was a change of pace. She was very, very nice, and her voice was rather soothing, but—as Rosanne had forewarned him—she did sound a little "loony." But, too, as Rosanne had promised, Howard did love the way she talked.

"You live on the Drive, Mr. Stewart, do you not?" she was asking him.

"Yes, in 153."

"Well, then, perhaps you would consider joining me for breakfast one morning. But if it is your preference that I come to your office—"

"Actually," Howard said, "it would be easier for me to swing by one night on my way home."

Pause. "Do you have a particular evening in mind?"

"Uh," Howard said, fumbling to open his calendar. "Oh, boy, let's see here." He whistled through his teeth. "Gosh, I didn't realize how . . ."

"Toward the end of June?"

"No, I'd like to see you soon." He wasn't kidding; he was eager to put a face to this voice. "That is, if you're not busy."

She laughed and Howard thought it was the nicest laugh he had heard in some time. "You must excuse me, Mr. Stewart," she said.

"I meant, you know, when you're going to be home."

She laughed again. "Mr. Stewart, I am always at home. The more appropriate question, I'm afraid, is whether or not you will find me at home in my right mind."

"Uh . . ." Howard said.

"Oh, dear," she said. "And Rosanne secured my sacred promise that I would be on my best behavior with you."

"Actually," Howard said, looking at his calendar again, "I could do it tonight . . ."

"This evening would be fine."

"No—sorry, I forgot." He sighed. "We got robbed today."

Pause. "Book bandits, perhaps?"

Howard laughed. "No, it was more—"

Bob was waving to him from the doorway.

"Could you hold on one second?" He covered the phone.

"A Cassy Cochran on 6. She says she *has* to talk to you for twenty seconds about some block party. And Patricia MacMannis stopped by."

"Okay." Back on the phone, "Uh, Ms. Miller?"

"Please call me Amanda."

Amanda.

"Amanda, could you hang on for a minute? I've got Cassy Cochran on the other line—do you know her?"

"Fridays."

"What?"

"Rosanne works for her on Fridays."

"Well, hold on, will you?" Click. Click. "Hello?"

"I feel ridiculous calling you out of the blue at the office," Cassy began, "but I can't seem to get ahold of Melissa."

"No, it's fine." Pause. "How do you do?"

She laughed. "I would be doing much better if Melissa was still president of the Block Association. Let's see here, Howard—you're doing the book-stall—yes?"

"Yes."

"Okay, just a quick question. My son Henry—"

"I met Henry last year. He's a nice guy."

"Thank you, I think so. Anyway, Howard, Henry's sorting the fiction and he needs to know if you want them separated into categories of any kind."

"If he's got the time, tell him to pull anything that looks like a mystery or a romance novel. But if he doesn't have the time, tell him not to worry about it."

"Mystery and romance. Got it. Okay, that's it. The books will be labeled and in cartons down in the basement of 162. The tables will be there, too, and the super will open—"

"I know the drill," Howard assured her.

"Terrific." Sigh. "Howard, thank you, I'll see you Saturday."

"You bet." Click, click. "Amanda."

"Howard."

Howard.

"Sorry to keep you holding. Cassy Cochran's calling about the block party Saturday. I'm doing the bookstall."

Another wonderful laugh. "You will recognize me as the dazed creature searching for Trollope."

Silence. Howard was thinking.

"Listen," Howard said, "my wife's already home talking to the police about our robbery, so why don't I just go ahead and . . . come and see you, say, six o'clock?"

"Six o'clock would be lovely."

Lovely.

"Where are you?"

"One seventy-three."

"Apartment?"

"The fourteenth floor."

Pause. "You don't have an apartment number?"

"No. Do you know the building the children call the ice cream castle?"

"The one with the towers?"

"Exactly. The north tower is my bedroom."

"You're kidding."

"No, not at all." Her voice lowered, playful. "The man who designed the building lived in here. It was all one big room, this floor. Very much like a chapel. When I first saw it, there were fourteen rows of chairs, all facing toward the window of the north tower." Pause. "But he never had any visitors. And all those chairs . . . They say he would lie on a blanket of velvet in the south tower, and play the flute through the night." Pause. "It's closed now, the south tower. Ghosts, they say. Insufficient structural supports, I say."

They both laughed.

"He had an altar of sorts, in the north tower, my bedroom. But, alas, that is too long a tale to be told at the present."

"Tell me the highlights."

"Pictures of Stalin, Coco Chanel and Marilyn Monroe."

"I'll be there at six."

A low laugh. "I thought you might be."

Howard was grinning when he hung up. He laughed aloud once, too, shaking his head. *Rosanne, old girl, you sure can pick 'em.*

"You shouldn't be smiling," Bob announced from the door. "You're ten minutes late for your lunch with Clark Bryson and there's a guy out here who's trying to dump two thousand—" He turned his head. "What did you say they were?"

Mumble.

"Two thousand pictures of airplanes," Bob finished. "He says they belong to you."

"They do."

"Nice to know we're expanding our horizons. Your wife's on 5."

Howard picked up. "Hi."

"You're not going to be happy, Howard. Detective Mendez says he knew exactly what he was doing. He bypassed the silver—because of the monogram—knew the real pearls from the fake ones, took my good bracelets, the earrings Daddy gave me last Christmas—all untraceable. Thank God I put Mother's jewelry in the safe deposit box."

"Well," Howard sighed, "we were lucky then."

"You weren't lucky, Howard. He took *all* of your stuff."

"My stuff? Like what?"

"All of your silver dollars are gone."

Ouch. He had been collecting them since he was four years old. There had to have been over three hundred, worth something—

"All of your cuff links and tie clips. Your school ring, your Nikon—"

Ouch.

"And your Sony from the study, which is destroyed. The screen's in a million pieces in the lobby. And do you have your pens with you?"

"No."

"Then he took all of your Cross pens too."

Good. He hated them anyway. Daddy Collins gave him one on every holiday. Always had them engraved "H N S." It was no mistake; Howard was quite sure Daddy thought his middle name was Nils, instead of Mills.

"Daddy's sending over people to install an alarm system this afternoon. He says we should have had it done a long time ago and he's right."

Howard started flipping through the mail folder on his desk.

"And the police seem to know all about Rosanne's husband," Melissa said. "Apparently we're not the only people he's robbed."

"Damn it, Melissa, how do you know?"

"Detective Mendez, unlike you, seems to be *very* interested in the fact that he was here yesterday."

"Did it ever occur to you," Howard began, shoving the mail folder and sending papers flying off his desk, "that no one would be stupid enough to rip off the place where his wife works?" Howard gripped the phone cord and stood up. "Surely even you can understand that one doesn't rob in order to get caught."

"Did you leave the front door unlocked this morning?"

"What?"

"Did you leave the front door unlocked?" Melissa repeated.

"Don't be stupid. It locks by itself."

"Don't *you* be stupid, Howard. There's no sign of a break-in. So unless it was Rosanne herself—and I wouldn't put it past her—"

"Stop it! Just stop it!" Howard yelled.

All the typewriters on the floor stopped.

"I'd accuse anyone—even you—before I'd—oh, hell, Melissa!" Howard slammed the phone down.

"Yes," Howard heard Bob saying outside. "Please tell Mr. Bryson that Captain Stewart—right, Captain Stewart—will be taking off shortly and will land at the Barclay in approximately ten minutes. Right. Thank you."

The sound of the office typewriters resumed and Howard grabbed his jacket.

9

IN WHICH AMANDA AND
HOWARD BECOME ACQUAINTED
AND MELISSA HAS HER WAY

Amanda looked at the boxes of Catherine like a mother who wished her child would behave better.

She spent the entire afternoon trying to pull together the first three chapters for Howard Stewart to read. The operative word in the latter was "trying"; once Amanda had Chapter 1 safely in the folder, she discovered Chapter 1 from 1981 and liked it better. And then she came across the 1983 version, which was radically different from the other two, prompting her to read succeeding chapters to see what it was she had been trying to do in 1983. The result was that Catherine was soon spread out all over the floor in the writing room, Amanda was near apoplexy with time running out, poor Mrs. Goldblum was informed that tea was canceled, and Rosanne was given the opportunity to lecture Amanda on the virtues of Reader's Digest Condensed Books.

By the time Amanda threw herself in the shower at five o'clock, the "pages" for Howard Stewart numbered something over four hundred. (Chapters 1, 2, 3, à la 1981, 1983 and 1986; outlines of intent from 1978, '80 and '85.) *Amanda Exposed,* she thought she should write on the folder. By the time she was dressed, Amanda decided to hide the "pages" in the kitchen and if—only if—Howard Stewart expressed a desire to read part of Catherine would she bring them out. (Amanda had a vision of opening the door, pages in hand, and Howard Stewart fainting.) Amanda also filed his letter away—the one that had GARDINER & GRAYSON, PUBLISHERS emblazoned across the top—which had been hanging over her desk.

Howard Stewart arrived promptly at six and Amanda found him charming. Warm, clever, earnest—what was there not to like? He was her age, she thought, perhaps a year or two younger—perhaps a year or two older. And she liked his looks. The way he was dressed—tweed jacket, loose-fitting pants—was enticing, but a large part of his appeal to Amanda had to do with the possibility of a change in costume. Take off his glasses (marvelous eyes) and put him jeans, boots and a hat and he'd make a fine cowboy. Let the five o'clock shadow grow into a beard, stick an ax in his hand, and he could be Pa in *Little House in the Big Woods.* Slick his hair back, dress him in a tuxedo, hand him an elegant walking stick, and plop him down in a speakeasy in the 1920s. Cloak him in furs against the cold winters of imperial Russia and . . .

Amanda noted how well he handled her, kept her on track. He was very direct about Catherine, about Amanda's relationship with her, about Amanda's relationship with the work. Every time Amanda lapsed into excuses about why the book was taking so long, Howard Stewart gently forced her into the present, about *today,* about her work habits and how (and if) they were changing, could be changed. At one point, while pacing in front of the fireplace, Amanda got so flustered she knocked over the fire irons. Howard jumped up, steered Amanda down into a chair, and said, very gently, "I apologize. I'm firing too many questions at you. This book is your life and doesn't deserve to be rushed, not even when talked about."

He held her shoulders while he said this.

If Roger had done the same thing, Amanda would have been waiting for him to kiss her. But the thought did not cross her mind with Howard Stewart. In fact, what she was thinking about was how much she yearned to curl up in his arms and cry. She wanted to tell him that Catherine would never be written, never be finished. That there was no point to this discussion, because if Catherine were to be finished, then Amanda would be left alone, and she would be finished too.

She did not curl up in his arms. She did not tell him this. She got him another glass of white wine and gave him a tour of the apartment. He seemed to know a good deal about antiques (in each room he headed straight for the best pieces) and made comments that let Amanda know that his appreciation was sincere.

He adored the writing room. Poking about, noticing all the boxes and files and shelves of papers, he asked her what else she was working on. When Amanda admitted that it was all Catherine, Howard merely smiled and nodded, saying, "I think you've been living alone with her for too long. And I think it's wonderful you've decided to let someone meet her."

Couldn't this man just stay here forever? Read in the corner?

She brought out the "pages" from the kitchen and handed them to him without a word. "Good," was all he said, tucking the manuscript under his arm. "And now, fair is fair. *Where* is the altar?"

For a minute Amanda didn't know what he was talking about. She was too caught up visualizing Howard sharpening pencils at her desk. Amanda understood, finally, and led him to her bedroom. When she turned on the lights, Howard covered his face and groaned.

Amanda didn't know what to do.

Picking up on her confusion, Howard quickly said, "It's the most remarkable room I've ever seen. I could move in here, lock the door, and be perfectly happy for twenty years."

Amanda smiled.

When Amanda had the contractors erect the walls, and hence create the rooms of her apartment, she had driven them to distraction over this room. The walls had to be torn down twice before she was happy with them. Rather, with it. Extending out from the front arc that made up the facade of the tower, the room had one continuous curving wall. In essence, the room was one sixty-five-foot circle, a third of which was the ironwork and glass of the tower windows; a third of which was built-in bookshelves of various sizes and shapes, and the last third of which was taken up by a stone fireplace and a four-poster bed. Ivy hung everywhere; Victorian paintings hung at odd junctures over and through the bookcases; there were candles everywhere, too.

Howard scanned some of the books and noted aloud that they were in alphabetical order by author. "The only way I can find anyone," Amanda said.

He looked at her then for a moment, his face unreadable. "Anyone," he murmured. "You speak of them as people too."

Amanda nodded.

His expression changed then and the corners of his mouth turned down.

He seemed to be trying to shake whatever the thought was that he was holding.

They went back to the kitchen, where Amanda refilled their wineglasses. Howard's eyes rested on a note that Rosanne had written. He looked at his watch.

Amanda handed him his glass. "I don't mean to keep you," she said.

"Are you kidding?" Howard said. "I told you—I could stay here for twenty years." He looked around suddenly, seemingly nervous. He put the manuscript down on the table and sat down in one of the chairs.

Amanda lifted herself up to sit on the counter above him.

"Maybe I should talk to you," Howard said.

Amanda blinked several times. "What, pray tell, have you been doing for the last few hours?"

He looked down to his feet. "I've got a problem."

Amanda waited, curious.

"My wife's got it in her head Rosanne's husband robbed us and I'm not sure what I should do about it."

Amanda sipped her wine. Quietly, "Do you think he did?"

Howard looked up at her. "No."

"Then what is the problem?"

He rubbed his eyes behind his glasses. Shaking his head, "You don't know my wife."

"From the sound of it, perhaps it's fortunate I don't."

His head kicked back with a laugh.

Amanda jumped down from the counter, picked the phone up off the counter and placed it on the table next to him. "222-5673, Room 709."

Howard picked up the receiver and punched in the number. The operator buzzed the DiSantos room but there was no answer. Howard had to call back a second time to leave a message. He hung up the phone and both he and Amanda, now leaning against the counter, looked at it.

Howard finally spoke. "Ever wish you could just—disappear? Vanish?"

Amanda merely smiled.

They talked for another twenty minutes about the Stewarts' robbery, about how much they both loved Rosanne (a great deal of laughter in sharing their views of her), and about the dubious circumstances of the DiSantos home life. They agreed that Howard should stand up to his wife on this; they agreed that Rosanne deserved every possible break in life; and somehow the subject veered and Amanda was promising to help Howard at the bookstall on Saturday at the block party. By this point the two were sitting almost knee to knee in chairs. Another glass of wine had been consumed; their faces were slightly flushed. It was approaching nine-thirty.

"Will I be working side by side with your wife?" Amanda asked.

"No, thank God. Melissa's got some grand scheme going with the Junior League. Cookbooks and food and dressing up like recipes or something."

Pause. Smiles.

Amanda fingered the stem of her glass. "May I ask you something?"

"Sure."

"Do you consider yourself . . . happy?"

He made a sound deep in his throat. "You mean am I happily married?"

Amanda didn't say anything.

"I don't think so."

Amanda nodded, sipping from her glass. "I wasn't either," she said.

Howard's eyes darted around as if he expected a husband to walk in.

"I'm divorced," Amanda said. "I've been divorced so long, I think I've always been divorced."

"Really?"

"Well, six years is a long time."

Howard murmured his agreement. After a moment he met her eyes. "I've thought about getting divorced."

Amanda's heart started to pound. And that wasn't all. Voice strained, trying to pull it off as a joke, "Your wife plays around, perhaps?"

Howard roared. "Melissa wouldn't play a piano," he said, slapping his knee. He continued to chuckle to himself and then, a moment later, his smile abruptly died. "We don't do anything, either one of us," he said.

Silence.

"Do you have children?" Amanda said.

"No. You?"

Amanda shook her head.

Silence.

Howard sighed. "I think I keep thinking it'll get better."

Softly, "Was it ever—better?"

"No," Howard said.

Silence.

"We were very fortunate, Christopher and I—that's my husband, Christopher. Was my husband. If we had had children . . ." She let her voice trail, shaking her head. She looked back at him. "Why haven't you had children? You seem like the kind of man who would want to be a father."

He thought a minute and then shrugged. "I don't know. We've never really even talked about it. I guess with Melissa's career—"

"She works?"

"Oh, does Melissa work. She's *very* successful."

"In publishing?"

"No, banking. She's with First Steel Citizen."

Amanda's surprise was evident. "I wouldn't have envisioned you with someone in banking."

He tossed back the rest of his wine and put the glass down heavily. "Me neither." He gave Amanda's foot a slight nudge. "What about Christopher, what did he do?"

"Christopher?" Amanda threw her head back to laugh. "Christopher didn't do anything."

"I don't believe that. He must have—"

She leaned forward. "It's true. Christopher did absolutely nothing while married to me, except—" She sighed and leaned back in her chair. "Oh, let us tread gently past the subject of what Christopher did."

"How did you live then?"

Amanda tossed her hands up. "I'm wealthy. I admit it. My grandmother died and left me all this money and Christopher married me and spent a lot of it. Not all of it, though." She gestured to the room. "I have this. I have more, too." She hastily covered her mouth. "Pardon me. I'm not a particularly good drinker."

"Nor am I."

Amanda pursed her lips for a moment. "It's a pretty terrible thing to know that someone married you because your grandmother died." She frowned. "It's really rather distressing."

"My wife's got money," Howard said, rocking back on the chair legs.

The cheery warm feeling (and feeling of other kinds) that Amanda was experiencing dissipated with this announcement. She was very polite, friendly still, but brought the evening to an end.

At the door, with the pages of Catherine tucked under his arm, Howard promised to read them before the block party on Saturday. Amanda would really come, wouldn't she? Standing there, listening to the tone of his voice, some of Amanda's good feeling returned. This was indeed a very nice man. A very nice man who genuinely seemed to want to help her with Catherine.

"You must not feel as though you have any obligation to me," she said.

"I don't," he said. "But, in any event, I've met one of my more wonderful neighbors, haven't I?" He held out his hand and Amanda shook it. "You don't know how much fun this has been for me tonight. I really needed to be cheered up—and I was." He grinned. Then he saluted. "Until Saturday."

Without thinking, Amanda curtsied.

"Good night," he said.

"Good night," Amanda said, closing the door.

He is attractive, she thought.

But then, so had been Christopher.

It was the apartment, it was her breasts, and it was the wine, Howard told himself all the way home.

What was the matter with him? His heart was racing, his stomach felt achy. Howard felt nuts.

She was bright—obviously, granted. Eccentric. A recluse. Hardly the stuff women of dreams are made of.

But she was very, very, very pretty. Not beautiful. Though she had verged on it, the way she had been standing by her desk, against the light. In the kitchen, too, when she was sitting on the counter. Looking down. Such strange eyes. That mouth.

The rest of her body certainly wasn't hard to take either.

"Rosanne's here," Melissa announced at the door, arms folded. "I think we should stand together on this."

Howard dropped his briefcase, laid Amanda's manuscript on the table, and brushed past Melissa without comment. Rosanne was standing in the middle of the living room, looking small, spent. She made no effort to greet him: she simply set her tired eyes upon him. Howard went to her and touched her arm. "I'm sorry," he said.

Melissa marched in, plunked herself down on the couch, crossed her legs and then her arms too for good measure. "Well," she said.

Rosanne continued to look at Howard. "You could have called me before sendin' the cops over."

"We didn't send the police," Melissa said. "The police asked us if there were any unusual visitors recently and we simply told them that your husband was one of them."

"I did call you," Howard said. "No one answered and I left a message."

"You called her, Howard?"

Howard looked at Melissa. "Yes, I did." He shoved his hands into his pockets."

"Thanks," Rosanne murmured. Then she addressed herself to Melissa. "I don't think my husband had anything to do with this."

Melissa tossed her head. "That's for the police to decide. We have nothing to do with it."

"I don't think your husband had anything to do with it either," Howard said.

"Well," Melissa said, rising from the couch, arms still folded, "regardless of what anyone thinks, I *know,* Rosanne, that you'll agree with me that it would better that you not work here until this matter is cleared up."

"Melissa—"

"No, Howard."

Howard touched Rosanne's arm again. "She doesn't mean it. Of course you'll stay on."

Melissa's eyes narrowed at the opposition. She circled the couch and stopped behind it. "Rosanne is not to return until this matter is settled. Do I make myself clear?"

Howard looked to the ceiling. "Melissa—"

"Let's just get real, Howard, shall we?" The tone of Melissa's voice could cut steel. "You couldn't pay for the electricity around here." To Rosanne. "I'll send you a check for one week. I think that's more than fair." She walked out of the room; a few seconds later they heard the bedroom door slam.

Without a word, Rosanne turned to go.

"Rosanne," Howard said, following her, "don't worry. We'll straighten this all out. Just come back on Monday. Everything'll be all straightened out by then."

Rosanne continued down the hall.

"Rosanne—"

"Don't you get it, Howie?" Rosanne said, wheeling around. She backed up a step and fumbled for the doorknob. "There's nothing to straighten out. Your wife hates me, and I hate her. She wants me out of here and you can't stop her."

Howard sighed. "Rosanne, look—"

"And I don't care how smart she thinks she is," Rosanne sputtered. "There's something all twisted up inside of that woman." She yanked the door open. She looked back at him, softening slightly.

"I'm sorry, Howie, but that's the way I see it." She was breathing heavily. "I like you, Howie—always did. But if you don't do somethin' about that bitch, you're gonna get all twisted up inside too."

She waited a moment, but Howard couldn't say anything.

" 'Bye," she said, closing the door.

A moment later she knocked. Howard opened the door and Rosanne handed him her keys to the apartment.

Amanda settled down into the six pillows on her bed to read Charlotte Brontë's *Villette*. In the course of wading through Catherine this afternoon she had come across a reading a list from one of her graduate courses at Columbia. Seven years late, but better late—

The buzzer went off on her phone, prompting—as it always did—an image of Carl to flash through her mind. Amanda's phone system had been her first concession to twentieth-century high technology. The man who had come to install it, two years ago, had been named Carl; Carl had to give Amanda six "phone lessons" to understand how to operate it without zapping people off left and right; and then Carl had come back every other Monday until Amanda bought her word processor from Roger.

There were three different lines on the phone—one for the world, one for her parents and one for special friends (Mrs. Goldblum, Rosanne and Claremont Riding Academy)—so that when the phone rang Amanda had a very good idea as to whether she wished to pick up or not. (She rarely picked up on "the world" line. The engineer she had hired to assess the north tower, Mark [predecessor to Carl], was still calling—after three years!) The phone also had a tie line to the house phone in the lobby, and it was this line that was buzzing.

She almost didn't answer it. It was near midnight and she couldn't imagine it being good news. More likely it was notification that Roger had been hauled out of the lobby by the police. She took a breath and picked up.

"A Mr. Stewart is here to see you. He says if it is too late he will come back another time."

Stewart—Howard? *He must love the pages,* she thought. "No, it's fine, send him right up."

"Yes, miss."

Amanda scrambled out of bed and grabbed the robe at the foot of it. She brushed her hair fast and furiously, ran a quick check in the mirror and sailed off for the front door. When she heard the elevator, she counted twice and then swept open the door with a big "Hello!"

Howard was holding some pages of her manuscript in his hand. His tie was gone, his shirt was open at the top and he was drunk.

"Found it that bad, did you?" Amanda said.

"Don't let me do anything stupid."

Amanda rubbed her eye, smiling.

"Can I come in?" he asked.

Amanda, still smiling, stepped back from the door. "Surely." She watched Howard drift down the hall. "Why don't you go to the kitchen? Do you remember where it is? Turn left." He did not remember and apparently did not know left and so Amanda had to steer him there.

"I'm afraid I'm a little drunk," he said. "But I still know wonderful writing when I see it."

"Good," Amanda murmured, pushing him into his old chair in the kitchen. "May I offer you some coffee?"

Howard smiled like an idiot.

"Or perhaps some tea, with honey and milk?"

"Mmm," Howard said, taking off his glasses and dropping them on the floor. It took a bit of time and effort, but he managed to pick them up. "I've never done this," he announced.

Amanda went about making tea. "Did something happen?"

"Oh, nothing in particular. My wife sent the cops to Rosanne's, Rosanne came over, Melissa fired her, Rosanne called me a wimp—other than that, nothing's happened."

"I'm sorry to hear that," Amanda said.

Howard rambled on for a while, the bits and pieces that he shared adding up to something quite ugly in Amanda's mind. By the time he was finished, Amanda had decided she must see Rosanne the following day. At Mrs. Goldblum's if need be.

Amanda shared the pot of tea with Howard. As upset as she was about Rosanne, she nevertheless found herself hinting about the pages of Catherine she had given Howard.

"It's the only good thing that happened today," he said. "I sat down in the study with her—"

Her, Amanda's mind registered.

"—and if I hadn't brought a bottle of wine with me . . . But I liked what I read. I mean, Amanda, I'm loaded and all, but I'm not that loaded. And then," he sighed, "it just seemed like a good idea to come over. At the time." He frowned. Then he looked at Amanda across the table. "I'm sorry. I don't know what's gotten into me. I've never done anything like this—"

"You've apologized at least forty times," Amanda said. "That's more than sufficient. Besides, if I were upset, I would simply have you thrown out."

Howard seemed surprised by this. "Really?"

"Really," Amanda said.

He smiled.

She smiled.

His eyes dropped down to her robe and then came back up.

Amanda swallowed.

Silence.

"I should go now," he finally said.

She closed her eyes and nodded. And then, opening them, she stood up. He just sat there, staring up at her. Amanda held out her hand and smiled. "No," he said, suddenly shaking his head, "it's all right. I mean—I'm all right." And he got himself on his feet and followed her to the front door.

"You will come Saturday, won't you?" he asked her, pushing the button for the elevator.

"I'll be there," she promised, leaning against the door.

"I, uh—" He hesitated.

"Yes?"

He looked at her nervously, smiled and touched at his glasses. "Thank you for being so understanding about—uh, this."

"It's quite all right."

"I—shoot—" He dropped the pages.

Amanda just stood there, watching him gather the papers together. When he stood up, his attention focused on the jumble in his hands, Amanda let her eyes drop—

No.

She raised her eyes immediately.

The elevator arrived. "Good night," he said, stepping in. He turned around, ran a hand through his hair, and waved. "Good night!"

"Until Saturday," Amanda said, waving back.

Howard undressed in the bathroom. Flicking off the light, he stood in the darkness, waiting for his eyes to adjust. Then he opened the door, crossed the bedroom and slipped into bed. He put his glasses on the night table, settled in on his left side, facing away from Melissa, and pulled the covers up over his shoulder.

"Howard," Melissa said.

Pause. "Yes?"

"I don't want to fight with you," she said.

"I don't want to fight with you either," he said.

Silence.

The rustle of sheets; Melissa's hand on his shoulder. "We need to talk," she whispered.

Howard took a deep breath and let it out slowly. Finally, "I'm tired, Melissa. Let's talk in the morning."

Melissa snuggled up behind him, slid her hand up his chest and let it rest there. Howard felt the side of her face press against his back. In a moment he felt her hand inching its way down, unsure. He waited.

Her hand reached him, there. Her fingers touched him lightly. The response was immediate and growing. When Howard started to turn over, Melissa's hand slipped away. "I'm tired too," she said, rolling over to the other side of the bed.

10

WHAT MRS. GOLDBLUM'S
PRIDE WROUGHT

I t was a dreadful situation, Mrs. Goldblum knew, and yet she couldn't bring herself to make the calls she knew she would have to. Soon. Next week, no doubt.

Sigh.

There were no more stocks in the safe deposit box. There were no bonds left. There were sixteen love letters from Mr. Goldblum, the negatives of Sarah's wedding pictures and Mrs. Goldblum's engagement ring that had become too large for her to wear.

Bernard Meltzer speaks of Empire Diamond on his radio program. He says I can trust them for an accurate appraisal—

It could not come to that. Could it?

Sigh.

Daniel would be of no help. To tell him would only burden him with guilt about the money she had given him. Freely . . . She could hardly take the bread out of her grandchildren's mouths.

Could she call Ben, wonderful Ben? He was remarried, for several years, and had three children now. She could hear Ben saying to her, "I'm only glad you called. How much do you need?" Sarah had married well. Sarah. *Oh, Sarah, my baby, I miss you so much. Still.*

Ben was out of the question. It would break Daniel's heart if she asked Ben for help. They did not see eye to eye, those two. . . .

"Oh, my," Mrs. Goldblum said aloud, covering her face with her hands at the kitchen table. Missy rubbed against her leg. She smiled and leaned over to pet her on the head. "Little Miss," she said. Then the dizziness came back and she had to right herself, slowly, grasping the edge of the table. She would wait a minute and then prepare some milk and honey. That would make the dizziness go away.

Missy meowed. She was hungry too. Mrs. Goldblum couldn't get up yet to feed her and it made her sad that the kitty had to sit there and be hungry. Missy's eyes were looking up at her—"Did I do something wrong?" they asked. Tears started to rise and Mrs. Goldblum folded her arms on the table and slowly let her head sink down onto them.

You must pull yourself together, Emma Goldblum. There have been harder times than these. Deep breath.

Robert darling, please tell me what to do.

Several minutes passed.

Until you have time to think it through, you must cut back your expenses, she heard.

I have, Robert, I have.

All that you can?

Mrs. Goldblum was feeling a bit better when Amanda stopped by, darling girl. She had brought Mrs. Goldblum a basket of yellow and white gladiolus from Embassy Florists, to, she said, apologize for canceling their tea on Tuesday. Without thinking, Mrs. Goldblum asked her to stay for luncheon (there was nothing but the one Stouffer's soufflé for Rosanne), but Amanda declined, explaining that she had received a new sense of inspiration about Catherine and was eager to get to work. (They did not pursue this topic; Catherine pulled Amanda into a world where Mrs. Goldblum did not care to follow. When some of one's relatives have spent their lives running away from Russians, Mrs. Goldblum did not see any reason to pay them a visit— even by way of fiction.)

When Mrs. Goldblum saw Amanda to the door, Amanda said she had thought Rosanne would be there.

"She called this morning to say she would be late."

"Oh," Amanda said, averting her eyes.

Tell, Amanda. Explain the situation to her. She would give her right arm to help you.

"You're using your cane. Is your hip bothering you?"

"What, dear? Oh, this—" *Tell her.* Pause. "Yes, a little. Arthritis, you know." *I can't. Daniel would be so ashamed.*

"Would you ask Rosanne to telephone me? I left a message for her yesterday, but she must not have received it."

Mrs. Goldblum promised that of course she would, and hurried their interview to an end. Mrs. Goldblum felt terribly guilty; she imagined that Amanda could sense it, hence the strange expression on the dear's face. An expression Mrs. Goldblum recognized. Worry. She had seen it on her own face in the mirror every day since the arrival of that hateful letter from that awful Mr. Robin.

Rosanne did not appear until close to two. Mrs. Goldblum retired to the living-room couch, waiting, thinking about how to handle the task in front of her. Rosanne must have suspected something, she thought, because Rosanne this day was strangely quiet.

When Rosanne dragged the vacuum cleaner into the front hall, Mrs. Goldblum decided she must go through with it before she lost her courage. "Rosanne dear—"

"Yeah?"

"I won't require—that is, I mean to say, I won't be needing you to clean for the next few weeks."

Rosanne was silent, her mouth drawn in a tight line, her arms holding the vacuum attachments up against her chest.

Mrs. Goldblum's hand tightened around the tissues in her hand. Slowly, carefully, "It will only be for a short while. Dr. Campbell seems to think I should try to do the household tasks myself. For my arthritis, you see. Exercise of any kind—"

Rosanne let the attachments crash to the floor. "You could at least tell me the truth," she said, eyes flashing with anger.

Mrs. Goldblum looked down at her hands.

"Say somethin' to me, Mrs. G."

Still Mrs. Goldblum couldn't speak.

Rosanne walked over and stood in front of her, hands on her hips. "What did Amanda tell you this morning?"

Mrs. Goldblum, startled, looked up at her. "Amanda has nothing to do with it," she said softly.

"So you just want me outta here, huh?" Rosanne's eyes started to fill and she turned away. "Jesus, Mrs. G!" she cried suddenly, whirling back around. "After all this time, you don't trust me—do ya?"

"I do trust you, dear, it's just that . . ." She brought the tissue up against her nose, unable to look at Rosanne. She shook her head. "It's a family matter," she finally said.

Rosanne took a hard intake of breath and then bolted for the kitchen.

Mrs. Goldblum tried to stand, but dizziness forced her back down onto the couch. When Rosanne flew back through the hall with her things, heading for the front door, Mrs. Goldblum raised her hand, saying, "I will pay you for today, dear. It will only be for a few weeks."

Slowly, Rosanne turned around at the door. She was blinking back tears. "If you can't trust me, I don't want nothin' from you. *Ever.*" She yanked the door open, her bag hitting the wall. "And tell—" Her voice broke.

And then the door slammed and Rosanne was gone. Tears rolled down Mrs. Goldblum's face and she did nothing to wipe them away.

Rosanne strode home to 94th Street, banged her way through the lobby and, when the elevator didn't come, marched up the seven flights without pausing. She pushed open the door to their room and stood there in the doorway.

Frank was sitting at the table, exactly where she had left him, only now the side of his face was resting in the plate of spaghetti she had left him for lunch.

He was in the nod. The heroin nod.

Rosanne threw her bag to the floor and walked over to him. Yanking his head up out of the food by his hair, she said, "Where did you get the money for junk? Where?" She shook his head and his eyes parted slightly. "Answer me, god damn it, *where* did you get the money?" When he didn't answer, she shoved him out of the chair. He fell to the floor and Rosanne kicked him. Instinctively he curled up to defend himself.

"I hate you! Do you hear me? I hate you!"

Interested neighbors stood by the door, watching. Frank started crawling toward them. Rosanne spotted Creature. "Get him out of here before I kill him! Get him *out!*" Creature handed his can of Old English to the woman standing next to him and came in. He touched at the red stains on Frank's face, examined his fingers, smelled them, and then laughed.

Rosanne ran to the closet and started jamming clothes into a pillowcase. Creature got hold under Frank's arms and pulled him up to his feet. "Take my son," Rosanne was ranting, "take my money, take my job away from me —you're nothing but a goddam junkie and I've had it with you." With Frank's head lolling on his shoulder, Creature managed to stumble him out the door.

Rosanne threw the pillowcase out into the hall. "You're not going to wreck my life anymore, you hear me?" She ran back in and then back to the door. She pitched something wrapped in a red bandanna which Creature seemed to recognize, for he lunged to catch it.

"Take your goddam junk and your goddam junkie friends and never come back here—" Frank fell down again, his hands making a splat noise against the linoleum.

For an instant Rosanne's anger wavered. But when Creature hauled him back up and Frank said, "Lez go-da Sissy's," Rosanne said, "If you *ever* come near me or Jason again, I swear to God I'll kill you. I'll kill you, do you hear me?"

And, with that, she cleared the neighbors with one long, unflinching glare.

11

THE DILEMMA OF
SAMUEL J. WYATT CONTINUES

Sam left his office and made the long walk to the other end of the floor where Walter Brennan made his executive outpost. When Brennan was made president of Electronika International six months before, he had moved everyone out of this end of the floor, ripped down the walls, and built two new huge connecting offices—one for himself and one for Chet Canley, the senior executive vice-president. The door to Brennan's office was closed (as it always was) and Sam stood there, waiting for Brennan's secretary to get off the phone.

"Hello, Mr. Wyatt. What can I do for you?"

"Walter is expecting me."

The secretary's eyes dropped to the phone pad in front of her. "He's in conference with Mr. Canley."

"Right," Sam said, "he just called me."

"Let me just check," she said, standing up. She opened the door, stuck her head in, said something, and then waved Sam through.

Brennan and Canley were sitting on Brennan's couch, crouching over dozens of papers strewn across the coffee table. No one would ever accuse either man of being handsome. Brennan was rotund and his face, which perhaps might have appeared jolly at one time, was now decidedly on the Happy Halloween side. Canley was very tall and angular; in fact, his physique was much like the long cigarette he was lighting at this moment.

"Wyatt," Brennan said, glancing up from the papers in front of him.

Sam nodded.

Canley sat back against the couch, puffing his cigarette, watching Sam.

Sam just stood there, waiting for Brennan to look up again. Finally he did. He sighed, pulled off the Ben Franklin glasses he was wearing and tossed them on the table. "About the ZT 5000."

Sam stuck his hands in his pockets. "Yes."

"You are not to discuss the matter with anyone. Do I make myself clear?"

"Yes," Sam said, shifting his weight to one leg.

"Good," Canley said, pounding the arm of the couch once with his fist. "Then no more phone calls to Trinity Electronics."

Sam swallowed. "On the assumption that you're moving the assembly out of Pretoria, yes, you may assume that."

Canley blew four smoke rings.

Brennan, after a moment, threw himself back against the couch and then rolled forward again so as to get ahold of his ankle and pull it up onto his knee. He drummed his fingers on his crossed leg, squinting at Sam. "Or what?" he finally said.

Sam hesitated. He almost said, *Or I'll knock your fat head in,* but said instead, "Or I will be obligated to seek an immediate solution to the problem."

Canley let out a blast of smoke. "And, in your eyes, the problem is . . . ?"

Sam rocked back on his heels slightly. He took his hand out of his pocket and started counting. "One, we're breaking the boycott of South Africa. Two, when word gets out, you can safely assume that every major account will cancel its orders for the ZT 5000. Three, you can also safely assume that institutional investors will dump their stockholdings in Electronika. And four, you can try to go to sleep each night, knowing that you're supporting a government that makes it illegal for three fourths of its citizens to vote."

Silence.

"And if word does not get out?" Canley said. "And if moving assembly from the Pretoria plant means heavy financial losses?"

Sam rubbed his right temple. He opened his mouth to say something, stopped, and then did. "You moved the assembly to Pretoria, didn't you?"

Canley's and Brennan's faces were inscrutable.

Sam closed his eyes, nodding slightly, thinking about the dirt-cheap facilities available that had been abandoned by other companies. With near slave labor, too, no doubt. He reopened his eyes.

Finally, slowly, Brennan took down his ankle (a two-handed effort) and leaned forward again over the coffee table. He glanced at Sam, put his glasses back on, and picked up a sheet of paper. He glanced at Sam again before scanning it. "After the first wave of assembly, the ZT will be moved to Kenya," he said, dropping the paper.

"What constitutes a wave to you?"

Brennan looked over his shoulder at Canley. "The first year," Canley said, stamping out his cigarette in the ashtray.

Sam took out his handkerchief, wiped his forehead, and stuck it back in his pocket. "That's it then," he said.

"That's what?" Brennan asked, looking at him over the top of his glasses.

"My resignation."

Silence.

Brennan shook his head. "Don't be a fool, Wyatt." He stood up. "You've got a job to do. To market the ZT 5000, the biggest damn thing to hit photocopying. This," he said, gesturing to the papers on the table, "has nothing to do with you. It can't be helped. It's a bad situation, but we'll fix it."

Sam shook his head. "No," he said quietly. "You could unfix it. Now. You could move assembly to Kenya now."

Brennan walked around the coffee table and headed for the door. "I suggest you take time to think it through, Wyatt. He turned to face Sam. "You did, after all, inadvertently get us into this mess. And I won't take kindly to you leaving us with it."

Sam gave him a smile—of sorts. "This is, uh, a threat of some kind?"

"It is a word to a wise family man." Pause. "The machines don't come off the line for ten weeks," he said, opening the door. "I strongly advise you to take that time to reconsider your position." He gestured to the open doorway. "Have a good weekend."

There had never been executives like Brennan and Canley at Electronika International before. A year ago, when old Clyde Tyler announced his retirement—after thirty-one years as chairman and president—everyone had assumed that his son would take over. Clyde, Jr., had thought so too and was as surprised as everyone else when his ascendance was interrupted by the announcement that El-San Industries was making a takeover bid for Electronika. Electronika then took up the offer of ICL for a friendly stock swap to protect itself. ICL, as part of the deal, put three members on the Electronika board of directors and the next thing everyone knew, the board had elected to bring over Brennan from an ICL subsidiary, DarkStar Inc. Brennan, as president, brought Canley over with him from DarkStar and Clyde, Jr., lasted about a week before throwing in the towel.

Although Sam disliked and distrusted both Brennan and Canley at their first meeting ("What are they like?" Harriet had asked him. "Let's just say that after we shook hands I checked to see if my ring was still there"), it appeared that Sam would do well under them. Brennan, until a month ago, was forever stopping into Sam's office to talk "policy, spirit and progress," and often talked about the ZT 5000 as Sam's ticket to corporate glory.

But this, what had transpired with this assembly business, made no sense at all. Oh, yes, Sam did not doubt that Canley had moved the assembly to Pretoria to save money—with U.S. companies moving out left and right, there were plants to be had for peanuts—but it was such a stupid, arrogant, immoral move . . .

Did they really think they would get away with it?

Well, they could. If Canley could set up the assembly plant in the first place, no doubt he could also falsify the assembly notice on the manufacturing plate as well.

"Your wife called," Mabel said as he walked back into his office. "She says it's very important. But it's good news," she added.

"Hi, honey," Harriet said, taking his call. "Wait—hold on a minute." Sam heard her say to someone there, "Tell 'Good Morning America' they can have the First Lady if they take Lilah Tuttle too." Pause. "And try and see if you can tag on poor old Mr. Bindley into the deal." Louder, "And if they won't go for it, let me talk to them." Back on the phone, "Sorry, honey."

"Hi," Sam said.

"Sam, guess what? One of our authors, Belinda Sayer, wants to profile us for *Essence*. Our marriage, Sam," she said, laughing. "Black professional couples. And she says if we give a good interview she'll try to get us the cover."

Sam brought his hand up to his forehead. "I—"

"She wants to do the interview next week—wait, hold on, honey." To someone else, "I don't care what Layton says—no press release with a naked woman on it is leaving this building. It is *not* a Sperry book, it's from

G & G. Tell him—no, never mind. I'll talk to him myself." Back on the phone, "Sorry, honey." (Conversations with Harriet at the office were always like this.)

"Harriet, I don't want to do it."

Silence.

"I'm sorry, it's just not a good idea right now."

She was surprised and hurt. He could hear it in her voice. "Why is it not a good idea?"

Sam sighed, falling back into his chair. "I just don't feel comfortable doing it." A bright idea. "What if she asks about the early years? How are we going to do an interview and pretend we weren't separated?"

"That's why she wants us most of all. She knows nothing about your— you know—but she wants us to talk about the pressures of a two-career marriage. How we've made it work the last eleven years."

Sam shook his head. "No, I'm sorry, Harriet. Not right now."

Silence.

"What *is* it with you, Sam?"

"I just don't feel comfortable doing it right now."

A heavy sigh. "What should I tell her, that you're having an affair?"

"Not funny, Harriet."

"You bet's it not," she said. She sighed again. "Look, I'll tell her we're going to pass. And I apologize for what I said. It's just that I thought you'd be pleased." To someone else, "He is? Right now?" To Sam, "I've got to go. Sperry's on his way down to see me." Pause. "Are you still going to get the stuff together for the booth?"

"I'm leaving in a few minutes."

"Okay. Well, I'll see you at home. And don't let Samantha watch TV, all right?"

"Right," Sam said, hanging up the phone.

When Sam got home he changed and went to work in the basement. The China Break. The Wyatts' annual block party booth that year after year was a raging success. He and Harriet had devised it on the theory that all New Yorkers yearned to destroy something to vent their anger—in a socially acceptable way, of course.

Sam broke a plate against the wall in honor of Brennan and Canley.

What the hell was he going to do?

Resign, and Brennan would do a number on him. He had promised as much. Good, bad or indifferent, Brennan was still the president of Electronika International, and a word from him would see that Sam was unemployed for a long, long time. In his field, maybe forever.

Go ahead with the marketing plans on the ZT? That's why they had told him, wasn't it? To develop a plan of action in case word somehow leaked out?

He could look for an immediate solution. But without any of his contacts at Trinity, how could he get the information he needed?

And then there was the immediate, immediate solution. He could leak the information himself. Call the *Times* and point them in the right direction. "Electronika is secretly planning to operate an assembly plant in Pretoria . . ." They'd move assembly then, he knew—as fast as lightning.

Hmmmm.

If he was found out, he would never work again. That part was easy to imagine. No one would touch him—no matter how right he was—if he turned in his own corporation.

And then there was the story itself. If it was leaked—by Sam or anyone else—it would have to point out that Electronika's involvement with Trinity Electronics and the ZT 5000 had been the brainstorm of Samuel J. Wyatt. And Sam was quite sure that Brennan and Canley would make it appear that Sam himself had . . .

Sam went back up to the apartment. He still had time to catch Mabel before she left the office.

"Daddy!" Samantha squealed as he came in the door.

"Hi," he said, scooping her up in his arms and giving her a big hug.

Samantha screamed and laughed until Sam put her down. "Got a 95 in math, wanna see?" she asked, tearing out of the room.

Sam went over to the phone and punched in his office number. While listening to it ring and ring and ring, Althea came sauntering through the living room. "Hi," he said.

"Hi, Dad."

"Thanks for picking up Samantha at school."

"It's okay."

"Where the heck's Mabel?" Sam asked aloud. He hung up and redialed.

"While the cat's away . . ." Althea began, drifting to the kitchen.

Samantha came shooting back in, thrusting her math paper under her father's face. "Seeeeeee?"

"Hey," Sam smiled, "Samantha, this is great." He rubbed the top of her head. "How'd cha get so smart? The only things I thought were in there were giggles."

She let some of the giggles out.

He hung up and redialed the number for the switchboard. "We're all set for the China Break tomorrow."

"Goodeeeeeeeeee!"

"Samantha," Althea called from the kitchen, "come get your pear."

"Hi," Sam said into the phone, "give me Mary Connell's office, please." Pause. "Hi, Cindy? It's Sam Wyatt. Listen, I've been trying my office and no one's answering—"

"Mabel's *there,* Mr. Wyatt," Cindy said, "she hasn't left or anything. They're just working on your phones. The call-forward was supposed to redirect them to the receptionist, but I guess that's why they're fixing them."

"Whatever," Sam said, impatient. "Look, just tell Mabel to call me— please. I'm at home."

Samantha came back and turned on the television. *"Julia's* on, Daddy."

Sam hung up the phone and wandered over to stand behind Samantha. She was sitting cross-legged on the floor, eating her pear. Reruns. *Julia.* Diahann Carroll. (The walls of Samantha's room were adorned with photographs of her from *Dynasty.)* Okay. Samantha could get away with this while Harriet was not home—Diahann Carroll was always okay in Sam's book. "Don't tell your mother I let you watch," he said.

"Noooooo," Samantha said, eyes wide in the delight of secrecy. ("No child of mine is going to grow up a couch potato," Harriet would say. "One hour of TV after dinner and that's *it."* An odd philosophy, Sam had always thought, for a woman who had the TV and radio on all hours of the day and night to hear Gardiner & Grayson authors hawking their books.)

Sam went into the kitchen to make himself a cup of Sanka. Althea was sitting at the table, leafing through *Cosmopolitan.* She looked up briefly. "Dad," she said, considering an ad.

"Hmmm?"

"What would you say if I changed my major to premed?"

Sam put the kettle down and turned around. "Premed?"

"Uh-huh." Bite into a pear of her own.

"I thought your major was going to be history."

"It was."

"What brought this on?"

Munch, munch, munch. "Dr. Rosenberg wondered if I'd consider it."

"Who is Dr. Rosenberg?"

"My anatomy professor."

"You're taking anatomy?"

Althea let the magazine fall. *"Dad."*

"Sorry. I seem to have forgotten that."

"Well, you raised such a stink about my modern dance class . . ."

"It was not your dance class," Sam said, turning the burner on. "As you'll recall, you were planning on taking your first semester—what was it? Modern dance, painting, introduction to sex and how to make a dress?"

She offered him one of her more cynical looks. "English, biology, textile—"

The wall phone rang and Sam snapped it up. "Hello?"

"It's me, Mabel."

"Good. Listen, Mabel, I want you to take the Trinity Electronics files—"

"Oh, don't worry," she said cheerfully, "Mr. Canley already has them."

Sam's stomach flipflopped. "What do you mean," he said slowly, "Mr. Canley already has them?" He turned his back on Althea's inquisitive eyes.

"He came over with some guy after you left. He said you knew all about it, that you discussed it at your meeting."

Man, oh, man.

As soon as he hung up, Althea said, "Somebody stealing your files?"

"Borrowed them," Sam said. He finished making his Sanka and pulled out a chair to sit down at the table. He was well aware that Althea's eyes were still on him.

She closed her magazine. "Who is Mr. Canley?"

"The senior executive vice-president."

Silence.

"Mom's going be pretty upset if we have to move to Peoria."

Sam looked at her.

"Mr. Canley's the guy who sent Mr. Wellman there, isn't he? To Peoria?"

Sam reached over and pulled on her nose. "We're not moving to Peoria, Miss Busybody," he said, trying hard to smile.

At close to one in the morning, Sam was sitting alone in the living room, in the dark, looking out across Riverside Park. By Wyatt standards, it was very late indeed; by New York standards, it was still considered a Friday night to be reckoned with. Cars were streaming south on the West Side Highway, heading for the heart of the city.

Sam pulled his robe a little closer around him and continued to think about the need for his office telephones to be fixed.

12

NEWS AT THE COCHRANS'

I
t had been some Friday. To start it off, for the first time in over three years, Rosanne did not show. After Cassy tried her a number of times, left messages with increasing urgency, she finally gave up, rolled up her sleeves and started cleaning the apartment herself.

By eleven she was on the phone, checking with the forty-seven odd neighbors who were running booths or working at the block party the next day. Did they have everything they needed? Did they know what to do? Would they make sure that Cassy would never, ever again be asked to organize this horrendous escapade?

Every time she placed a call, it seemed, someone from WST called on the other line. Was Cassy aware that the AFD films had not arrived yet for the weekend film festival? Did Cassy know the air vents were all being replaced next month? (Next *month?* This had to be discussed at noon on her day off?) What was Cassy going to do about Chester's new contract? Had Cassy come to a decision regarding the removal of pay phones from the lobby of the building? Her boss, Steven Lubin, called too, simply to say what he always said when Cassy was out of the office. "If you're going to be indispensable, you can't leave us to fend for ourselves in this asylum."

Phone under her chin, Cassy took an inventory of the kitchen. After the block party, the neighbors who helped were all supposed to come back to the Cochrans' for a buffet. With Rosanne currently and mysteriously missing in action, Cassy assumed the worst for tomorrow and called the caterer in Rosanne's stead. And of the six casseroles in the freezer? Well, Michael and Henry could predict the next month's menu.

Alexandra Waring called in. Since Harriet Wyatt reported that Newton Thatimov was on tour to promote his 345th book and could not get back from San Francisco in time for the block party this year, Alexandra had become their sole starring attraction.

"Michael suggested one dollar for an autograph, two dollars for a handshake and five dollars to—" Alexandra had laughed, a wonderfully long affair that reminded Cassy of Garbo in *Ninotchka.* "He seems to think people would want to pay five dollars to kiss me on the cheek."

"Oh, Lord," Cassy had said, "I wouldn't make you do that."

"Good," she had said. "But do you want me to? Five dollars is a good deal of money."

"Alexandra, I would not ask anyone to be kissed by strangers. In Kansas maybe, but in New York? Good Lord. No, what I think we should do is stick to autographs for two dollars. Okay?"

"Fine with me." Pause. "What do you want me to wear?"

"Oh, anything you're comfortable in. No—you know what? I adored the blue dress you wore on your debut—"

"The navy one?"

"Yes, I thought it was stunning."

"So you're going to make me stand in heels all day."

"You can wear whatever—"

"I was kidding, Cassy, really. I don't mind." Pause. "Okay, I'll wear the navy number. By special request. Say, if it's as stunning as you say it is, maybe I can fetch two-fifty."

Alexandra handed the phone to Michael, who promised to be home by four to help out with the tables in the basement. Next came the police department, checking and rechecking the hours of the fair, the exact area that was to be barricaded off from traffic and the number of off-duty cops the association would pay for. Sergeant Baker made no secret of his fond admiration for Cassy, and it was with great effort that she succeeded in convincing him she needed no further assistance from him tonight after he got off duty.

Henry zoomed in from school at three and out again, down to the basement to sort the books for Howard Stewart's bookstall. Cassy went out herself, coordinating and rechecking arrangements with the building supers who were storing materials for various booths. When Michael failed to appear, and the evening grew later, Cassy took Henry and moved and labeled the tables for the booths herself. By nine they were finished. By quarter past ten Cassy was bathed and in bed. Five-thirty would come awfully early the next morning.

She dreamed that Henry married a German girl who looked suspiciously like Greta Garbo. ("Henry," Cassy said in her dream, straining her eyes, "I'm positive this girl is Garbo." "Her name is Hilda, Mom." "But I *know* it's Garbo in disguise and I think she's too old for you. She's only pretending to be sixteen.")

"Mom," Henry's voice was saying.

Cassy struggled to wake.

"Mom, come quick—it's Dad."

Cassy sat up like a shot. "Henry?"

"You'd better come."

There was a crash from somewhere in the apartment. Cassy turned on the bedside lamp and reached for her robe on the chair. Henry was already gone.

There was another sound—a kind of thunk—followed by the crack of glass, and then a harsh scraping sound. She heard Michael laugh. It was coming from the study.

Henry was standing outside the door to the study. He looked back at Cassy with a silent warning.

Crack. Scrape. Crash.

Cassy pulled Henry behind her and peered into the study. Michael was stabbing the photographs on the wall with a kitchen knife.

Cassy yanked Henry a few steps down the hall. "I want you to go to your room and lock the door."

"No. I'll stay with you."

Cassy put her hands on his shoulders and looked him straight in the eye and said, "I'll be fine. Go. *Now,*" and gave him a little shove. "Go on."

Crack. Slam.

Once Cassy heard the lock on Henry's door click, she went back to the doorway of the study.

Roughly half the pictures were still hanging. Glass and tattered photos and broken frames were everywhere. The point of the knife had broken off, but Michael was beyond caring. Holding the knife in both hands up over his head, he took aim and then swung down on another picture.

Crack.

It was a direct hit, splintering the glass and slashing through the back of the frame. It was of Michael accepting a Dupont Journalism Award in 1973. The picture was stuck on the knife and Michael laughed, flinging it off.

Crash.

"Mike," Cassy said softly.

He turned with a ghastly smile. For a second Cassy considered running, but then he lowered the knife.

"Sweetheart," she said, voice hushed, "what's happened?"

He swung away from her and faced the wall of pictures again. "I've decided to redecorate, that's all," he said, scraping the knife in an arc over the wall, sending three more photographs to the floor. "I'm sick of these pictures. Sick of the people in them." He stepped down hard on a picture and ground his heel into the glass. "It's all in the past, Cassy girl. They don't count for nothing."

Dazed, he looked at the mess around him. Sighing, he dropped the knife to the floor. Then, weaving slightly, he covered his face with his hands. "Oh, Cass," he said, "my contract."

Cassy hesitated, and then took a step toward him.

"Cassy," he wailed, looking up from his hands. Tears were spilling down from his eyes. "They fired me. *Fired* me."

In a moment Cassy was there, holding Michael, feeling the pain of his heart.

13

THE BLOCK PARTY

It was a gorgeous day, the sun shining and the sky teal blue. The apartment buildings were festooned with red, white and blue streamers, balloons and hand-lettered signs. Across the way, in Riverside Park, the trees were radiant with new leaves catching the morning light, and the birds, as they would all summer, were sitting in them, singing their hearts out.

The block party was, in actuality, three blocks long. The northbound right-hand lane of the Drive had been cleared of parked cars and was barricaded off by the police. The cross streets, too, 89th through 91st, had been cleared and were closed to traffic. Cars on the Drive slowed to look at the activity occurring along the front of the buildings, and some even pulled over and got out to see what was what. "We don't open until nine!" the harried volunteers yelled, frantic to meet the deadline, but fretting nonetheless about whether they should or should not make an exception to make a sale.

It was for a good cause, the annual block party, though no one seemed to remember exactly how it was they had come to pledge themselves to raising money for the Children's Clinic—a marvelous institution way up in Riverdale that, in truth, no one still living had ever visited. But every year Sister Mary came down, her habit gently aloft in the river breezes, and expressed such gratitude, such humility to the volunteers, that no one ever considered not carrying on for at least another year.

This year Cassy put Sister Mary and her heavenly influence to work. The block party headquarters was located in the lobby of the Cochrans' building on the corner of 88th, and so was the treasury. Every two hours the off-duty police officers were to collect excess money from the booths and bring it back to headquarters. Now last year, despite the presence of the police, two different desperados had made a play at trying to steal the treasury. So this year Cassy decided to try throwing the fear of God at them, and stationed Sister Mary outside headquarters, under the awning of 162, reclining in a La-Z-Boy from the Cochran living room.

The layout of booths and stalls and rides was the best in years. The booths and stalls stretched along the buildings of the Drive; the rides and activity booths were sprawled across the cross streets: 89th had the big wooden Train Ride (powered by ten stalwart daddies who would spend the day pulling trainloads of alternately delighted and terrified little people), and a huge, inflated tent of air pillows called the Space Walk; 90th had the Puppet Theater, the House of Mirrors, Needle in the Haystack, and the China Break (manned by the Wyatts); and 91st had Pop a Balloon, Shoot-Out at the OK Corral (water pistols and candles), and Lawn Bowling (on Astro-Turf).

Highlights along the Drive were MEET ALEXANDRA WARING OF WWKK-TV between 88th and 89th; Melissa Stewart's creation, THE JUNIOR LEAGUE'S "DANCE OF THE SPRING VEGETABLES" on the corner of 90th; and Howard Stewart's MORE BOOKS FOR THE BUCK, stretching for nearly a half block at 91st.

Thanks to Henry Cochran and his friend Skipper, the book tables were set up and ready to go at eight-thirty. For nearly two hours they had carefully organized and lined up (spines up) over seven hundred books on ten long tables. When they ran out of room, at Henry's suggestion, they organized paperbacks, spines up, in cartons to put under the tables, or on them as room was made by sales.

He was a nice kid, this Henry, and Howard was pleased when he asked if he could help Howard all day—that is, if he didn't mind. *Mind?* Of course not. "In fact," Howard had whispered to the two boys, "if you'll help me, I can get rid of the two flakes my wife recruited." And so Howard and Henry and Skipper became the official proprietors of the bookstall and the flakes—when they finally showed up—were redirected to the "DANCE OF THE SPRING VEGETABLES" to help Melissa.

As for Skipper, well, let's just say that what Skipper offered as a potential salesperson (which Henry claimed was a great deal), he lacked in social graces. At one point Skipper took a swing at one of the clowns in the booth next to them. "Tell him to stop banging his goddam cymbals in my ear!" Skipper complained. Howard intervened and the clown was moved to the other side of the CLOWNS COURTESY OF BRANTOWSKI CEMENT—"WE STICK TOGETHER" booth, and Skipper was assigned to work the other end of the book tables.

At twenty to nine Cassy swung by. "You're the only ones set," she said, throwing an arm around her son.

In a pale yellow sweater, gold hoop earrings, blue jeans and yellow Topsiders, Howard Stewart thought Cassy Cochran a knockout. They officially shook hands—yes, they agreed, they had seen each other around the neighborhood for years; Howard told her Rosanne had had him watch one of her editorials; Cassy said she knew Melissa (end of comment); Howard told her she had a great son and she agreed with him.

Looking into this woman's eyes, Howard was struck by how tired she appeared, and yet how beautiful she was—much more than she had been on television that day. It was funny—Melissa had no lines to speak of in her face, and indeed, Cassy Cochran did, particularly at the corners of her eyes, but they seemed only to make her eyes bluer and more intense. And more . . . No—you know what it was? Cassy Cochran looked like she lived a life —laughed and cried and loved—whereas Melissa looked like she—well, posed for life.

Henry said he was sixteen, so if Cassy had been, say, twenty-two, that would make her thirty-eight. Well . . . No, Howard thought maybe forty . . .

Howard commanded himself to stop thinking along these lines, mainly because he knew in what direction he was trying to rationalize: speculating and exploring the possibilities of what Cassy Cochran—the woman standing here in front of him, with a teenage son at her side no less—might be like in bed.

As Howard and Cassy and Henry stood there, smiling at one another and chatting, an irate woman dressed like a tomato descended upon them. Betty the Tomato, as her name turned out to be, had been sent as an emissary to file official protest about the Junior League being repeatedly zapped by a little monster wielding a Laser Tag gun. As the woman argued with Cassy over whether or not the six vegetables could handle this extreme danger themselves, Henry and Howard moved around to the inside of the tables where Skipper was lying against the wall of the building, holding his sides, hysterical over the antics of Miss Tomato. Henry started laughing next. And then when Miss Tomato, in her excitement, started rear-ending books off the table, left and right, Howard too had to turn away and laugh.

And then a familiar voice cut through the air.

"Howard! Howard!"

The voice was so shrill, even the boys stopped laughing for a minute to follow the sound of it. Melissa, in the form of a celery stalk, was approaching. Bound and wrapped in yards of green crepe paper, her progress was not achieved without difficulty. Particularly since she had to keep a mindful eye on the horrendous green spiky things that were shooting out of the top of her head.

With a hoot, Skipper clapped his hand over his mouth and keeled back against the wall.

Howard's and Cassy's eyes met. They both clamped down hard on their teeth to keep from laughing.

Henry, at this point, was under the table in tears. "Hey," Howard whispered, nudging him with his foot and choking back a laugh, "cool it, it's my wife."

"Melissa—thank God!" Betty the Tomato said.

"I have solved our problem," Melissa declared. "There!" She hurled a handful of plastic on the table in front of Howard. "I disarmed that Benson brat myself."

"Good!" Betty the Tomato said.

Skipper slid to the ground.

"We didn't have this kind of problem last year," Melissa huffed to Cassy. "Come on, Betty, we're about to start." Miss Celery took Miss Tomato's hand and led her away. "Oh, Howard," Melissa said, turning, her spiky green things bending in the breeze, "those vile Bensons will probably want to talk to you."

When it was safe, Howard and Cassy burst out laughing.

"I'm sorry, Howard," Cassy said, wiping at one eye.

"It's okay," he assured her. He kicked Henry with his foot. "Hey, you still alive down there?"

Cassy checked her watch. "Okay, gang, you're officially open in two minutes. Good luck. I'll stop by later."

"Okay, Mom," Henry said, standing up, wiping his eyes.

"Howard," Cassy said, motioning him away from the boys. She placed a hand gently on his arm. "Thanks for letting the boys work with you today. Henry wanted to work with the books, but since he—we—didn't know you, he felt shy about asking."

"I'm only glad to have him. Really."

"Good luck, boys!"

"Thanks, Mom."

"Bye, Mrs. C."

The liberty bell at the Colonial America booth rang and the block party officially began. People descended on the book tables with all the decorum of looters. Skipper raced up and down warning, and then threatening, the customers about how they were treating the books. "What I need," he yelled to Howard, "is a fly swatter for these guys!"

Someone tapped Howard's shoulder. He turned around. He felt his face flush and he said, "Amanda."

It was Amanda all right. No, she didn't look anything like Cassy Cochran. There was no great beauty, no great blaze of light from her eyes; she was just, just—well, lovely Amanda in the sunlight, looking even better to Howard than he remembered. Or making him feel even better than he remembered.

"As promised, I have come to render my services for this worthy cause," she said, holding her arms out to the side.

Howard looked down (he guessed that was what he was supposed to do) and saw that she was in the cheerful garb of a pale blue-green sweat suit and sneakers. He brought his eyes up, touched his glasses and noticed that she was looking more than a trifle nervous.

"We would love to take advantage of your kind offer," Howard said, taking her arm. He quickly introduced her to the boys, ran her through the book categories, price listings and cash box, and told her she was on her own, good luck. Smile.

Smile.

Wink.

Smile.

Thunk.

The crowd at the tables swelled to four people deep and the crew had their hands full. People were trying to drag cartons off to dig into them away from the crowd. Henry was good with them ("Sorry, these have to stay here"); Amanda was too nice to them ("Thank you for trying to assist us, however the cartons are not in need of transportation"); Skipper was downright vicious ("If you don't keep your paws off, I swear to God I'll cut 'em off") and Howard found himself yelling, "Please, please, this is a book sale, not a wrestling match!" The chaos had the four careening into each other in the struggle to keep up—"Sorry!" "Whoops!" "Excuse me!" "Whoa!"—and all but Skipper spent most of the time laughing.

"Do we have bags?" Amanda asked Howard, both bent over the cash box to make change.

Her face was inches away from his and he could feel her breath on his chin. He looked into her eyes and the change was forgotten. "No—wait, yes. I'll get them. But they're for purchases of ten dollars or more." Still, he didn't move. Nor did she. Skipper then helped them out by pushing Howard out of the way.

"Gotta keep in step if you wanna make the big bucks," Skipper told Howard.

It was nuts. Just crazy. An absolute madhouse. And Howard felt insanely happy.

Alexandra Waring made the Block Association over two hundred and seventy dollars by eleven-thirty. At first it was simply through her autographing publicity stills, but then, at Michael's suggestion, Old Mr. Gresham (as he was known in the neighborhood) had offered her twenty-five dollars to let him kiss her on the cheek. Alexandra took the twenty-five dollars, let him kiss her, and then she gave the eighty-some-odd-year-old man a kiss back *and* a hug. But since Old Mr. Gresham's eyes never left her chest during the latter, a rumor started that Alexandra Waring was letting men look down her dress and the line for her booth expanded accordingly. (Lest anyone think unkindly of Ms. Waring, a WWKK publicist ran about to make it known that she was only signing autographs and shaking hands.)

Michael had appeared shortly after ten, looking ashen and unwell. He had found Cassy at Alexandra's booth, whispered that he loved her, and then kissed her ear. His breath had told Cassy that the coffee mug he held was laced with brandy, but she was so relieved to see him up and about that she did not care. She had hugged him.

Alexandra had risen from chair, stepped out of her booth, and simply held his hand for a moment. "When you get resituated, Michael, I only hope I'm good enough to follow you there."

For that one moment—suspended in the noise of the crowd and of the pesky clown beating a drum behind them—Cassy could think of nothing nicer than for Alexandra Waring to move into the Cochran household.

Michael had moved a chair next to Alexandra in her booth and, with his thermos and mug, remained at her side throughout the morning. Cassy had watched them and noticed the remarkable kindness and sensitivity the young woman possessed. Alexandra did nothing flirtatious, nothing that could be misconstrued; she merely made Michael the center of her attention, of her calm reassurance, and of her gentle humor that made him smile and chuckle despite his misery.

And Michael was miserable. Cassy knew the slouch of his shoulders was new; she knew his expression—as if he were half ready to be struck at any given moment—had been acquired in the night. Self-righteous rage, arrogant accusations—Cassy had been prepared for anything but this. A broken-spirited, quietly despairing middle-aged man. A man she didn't recognize, but whom Alexandra apparently did.

Cassy thanked the heavens for Alexandra's being there.

She made the rounds again near noon to see how everyone was doing. At the Junior League booth, Melissa Stewart was seething with rage. Someone, while the vegetables were doing their spring dance, had stolen their deviled eggs. When Cassy became confused ("I'm sorry, do you mean a dancer was taken? Or real food?"), Melissa had screamed at Cassy that she was the most inept, utterly moronic chairman they had ever had. At that, Cassy turned the case of the missing deviled eggs over to a policewoman and departed.

Everyone else seemed to be doing brilliantly and having a great deal of fun. ("No heart attacks yet!" the Train Ride people cheerfully reported.) The Wyatts were positively making a fortune with their China Break. As Cassy approached, an elderly woman, being helped by Sam, was in the process of throwing a softball (with her eyes closed). She clipped a cup right off the hook and the crowd went wild with cheers and applause.

"Everything's fine," Harriet told Cassy. "We did have one scare, though. A woman dove into the line of fire and nearly got brained. Apparently one of our plates on the rack was some kind of Wedgwood china. She gave us twenty dollars for it."

Althea Wyatt came charging up and handed Cassy twenty-eight dollars. "My friend Alice brought some buttons to sell. This is from her." Cassy slipped the money in her back pocket while Althea took the liberty of pinning a button on Cassy's sweater. JANE WYMAN KNEW, it said.

The children, in particular, seemed to be having a wonderful time pulling their parents in one direction and then another, squealing, "Mommy! Daddy! *Look!*" And the parents didn't seem to be having a bad time of it either. And since this year no wine or beer was being sold, the bands of teenagers they had had trouble with the year before were nowhere to be found.

It was also a great day for politicians, Cassy thought, because there were two great ones to be seen: Council Member Ruth Messinger and Congressman Ted Weiss. The neighbors' opinions apparently coincided with Cassy's, since both—stuck on two separate blocks—were surrounded by wide-smiling constituents eager to express their admiration. (In light of current New York City political weather—heavy subpoenafall—the neighborhood was even more proud of these sterling public servants than usual.)

But the noise—wow. Cassy could feel it in her chest at times: the steady hub-hub-hub of the crowd; isolated peels of laughter and squeals of glee; a shriek; a gasp; applause; the boom-boom-boom and clang-clang-clang of those frisky clowns who were perpetually wandering about.

The block party was a success, Cassy knew. Really, truly, a wonderful success, and it made her feel oddly close to crying when she thought of Sister Mary under the awning in the Cochrans' La-Z-Boy. Cassy *would* go to the Children's Clinic. Soon. She wanted in the worst way to see how this festival would translate into help for those children.

At the book tables, Cassy smiled at how happy Henry appeared to be. Howard was talking to him, apparently about the book he was holding, and Henry's eyes were bright with interest. Howard tucked the book under Henry's arm and gave him a pat on the shoulder.

"Hi," Cassy said.

"Mom—look. Howard found a first edition of *Islands in the Stream* and he gave it to me." He flicked the pages back to the copyright page. "See?"

"Maybe Howard will inscribe it for you," she said, putting her arm around him and looking up at Howard. "He's an editor, you know."

The way Henry's head swung in Howard's direction indicated that this was an idea that appealed to him.

"Later," Howard promised.

"I gotta get back to work, Mom," Henry said.

Cassy and Howard watched Henry a minute, and then Skipper stole their attention by berating a young woman for being such a hog about all the Agatha Christies.

I never did talk to his mother, Cassy thought.

A policeman arrived to collect the cash and Howard brought him back around the tables for the transaction. A woman Cassy didn't recognize came up to Howard at the cash box. She looked at Cassy and offered a tentative smile. She said something to Howard; he said something back and then the woman smiled broadly at Cassy and came over to her.

"Hello," she said, extending a hand, "I'm Amanda Miller, more commonly known as Tuesdays."

"Oh, hi," Cassy said, smiling, "I'm Cassy Cochran, Fridays."

"Yes, I know."

The two women watched the men work the tables. "You're a good sport to help us out," Cassy said.

"Oh, I don't mind. I would have done it before had anyone asked me to."

Cassy nodded. And then, "Henry's my son."

"I know. Rosanne speaks of him a great deal, you know." Pause. "I find him completely charming."

"Thank you." Cassy hesitated and then said, "Amanda, did you see Rosanne this week?"

A wave of seriousness passed over Amanda's face. "Why do you ask?"

"She didn't show yesterday and I can't seem to get ahold of her."

Amanda sighed and looked momentarily down at her sneakers. "I'm very sorry to hear that." She led Cassy away a few steps from the booth, saying, "Perhaps I'd better fill you in on what happened this week."

Amanda told Cassy the story about the robbery at the Stewarts' and the aftermath. Cassy's expression grew more concerned and her temper began to get the best of her. "That shrew," she said of Melissa Stewart. "I've got half a mind to go down there and beat the living daylights out of that woman. How could she do that?" Amanda pressed on with her story, and the two women began comparing notes about what they should do. Both promised that if either one of them got ahold of Rosanne, she would call the other.

Walking back to the tables, Cassy asked Amanda if Howard Stewart was as nice as he seemed.

"He is," she answered, looking at him.

"Rosanne always said so," Cassy said. "Howard and the Bitch, she always calls them."

Amanda seemed startled by this. "Does she?"

At that second Cassy leaped to a wild conclusion. She tried to remember what Rosanne had ever told her about Amanda, but none of it, Cassy suspected, would be as telling as Amanda's expression at this moment. Cassy smiled to herself. Perhaps Melissa's punishment was already under way.

Cassy made her way back down the Drive, carefully circling the hungry crowd buying food at the Junior League booth, and arrived at Alexandra's booth to find a sign saying she would be back at two o'clock. She came upon Michael and Alexandra inside headquarters, sitting on the lobby stairs, Michael drinking a Heineken and Alexandra eating a—

"Where did you get that deviled egg?"

Alexandra struggled to swallow, covering her mouth with a napkin. "A little boy just came in here and sold it to me. Why?"

Cassy roared and Michael and Alexandra looked at each other.

"I love it!" Cassy declared, plunking herself down next to Alexandra. "Street urchins selling Melissa Stewart's stupid eggs. She's been screaming all day about them being stolen. How much did he charge you?"

"Two dollars."

They all laughed until Michael added, "I better ask that kid for a job."

From the sound of his voice, Cassy knew he had been seriously drinking. *Well,* she thought, *if he stays with Alexandra, he'll be all right. Wait a minute. Why am I dragging poor Alexandra into it? Whose husband is he?*

Cassy got up, moved in front of her husband, bent over and, holding his face in her hands, kissed him briefly on the mouth. Then she knelt down in front of him and wrapped her arms around his knees.

Alexandra was politely examining her napkin.

Cassy kissed one of his knees, looked up and said, smiling, "You're going to be able to do the work you've always wanted to do, Michael. No more office stuff, lucky guy." A sigh.

Alexandra was now looking at Cassy.

"People have been after Michael for years to go independent," she explained.

"Cass," Michael said. His voice was low and tired. "I want you to steal Alexandra away from KK. I know how to break her contract."

Cassy raised her eyebrows. He closed his eyes, nodded, and opened them. "I can't stand the idea of those bastards having her."

Cassy turned her head to look at Alexandra. Her face was impossible to read. Cassy rested the side of her face on Michael's knee. "I'm not sure Alexandra would be happy at WST," she said, watching her.

"She'll push your ratings through the roof—"

"No, Michael, that's not what I mean," she said softly. She raised her head to speak to him but kept her eyes on Alexandra. "I think it would be a waste to keep her in local news for much longer. She needs to get out in the field, national news. And then, later, documentary, investigative or straight. My instincts tell me she'd be fabulous at either one."

Michael turned to look at Alexandra too.

"Of course," Cassy added, "my instincts could be wrong, though I would hardly say so if I thought they were."

They waited for Alexandra to say something, but Alexandra appeared to be a bit tongue-tied.

"Mike," Cassy said, turning to him, "why don't you do it? Jack O'Hearn would underwrite you in a second."

Michael considered this and shifted his legs a bit. Alexandra was staring off into space.

"Alexandra," Cassy said.

"Yes?"

Those eyes . . . So young and bright and alive.

Alexandra Waring, you must do this. You must go on to better things before they suck the life out of you and make you tired and afraid.

"What do you think?" Cassy asked her.

She smiled, shyly. "I think you may be overly generous regarding my capabilities."

Michael slapped Cassy on the shoulder and laughed. "That's exactly what she said to me out in Kansas when I offered her a job."

Cassy and Alexandra were still looking at each other. "Really?" Cassy asked her. "Is that really what you think?"

The slow smile that emerged from Alexandra felt like sunshine to Cassy, so pure was its warmth. "No," she said.

Cassy did a drum roll on Michael's knee, got up and leaned over to kiss him on the mouth again. "I think you two have a great deal to talk about," she announced. "But don't talk too much—save some of your discussion for tonight, so I can hear." She nudged Michael's leg with her knee. "So-right?"

"So-right," Michael said.

The crowds outside were as thick as ever. Cassy sat and talked with Sister Mary for a little bit, about how well the booths were doing, about how much Cassy was looking forward to visiting the Children's Clinic. At that announcement, Sister Mary reached forward and took Cassy's hand in her own. "Will you really come, my child?"

"Yes, I want very much to."

Sister Mary smiled. "It will mean a great deal to us all. Bless you for being so kind."

Cassy spent the next two hours pretending to check up on things but in reality sifting through a series of troubling thoughts brought on by her talk with Sister Mary. What Sister Mary had said, about it meaning so much for her to come and visit, had struck a chord in Cassy, one that was painful.

Yes, Cassy would make the visit. And no doubt she would bring along a reporter and mini-cam to do a story on the clinic and drum up some contributions from the public. The pain came from wondering why she had stopped doing things like this. She *always* had, up until—well, when *was* the last time? The home for runaways? She must have been thirty-six. Over five years ago.

When had she become so wrapped up that people no longer even bothered to seek her help? Here Rosanne was going through this ordeal and, after all this time, she would rather disappear than ask Cassy for help. And Skipper —why hadn't she followed through on talking to Deidre Marshall?

I can't even help Michael.

And, oh, Lord, what was she really doing to poor Alexandra? Should Alexandra really gamble her career on Michael? *No.* Would Alexandra give Michael one last ace to play in his career? *Yes.* If Michael went down, did Cassy want Alexandra to go down with him instead of herself? *Yes.*

But she had the strength, the energy to pull it off. Cassy felt sure about that. Alexandra was like her, like Cassy, in the old days.

"*Catherine Littlefield Cochran,*" her mother had screamed at her on her last visit three years ago, "*someday you are going to wake up and realize the price you've paid for being such a fool.*"

"*Such a fool about what, Mother?*"

"*Throwing your love away on a bottle.*"

"*Oh, Mother.*"

"*I know. Believe me, I know! The same thing that happened to me is happening to you and I won't just stand by and watch it happen!*"

Maybe she should hire Alexandra at WST. Maybe she should put Alexandra into the hands of a good agent. Maybe Alexandra *had* an agent. Maybe . . .

Could Alexandra really be so trusting as to place her future in our hands?

Oh, Lord, Cassy thought, watching children trying to extinguish candles with squirt guns, *if you're really there, please let us get through this without hurting anyone else.*

Henry was leaving for Colorado in a week, and much as Cassy had been dreading it, now she was relieved he would be so far away. It would be a long summer. Even if Michael did find another job, or decided to go out on his own, Cassy felt sure it wouldn't happen before fall, when people were back in town. And heaven only knew how Michael would see fit to spend his time until then.

What stories would be circulating about Michael? she wondered. *"They couldn't agree on the renewal terms of his contract,"* she practiced in her head. *Who are you kidding? They wouldn't renew his contract, period. Everybody will know that, and everybody will know why.*

After having a bite of lasagna at the ITALY, ITALY booth, Cassy started making her way back down to headquarters. In the sunshine of the afternoon it seemed as though every child on the West Side had been brought outside. Strollers zigged and zagged through the crowds, carrying bright little eyes roving in wonderment; snugglers on mothers' and fathers' chests cruised through, with newborns snoozing in warm oblivion; and backpacks trotted in and out, the heads of their precious cargo jigging and jogging from side to side.

My baby is six feet tall and is going to learn how to survive in the wilderness with a knife and a piece of string.

At three-thirty the line at Alexandra's booth was even longer than it had been in the morning. She was in fine spirits (the New York *Post* had just finished taking pictures of her with Sister Mary) and claimed that her hand was holding out just fine against writer's cramp.

Michael, on the other hand, was a mess. He could barely keep his head up. Cassy tried to get him out of his chair, take him up the apartment, but he made such a scene that Alexandra urged her to leave him where he was. So Cassy stood there, posted like a guard at his side, her stomach aching with the fear that he would do something outrageous.

He did. It started with a man who paid his two-fifty for Alexandra's autograph. She signed her picture, handed it to him, and was about to shake his hand when Michael grabbed her arm. "Jesus, Alexandra, I'd get this one checked for AIDS before I'd let 'im near me."

Alexandra jerked her arm away, clearly annoyed, and frowned at Cassy.

"Michael, come *on,"* Cassy said, pulling him out of his chair. Literally. He fell right out of it. One of the off-duty cops came to Cassy's aid in picking him up. Michael pushed the cop and the crowd started backing away from the booth.

"Keep your filthy hands off me!" Michael said.

"Mike," Cassy pleaded, "come on, we have to get out of here." He allowed Cassy to lead him away a few steps, but then he spotted little Samantha Wyatt standing there in wide-eyed fascination. "What are you looking at?" he demanded.

"I'm sorry," Cassy said to the cop, "he doesn't know what he's doing. Could you help me with him?"

Michael jerked away from her and pointed at Samantha. "What's that nigger child looking at?"

There was a blur and a scream and Cassy was thrown to the pavement. She was stunned for a moment, not sure of where she was. "Cassy," she heard Alexandra's voice say from somewhere. She felt hands helping her to turn over and sit up.

Sam Wyatt was sitting on top of her husband, alternately slapping his face with the palm and back of his hand. Slap, slap, slap, slap, slap—Cassy sat there, mesmerized.

"For God's sake!" Alexandra yelled close to her ear.

The cop grabbed Sam from behind and another cop broke through the crowd to help pull Sam off. Michael just lay there on his back, blinking up at the sky, blood flowing from his nose and oozing out of the right side of his mouth.

Alexandra, on her knees, had her arm around Cassy. "Are you all right?"

Cassy hid her face in Alexandra's shoulder and whispered, "I don't think I can deal with this."

Alexandra got Cassy into a chair and someone handed her some tissues to wipe the blood from her palms. The cops led Sam away somewhere and two men from the crowd helped Michael to his feet. He staggered over to Alexandra's chair and Cassy held his head back, pressing the tissues against his nose until he could hold them himself. Uniformed cops arrived and Alexandra talked to them.

"Come on," Alexandra said gently to the Cochrans, "Officer Blake is going to run us up to the emergency room. You should get an X ray." Cassy stood up, and Michael, silent, eyes vacant, let Cassy lead him by the hand.

Walking through the police barricade to the Drive, with Michael between her and Alexandra, Cassy saw Melissa Stewart in the crowd. Cassy made them stop for a moment. "Henry, our son, is working with your husband," she said, voice hoarse. "Would you tell him the plans have changed and that he is to go to Skipper's?" Melissa just stared at her. A tear trailed down Cassy's cheek and she wiped it away. "Would you tell the others that we're sorry, but we have to cancel the buffet? Would you do that for me, Melissa?"

Melissa's eyes darted to Michael. "Yes," she said.

And Melissa did. With her spiky green things flailing wildly with purpose, she stopped at every other booth and said, "The party's off tonight. Cochran's drunk and Cassy had to take him to the hospital. Pass it on."

Melissa was also fed some details regarding the fight itself (which she had missed), so by the time she reached the book tables she was more than curious to see which boy it was whose drunken father had so savagely attacked Sam Wyatt's baby girl.

Howard was standing in a little tête-à-tête with two women Melissa had never seen before. One was an old lady, on the outside of a table, of no interest to her; the other, standing inside the table by the cash box, was of interest to her, seeing as how her husband was talking to her.

"Howard," she said.

"Melissa—hi." He seemed startled. He was startled. But he took a step back, pulled the celery stalk closer, and said, "I'd like you to meet my wife Melissa. Melissa, this is Mrs. Goldblum, who lives in—"

"One eighty-four."

"And Amanda Miller, who lives in 173."

"How do you do," Melissa said without a trace of cordiality. Her eyes were busy checking out this Amanda's body. "Howard," she then said, turning her green self to her husband, "which one is the Cochran kid?"

"He's over there, why?"

Glancing at Amanda briefly, checking out her face this time, Melissa said, "His father attacked Sam Wyatt's little girl and Sam knocked his head in. He was drunk out of his mind," Melissa added loudly.

"Oh, my," Mrs. Goldblum said.

Amanda shot over to Skipper, who had overheard this.

Howard told Melissa to keep her voice down and they started to argue.

"Skipper," Amanda said, "don't say anything to Henry about—about what Mrs. Stewart just said. She's probably exaggerating."

"It's true," Skipper said, shrugging. "Mr. C's always drunk. It's no secret." He turned away to wait on customers.

"Skipper," Amanda said sharply.

"I won't," Skipper said, clearly exasperated.

Henry came back to the cash box for change. He smiled at Melissa the Celery Stalk. Melissa stared at him.

"My wife, Melissa Stewart. Melissa, Henry Cochran, the mastermind of this operation."

Henry said hi and got his change. Howard told him that his mother's and father's plans had changed and they wanted him to go to Skipper's tonight.

"Fine," Henry said.

"And," Howard added, "I'd like to take you guys out for a bite to eat after we clean up. To thank you for your help."

"Great," Henry said, eyes lighting up. "That'd be great. Thanks."

As Henry was walking away, Melissa said, "I don't suppose you're expecting me to attend this little soiree. We're due at the Griffins' at eight."

"Melissa, what do you want me to do? If what you say is true, I—"

"What business is it of yours, Howard?"

Mrs. Goldblum slumped and fell across the table. The crowd gasped; Skipper managed to grab her arm before she slid off. Howard lunged and caught hold of her under her arms and Amanda ran around the end of the tables, screaming at people to get out of her way. Henry jumped up on the table and, cupping his hands, asked if there was a doctor in the crowd.

"Melissa," Howard yelled over his shoulder, "go in the lobby and call 911!" Henry leaped off the table and waved Melissa to follow him into the building.

A woman introduced herself as a nurse and Mrs. Goldblum was gently lowered onto a makeshift bed of sweaters and jackets. Amanda accepted another jacket from an onlooker, knelt down beside Mrs. Goldblum, and covered her with it.

Mrs. Goldblum's eyes fluttered. "I must have fainted," she said quietly, watching the nurse taking her pulse.

Amanda smiled and signaled her to be quiet.

"I really am quite all right," Mrs. Goldblum said.

"Shhh," Amanda said, stroking her forehead, "you just lie there and rest a moment."

The nurse asked Mrs. Goldblum some questions and came to agree with her that she had just fainted. The ambulance arrived, backing in through the crowd. Mrs. Goldblum valiantly argued that if she were just taken home she'd be fine.

Amanda wouldn't hear of it. "If it were me," she said, holding Mrs. Goldblum's hand between her own, "wouldn't you want to make sure I was all right?"

Mrs. Goldblum closed her eyes, smiling, and softly sighed. "Yes, dear, I suppose I would."

The attendants carefully lifted Mrs. Goldblum onto the stretcher and Amanda walked back to the ambulance with them, holding Mrs. Goldblum's hand. As they hoisted the stretcher into the ambulance, Howard touched Amanda's arm. "As soon as I find someone to help the boys," Howard said, "I'll meet you at the hospital."

"Thank you," Amanda said, giving his hand a squeeze.

Howard helped her up into the ambulance. "Wait—where am I going? Roosevelt?"

"St. Luke's," the attendant said. "Emergency room on 113th and Amsterdam."

"Right," Howard said. He looked up at Amanda. "She'll be fine, you know."

"Of course," she murmured.

The doors closed and, lights flashing, the ambulance slowly pulled out onto Riverside Drive.

14

ST. LUKE'S HOSPITAL

"Y ou're lucky," the orderly told the Cochrans. "The Saturday night massacre doesn't start until six. You can go in now." A nurse opened the door and waved them into the examining area.

Cassy looked back to Alexandra.

"I'll wait out here."

Cassy nodded and went on with Michael.

"Pretty busy on Saturdays," Alexandra said to the orderly.

He nodded, scribbling on a clipboard. He looked up. He looked down. He looked up. "Do I know you?" he asked.

"I don't think so," Alexandra said. "I just moved here. From Kansas."

He rested his elbows on the standing desk and gave her his full attention. "Ever run into Auntie Em?"

Alexandra smiled. "Yes. She's very nice." She scanned the waiting room.

It was not a particularly uplifting room. But then, it is very hard to enliven any room whose purpose is to take in the ill, the maimed and the less than sane straight from the streets. It was an oblong room, with the orderly at one end, the door to the examining room on his left and the glass door to the outside on his right. Near the glass door, suspended from the ceiling, was a large color television set which, at this moment, was blasting a baseball game. The right wall of the room was made of a lively blue glazed brick, along the upper part of which were windows looking out at St. John the Divine across 113th Street. The left wall had a large glass partition where administrators and medical people were on view. The floor, though astonishingly clean, was still—no matter what they did—the same linoleum that one comes to associate with any form of American incarceration, from schools to prisons. There were many, many plastic chairs and the people sitting in them did not seem very happy, but neither did they seem very unhappy.

"Are all these people waiting to see a doctor?" Alexandra asked.

The orderly chuckled and pointed his pencil with discreet subtlety. "That one there," he said in a low voice, "drops in when he's lonely. That lady decided today's the day she wants a physical. Those three are waiting for someone inside. That gal—the one with the sunglasses—is waiting around to see if she can buy any of the patients' prescriptions from them. I have to wait until she tries before I can throw her out. And see the guy in the back?"

"Yes."

"He's writing a novel about a hospital. And that one—the girl on the other side—she's working on her master's degree on urban health care." He smiled at Alexandra. "But don't worry," he said, looking at his watch, "we'll be up to our necks in patients in about an hour."

"And then . . ."

"And then," he said, "the Saturday night massacre officially begins and it will be standing room only—until about nine tomorrow morning."

Alexandra scanned the room again. "Do you have enough doctors?"

His head kicked back with a snort. "Ever see *MASH?*"

"Yes."

"Well, that's what it's like in this part of town. We don't need more doctors, we need less wounded. Every since Crack Alley opened up—" He ran his hand through his hair. "You don't live in Brooklyn Heights, do you?"

"No, I don't."

"I swear I know you from somewhere." He tapped his pencil. "Maybe that means I should know you."

Alexandra smiled. "I guess I'll sit down and wait for my friends now."

The orderly bit his lip a moment, shrugged to himself, and went back to his papers.

Alexandra sat along the brick wall and watched the people behind the glass. In a minute or two a long wail of pain came from the direction of the examining rooms. It was a woman's cry. When it stopped, the people in the waiting room uncomfortably exchanged looks but then, a moment later, lapsed back into their private worlds.

After a bit Alexandra got up to walk around. Through the glass door she saw an ambulance pull into the carport outside. She walked to the door and watched as a stretcher was unloaded and carried inside, a young woman trailing behind it.

Alexandra sat down again and tried to watch the baseball game.

"Channel 6 news!" the orderly suddenly yelled.

Alexandra turned. The orderly snapped his fingers and pointed at her. The entire waiting room looked at her. She got up and reapproached the desk.

"Alice, right?"

Alexandra shook her head.

The glass window slid open. "Alexandra Waring," said a nurse, poking her head out.

"That's it!" the orderly said, pounding the desk.

"The lady on the news," the woman wearing sunglasses said, standing up.

"Who?" asked the old man who was lonely.

"In the subway ads," the novelist called out.

The nurse came out to get Alexandra's autograph, a request that was soon echoed by many of the people in the waiting room. The orderly donated his pencil and some paper and a corner of his desk.

"I was just talking to her," the orderly was saying to the nurse. "I knew I knew her face—"

The door to the examining rooms opened and the small figure of a woman cautiously emerged. She briefly looked up at the commotion, at Alexandra, her eyes and face mottled with red. She quickly lowered her head, then circled around the people and slipped out the glass door.

A moment later a doctor's head appeared around the door. Looking around, he said, "Clem—did you see Mrs. DiSantos?"

The orderly looked around. "No."

"If you see her, tell her I need to see her before she leaves," the doctor said. He frowned at the little autographing session. "What the heck is this? Clem, get these people to move outside. This isn't Hollywood."

Alexandra promised everyone an autograph on condition that they take their seats and be quiet. It worked and she went to work, moving from chair to chair until she met a woman who said she didn't want her stupid autograph, and so then Alexandra reseated herself and tried to watch the baseball game.

Loud voices were emanating from the glassed-in area behind her. She turned in her chair to see the woman who had climbed out of the ambulance before. And then Cassy landed in the chair next to Alexandra, startling her.

"His nose isn't broken," Cassy reported, sighing. "They're just giving him a couple of stitches in his cheek."

"He's okay," Alexandra said.

Cassy nodded. "Yes, he's okay."

"Clem," the doctor said from around the door, "did you find Mrs. DiSantos?"

Cassy sat up.

"She's not here, Dr. Karrel."

Cassy jumped out of her chair and went up to the orderly. She said something to him. He said something and then went back to the examination area. In a minute he reappeared and said something to Cassy. She drew her hand up to her mouth.

The woman from the ambulance came out of the door (looking very upset), crossed the room behind Cassy and went out the glass door.

Alexandra saw Cassy cover half of her face with her hand and hurried over to her side. "What's wrong? Is—?"

"It's not Michael," Cassy said. I just—when they said Mrs.—I wondered—"

"Cassy?" Alexandra had taken hold of her arm.

"Our cleaning woman," Cassy said, dropping her hand. "Her husband just died. In there. Just a few minutes ago."

"Oh, no," Alexandra said. "I'm sorry."

A mother came in with a little boy screaming at the top of his lungs. The women moved out of the way so the mother could talk to the orderly.

"I didn't know him," Cassy said. "But Rosanne—she's had such—" She sighed. "I can't believe it." She shook her head.

"Cassy," a man's voice said. They both turned.

"Howard," Cassy said.

"I just left Henry. He's going to Skipper's. Is your husband—"

"He's fine. He's just getting some stitches."

Alexandra's head was turning back and forth with the exchange.

"Is Amanda here?"

"Amanda?" Cassy said.

"They were bringing in a friend of hers—oh, what's her name?—a nice old lady who's a neighbor of hers. She fainted at the bookstall and they were bringing her here."

"In an ambulance?" Alexandra asked him.

"Yeah."

"I think I saw her," Alexandra said. "If it was she, she just left."

"Left for where?"

"I don't know." Alexandra pointed to the glass partition. "She was in there, before, talking to those people."

Howard walked over there.

"Poor Rosanne," Cassy murmured.

"What happened to him?"

"I don't know. They wouldn't tell me." She yanked the clip from her hair, stuck it in her mouth, put her hair up, and clipped it back into place. "I wonder if I should go and try to find her."

"Tomorrow might be better," Alexandra said.

Sigh. "You're probably right." She looked at Alexandra as if she had just noticed that she was there. "You were wonderful to come up with us, but you should go on home now."

"No," Alexandra said.

Cassy looked at her.

"Unless, of course," Alexandra said, "you'd like me to leave."

Cassy smiled slightly. "God, no," she said, touching her arm and turning away.

Howard came back. "Amanda's at the main admitting desk up the block. You sure everything's okay?"

"Yes," Cassy said on an intake of breath. "Michael's fine." She hesitated and then took Howard's arm and steered him toward the glass door. Alexandra watched as Cassy talked to him. Howard's face blanched and he turned away from her for a moment. He shook his head, pressing his fingers against the bridge of his nose. Then he took off his glasses and wiped his face with a bandanna from his pocket. They talked a minute more and he left.

Cassy said something to the orderly and came back to Alexandra. "Get some fresh air with me, will you?" she asked.

They went outside and looked one way up the street and then down the other. Leaning against Alexandra, Cassy said, "I really just want to sit down anywhere but in there for a minute." They settled on the curb outside the ambulance carport.

"Look at your stockings," Cassy said.

Alexandra's knees looked like the remains of a nuclear blast, with huge runs streaking up and down.

"And your beautiful dress," Cassy sighed. She patted Alexandra's hand and then held it. "Did you ever think, when you were in Kansas, that one day you'd be sitting on the sidewalk outside an emergency room in New York City, holding hands with the station manager of WST while she had a nervous breakdown?"

Alexandra brought her hand back to massage the back of Cassy's neck. "Yes," she said.

Cassy closed her eyes and softly laughed. "Oh, Lord, that feels good." After a little bit she said, "That's enough, thank you," and let her head fall against Alexandra's shoulder. In a moment she opened her eyes. "What's going to happen to us all, I wonder?"

"I don't know," Alexandra said quietly.

Cassy closed her eyes again and they sat there like that awhile.

The glass door opened and Michael emerged, featuring a massive "X" of adhesive tape over his nose. He stood there, blinking, holding a cold pack to his cheek.

"Cassy," Alexandra said, and Cassy's eyes flew open and the two women got up to meet him.

At the main admissions desk, Amanda was in such a tangle of fear and despair that it took nearly ten minutes for Howard to make out what had happened.

They arrived at the hospital.

The doctor saw Mrs. Goldblum.

The doctor told Amanda Mrs. Goldblum appeared to be suffering from malnutrition and should be hospitalized for a week.

The nurse told Amanda there was a problem with Mrs. Goldblum's medical coverage.

Amanda told them she would take care of Mrs. Goldblum's expenses.

They told Amanda to go to the admissions desk in the hospital.

At the admissions desk they told Amanda that Mrs. Goldblum had fallen in the examination room and had broken her hip.

Amanda was crying.

Howard led her away from the desk, forced her down into a chair and tried to calm her down. Amanda had to believe that everything would be all right. They would take care of everything. Mrs. Goldblum would be fine. What happened often happened with older women, and they should be grateful it was something that could be fixed.

"But, Howard," Amanda wailed, "she was starving. Don't you understand? She was starving to death." She drew her legs up in the chair, bound herself up like a ball and sobbed.

Howard got up to talk to a nurse at the desk. He got on the phone with the doctor in the emergency room. He talked with the nurse some more and then went back to Amanda.

"Mrs. Goldblum was supposed to rest in the examining room until they moved her upstairs to a room. She said she would, but when the nurse left her, she apparently tried to leave, fainted, and fell. It wasn't anyone's fault."

"I've got to see her," Amanda said.

"She's sedated now," he said, sitting in the chair next to her. "They're setting her hip and are going to move her into a room. You can see her first thing in the morning." Pause. "Amanda," he said softly, touching her knee, "she's going to be fine. Really. Don't be frightened. She will be all right."

Amanda clapped her hands over her face. "How could I not have noticed?" she said. "How?"

"She wasn't starving, Amanda. The nurse says it often happens with older people who live alone. They just stop eating balanced meals. Malnutrition doesn't mean she was starving—just that she wasn't eating properly. At least here, in the hospital, they can build her up and make everyone aware of the problem—most of all, Mrs. Goldblum."

Amanda uncovered her face and Howard took the used Kleenex out of her hand, tossed it into the ashtray and handed her the bandanna from his back pocket. She wiped her eyes and blew her nose.

"Amanda."

She looked at him.

"We've got to make some decisions about her room. We need to talk to the nurses. Do you think you can?"

She nodded, wiping at her eyes again.

The nurse was waiting for them with a pile of forms.

"Mrs. Goldblum doesn't have any medical coverage," Howard said, reconfirming the fact as it had been told to him.

The nurse nodded. "She's not registered with Medicaid. In fact, she doesn't appear to be registered with Social Security."

Howard looked at Amanda and she shook her head, holding the bandanna against her mouth.

"I think," the nurse said, glancing at her colleague, "we can straighten this out while she's here—technically speaking, she has no coverage whatsoever, nor, as she told them downstairs in emergency, does she have any means of paying."

Amanda muffled a sob with the bandanna. Howard put his arm around her. "You heard what she said—we'll straighten this out."

"She had no money, Howard," Amanda whimpered, looking away.

Howard looked at the nurse. "So what now?"

"Well," the nurse said, trying to sound cheerful, "our policy is to help whoever needs our help." She smiled. "So we're not the biggest moneymaking hospital around, but"—she looked to Amanda—"we are one of the best. Really. Your friend will receive excellent care here."

Howard nodded. "What kind of room can you put her in?"

"Well," the nurse said, "under the circumstances, we'll have to put her in one of the min-turn wards."

"What's that?" Howard asked. Amanda started to shiver and he pulled her tighter against him.

"An open ward."

"No," Amanda said. "Put her in a private room."

"Well," the nurse said with caution, "what we need for that is some sort of—"

"I'll take care of whatever expenses there are," Amanda said through the bandanna.

"What?" the nurse asked, leaning forward.

Amanda lowered the bandanna. "I said, I'll pay for everything." The nurse and Howard exchanged glances as Amanda looked down at her sweat pants and frowned. "I have nothing with me—what do you need?"

"Um—" the nurse said.

"American Express?" Amanda asked. "I have a gold card. I have a gold MasterCard. Dear God," she said, voice breaking, "I've got all the money in the world." She threw herself against Howard's chest and he brought his arms up around her. "Why didn't she tell me?" Amanda wept.

15

CASSY SAYS SHE THINKS
SHE KNOWS WHAT ALEXANDRA
IS GOING TO SAY

"You have to eat dinner with us," Cassy was saying to Alexandra in the cab driving home. "I forgot to call the caterers. We've got food for sixty."

"So you're not perfect," Michael muttered, looking out the window.

Cassy, on the other side of Alexandra, leaned forward. "What?"

Michael turned. He was going to have a black eye, the outline of which was darkening by the minute. He lowered the cold pack from his cheek. "I said, so you're not perfect after all." Pause. "A fact Alexandra perhaps should be made aware of." He turned back to the window.

Cassy sat back in her seat without a word.

After a minute Alexandra said, "I am rather tired. Perhaps we should do this another night."

Both Cassy and Michael looked at her.

"Well," Cassy said, "maybe—"

"Oh, Christ," Michael said, "you can't leave me with her." He imitated

Cassy's voice. " 'Michael, I think you should do this—Michael, I think you should do that—Michael, *sweet*heart—' Who the fuck needs it?"

Silence. Alexandra was looking down at her hands. The Cochrans were looking out their respective windows. The cab turned down 87th Street, and then right again onto the Drive. The police blockades were down and only a few neighbors were still out, picking up trash. The cab pulled up in front of their building.

Michael started to reach for his wallet.

"I'll get it," Cassy said.

"I can pay for the goddam cab, can't I?" Michael yelled at her.

Cassy fumbled to open her door. Alexandra reached over to unlock it for her.

"No," Michael said to the driver, "I changed my mind. I'm driving on."

Cassy tossed her head. "Great, where are you going? Sam Wyatt's for round 2?"

Michael glared at her. "You are such a cunt," he said.

"Fine." She yanked the handle of the door. "I don't care what you do," she said, getting out.

Alexandra started to slide out. "Don't," Michael said, taking hold of her arm. "I'll take you home."

"I don't want to go home," Alexandra said, taking her arm back. She climbed out and closed the door behind her. The cab pulled away.

"Well," Cassy said, standing there, scratching the back of her head, looking at the entrance to her building.

"Cassy," Alexandra said.

"Hmmm?"

"Come on." She pulled on Cassy's arm and Cassy looked at her, not understanding. "Come on," Alexandra repeated. "Let's just get away from here for a while. Let's just *go.*"

A flicker of a smile passed over Cassy's face. Then she shook her head. "No, I've got all that food upstairs . . ." Cassy looked back at her.

Alexandra was smiling, eyes twinkling. It was the look of someone who suspected she was about to get her way. "Come on," she said, taking Cassy's arm.

"But where will we go?" Cassy said, being pulled along.

Alexandra laughed, stopped and looked at her. "Anywhere," she said. And then she resumed pulling Cassy along. "We'll get my car and take it from there."

They walked up 88th to West End Avenue and then over to a garage on

87th Street. Alexandra's car turned out to be a navy-blue MG and Cassy covered her face when it came down on the elevator. "You don't expect me to get into that thing, do you?"

When Cassy got in, she felt as if she were sitting on the ground. It was comfortable, in fact rather marvelous, but she rolled her window down for a sense of a little more space. Alexandra got in and started unhinging two large metal hooks over the windshield. "Oh, you're not—" Cassy protested.

"Oh, yes, I am," Alexandra said, laughing. She unsnapped and unzipped this and that and then hopped out to bring the top down. "Okay," she said, getting back in, "buckle up." Alexandra snapped her seat belt into place, helped Cassy with hers, took out a pair of sunglasses from the glove compartment, put them on, revved the motor, put the car into gear, and grinned.

"Kidnapped by Darth Vader," Cassy said.

Alexandra laughed and drove the car out of the garage.

It was wonderful. Cassy felt as though she were flying. The wind blew against and around her face and the buildings loomed like canyon walls and children waved to them and it was free and open and it was wonderful.

Alexandra headed east on 86th Street, toward Central Park. "How about my house?"

Strands of her hair lashing against her face, Cassy's eyes crinkled with a smile. "Sure."

They stopped for a light at Columbus Avenue and two boys behind them in an old Valiant honked and waved. The driver leaned out his window and called, "Hey! How about having some fun?"

Alexandra smiled into the rear-view mirror; Cassy peered around the headrest and whipped back around again. "Good Lord—I'm old enough to be his mother."

"Hardly," Alexandra said, sunglasses in Cassy's direction.

The light changed and they shot ahead, the boys tailgating them.

"This happened to me in Nevada a few years ago," Cassy said over the noise. "I was driving a friend's Porsche and this car was following me. When I stopped at a light, this teenager pulled up beside me, took one look at me and nearly had a heart attack." She laughed.

"Don't," Alexandra said, downshifting for the approach of the Central Park West light.

Honk, honk, honk went the boys' car.

Alexandra looked in the rear-view mirror, pulled over into the right-hand land, and slowed almost to a stop. The boys behind them cheered.

"Alexandra, you're not thinking of—"

As they crept to the corner, the light turned yellow. Alexandra revved the motor, slammed into first and the car shot across the intersection just as traffic on Central Park West began to move. They sailed into Central Park, the traffic closed up behind them, and the boys were stuck at the light.

The cool air of the park rushed over Cassy and she laughed. "It's fun running away with you," she called.

When they reached the other side of Central Park, Alexandra turned down Fifth Avenue, drove past the Metropolitan Museum, and then turned back into Central Park at 79th Street. "Just for a while," she said to Cassy. And inside the park she took the turnoff for Central Park South and then took another turnoff and headed north, and another heading west, and on and on until she had taken Cassy on a motor tour of the whole park.

Cassy loved it.

"You're cold," Alexandra said later, glancing over at her. "It's getting too dark to be safe doing this anyway. I'm heading for home."

Alexandra lived at the corner of 86th Street and East End Avenue. Her apartment, she explained, actually belonged to her uncle Arnold. He had lived there for forty-three years. Now he was back in Kansas, to be near her parents, and Alexandra's lawyer was in negotiation with the owners about transferring the lease.

They parked in the building's underground garage. Cassy watched as Alexandra put the top back up and then they took the elevator up to the sixth floor. Outside Alexandra's door was a stack of newspapers, each neatly slipcased in plastic wrap. Cassy picked them up: the Washington *Post;* the Los Angeles *Times;* the Chicago *Sun-Times;* the Houston *Chronicle;* the London *Times;* and last, but not least, the Kansas City *Star.*

Alexandra sure liked white. The apartment was open and breezy in a way that reminded Cassy of a British colonial outpost in the tropics. The floorboards were light, there were what appeared to be close to a million plants, and then, of course, the white—the walls, the rug, the couch . . . No, Cassy decided, this was not a home intended for children. Certainly not a little boy. (She thought of the nice purple elephant Henry once drew on their living-room wall.)

What Cassy assumed was meant to be a dining room was now Alexandra's work area. There was an enormous white (of course) table (a dining table?) that had a blotter and word processor on it, three stacks of magazines and journals, and several folders bulging with papers. There were a VCR and a small TV in the corner, bookshelves of videotapes, a set of

Encyclopedia Britannica and *World Book,* an Oxford Dictionary . . . and plants. Yes, Alexandra certainly liked plants.

The kitchen was small and cheery and—surprise—white. Even the TV set on the counter.

The bedroom was a fair size, with a nice view of Carl Schurz Park and the East River. The room, surprise, surprise, was pale blue. There was a double bed with shelves at the foot of it, where sat another small TV and more magazines and a pile of books. A chaise longue was under the window, beside which sat a small table and more books.

Cassy's eye landed on the phone next to the bed. As if reading her thoughts, Alexandra said, "Go ahead. I'm going to change into some jeans —in the bathroom—and then start dinner. Bluefish okay with you?"

Cassy called the Marshalls' and managed to recreate the story of the afternoon for Henry in a way that did not at all accurately reflect what had happened, but it did, at least, prepare him for seeing his father looking like a prize fighter.

Afterward, Cassy sat on a stool and watched Alexandra cook dinner. Alexandra asked her if she would mind eating on TV tables in the living room. Cassy said no, and Alexandra checked the asparagus, replaced the lid on the steamer and turned to her. "At the risk of sounding rude, would you like to talk or would you like to watch a movie?"

Cassy thought a movie sounded terrific and Alexandra sent her off to choose one. When dinner was ready, Cassy was still wading through the tapes, unable to make up her mind. There seemed to be eight categories in Alexandra's collection—Colbert, Crawford, Davis, Dietrich, Garbo, Harlow, Hepburn and Lombard.

"We want something short," Alexandra said.

"Oh, gosh, I don't know—they're all wonderful. I—I don't know, you choose."

Alexandra skimmed the titles and picked one. *"Red Dust,"* she said, "I bet you haven't seen that for years. And it's not even an hour and a half."

And so they sat in the living room and watched a large Mitsubishi TV and shared their dinner and coffee and fruit with Clark Gable, Jean Harlow and Mary Astor. While Cassy enjoyed the movie immensely, she was also very much aware of the mess waiting for her at home—sigh—and the office. And Rosanne. Her thoughts drifted to her. . . .

She helped clear the living room, and while Alexandra washed the dishes, Cassy had her permission to poke around. Cassy was stalling about going home (to God only knew what), and she knew Alexandra knew it. They were both yawning their heads off.

Cassy started looking at the photographs hanging just outside the kitchen in the front hall.

"I can spot your mother a mile away," she called out.

A laugh. "We all look like Mom," Alexandra called back.

"But you have your father's mouth. This is your father—this man sitting at the desk?"

"Yes."

"What does he do?"

"He used to be a congressman. Now he's in private practice again. As a lawyer."

Alexandra came out into the hall, drying the steamer.

Cassy's brow furrowed. "Your father isn't Paul Waring, is he?"

"Uh-huh."

"You're kidding."

"No."

Cassy looked at his picture again. "I remember his health insurance bill."

"That got killed," Alexandra finished, returning to the kitchen. "They called him a socialist."

"Is he?" Cassy laughed.

"No."

After a while, "How many brothers and sisters do you have?"

"Three brothers, one sister. Paul's the oldest. Then Elizabeth. Linc— Lincoln and David. And then me." She came out again, holding the dish towel. She pointed to a group wedding photograph. "That's Mom, Dad, my grandfather, Paul—he's an assemblyman; that's Linc, he's a rock singer; David's a lawyer; and Elizabeth teaches high school English."

"Lincoln's a rock singer?"

"I know," she laughed. "You'd never know from that picture. He has orange and purple hair, last I heard."

Cassy smiled. "Anyone married?"

"They're all married. Right out of college. Linc got married in college." She pointed. "These are my nieces and nephews."

"Wow," Cassy said.

"I know. The Warings are known for propagating at an alarming rate."

"Hmmm," Cassy said, straightening up. "It's sure a good-looking family."

Alexandra smiled, folding the towel.

"Who's that?" Cassy asked. It was a picture of a young blond woman waving from a dock. "She's very pretty."

"An old friend," Alexandra said, moving near Cassy to look at it.

Cassy waited for details but none came. "What's her name?" Cassy finally asked.

"Lisa," Alexandra said, walking out.

Cassy looked at the picture again and fiddled with one of her earrings, thinking. She leaned closer, examined the picture again, and then walked out to the kitchen. "Alexandra?"

"In the living room," came the answer.

She was rewinding the video cassette.

Silence.

"I liked Gordon very much," Cassy said.

Alexandra was watching the digital counter. "We knew each other at Stanford." She glanced over. "He's been great to me since I moved here."

Silence.

"Quite frankly," Cassy said, lowering herself into an easy chair, "I was jealous that night." Alexandra's head shot around. "All the way home I wondered what it would be like to go home with Gordon instead of Michael."

Alexandra turned back to the machine.

Cassy crossed her legs and smoothed the denim on the top. "Does that sound awful to you?"

"No. It sounds very normal to me." The tape stopped and Alexandra pushed the eject button. "Gordon liked you too. If you want . . ." she started, putting the tape back in its case. She smiled at Cassy. "Well, I mean, if you ever—" She laughed, embarrassed. "Of course you could have anyone you want," she finished, moving across the room to put the tape back.

Cassy laughed slightly and then said, "You certainly don't sound very attached to him."

"I am," she called from the work area, "but not the way you think." Pause. "I was once—we lived together, actually. But," she said, coming back into the room, "that was a long time ago."

Cassy watched Alexandra as she walked over to the couch, drumming her fingers on the arm of the chair. "I really should be going home," she said.

Alexandra sat down and tossed a pillow in her hands. "You're welcome to stay as long as you would like. Or come again. Any time."

Cassy let her head fall back against the chair. "It's been quite a day."

"Yes," Alexandra agreed, catching the pillow.

Silence.

"You really haven't ever slept with Michael, have you?"

"Cassy!"

"Sorry." She got up and pulled down her sweater. She smiled and walked over to the couch. "I'm sorry, it just occurred to me that it would kill me if I found out later that all along you had been—you were—" She sat down on the end of the couch. "What I mean to say is—thank you for everything you did today, for being so wonderful. I don't know what I would have done without you."

Alexandra drew her back up against the end of the couch. "You're welcome."

"And I'd like to be a friend to you too. Help you, if I can." She looked down at her hands, turning her wedding band. "There's something I need to tell you."

Silence.

"Alexandra—" She raised her eyes. "Don't go with Michael. Under any circumstances, don't go with him. Not now. Not the way he is." She lowered her eyes. "It was inexcusable for me to talk the way I did today—bringing up that idea." Pause. "I wasn't thinking—" She pounded her thigh with a fist. "Damn it," she said, looking up at Alexandra, "I *was* thinking. I was thinking of him, of his career—at the risk of yours." Pause. "I can't tell you how sorry I am."

Alexandra smiled.

The eyes.

"There's nothing to be sorry about," she said gently. "We were only talking."

"Still . . ." Cassy touched the leaf of a plant on the windowsill behind them.

Silence.

"Cassy."

Alexandra had her arms wrapped around her legs and was resting her chin on her knees. She dropped one hand to pluck at her sock. "There's something I want to tell you—about me." Alexandra's eyes skipped up briefly—checking to see that Cassy was listening—and dropped again. "You'll be able to blackmail me for a thousand years."

Cassy waited.

"I, uh—" Alexandra exhaled, slowly, and bounced her chin on her knees three times, debating.

Silence.

After a moment Cassy said, "I think I know what you're going to say." Alexandra's eyes met hers.

"It's okay," Cassy said. She smiled. "This is New York, you know."

Quietly. "Do you really know?"

Gently. "That you're gay."

"Oh, God," Alexandra groaned, "is that what you think?" She fell back and looked to the ceiling. "One affair makes me gay?" She sat up. "Please don't say that. Even I don't know what I am—please."

"I'm sorry," Cassy said, "I spoke too quickly. I just—well, I thought— there was—you—I don't know, I—" She sighed, smiled and then shrugged. "What the hell do I know? You tell me."

Alexandra looked agonized. She ran a hand through her hair. "This wasn't such a great idea," she said, blinking rapidly. She took a deep breath and let it out. "Well, anyway, now you know who Lisa is. Was."

"Alexandra," Cassy said quietly, reaching forward to touch her arm. Alexandra looked out the window. "It doesn't matter. It really doesn't. Who you love is not important—the fact that you can love is. Really. The rest of it—" She gestured with her hand. "Look at me. I've been Miss Goody Two-shoes my entire life and look what it got me." She shook her head, slowly. "Alexandra—you've got to live the life that makes you happy. And whether it's a woman or a man—whose business is it?"

"The whole world's," came the reply, "or at least the tri-state area's."

"Are you worried about that?" Cassy leaned forward. "Alexandra, dear darling girl, I hate to tell you, but you're not the first—bisexual—woman to be in the public eye." She fell back with a laugh. "You're going to have to do better than that to win sympathy from me."

Silence. Alexandra brought her hands to her face and Cassy realized she was crying.

"Don't," Cassy said softly.

"It's easy for you to say," Alexandra said, springing from the couch. "Nobody gives a damn about what goes on in your marriage, just so long as you're married." She whirled around, covering her mouth with her hand. "Cassy, I'm sorry," she said, sinking back down onto the couch. "I didn't mean that. I'm just—I'm—" She lowered her face into the crook of her arm on the back of the couch.

Cassy leaned forward, patted her back and let her hand rest there a moment. Alexandra's shoulders were trembling. "It's okay, Alexandra, it's okay," she murmured. "We're both so tired—so much has happened to-day." Pause. "You must know though, Alexandra, that what you've told me makes me respect you all the more. Admire you all the more." Pause. "You're a wonderful young lady, you know. And you've got one of the biggest and brightest careers ahead of you . . ." Sigh. "And I understand," she said, patting her back again, "how difficult things are for you right now. Living in a strange place . . . all the excitement . . . all the pressure that's on you . . ." Cassy withdrew her hand.

Alexandra sat up and wiped her eyes with her sleeve. She cleared her throat, swept her hair up with both hands and held it there. She sniffed. She took a deep breath and let it out slowly. Then she dropped her hands into her lap. "But would you understand," she said, "if I told you I think I'm falling in love with you?"

16

AMANDA AND HOWARD
AND MISSY THE CAT

Before Amanda and Howard left St. Luke's Hospital, an orderly had run up from the emergency room waving Mrs. Goldblum's keys. "She kept talking about her cat and I promised I would get these to you," he had said, handing them to Amanda. "You'll take care of the cat, won't you?"

And so Amanda and Howard were standing in Mrs. Goldblum's apartment, and Amanda was staring at the cat as if it were from outer space. It meowed. "I think it knows," she said, wincing.

Amanda didn't know anything about cats. On her grandmother's farm they had run wild and eaten field mice. Howard had grown up with a dog, not a cat, but had enough of a suburban heritage to remember his friends who had had one—and he tried to remember all the things they would need. Let's see, there was food. And something to carry the cat in—a box or something. Oh, and yes, something for the cat to go to the bathroom in.

They could only find half a can of cat food in the refrigerator. The kitty litter box was a mess, and there didn't seem to be any extra litter around. And then Amanda sat down and started to cry that Mrs. Goldblum

couldn't come back here and live alone and where was she going to live
. . . Howard stood next to her and rubbed the back of her head, talking
softly, telling her that everything was going to be all right and that, right
now, at this very moment, everything was all right. Mrs. Goldblum was safe
and sound.

They gave the cat the half can of cat food and set out to find a store that
was open where they could get what they needed. They ended up throwing
themselves on the mercy of a delicatessen owner who kept a cat in his store.
(It was sleeping in the window, under the heat of the lights, in the grapefruit
bin.)

The deli owner gave them a box to put "keety" in. He handed them cans
of cat food and some dry food in foil envelopes called Tender Vittles. ("How
utterly bizarre," Amanda said to Howard, looking at the packages, "hillbilly cat food.") He lugged out a twenty-five-pound bag of kitty litter, and
they all agreed that a gigantic aluminum-foil roasting pan would do for a
litter box. "Vat else?" the deli owner pondered.

"Don't I need a toy or something?"

"Take dis," he urged, scooping up a Super Ball from the rack by the
register.

They went back and got Missy the cat. Missy did not like the box at all,
and howled and scratched inside of it until Amanda was tearfully convinced
she must be killing it. Howard said the cat probably thought it was going to
the vet's, and took the box from her. Amanda struggled with the sack of
kitty litter and the other deli purchases and they pressed onward down the
Drive.

Missy loved Amanda's apartment. As soon as they opened the box in the
front hall she sprang out of it and shot down the hall to the living room.
Amanda and Howard scrambled after her, arriving in time to see her climb
up the curtains. Howard stretched up and just missed grabbing her as she
leaped to the ground and skidded out through the passageway to the
kitchen. She ran flat out—ears back—to the writing room, sailed up onto
Amanda's writing desk, hit manuscript pages, slid all the way across, and
landed softly on the ground on the other side. Her back paws furiously
clawed the wood floor for a running start and then she was off again, her
rear end swinging around the doorway. She flew down the back hall to the
bedroom and, at long last, came to rest under Amanda's bed.

On their hands and knees, peering under the bed and seeing nothing but
two shining eyes, Amanda and Howard decided to leave her be.

They put down some newspaper on the kitchen floor and set out a saucer of water and some of the hillbilly cat food. Cupping his hands around his mouth, Howard tried out various ways of calling her—while Amanda laughed and laughed—and then, when he started making psst—psst—psst noises, all of a sudden there was Missy the cat, arching her back, rubbing against the kitchen doorway. She spotted the food and trotted over, tail held high, and sniffed at it. Then she went over and, to Amanda's delight, rubbed against her leg. "She likes me," she said, bending and tentatively patting the cat on the head.

They decided to set up the kitty-litter operation under the sink in the powder room off the writing room. "We have to show her where it is," Howard said when they were finished, and he went back to the kitchen to get her. He plunked her down into the litter, the cat sniffed, scratched once and then bolted, sending kitty litter everywhere.

"I thought cats were supposed to be clean," Amanda said.

Back in the kitchen, Amanda poured them each an Amstel Light and fixed a platter of sliced apples, pears, bread and cheese, and Howard tried calling home. No answer. No answer. "Melissa went to the dinner party," he said, hanging up.

They sat down at the kitchen table and talked about the afternoon. The food did much to perk them up; Amanda's color had come back and so had her smiles. Howard carved a face out of a piece of apple and held it up to her mouth. "Hi," he said.

Amanda looked at it and said hi back. And then she ate it.

When they finished eating, when they were both on their second beers, Howard carefully, calmly, told Amanda about Rosanne's husband. He was nervous that Amanda might break down again, but he was wrong. She didn't. Instead, she just looked sad, sighed, and listlessly toyed with the cheese with the knife. "It was bound to happen, sooner or later," she finally said. She dropped the knife on the plate. "He was a drug addict, you know."

"Was he? Melissa said something about that once."

Amanda nodded, still staring down at the cheese. "Yes. I posted bail for him once. They told me that, the police did. They warned me I'd never see the money again." Amanda got up from the table. "I am feeling a bit strange," she said softly. "Would you mind if we sat in the living room?"

Howard followed her in and Amanda turned on a single lamp. He sat down on the settee. Amanda set a match to the wood in the fireplace and stood there, hand on the mantel, watching it for a few minutes. She put the screen back in place, took an afghan out of a cabinet under the secretary, and then curled up in the wing-back chair across from Howard to watch the fire.

"It's a terrible thing to say," Amanda said quietly, "but perhaps it's for the best." She brought the afghan up higher over her shoulders, eyes still on the fire.

Howard sipped his beer and rested the glass on his leg.

"Have you ever lost anyone?" Amanda murmured.

"Just my grandparents."

"Hmmm. Me too. My grandmother—Nana—" For the first time, she looked over at him. "When Nana died, it wasn't real to me. I told myself she had just gone away. I suppose that was the only way I could accept it." She looked back to the fire and snuggled her head against the wing back. "It didn't really sink in until I left Christopher. I went down to Nana's, to the farm . . ." She squeezed her eyes shut.

"You loved your grandmother very much."

Amanda nodded. She opened her eyes and Howard could see them glistening in the firelight. "And she was awful, really." She sniffed and turned to Howard. She laughed under her breath. "Nana was terrible to my mother —she disowned her when she married my father. Because he was Jewish." She chuckled and shook her head. "She sure loved me, though. And she loved Mother too. And my father, eventually." She dropped her voice. "Her nose was just terribly out of joint over Mother not marrying a Baltimore buffoon."

"What about your grandfather?"

"Oh, Grandfather?" Amanda rubbed her forehead. "Grandfather never spoke, not that I can recall. He was always shut up in his study. Mother says she thinks he had something going with the cook." Another chuckle. "Nana used to say that Grandfather was more sociable dead than he was when he was alive."

Howard laughed.

"I never knew my father's parents. They died when he was very young. Of influenza, can you believe it? And Father's brother died in the war."

"Who is that?" Howard asked, pointing to the portrait over the fireplace.

"Nana's mother, Amanda Tinker." She bowed her head. "My namesake. It has been said that I resemble her."

"You do," Howard said.

"She was positively scandalous in her day, but everyone adored her, even Nana. Though," she laughed, "it was a little hard on her to have a mother who was known to entertain certain gentlemen to whom she was not married. Mother said she had a boyfriend up until the day she died—at eighty-one. Reginald was the name of the last one. . . ."

Amanda closed her eyes and Howard thought she had gone to sleep. He sat there for a half hour, sipping his beer, watching her.

He took his glass into the kitchen and used the bathroom. He found the cat in the writing room and picked her up and petted her, looking around at the shelves. He put the cat down and went back into the living room.

Amanda had not moved. Howard stood over her, watching her gentle breath rise and fall under the afghan. He reached out toward the hair that had fallen over her face, but refrained from touching it. He walked over and rested his hands on the mantel, looking down into the fire.

"I don't want you to leave," Amanda whispered.

He didn't move. And then he said, "I don't want to leave either." When he turned around Amanda was in the same position, but her eyes were open, looking at him. He went over and sat down on the edge of the chair. He looked into her eyes for a long moment and then bent, slowly, and brushed his lips over her forehead. Then he sat up again.

Amanda looked at him for a long time. Then she brought up a hand from under the afghan, slipped it up around the back of his neck, and pulled him down to her. They kissed a long, gentle, dry kiss. And then Howard kissed the side of her mouth, and her cheek, and her temple, and her ear and then her mouth again. He took off his glasses. Amanda brought out her other arm from under the afghan and put it around him and Howard took her in both of his arms and they clung to each other and kissed each other and tried to climb inside each other.

They stayed in the chair for almost an hour. And then, gently, Amanda eased Howard back so she could see his eyes. "It is Saturday," she said, "and you are Howard Stewart, and I want to make love with you." He whispered something about contraception. She whispered for him not to worry, it was taken care of; she slid out of the chair, holding his hand, and sat down in front of the fire. Howard looked at her a moment, still holding her hand, and crawled down next to her. Amanda lay down and pulled him on top of her, and they kissed.

It happened too fast. Howard was fumbling with his belt; he was free of his pants; Amanda's were down; and he was inside of her. And he came. Just like that.

"I'm sorry," he said, forehead pressed against the rug next to her head.

Amanda lay there, touching his hair. She pushed his shoulder, making him raise his head to look at her. Holding the sides of his face in her hands, she smiled. "You sure know how to flatter a girl," she whispered, kissing him lightly.

Howard closed his eyes, groaned, and let his forehead bang down on the rug.

"Howard," Amanda said.

He opened his eyes.

"Look at me, please."

He raised himself up on one elbow and did so, tracing Amanda's nose with his finger as he did so.

"Would you do something for me?" she said. "Would you let me have my way? Do exactly what I tell you?"

He nodded, swallowing.

"Wonderful," she said, kissing him. "Follow me."

They put their clothes back in place, smoothed each other's hair, restored Howard's glasses to their proper place, and Amanda, with a faint smile, took his hand, led him to the writing room and sat him down at her desk. Howard sat there, watching her, as she commenced to turn on every lamp in the room. Then, scanning the shelves of Catherine, Amanda took down a section of manuscript and plunked it down on the desk in front of him. She flipped open the inkwell compartment at the side of the writing surface, extracted several No. 2 pencils, and placed them on the desk as well. "Read, please," she said, walking out of the room.

Howard sat there, slightly dazed. He looked to the doorway, pushed at his glasses and called, "You sure know how to flatter an editor."

A laugh from the kitchen. Amanda reappeared at the doorway. "We are having an editorial session," she announced. "So please read, and I will rejoin you in a few minutes."

Howard shook his head, smiling, and started to read. It was a chapter about how Catherine the Great had selected her lovers from the Imperial Guard. By the second page he was hooked.

She came back in a half hour. He turned at the sound of her approach and his expression must have been blatantly surprised, for she laughed and said, "Do not fear, Howard, it is only me."

She was carrying a pot of coffee and coffee things on a silver tray. But she was wearing yards of a white silk—something. A caftan? A robe of some sort? It was difficult to tell. But it was white, and it was silk, and it trailed. There was a very deep V plunging between her breasts, and there was a sash of blue silk around her waist. She placed the tray down on the corner of the desk, drew up a chair to the left of him and sat down. As she leaned forward to pour the coffee, Howard did not fail to notice the view of her left breast as she did so.

"Uh," he said, swallowing, "was there really a Countess Bruce?"

"Oh, yes," she said, pulling a cup and saucer back to Howard. She leaned across his arm—her right breast gently resting on it—to see what page he was on. "Hmmm," she said, reaching for the cream, her breast sliding down his arm to get it, and sliding back up to bring it to him. She sat back then and crossed her legs toward him, revealing that within the many folds of this white silk something there was a slit down there as well. She smiled at him—as though she had only just made his acquaintance.

"Uh," Howard said, rubbing his chin, looking at the manuscript, "I'm not sure if people will believe this. I mean, the countess slept with the guards first to see if they were any good?"

"Yes," Amanda said, raising her coffee cup. "After the physicians checked them for venereal disease." She took a sip. "And then Catherine would come in to watch—to see for herself. They didn't know, usually, for she had a secret door into—" She laughed, softly, putting her cup down.

Howard was looking down at her breast again, marveling.

"She had many secret doors in the palace. She would watch Madame Protassov as well." Pause. "Howard?"

His head jerked up. "Um," he said, touching his glasses, "right. Well, the way you have it here—uh," he said, picking up a pencil and jiggling it. He dropped the pencil, rubbed his eyes under his glasses and looked at her.

She smiled, looking vaguely puzzled, tilting her head as if it would help her to understand him better.

"Okay," he said, taking a breath and picking up the pencil again. "I think you're perhaps sticking a little too closely to the facts." He hazarded a look at her. She was looking at the manuscript, absently rubbing her collarbone. The movement offered glimpses of her breast again, and the motion of her fingers, spreading and contracting, spreading and contracting, had decidedly derailed his train of thought. "I think," he started. He cleared his throat. "I think you need to . . ." She lowered her hand, shifted slightly, and leaned closer to the manuscript.

Now he could see both. Hanging there. Full. Beautifully heavy. Beautifully full and heavy and there, right there in front of him.

"If this part troubles you," she said, drawing herself up, "then I'm afraid the hairdresser will positively make you despair." She looked at him with the most innocent of expressions.

"Hairdresser?" His voice sounded very far away.

"Yes," she said, recrossing her legs and reaching for her coffee. Now her leg was gently pressed against his. "Catherine was obsessed with the fact that she had to wear wigs. Her own hair—never mind." She sipped her coffee, replaced her cup and propped her elbow on the desk to support her chin.

Howard didn't dare look anywhere but her eyes. Yes, he might well be having a heart attack, he decided. He felt her foot gently curling around his shin. "Go on," he said.

"She didn't want anyone to know. And so," Amanda said, pausing to let her tongue run along her upper lip, "she locked her hairdresser in an iron cage in her room. For three years."

"Did she?" Howard said, letting Amanda take his hand.

"Uh-huh," she said, looking into his eyes. She brought his hand up and pressed it against the silk over one breast. "She did not want him to gossip about her wigs," she murmured, pressing his hand harder, moving it in a circle.

Their eyes were still locked.

Amanda swallowed. Her voice faint, "So she kept him in a cage in her bedroom."

Howard let a shaky breath escape. "Really," he said.

"Yes." She closed her eyes then, mouth slightly parting.

Howard watched her face as he slid his hand under the silk to hold her breast. She took a deep breath, eyes still closed. He touched her nipple and she squirmed slightly in her chair, a low sound coming from her throat.

She opened her eyes. With each movement of his hand, there was a trace of a wince and a creak from her chair, but she did not stop looking at him. "Maybe I should have—" she started to say, breaking off as Howard worked again at her nipple. Her eyes fell half closed. "Written a biography," she murmured.

"No," Howard whispered, "I don't think so." He glanced down, twisted at the waist, and brought his other hand up to her other breast. If—with each deep movement of his hands, of his fingers—Amanda had not made soft sighing sounds, he might have thought she was fighting death. Her eyes were barely open; her leg had, at some time, hooked around his and was locked into position; her left hand was in a fist, bearing down on the desk.

"I, I—" she said, her eyes opening. She was breathing heavily. "I'm not sure I can continue working." And then she closed her eyes, reached up to his head, and pulled him down to her breasts.

He was half out of his chair, but still, he managed. He parted the silk, freed one breast, and sank his mouth onto it. Her back lurched in an arc, and her chair creaked—creaked—creaked—as she strained against the back of it. "Oh, my," she said, pulling his head harder against her. "Oh, my, yes."

Mouth still at her breast, Howard slid his hand down between her thighs. They were clamped shut. His hand shot under her knee, lifted her leg, uncrossed it, and then slid back, his palm plunging smoothly down against her.

Amanda groaned, pulling his hair.

He left her breast, mouth running up her chest, her neck, and finding her mouth. "Come on," he said, hoarse, sliding out of his chair. He leaned over, slid an arm behind her back and under her legs, muttered, "Three," and heaved her up into his arms.

Amanda's head fell back, laughing.

He carried her out of the writing room and down the hall. Amanda had her arms around his neck now and was gently licking his ear. "All the way down," she whispered, when he paused at the first door. "All the way down."

There was a fire burning in the bedroom. And the bed was turned down. Howard stood inside the doorway, still carrying her, and laughed. "It appears I was expected," he said, kissing her.

"Mmm," she said, tasting his mouth.

He walked over to the bed and laid her down. He took off his glasses, put them on the night table, and started to unbutton his shirt.

"No," Amanda said, bolting upright. "No, please, let me." She slid off the bed and stood in front of him. She undid the buttons and then looked up at him, smiling, as she drew the shirt down off his shoulders. She tossed it on the floor. "Up," she said, patting his arms, and he raised them, and she took her time pulling his undershirt up over his head. That, too, ended up on the floor, and Amanda got distracted by his chest, by kissing it. He used the time to untie the sash around her waist.

Sinking to her knees, Amanda unbuckled his belt and let it hang. She slid her hands around his waist and rested the side of her face against the rise in his pants, sighing. Then she kissed the rise and unzipped his pants, taking hold of them at his waist and tugging them down to the floor. He stepped out and kicked them behind him. And then she held him around the waist again, nuzzling the fabric at the place where it strained most. She sighed again, softly. "Mmm," she finally said, pulling back, working his Jockey shorts down. Then she gazed at the sight before her, made a sound in the back of her throat, and looked up at him.

The fire crackled; the light flickered.

"You are magnificent," she said.

She bent down to kiss his ankle and gently dragged her mouth up over his shin, his knee, his calf, his thigh, to there.

He was a wonder. She closed her hand around him, her thumb scarcely reaching her middle finger. Lifting him gently, she kissed him, very softly, underneath, first one side and then the other. She drew back slowly, her mouth breezing over him, lifted him slightly, and then opened her mouth to take in of him what she could.

His buttocks locked and his head kicked back with an intake of breath. His hands were buried in her hair. "Amanda," he whispered, feeling her mouth moving around him. "Oh, Amanda." And then he eased her head back, slid his hands under her arms, and lifted her to her feet. He looked at her, kissed her around her mouth, took her in his arms, and held her for a long moment. "Amanda," he sighed, rocking her gently.

She stepped back and raised her arms. "Please," she whispered. He lifted the silk over her head, and she laughed, softly, as he tried to find an end to the material. Finally it was off and she fell back onto the bed, her arms outstretched.

He crawled onto the bed between her legs. Crouched on his knees, he leaned to kiss her mouth and then her neck. She drew up her knees to either side of him and squeezed. "Please, I want you now." And she lowered her legs, pushed him slightly to the side, and pulled his hand down to touch her. "I am so ready for you," she whispered, urgent, pressing her forehead into his shoulder. "Please."

He moved on top of her and, resting his weight on one elbow, made way for her hand that was reaching down for him. She held him, murmuring something he could not hear, and led him to the way inside her. She was breathing heavily and made a sound, releasing him, and brought her hand away to rest on the small of his back. Howard looked down into her eyes and then gently pressed into her, not far; he eased back and then pressed forward again, moving a little deeper; back, and then down, slowly, further, deeper, into her. And then he pulled back and pushed himself all the way inside of her, making Amanda's face crumble and her head jerk to the side.

He started to move, slowly, steadily, gaining a rhythm that altered her breathing. "Howard, yes," she breathed, moving with him, thighs tightening around him. "Yes," she said with each drive into her, "yes, yes, yes . . ."

He was moving faster now, a slick friction between them. "Yes—How—ward—yes—yes . . ."

Her head started to move from side to side, and he took tighter hold of her, lowered his head, and broke into hard pace. She started muttering, groaning, and her hips started to climb, and climb, and climb and then her body went rigid and she gasped, "Hold it—hold—" and he froze, and she was fighting for her breath, hanging there, straining, teetering, and then she cried, "Now," and he plunged down into her and she was clinging to him, shuddering, her sounds frantic, and he felt her spasms grip around him and then he was climbing and it was coming and he groaned and he thrashed and he twisted, straining into her, and he came, in waves, he came, teeth clenched, he came, pouring his everything into her.

He slowed, ebbed, slowed, slowed to a stop. A tear trickled down his cheek. He shuddered again suddenly, pressing into her once more, and he stayed there, holding there, clinging there. To her. He choked back a sob.

"My darling, my darling," she whispered, stroking his hair, kissing the side of his face. "My darling." And she pressed her face into the side of his and he could feel the tears that were not his but hers.

17

HARRIET AND SAM

Sam was sitting in bed, arms folded, glaring at the bookcase across the room. "You're wasting your breath," he said.

Whether she was or not, Harriet was going to continue, he knew.

She was not in her most imposing dress. The flannel nightgown had little Mickey Mouses dancing on it (picked out as a gift from Samantha); and her hair was wrapped in toilet paper, secured with bobby pins. She smoothed the sheet in her lap. "But you know better, Sam. You know he didn't know what he was saying."

"He called our daughter a nigger."

"Sam—" He wouldn't look at her. "He's as ill and confused and frightened as you once were."

"I was never that bad," Sam said. He climbed out of bed and walked out of the bedroom. After a moment Harriet got up too, put on a robe and followed him out. She found him in the kitchen.

Leaning against the doorway, she said, "I'm only suggesting that maybe one of your friends could help the Cochrans. Not you."

Sam was standing with his back to her, looking at the calendar on the refrigerator door. "It doesn't work that way. People get sober because they want to, not because they need to." He turned. "I'll help anyone who asks me—I don't have to help anyone who abuses my kids."

Harriet sat down at the kitchen table and propped her head up on her hands. "You also don't have to attack them."

He turned back to the calendar. "Do you think I feel good about it? When I heard him—I lost my temper," he said.

"Yes, Sam, you lost your temper." Harriet sighed. "And you don't want to talk to *Essence*—"

"Not that again," he muttered.

"And you don't want to talk to me, either."

He yanked the refrigerator door open and then slammed it shut without looking inside. He crossed his arms and fell back against it, making the refrigerator rock slightly. "I'm under a lot of pressure," he said.

"Glad to hear you say so," she said, sarcasm edging in. "It explains everything."

"At work," he added.

Harriet sighed again, massaging her hand. "I'm not moving to Peoria, Sam."

He stared at her for moment and then uncrossed his arms. "We're not moving to Peoria. Althea just—"

Harriet slammed her hand down on the table. "Damn it, Sam! I know that. But what I do want to know is why I have to hear from Althea that something's wrong at work." Pause. "Why won't you talk to me?"

Sam pushed off the refrigerator. "I didn't tell her anything."

She looked at him, mouth open. Then she threw her hands up in a gesture of frustration. "What *is* it with you? What could be so wrong at work that you can't talk to me about it? I know you, Sam Wyatt, and you haven't acted like this since—"

She stopped herself, but what words she had said hung in the air between them.

Sam opened the refrigerator and took out a bottle of mineral water. He unscrewed the cap, tossed it in the garbage and took a long swallow. Lowering the bottle, he said, "Do you trust me?"

Quietly, "Yes."

He nodded, slowly, eyes on the floor. He raised them. "I've got a problem I need to work out for myself."

Harriet looked as though she might cry. But she didn't. She closed her eyes for a moment, raking her teeth over her lower lip, and reopened them. "Okay," she murmured. "Okay."

"I just can't talk about it now," he said, shoulders slumping, moving toward the door.

She caught his hand as he went by and pulled him back a step. He looked at her, eyes tired. "It's not us, Sam," she whispered, "is it? Just tell me that much. We haven't—" Her mouth pressed into a line.

Silence.

"No, honey," he said, brushing her cheek with the back of his hand. "It's nothing like that." He paused, tilting her head up. "Trust me," he said.

She nodded and Sam left the room.

PART II

18

THE MEMORIAL SERVICE

It took almost a month, but Rosanne managed to pull things together to hold a memorial service for Frank.

After trying for a week to track down the scattered remains of Frank's family, she had given up and had his body cremated. The undertaker was still holding his ashes, waiting for instructions. Instructions Rosanne was not sure of. She was still waiting to hear from Arlington Cemetery in Washington, D.C.

"Cardiac arrest," was what it said on the death certificate and that was the line Rosanne used. And it was true. During the frantic efforts of the emergency-room team to keep Frank alive, to drain the deadly dosage of heroin and cocaine in his body, his heart had stopped. They had tried everything, for almost an hour and a half, but Frank slipped away.

Four times before Rosanne had been in that emergency room, willing her husband back to life. Four times before the tubes they had put inside her husband had sucked the toxins out of him in time. Four times before the death rattle in his chest had been driven out. And this last time, after Dr. Karrel pronounced her husband dead, Rosanne had kept on sitting there, waiting for Frank to come out of it. But he didn't and Dr. Karrel kept saying, "Mrs. DiSantos, Mrs. DiSantos," and then in one awful moment it registered—Frank was really dead this time.

It was the undertaker who had suggested she talk to the pastors of Riverside Church about a memorial service. Rosanne did so, cautiously. The church of her own childhood faith was out of the question. In the beginning of her troubles with Frank she had gone to that church, seeking guidance, seeking help. What she had got was harsh judgments and a declaration of God's wrath against a life of sin. ("No," Rosanne had said, pleading her cause, "he's a veteran who got addicted to drugs while fighting a war for his country.") Rosanne refused to lie about Frank to a church. If prayers were to be offered in his name, they had to be offered by those who believed in a more merciful God.

She told a pastor of Riverside Church the truth about Frank, about their religious history, about their nonattendance at any church for years. The pastor did not seem surprised, or ruffled by what Rosanne said. He merely nodded, smiled gently at times, and made sounds of understanding. When Rosanne had finished, he told her that God's love worked through people, and they would be happy to do whatever they could to help Rosanne through her time of grief. He only hoped this would help reassure Rosanne that God indeed loved her and Jason, that He was always there for them, and that Frank was one of His children too, at peace now in His eternal embrace.

A memorial service for Frank DiSantos would be held in the chapel of Riverside Church.

Rosanne could not bring herself to write notes to people, so she had a simple announcement printed that said Frank had passed away and there would be a memorial service. She sent one to the Cochrans, to Amanda, to Howard, to the Wyatts, and finally, after agonizing awhile, to Mrs. Goldblum. Then she sent one to every person in her address book—one that hadn't been updated for years—and hoped the announcements would find their way to all who cared.

She traveled to Brooklyn only once in those weeks, to see her son, to try to explain to him that his daddy had died. What it meant. It nearly broke her heart to look into those trusting five-year-old eyes (Frank's eyes) and say that Daddy had gone to heaven to live with God. After, Rosanne took Jason out to buy him a navy-blue suit and made arrangements with his foster parents about the day of the memorial service.

Jason's temporary guardians, Ruth and Gary Rubinowitz, were at first very sympathetic, very supportive to Rosanne. But then, when Rosanne said she was planning to take Jason back at the end of July, their attitude decidedly shifted. Rosanne said she had to work out new living arrangements, a new apartment—and of course they would see Jason whenever they wanted. . . . It wasn't anything the Rubinowitzes said, but when they nodded and said they understood, a look was exchanged between them that sent a chill into Rosanne's heart. But of course they would be sad, Rosanne thought, and she left their home trying to dispel her anxiety.

Rosanne laboriously wrote out the details of Frank's life for the junior minister, Reverend Harris, who volunteered his services. She hunted through the photographs she had, found one photograph of Frank that she loved (just after his release from the army—how handsome, how healthy, how happy he looked then!) and had it blown up into a 1-1/2 × 2-foot photograph for the service. The minister arranged for an organist and Rosanne went along with his suggestions for music.

She went to Macy's and, with Mrs. C very much on her mind, bought a black dress, shoes, stockings, and purse. And, with Mrs. G very much on her mind, she also bought a black hat and gloves.

Rosanne ignored all but the long-distance phone messages that were collecting at the Krandell Arms front desk. A stack of letters and notes had also accumulated, but all except those postmarked from outside of the city remained unread, unopened. One night, late, someone knocked on her door and called out to her—it was Amanda, Rosanne recognized—but Rosanne had just lain in her bed, shivering, and had not answered.

Not yet. Soon. But not now.

Rosanne had tried to track down by phone Frank's best buddies from Vietnam. The first, Freddie, had sounded drunk on the phone (at eleven in the morning) and so Rosanne had not pressed an invitation to the service. But then she located Ron, Frank's second best buddy, in Ithaca, New York, and his response to the news had comforted Rosanne. He had been upset— his voice broke when he asked what had happened—and he said of course he would be at the service, and yes, he would feel honored to say something about Frank. Rosanne's efforts failed to turn up any other army buddies.

Two days before the service, on Wednesday, Frank's older brother surfaced in Chicago. Rosanne's announcement had reached him; it had been forwarded from his address of ten years ago in Nashville. He also said he would come to the service, and sure, he would say something about Frank— but no, he was sorry, he had no idea where his other brother was.

The memorial service was on Friday, July 4, and it was a brilliantly sunny

day. It had never registered with Rosanne that it was a holiday—much less
the day of the Liberty celebration. When she left the Krandell Arms that
morning for the church, she was confused and a bit frightened to see hundreds of people streaming down 94th Street to Riverside Park. Cars were
parked everywhere; groups with hampers and straw hats and blankets and
radios and chairs and binoculars roamed; apartment windows all along West
End Avenue were flung open, parties going on inside.

"Operation Sail," one man told her, looking at her as if she were crazy.
"The boats—the tall ships—they're sailing up the Hudson at noon." (Here
everyone was jumping about in Bermuda shorts and this tiny woman was
dressed in black, from head to toe.) "Lady," he added with some urgency,
"the Statue of Liberty's a hundred years old today—where are you from,
anyway?"

Rosanne was thoroughly shaken by the time she reached the chapel on
122nd Street. Convinced now that no one would come, no one would come
to say good-bye to Frank, she cursed herself for not reading the mail. At
least she would have been prepared.

Reverend Harris met her in the lobby and took her inside the chapel.
Chairs were still being set up, but Rosanne was awestruck at how beautiful
the sanctuary was. Over one hundred years old, its walls were works of art
unto themselves, and the stained glass windows were magnificent. The minister guided Rosanne down the aisle to the altar and then stood there, hands
folded, waiting for her reaction.

Candles were lit all across the altar, casting a warm, comforting glow
around a large gold cross. In the center of the altar, held by an intricately
carved mahogany easel, was the photograph of Frank. It was surrounded by
vases and baskets of flowers. "You've done too much—" Rosanne started,
swallowing.

"They were sent by your friends," the minister said gently, taking her
hand. He took her to meet the organist, a parishioner, a middle-aged man
who murmured how sorry he was.

The Rubinowitzes arrived with Jason and the minister led Rosanne and
her son through a door on the altar into a small study. Rosanne sat down in
a leather chair while the minister showed Jason a model of the church. The
organ music began and Jason looked to his mother. She patted her lap and
he came over to climb into it. Rosanne put her arms around him and absently kissed the top of his head.

In a few minutes Reverend Harris slid open a panel and looked out into the chapel. He turned to Rosanne and smiled. "Many of your friends have come," he said, stepping back and making a gesture for her to come and see.

Rosanne went to the panel.

Joey, Frank's brother, was sitting in the second row with a woman Rosanne presumed to be his wife, and a young girl, perhaps twelve years old, who was clearly his daughter. Joey looked good; the years had treated him well.

Across the row, on the other side, were a man and a fair-haired woman. It was Ron—balding—the same face that grinned in the photographs taken over one wild weekend leave in Saigon so many years ago.

There were the Rubinowitzes, looking around at the other people.

Amanda was seated behind Joey, looking serene and lovely in her Tuesday-tea black dress and pearls. Joey leaned over to say something to his wife and Rosanne nearly gasped when she saw who was sitting next to Amanda. It was Howie. He was holding Amanda's hand, whispering something to her, and then Rosanne could have sworn she saw him kiss her ear.

Rosanne stepped back from the panel for a moment to consider this. For the first time in weeks, a faint smile crossed her face. She looked back outside.

Mrs. C was coming down the center aisle. Alone. Rosanne knew Henry was away; she figured Mr. C was taking a quick pull somewhere. Mrs. C was beautiful in the pale gray dress she wore but seemed—well, kind of fragile or something. She took a seat, looked up at the altar briefly and then lowered her head in prayer.

And, oh, boy, there was the gang from the Krandell Arms, skulking along the back and then sitting down in the back. Buzzy, Creature, Ernie, Lenny and—oh, no—Sissy, tottering about and looking like hell.

Ceily and James were sitting toward the front. James was coloring in a book in his mother's lap. Ceily looked great.

The Wyatts were coming down the aisle now, with Harriet leading the way in a black suit; Samantha, clinging to her mother's hand, wearing a blue dress; Althea was in a flaming red number (must have had a fight over that one); and Sam, in a navy-blue suit, was straightening his tie, looking around at the chapel.

Maxie from the newspaper stand, and his wife, were there.

Dr. Karrel from St. Luke's was there.

Could that be . . . It was. Nicole, one of Rosanne's sisters, about forty pounds heavier and with an overweight man Rosanne did not know. Who the teenage boy and girl sitting next to them were was anyone's guess, since Nicole was only twenty-three—no, twenty-four now.

Zigs and Carson swaggered in and sat down toward the front.

No Mrs. G.

The minister said it was time to begin. Rosanne looked down at her dress, pulled on her gloves, and beckoned Jason to her. She fussed with his hair, straightened his little tie, and bent to kiss him. She took his hand and stood at the door.

"Ready?" the minister whispered.

Rosanne nodded and he opened the door. Without looking at the congregation, she walked into the chapel, sat down in the front row, and helped Jason up into the seat beside her. He behaved like an angel.

The organ music stopped and Reverend Harris' robes flowed across the altar to the pulpit. He welcomed everyone and opened with a short prayer. He told them why they were gathered together today and offered his condolences and his comfort. "Frank Salvatore DiSantos . . ."

His name sounded strange to Rosanne, as if she had never met him.

The minister gave a short eulogy, describing Frank as a man of great courage and of gentle humor, a man who had done his best in a difficult world. A son, a brother, a brave soldier, a husband, a father . . . After he led the congregation in another prayer, he invited people to come up to the altar and share their memories of Frank.

Rosanne turned to look at Joey, but it was too late. Sissy, in blue jeans and a knit shirt that had seen better days, came lurching down the aisle. Rosanne turned back around and closed her eyes. Sissy stomped up the stairs of the altar, went up to the photograph, and cried, "Frank!"

"Mommy—ouch," Jason said, and Rosanne relaxed her grip on his hand.

Sissy was just standing there, zonked out of her mind, staring off to the heavens. The minister carefully took her arm and guided her down from the altar.

Joey tripped on the chair in front of him but did much better on the way to the altar. He stood by Frank's picture and cleared his throat several times. His face grew more and more red.

"I'm Frank's older brother Joe," he said. He cleared his throat again and spoke, louder. "Of all of us, Frank was the smartest kid in the family. But he was also the dumbest when it came to—courage. We used to go down and play on the old freight train tracks. And like the fools we were, we used to stand on the rails, waiting for trains to come. And one would come and we'd stand there as long as we could. And then Louie would run away, and then

Mickey would jump off and then *I'd* start running—but there would be Frank, standin' there like Superman, trying to stare down the train. And then at the last second, the very last second, he'd jump off the track and the train would come roaring through."

Pause.

"And I was seven years older than that squirt!"

People chuckled, softly.

"He was a good kid. I'm glad he was my brother." Pause. "I'm glad he's left a son behind." He looked at the photograph, tapped the corner of it and said, "He was the best-looking kid, too." Softly, "Wasn't he?"

Joey came down from the altar, ringing his collar with his finger. As he passed Rosanne, she smiled and nodded her head.

Ron rose from his chair. He was impressive. Tall, good-looking, neat, obviously successful at something, he strode up to the altar with a manly gait and faced the congregation without a shred of nervousness.

"My name's Ron and I served in Vietnam under Sergeant Frank DiSantos." There was a slight murmur.

Rosanne smiled.

"We were in the infantry and, for those of you who don't know what that means, it meant we fought in places where more soldiers died than survived." Pause. "I'd like to share good memories about that time, but, to be honest, I don't have any. I saw my friends be killed—my brother was tortured to death in a prison camp—and half of my platoon was slaughtered on April 4, 1972, and if it hadn't been for Frank DiSantos, I wouldn't be standing here today. I would have come home in a body bag.

"We were ambushed on maneuvers. We had just come out of the jungle and were crossing a field and—" He snapped his fingers. "Our point man's head blew off and then most of us were down. It happened that fast. The VC had two M-79's on us—two of our own grenade launchers—and I took a hit in the chest and leg and was just lying there in this damn field, not able to move, with no place to hide even if I could."

A pause. A smile. "And then all of a sudden I'm being pulled away by the back of my shirt. It was Frank, out there in the middle of this shooting gallery, on his stomach. Out there to get me." Pause. "And he did. He dragged me out of the field, stashed me, and then went back out and got two more guys before one of our gunships came and took out the VC."

"A medevac chopper picked us up and I was in the hospital for three months. While I was there I found out Frank had been hit, too, that day—he had been carrying a piece of shrapnel in his thigh the whole time."

Rosanne knew exactly what the scar had looked like, exactly what it had felt like under the touch of her hand.

Ron paused to wipe his forehead with the handkerchief from the breast pocket of his suit. "He saved my life. He saved a lot of men's lives." He looked at Rosanne and Jason in the front row. "His son should grow up knowing that his dad was a hero."

The chapel echoed sounds of throat clearing and muffled coughs.

Ceily walked up to the altar. "I'm Ceil, a neighbor of the DiSantoses. I just wanted to say that once when I was short on cash Frank bought me and James enough groceries for a week. He never let me pay 'im back, either. Frank was like that. You know, anything he had, he'd give some to whoever needed it. He was a hell"—she winked at the minister—"heck of a guy and did the best impersonation of Buddy Holly I ever saw." Chuckles. She looked at the photograph. "I'm going to miss him a lot. It just won't be the same without him."

Rosanne reached out to touch Ceily's hand as she went by.

A minute passed in silence and Rosanne thought the service would come to a close. But then she heard high heels on the marble floor and she saw Mrs. C slowly walking down the aisle. She stepped up onto the altar and turned around, holding pieces of paper and glasses in front of her with both hands. She smiled slightly and said, "My name is Catherine Cochran and I am a friend of the DiSantos family." Her voice rang loud, clear, cleanly through the chapel. "There are three people who were unable to be here today, and each asked that a few words be read in their absence."

She slipped on her reading glasses. The papers in her hands shook. "The first is from my husband Michael, who is out of town. He says, 'I never had the honor of meeting Frank DiSantos, but I have known his wife Rosanne for years. And from knowing her, I know he matched her in compassion, strength, humor and love.' "

Rosanne wiped at a tear and pulled Jason onto her lap.

"The next is from my son Henry. He wished to say, 'I liked Mr. DiSantos a lot. He was friendly and always very funny. He once helped me write a report for school about the Vietnam conflict. He knew all about the battles and the troops and he told me exactly what I should write about. I got an A. I also learned what the word "bravery" means.' Cassy recited the next two lines while looking at Rosanne. " 'I hope I grow up to be as brave as he was. I know his son Jason will be.'

"And the last one," Cassy said, unfolding a letter, "is from one of our neighbors, Mrs. Emma Goldblum, who is recovering from a minor illness.

She says, 'In the fifty-four years I have lived on Riverside Drive, I have never known a finer family than that of the DiSantoses. The passing of Mr. DiSantos is of great sadness to us all. But the friends of the DiSantoses are comforted by the legacy he left behind—his beautiful, loving wife Rosanne and his blessed little boy, Jason. In them, the memory of Mr. DiSantos will be kept alive, nourished by love, and made everlasting in our hearts."

Rosanne lowered her head on top of Jason's, her tears flowing freely.

Cassy took off her glasses. She was fighting back tears, but her voice did not betray her. "I only wish to say that I too will always love Mr. DiSantos —for it was through him that his family came to be such an important part of mine. A place, I pray, they will always remain. Thank you."

Rosanne was now openly sobbing. Cassy stepped down from the altar and slid into the chair next to her. She took Jason onto her own lap and put a protective arm around Rosanne.

The service was closed with the Lord's Prayer.

19

THE RECEPTION

Rosanne stood there, dazed, holding Jason's hand. People came up and hugged her, told her how sorry they were, how beautiful the service was . . .

Sam had to explain twice about the buffet before Rosanne could understand what he was talking about. He extracted a card from his pocket and held it up.

WYATT
182 RIVERSIDE DRIVE
APARTMENT 10A
NEW YORK, NEW YORK 10024

"Everyone is coming back to the house," he said again. "Harriet and the girls have been cooking for a week. They've gone ahead and are waiting for us."

"Who?" Rosanne said, trying to clear the fog in her head.

"All of us," Sam said gently. He hiked up his pants and squatted to address Jason. "Hello there, young man."

Jason turned his face into his mother's dress.

"I bet I know someone who's hungry . . . someone who could go for a piece of fried chicken . . . or maybe some ice cream. . . ."

One eye appeared over the fabric.

Sam glanced at his watch. "What do you say, Jason? You want to come to our house and watch the tall ships come up the river? Hmmm? What do you say?"

Jason rubbed his eye, smiling.

"Then it's settled," Sam declared, rising. He took Rosanne's arm. "The station wagon's just around the corner, in front of the church," he said, leading her out of the chapel to the street. Rosanne shielded her eyes against the blaze of sunlight; Sam kept a hand on her. "The kids are all set up to watch the ships," he said, "so you can have a little time with your husband's friends."

In the front of Riverside Church, on the Drive, the threesome walked along one of the highest rises of the valley. The Hudson was gorgeous, bespeckled with small boats, but then—there in the center—through the trees, they could make out a majestic clipper ship, sails billowing, gracing its way up the river.

Without asking permission, Sam swept Jason up into the air and held him up over his head. "Can you see, Jason?"

After Jason got over his startle (and decided not to cry), his hand shot out to point. "Mommy, look!"

Sam laughed and settled Jason on his shoulders.

Driving down to the Wyatts', after every turn Sam made, he placed his hand on Rosanne's forearm—as if he thought she might make a break for it. He talked to Jason the whole while, telling him about the boats he would see. And about what flavors of ice cream they had.

Rosanne edged a bit closer toward the window, resigned to the fact that Mr. W had her trapped.

Rosanne saw it all but felt very little. Mrs. W hugged her for a long time at the door. Jason shot off to the living-room windows where Althea and Samantha were in charge of Operation Sail (six chairs, six pairs of binoculars and a standing telescope). Creature was sitting by himself in an easy chair, drinking a bottle of beer, watching the kids. The Rubinowitzes were on the couch, balancing plates of food. Ron and his wife came out from the kitchen with Joey; they all hugged Rosanne and she clung a second or two longer to Ron, thanking him for all he had said. Joey's wife was introduced. Amanda and Howie arrived with a case of soda and a carton of fruit juices. Nicole grabbed Rosanne from behind and wailed and then Mrs. C arrived carrying foil-covered trays and someone put a cup of coffee in Rosanne's hand and Jason begged her to come and look and Mr. W whispered was she all right and Rosanne said she didn't know. People held her hand, rubbed her back, and kissed her. "Hello. Yes. Thank you for coming. Thanks. Yes. He's over there. Thank you. I better get the door. No? Thank you. It was. I was glad you could come. It has been a long time. Thank you. Fine. I think so."

"Sam," Cassy said, crossing the kitchen.

He was in his shirt sleeves, carving a ham. "Cassy," he said, glancing up from his work. "I'm glad you came."

"I could hardly refuse after your note." She moved in a little closer to the counter. She raised her hand slightly to say something, saw that it was shaking, and reached down to hold onto the edge of the counter. "I don't know what to say—except to thank you for your understanding. Your kindness."

"My kindness?" he said, looking over at her. "I attacked him." He thought about this a moment, resting the knife on top of the ham.

"I'd like to apologize to Samantha," Cassy murmured.

"No," Sam said, shaking his head, "that's not necessary. We talked with her and she understands." He resumed carving. "An alcoholic can be the most terrifying creature in the world—until, that is, you realize he is an alcoholic and then all the insanity makes perfect sense."

At the word "alcoholic," Cassy visibly recoiled.

It did not escape Sam's notice. He put the knife and fork down, sighed, and wiped his hands with a dish towel. "Cassy," he said, lowering his voice, "I'm an alcoholic."

Cassy didn't look as though she was going to last long.

"I haven't had a drink in eleven years, but I'm still an alcoholic. A recovering alcoholic."

Cassy was staring down at the ham. "How did you stop?"

Sam laughed to himself. "Well, it's kind of a long story, but the upshot is that after Harriet left me"—Cassy looked up at that—"after my girlfriends left me, after my boss threatened to fire me, after my doctor told me my liver was in trouble, my blood pressure was through the roof . . . Oh, hell," he laughed, tossing the dish towel on the stove, "I don't know. I just finally woke up one afternoon, sick and tired of being sick and tired. And lonely. And messed up." He shrugged. "The next thing I knew my boss was signing me into a rehab."

"But how—" Cassy began, but Harriet came zooping in with a platter.

Harriet looked at the two. "Don't let me interrupt—I just need a refill," she said, transferring ham onto the platter.

"Harriet and I thought maybe you might want to stay for a little while after everyone leaves—and talk a bit."

"You'll feel better, I think," Harriet said. She finished with the ham and turned to Cassy, offering a sympathetic smile. "I know it's difficult, Cassy, to talk about it, but you have to believe me when I say there's nothing that's happened in your household that hasn't happened in ours. Sam and I . . ." She gazed at her husband, eyes distant. "We"—she sighed, smiling, swinging her eyes back to Cassy—"we've been through it all."

"And are alive to tell about it," Sam added.

Harriet patted Cassy's arm, said, "Please stay," and left the kitchen.

Sam moved over to pick up a scrap of ham from the carving board and pop it into his mouth.

"I just don't know what to do," Cassy whispered, holding a hand to her temple. She brought it down to cover her mouth. She coughed. She kept her hand pressed against her mouth for a moment longer and then dropped it. "Michael's already lost his job." She paused and then reluctantly looked up at Sam. "And he's gone. I don't know where he is."

Sam sat her down in a chair and poured her a tall glass of seltzer, chock full of ice. He watched her drink some and then sat down beside her. "Has he ever left before?"

Cassy shook her head. "Never." She drank some more seltzer. "It's been a week."

"Okay," Sam said carefully. "Look, Cassy, I know how upset you are, how scared you must be. But frankly—and I know this will sound strange—right now I'm more concerned about you than I am about Cochran."

Cassy put the glass down in front of her and held it with both hands.

"You know," Sam said, crossing his arms and resting them on the table, "Cochran's been drinkin' for years and, if he's the kind of drinker I think he is, he's just holed up somewhere, drinking as much as he damn well pleases, hoping he's scaring the hell out of you—which he is."

This apparently made some kind of sense to her, for Cassy's expression eased slightly.

"Cassy." Sam's voice was firm but gentle. "Stop and think a minute. What do you really think he's doing? Do you really think he's lying in a ditch somewhere? You've called all the hospitals, I bet"—Cassy nodded, yes

—"and somewhere, somewhere you must know that he's playing some kind of game with you. The question is, do you really want to play it anymore?"

She took a sip from her glass.

"What would happen," Sam continued, "if—instead of running yourself into the ground with worry and 'what ifs'—you decided to spend this time taking care of yourself, getting some rest, recharging your batteries, so that when something *does* happen, when there *is* something you can do, you'll be ready to do it?"

Cassy sighed. "Michael did call my son—Henry—two days ago. At camp."

Sam smiled. "So he is alive."

A faint smile. "Yes."

Sam bit his lip, watching her for a moment. "Look, Cassy, I think what we should do right now is take a little vacation from all of this. Just for an hour or two. If you want, we can write it down. 'Three o'clock—resume agonizing over Michael.' "

Cassy laughed, sort of.

"Why don't we go and join the kids and watch the ships for a while? Maybe even laugh—just once," he hastened to add, offering a smile of encouragement. "Maybe we can look out and see how beautiful the river is, and the sky, and the trees, and the sun—and my daughters, of course, who take after their father."

Sam got up.

In a minute, Cassy got up too.

"We have something to tell you," Amanda said to Rosanne, pulling her down beside her on the Wyatts' bed. Howard closed the bedroom door.

"I know all about it," Rosanne said.

Amanda and Howard exchanged looks.

"Well, geez," Rosanne said, "Howie's only sittin' there pawin' ya in church for Pete's sake. Any"—she leaned forward to accentuate her point to Amanda—"*knave* could figure it out."

Howard blushed scarlet and Amanda made a high-pitched sound in her throat. "Oh, my," Amanda finally said, turning away to smile.

It took a few minutes, but Howard and Amanda got unflustered enough to tell Rosanne their news: the police had caught the burglars who had broken into the Stewarts'. Window washers. They caught them up the Drive and found Howard's "stupid Cross pens—wouldn't you know, that's what

I'd get back—" in their possession. They had come down from the roof on a scaffold and slipped in through the bedroom window.

Howard ended his story by saying that he was sorry, for everything. He felt if it hadn't been for—

"No," Rosanne said, cutting him off. She patted his arm. "No, Howie," she murmured, tears rising. "He had—Frank was in trouble before the robbery." She rubbed her eye and dropped her hand. "I can't blame anyone, else I'd have to blame myself." Pause. "It was going to happen anyway," she finished.

After a moment Rosanne looked to Amanda. "I wish you'd tell Mrs. G, though. About the burglars." She remembered something. "And what's this about her being sick?"

"She broke her hip," Amanda said.

"Aw, no," Rosanne said, holding her hand to her brow.

"But she's fine," Amanda hastily added. "They performed a hip replacement operation and she will be better than ever. But she must stay on in the hospital to recuperate." She gave Rosanne's hand a squeeze. "Rosanne, she is just fine. Really. Actually, she's having a rather grand time of it up at St. Luke's." Pause. "And she'd like very much to see you."

Rosanne got up from the bed and went to the window. Leaning on the windowsill, she said, "She fired me, ya know."

Amanda frowned and looked at Howard. He shook his head, shrugging. Amanda got up and went over to her. "When?"

"Right after the robbery. I figured you told her and—"

"Oh, no, Rosanne," Amanda said, reaching for her hand. "No, no—I never told her anything about it." She paused, thinking. "Oh, dear," she sighed, "I believe I understand it now. Rosanne—" She made Rosanne face her. "Mrs. Goldblum didn't want anyone to know of her—" Pause. Tentative, "Her husband's pension was discontinued, you see."

Rosanne frowned. "You mean she was broke?"

"Well, yes."

"Ohhh," Rosanne, said, nodding, looking back out at the river. "Ohhh," she said again. "Oh, man," she then said, pulling away from Amanda, "poor Mrs. G. I thought—and geez, there I was yellin' at her." She shook her head, moving toward the door. "I'm gonna go see her tonight." She opened the door. "St. Luke's?"

"Yes," Amanda said.

Rosanne nodded.

Howard stood up. "Rosanne, I, uh—"

Rosanne waved a hand at him. "I won't tell nobody, Howie, if that's what's worryin' ya." She threw her head in Amanda's direction. "About Sleepin' Beauty, I mean."

"No," he said, rubbing his jaw, "that's not it. I just wanted to say—not that you'd want to—but, anyway—I'd sure like it if you'd come back on Mondays again."

"Ha!" Rosanne said, falling back against the door. "With a bazooka, I will!"

"Well, I didn't think so—" Howard began.

Rosanne shook her head, looking across the room to Amanda. "What is it with this guy?" she said, jerking a thumb in his direction. She looked back at Howard. "Listen, Howie, I'll let ya in on a little secret. After the prince woke up Sleepin' Beauty, he didn't go back to the gingerbread house to live with the witch."

"Rosanne—" Howard sighed, sliding a hand into his pocket.

"Rosanne, nothin'," Rosanne said, closing the door behind her.

Silence.

Amanda walked over to Howard and took his hand. He looked at her, his expression sad. "She's right, you know," he said.

Amanda dropped her eyes. "No," she murmured, "she's not."

Ron had just finished explaining that he was a division sales manager for Kop-Tech. "You're making my life difficult, you know," he said to Sam, facing him on the couch, "with that ZT 5000 you're bringing out."

"That's Dad's," Althea volunteered, watching the river through binoculars. "Jason," she said, "look at the one coming up now."

Cassy, sitting in a chair, lowered her binoculars to look at the magazine in her lap. "I think it's the one from Spain—the *Juan Sebastián de Elcano.* It says it's named after the commander of the only ship that returned from Magellan's expedition."

"Buenos días," Samantha said, dancing about.

"I can't see!" Jason cried.

"Here, sweetie," Rosanne said, kneeling behind him. "Let me point you in the right direction."

"Three hundred fifty-one feet," Cassy was reading. "Mast, one hundred sixty. Crew, three hundred forty-three."

Ron was looking at Sam. "You're the guy behind the ZT?"

Sam was tracing the inside of his cheek with his tongue. "Well, I had something to do with it."

"He's getting a huge raise for it," Althea said, bringing her binoculars down. "Aren't you, Dad?"

Sam shrugged.

"Much as I hate to admit it," Ron said, "it's a great machine. Caught us by surprise, too. Not to sound arrogant, but we frankly never considered Electronika much of a threat."

"Well," Sam said, "the photoelectronics division has had its troubles. We were sort of in a do-or-die place with it. And it seemed, if it was ever going to find its legs, the ZT was the way to go. But we'll wait and see."

"I see it!" Jason yelped.

"What's next, Mrs. Cochran?" Althea asked.

"I'm not sure," Cassy said, flicking pages, squinting at the pictures of the sailboats. *"Capitán Miranda* from Uruguay, I think."

"Jason, sweetie, you're gonna strangle yourself with the strap."

"I saw the test machine you put in the library at Ithaca College," Ron said. He lofted his eyebrows at Sam. "What's your service contract like?"

Sam laughed. "Why, has it broken down?"

"Not yet, not that I know of," Ron said. "When I was there, they were turning out full-size copies of the New York *Times* from microfiche." He shook his head at the memory. "To tell you the truth, Sam," he said, dropping his voice, "I nearly choked when I saw it."

Sam smiled briefly and sipped his ginger ale.

"Wait a minute," Cassy said, looking up from the magazine. "Are you talking about that machine that takes those huge rolls of paper? Cuts it any size?"

"From a postage stamp to a city newspaper," Sam said.

"What's it called?"

"The ZT 5000."

"Yes," Cassy declared, "right, Electronika. We're getting one installed in the news department, in research." She frowned slightly, trying to remember. "They're linking it to our computers. . . . The data base, retrieval and tie-line systems? Does that sound right?"

Sam said it sounded in the vicinity of being right.

"All I know," Cassy said, taking a brief look through her binoculars, "is that it's supposed to save us time and money." She smiled at Ron. "That's what I do for a living—sit around and sign anything that promises to save us time and money."

"She runs a television station," Sam explained.

"Really?" Ron took a second look at her. "That's some job."

Cassy raised her binoculars. "Not really. Not when your heart is still in news." Pause. "I used to be in news." She tapped Samantha on the shoulder. "Look at that green raft down there."

"Mrs. C's on TV all the time," Rosanne said, tucking her legs underneath her on the carpet.

"Really?" Ron's attention to Cassy was ever increasing.

"Editorials," Cassy said. "Can you see it, Samantha?"

"No," she said.

"Come here, sweetheart. Okay, look down there. Can you see? There's a clown on the raft. See?"

"I wanna see the clown!" Jason said.

Rosanne got back up on her knees to help him.

"Cassy," Sam said, "do you ever get involved with the news department anymore?"

"I . . . see . . . it . . ." Samantha taunted Jason.

"Mommy!"

Cassy steered Samantha a step back and rose from her chair. She walked over and stood by the coffee table in front of Sam and Ron. "I try to, every once in a while. If a story really interests me, or sometimes when I think a certain kind of story should be done. Sid—our news producer—is nice to me that way and," smiling, "patronizes me on occasion." She leaned over to pick up an hors d'oeuvre. "We worked together years ago in Chicago."

Sam was jiggling his glass, making the ice clink. "You do much in the way of investigative reporting?"

Cassy nodded, swallowing. "Sure," she said. "In fact, since we don't have the resources the affiliates do in town, covering the daily news, it's really the area where we can hold our own. And sometimes," she added, touching at her hair, "we do more than hold our own." Her expression was brightening by the second.

"On an investigative story, usually—hopefully—you're the only ones working on it and it gives you a little more time and control. Unless, of course, whatever it is we're uncovering blows up before we have a chance to figure out what it is we're uncovering." She laughed. "Which was the case last year on the Traffic Violations Bureau bribes." An aside to Ron. "In case you haven't heard, our city government appears to be the official career counseling and job placement center for organized crime."

"Upstate we hear your city government *is* organized crime," Ron laughed.

"But we've had our share of successes, too," Cassy continued, putting a hand on her hip. "The milk mafia story was ours; the cocaine trafficking at the Stock Exchange; the seventy-six-thousand-dollar pothole—"

"Mrs. Cochran," Samantha called from the window.

"Yes, Samantha."

"Come look at this boat—please."

Cassy smiled at Sam and Ron. "Duty calls," she said.

Sam nodded, jiggling his glass again, thinking. "Hey, Cassy," he said a moment later.

She turned.

"Do you do any international stories?"

"If they tie in to the tri-state area," she said, bending to follow Samantha's line of sight.

20

AFTER THE RECEPTION
PART I: HOWARD

Sad as the occasion had been, Howard felt like skipping home from the Wyatts'.

Amanda, Amanda, Amanda, he sang in his mind.

He would go home, take a shower, change his clothes, have dinner with Amanda, and afterward make love to her. *Grand Hotel* was on television at eight o'clock. They would bring the TV into the bedroom (Howard didn't think he knew anyone who still had a black and white TV, much less one kept in a closet) and prop themselves up on pillows on the floor in front of it. They would eat popcorn and watch the movie and Howard would gradually forget the movie and lose himself in Amanda and . . .

He would spend one entire, glorious night with her.

Melissa was at the house on Fishers Island with her father. *(Hooray for Daddy!)* She had made one last attempt that morning to force Howard into going, but he was firm about his intention to attend the memorial service.

"Oh, Howard," Melissa had said, "even you have to admit it's stretching a point to stay home on the Fourth of July for the cleaning woman."

But Howard countered with the argument that it was the least they could do, seeing as they were the ones who had falsely accused the man of robbing them—

"If he didn't rob us, he robbed someone else," Melissa had said.

Howard had lost his temper then and had really given it to Melissa, telling her that if she wanted to be heartless that was fine with him, but she shouldn't expect him to be. And *then,* scaring the hell out of him, Melissa had expressed reconsideration, saying that perhaps Howard was right, maybe she should go to the service too, and that they could drive out to the house afterward. So, maneuvering around, Howard had started agreeing with her, telling her how much it would mean to Rosanne for Melissa to apologize and Melissa, getting more and more indignant, had finally exploded—"I will not apologize for what was perfectly rational behavior!" And then he yelled she *had* to, and Melissa said to hell with that, she was leaving for the house right this minute.

After she left, Howard had gleefully danced around the apartment.

Amanda, Amanda, Amanda.

She was, quite simply, the most completely wonderful woman in the world.

Oh yes she was.

It was too good to be true, he often thought. It seemed impossible that, after all these years, a woman like Amanda could suddenly appear in his life, offering to fulfill the dreams that until now had caused him such despair. There was their sex life, certainly; if it had been unreal that first night, then it had become positively fantastical. Why didn't their passion ebb? Why was their desire so constant, yet so different, every time? How could it be possible that someone so well mannered, so obviously "well bred" (he winced, thinking that he was using a Melissa term), could be so endlessly, wildly passionate? And her books, her writing . . . Amanda was as much in love with the world of print as Howard was—if not more so. She was terribly excited to hear anything about Howard's work; and vice versa, Howard was terribly excited to hear about hers. Her library, her writing room, the whole place—it was as if Amanda's apartment had been created from the knowledge of his fantasies. Amanda herself seemed like a creation of his romantic imagination.

But . . .

There were traces of a dark cloud in their world. There were things Amanda had said that nagged at him, made him feel jealous.

She said something about Howard's Jockey shorts making her feel as though she were molesting a minor. When Howard asked why, she laughed and said men didn't usually wear them to the office. (How the heck did she know?)

And then, after he asked her, Amanda had told him she had an IUD. When he expressed concern about it—hadn't Amanda read about how dangerous they were? no, Amanda had not—she said she had only had it for two years, after someone else had worried about her being on the pill.

Who was the someone who had worried about her being on the pill?

Someone who did not wear Jockey shorts to the office, obviously.

But who? She would never say anything. In fact, she talked as though there had not been anyone in her life since Christopher. But, obviously, there must have been—why else would she have been on the pill, got an IUD?

Could that someone still be around?

No. He couldn't be.

But could he?

She had made herself accessible to Howard any time of the day or night for the past month, except—except . . .

On Mondays. She absolutely forbade him to come on Monday and made no excuse why. It was very strange, the look that came into her eyes, when he pressed the issue. Almost . . . frightened. But then, as always, she would quickly, easily distract him.

It was impossible not to be distracted by Amanda. It could very well be that he was involved with the most utterly beguiling creature to walk the face of the earth. And it was not merely sexual—though, again, God knew, Amanda's body seemed to have been created for pleasure that way, for herself as well as for him. No, there was something about the way her mind worked that fascinated Howard. There were slides in it; she could slip through time, through eras, real and imagined, and reappear in the now with the blink of the eye, and with a joy that was contagious.

"I didn't say she was mad," Patricia MacMannis had said to him. Howard had passed on the pages of Catherine to her, explaining that he wasn't exactly unbiased about this submission. Patricia had read the material and raved about it, and had, quite eagerly, met Amanda with the intent of signing her up as her own. "I said, if I hadn't gotten the chance to talk with her, to see what a lovely person she is, how clearly gifted she is," Patricia said, "I might have thought she was. For heaven's sake, Howard, she appeared at the door dressed like Isadora Duncan."

Yes, it was true. After their first night together, Amanda had started wearing, well, costumes. Not all the time, just some of the time. And when she did, she seemed so completely happy and free. Howard had seen Isadora several times by now, and he had also seen Emily Dickinson, Scarlett O'Hara, Anna Karenina, Emma Bovary and—he was pretty sure—Colette (using Missy the cat as a prop). Amanda herself was always there, however, during these escapades, uttering small asides to Howard about who it was she was portraying, and, if it was not "playing" right, she would simply take whatever it was she was wearing off.

Yes, off. To reveal the body he had become obsessed with. But was it her body? Partly. It felt as though it were the means of reaching her, finding her, way, way back inside. To that beautiful, beautiful, vulnerable woman; to that vulnerable woman who looked into his eyes and into his heart, reading it, and then drawing it out and into her own, surrounding it, sealing it with hers in the warm glow of trust.

Of love.

Spirits back on high, mind envisioning Amanda in his arms, Howard asked after the elevator man's family, asked about his state of health, and when they reached his floor, Howard made a point of telling him how very well he did his job and how much he appreciated it. (He gave him a ten-dollar bill as he got off.)

He let himself into the apartment and quickly opened the panel of the alarm system. (If within thirty seconds Howard failed to punch in the proper security code, a silent alarm would go off, the security people would call the police and, Howard presumed, Daddy Collins would have him arrested for breaking in.)

The light of the alarm was not on. He hit the side of the box, wondering if the light had burned out already. No . . . Howard shrugged and closed the panel, tossed his keys onto the table and walked on, humming.

He turned into the living room, thinking about underwear.

"Surely the service couldn't have been this long."

Howard nearly jumped out of his skin.

Melissa came in from the kitchen, carrying a large vase of freshly cut flowers. "Hi," she said, walking over to put them down on top of the television set. She was still in the green blouse, pink skirt and green sandals of the morning. It was amazing how tan she was; Howard, in comparison, was rather anemic-looking.

"Hi," Howard managed to say. "There was a reception at the Wyatts'."

Satisfied with the way the flowers looked, Melissa turned and smiled. "You look so handsome in a suit," she said, coming over to him. "I wish you'd wear them more often." She picked a piece of lint off one lapel, rested her hands on his chest, and looked at him. "I came back," she said.

"Yes, so I see." He hesitated, kissed her on the cheek, and backed away to the kitchen. "Why did you change your mind?"

She followed him. "Oh, I started thinking about our argument this morning, and that we've never been apart on the Fourth of July."

"Do you want something to drink? I'm having a beer."

"No, thanks. Anyway, I was thinking that the Lynleys wouldn't be much fun without you—"

Howard reached into the refrigerator. "Without me? Melissa, I hate dances, you know that—"

"I would miss you, Howard . . ."

He opened the bottle of beer and took a deep drink.

"I changed my mind," she said, "I'd like a glass of wine."

Howard nodded and went about complying with her request.

"And Daddy loves the Lynleys," she continued, sitting down at the table and crossing her legs. "Make it a spritzer, Howard."

"Spritzer," Howard repeated.

"So I knew he would have a good time. I told him we'd drive out in the morning." Pause. "You haven't been out since Memorial Day." She was watching Howard, intently. "Howard." He glanced over. "I thought about watching the fireworks with you in the bedroom tonight. That's why I turned the car around and came back."

Eight years and tonight's the night Melissa decides she wants sex.

"So how was the service?" she asked, crossing her legs and bending to run a hand down one.

"Oh, nice. Very nice, actually. The chapel up there's really something. There were a lot of flowers, they played a lot of Bach, and the minister gave a good eulogy. And then people got up to say a few words." He finished stirring the spritzer—with a Collins swizzle stick—handed it to Melissa, and retreated back to the counter and his beer.

"Thank you," she said.

"He was a sergeant in the army, in Nam, apparently," Howard continued. "This guy got up and told a story about how Frank had saved his life. It was very moving."

"I'm sure," Melissa said coolly, sipping.

"Cassy Cochran got up and read some notes from people."

"Not from her husband, I bet," she said, snickering.

Howard pushed at his glasses. Something was up. Melissa's eyes rarely twinkled for nothing. "She did read a note from him."

"Sure," Melissa said, "just like you read a note from me."

"What are you talking about?"

She crinkled her nose. "Did you put any wine in this?"

"Yes, I put wine in it." Pause. "Do you want me to pour some more in?"

"No, don't bother," she said. "Anyway, I can assure you, Michael Cochran did not write any note. He's long gone."

"What?"

"He ran out on her. A week after the block party." Pause. "Gone, Howard. Scram. Vamoose. Bye-bye. Whatever you want to call it, he's gone." Under her breath, "Not that I blame him."

Howard shifted his weight and stuck a hand into his pants pocket.

"I ran into Didi Rogers at the Korean market," Melissa said, "and she told me the whole story. And it's quite a story." She threw her head back and laughed. It was her Daddy Collins laugh, a guttural affair that was reserved for the privacy of their home. Otherwise, Melissa expressed amusement in the same dry, passive tee-hee-hee manner of her friends.

"Howard—he threw a TV at her. And missed! It went crashing out the window and down into the street. Malcolm Rogers was nearly killed."

"What?"

"It's true, Howard! Malcolm was getting out of a cab and he heard this crash and looked up and saw this TV flying down out of the sky. It landed not even six feet away from him. And everyone started screaming and looking out their windows." Melissa was getting very excited. "So then, when everybody's outside wondering what the hell happened, Cassy came out and said the TV had accidentally fallen off a shelf or something. Well, no one believed that, but then—get this—"

"Well, it could have—" Howard began.

"No, wait, Howard, listen! So they're standing there listening to her and who should come out but Michael, drunk as a skunk, screaming at the top of his lungs that he's going to kill her."

"Oh, God—"

"Wait! You haven't even heard yet—" Melissa slapped her hand down on the table. "So Michael tries to get her, and Malcolm and the taxi driver—a *taxi* driver—gets in between them and Michael's screaming and yelling and so finally Malcolm said if Michael didn't calm down he was going to call the police. So Michael finally calmed down and apologized, and they let go of

him. So then Michael walks over to Cassy, as calm as could be, and
WHAM!"

Howard cringed.

"He slugged her! Decked her! Right there in front of all those people!"
Melissa could barely get her breath, she was laughing so hard.

"Oh, God," Howard said.

"And then he ran off. And no one's seen him since," she added, near
choking, holding her hand against her chest.

Howard shook his head and loosened his tie. He sighed.

"Didi says—"

"Screw Didi," Howard muttered. "I feel badly for Cassy."

"Oh, Howard," Melissa said, taking a gulp of her drink. "Anyone who'd
marry a creep like that deserves it. God, he's so ill bred."

Howard yanked his tie off and started to walk out of the kitchen.

"And she's always on her high horse. Well, it only goes to show—"

Howard whipped around. "Will you shut up?"

Melissa's eyes widened. "Don't speak to me like that."

Howard looked at her, raised his arm to lean against the doorway and
said, "Why the hell not? You deserve to be spoken to like that." He straightened up, took a step forward, gesturing with the hand holding his tie. "You
sit there and make a joke out of someone else's misfortune." Pause. "That's
sick, Melissa. Sick."

Melissa was staring at him as though he were crazy.

"Other people's troubles are not for your entertainment, Melissa. Things
happen to people. Cassy Cochran's a nice person and her son is a nice kid
and the man those two nice people love is sick. There's nothing funny about
it—there's nothing amusing about it—there is nothing to laugh at." He
threw his tie down on the table and walked out.

Melissa leaped out of her chair to follow him. Howard went to his study,
slammed the door, and locked it. "That's your answer to everything, isn't it,
Howard?" she screamed from the other side of the door. "Just run away and
hide!"

He unlocked the door, flung it open, and sent it crashing against the wall.
Melissa stumbled back and Howard grabbed her arm. "You better hope to
God that I hide, because if I don't I'm very likely going to deck *you.*"

"How dare you talk to me like that!" she screamed, pulling away from
him.

Howard lunged for her arm and yanked her around to face him. "I have
had it with you, Melissa. I won't put up with this anymore."

"With what?"

"With *what?*" He pushed her back against the wall and held her there. "With bullying Rosanne, with telling the police to arrest her husband, with you not even having the decency to apologize to her, with you laughing at the Cochrans—what do you mean, with *what?*"

Melissa slapped his face.

"And me," Howard said, glaring at her, the side of his face turning scarlet. "Me, Melissa. I am not going to take your shit anymore." He released her.

"That's not the issue," Melissa hissed, grabbing his arm. "The real issue is how long can I put up with a little boy who can't earn a decent living, who can't handle any responsibility whatsoever—and whose long list of friends is comprised of the cleaning woman and some old bitch who's in heat—"

Howard shoved Melissa out of his way and went into the bedroom.

"Now what are you going to do, lock yourself in the bathroom?" Melissa demanded, following him.

"I'm getting the hell out of here, that's for sure!" He banged open his closet and flung a duffel bag out onto the bed.

"Oh, don't tell me," Melissa said, sarcasm supreme, "now the little boy's threatening to run away from home."

"You got it." Howard yanked out a bureau drawer and started throwing pairs of underwear on the bed. "I have had it with you, Melissa. Had it!" He slammed the drawer shut and moved on to the next—socks.

"She's too old for you, Howard."

Howard stopped what he was doing. He turned around.

"Christ, she's probably in menopause," Melissa said, plunking herself down on the other side of the bed, folding her arms.

Howard pushed the drawer closed behind him. "You really are sick," he said, moving back to his closet.

"Oh, I'm the one who's sick. And you're perfect, Howard." She made a humming noise. "Well, she'll find out soon enough."

Howard starting pulling shirts out of the closet.

"But she is too old for you, Howard, no matter how attractive you think she is. She's going to have skin like a rattlesnake."

He stared at her. "You're really nuts, Melissa. Absolutely nuts."

"I saw you two at the block party. The only thing you didn't do is hump her there in the street." She kicked off her shoes and brought her legs up onto the bed. "I *saw* you, Howard, the way you two were mooning over each other that morning."

"Christ, Melissa!" Howard hurled a hanger across the room.

"Thirty-three years old and you still can't pack," she said, adjusting the pillows behind her. Silence. Then, looking at her nails, "So that's why her husband's a drunk. She sleeps around. I always thought so."

Howard slapped his head with his hands. "You are unbelievable! Look, Melissa, get this through your head. I don't know Cassy Cochran from Moses. I don't even know her. Do you understand me? I don't have anything to do with her. As far as I know, Cassy Cochran is exactly what she says she is—married, a mother, and on TV. Period. So cut it out," he finished, slicing his hand through the air.

She watched him shove his clothes into the bag. "Well, there's got to be somebody," Melissa mused. "You couldn't go to the corner without someone holding your hand."

Howard continued packing.

"But if it's the cleaning woman, don't tell me," Melissa added. "I don't think I could take that."

Howard got his toilet kit down from the top of his closet and headed for the bathroom.

"But who could it be?" Melissa asked herself.

Silence.

"Didi," Howard said from the bathroom.

Melissa laughed.

Silence.

"Howard?"

After a moment, "What?"

"A skyrocket just went off across the river."

Silence.

"Don't forget your dental floss."

There was the sound of the medicine cabinet being closed.

"And you should take your blue striped shirt. The gray one too. They're in your bureau. The shirts you packed don't match your pants."

Howard appeared at the bathroom door.

Melissa was smiling. "Come here," she said quietly. "Come on, Howard, take pity on your poor wife." She patted the bed. "Just for a minute and then you can run away from home. Promise."

Sighing, Howard went over by the bed. Melissa reached for his hand and pulled him down to sit. She slipped her hands around his waist and leaned forward to rest her head against his chest. "I don't want to fight with you. I love you," she said.

They sat like that for a minute.

"Can't you run away tomorrow?" Melissa whispered, her hand sliding down to massage him between his legs.

Howard closed his eyes.

"We could have such a nice time tonight," she said.

"I'm sorry, Melissa," Howard said, slowly detaching himself from her. He got up from the bed and walked back around to his bag. "I'm too upset. I need time to cool off. To think. Just for tonight. I'll check into a hotel or something."

"A hotel?" Melissa's eyes went wide. "That's crazy, Howard, you can go into the study."

Howard sighed, picking up a pair of Jockey shorts and stuffing them into his jacket pocket. "I'll be back in the morning." He unzipped the toilet kit and took out his toothbrush.

Melissa was on her feet. "You're checking into a hotel because Cassy Cochran's husband left her. This is insane, Howard."

"I'll be back in the morning," he repeated, throwing the duffel bag onto the floor of his closet.

"We've had much worse fights than this—"

Howard walked around the bed and past Melissa to the hallway. "I need to think, Melissa."

"But shouldn't you call to see if they even have a room? It's the holiday," she said, following him. "Where will you be? Where can I call you?"

Howard was through the living room and breaking down the home stretch. "I'll call you."

"Howard!" Melissa cried, voice ringing down the hall. "I don't understand this! After eight years, suddenly you have to go to a hotel to think?"

Opening the front door, "I'm upset."

"You're *always* upset!"

Howard rang for the elevator. Melissa stamped her foot in the doorway. "I demand you tell me what's going on!"

He sighed, looked over at her and said, "I'll be back in the morning, when I'm calmer. And then we can talk. But not now. I can't take this."

"Can't take *what?*"

"Melissa—don't scream. Just calm down and I'll see you in the morning. I'll call you—"

The elevator arrived.

"When?"

The doors closed and, on the strength of Howard's earlier interest, the elevator man started talking about his family.

"When?" echoed in Howard's ears. Outside of bed, he didn't think he had ever heard Melissa so close to tears.

"Howard!" he heard for real, coming from the floors above.

His hands were shaking; all of him was a-jitter. He wasn't sure of what he had said. He wasn't sure how he had actually got himself out of the apartment. But he had. He had. Because here he was, leaving.

21

AFTER THE RECEPTION
PART II: AMANDA

He was the most affectionate man she had ever met.

Amanda smiled when she thought about it, about how Howard clung to her, any part of her, at any time he could reach her. In his arms; holding her hand; brushing a strand of her hair with his lips; even his eyes clung to the sight of her from across the room.

He made her happy. And she did not think it had to do with sex. She *wanted* to think it was sex; she had tried, those first two weeks, to rationalize what felt like her insane behavior—to welcome him, wait for him, at any time of the day or night.

Except Mondays.

That had been the first clue that "something" was happening between them, her horror at the thought of Howard coming to her on that day. Like the others. As if Howard was merely a replacement for Roger.

Roger. The thought of him made Amanda feel ill. The thought of him, of herself with him, utterly repulsed her. After that first night with Howard something had closed in Amanda, like a tomb door, shutting away what appeared to be—looking back—a process of death. Christopher was behind that door too.

But how could she fully accept what was happening to her? That everything that Howard said to her, every way that Howard touched her, seemed so new, different, wondrous? Had not men said to her many of the same things he said to her? Yes, they had. So why, coming from him, could she believe in them, remember them, mull over and savor them for hours after he had gone?

Dr. Vanderkeaton said that Howard spoke the same language as Amanda. And what language was that? Amanda wanted to know. A broken heart finding regeneration, the good doctor had said. She had said a great deal more than that, but Amanda had not listened very closely, so taken was she with that casually offered insight.

A broken heart finding regeneration.

When Amanda was six, Tinker, watching her daughter dancing about on the lawn, had called her up to the veranda. Sitting Amanda in her lap, Tinker had rocked them both, and opened a book to show Amanda a photograph of Isadora Duncan caught in a supreme moment of grace. "My dearest angel," Tinker had whispered, stopping the chair, kissing Amanda's little hand and bringing it down to the photograph, "this is what you are like. This is your spirit and this is your laughter."

After a week with Howard, the Isadora of her childhood and young life had reappeared. Amanda did not think she was Isadora Duncan; but Amanda did feel like that photograph—spirit soaring, energy radiating, a burst of wonder at this splendid thing called life. She had laughed wildly, searching through her closets for Isadora's things, and Howard had lain there, naked, across her bed on his stomach, watching as she dressed. And then he had laughed and laughed as she danced around the tower windows, and then Amanda had collapsed, out of breath, into his arms.

Howard somehow seemed to know all there was to know about Amanda. It wasn't just that he had recognized Isadora without aid from her, it was that he knew that Isadora was a part of Amanda, deep inside of her, that was being pried loose by him and was struggling to come out. Out in the open. And it was not just Isadora. There were others, many others.

"You are going to have a wonderful day writing," he had said, coming into the writing room, tying his tie before dashing to work. She had already been at her desk, writing longhand, with Missy the cat in her lap. He had leaned over and kissed her on the forehead. "Colette had that same ability to make reality the kingdom of her imagination." Amanda had smiled at him but had inwardly trembled at how effortlessly he could read her. (Colette? How had he known? *How?* Because of the cat?)

"Be careful," Dr. Vanderkeaton had said, "be careful, Amanda." But Amanda wasn't being careful and was growing more fearful by the minute. Of Howard. Of this dear, handsome, brilliant man. Of this deeply affectionate, caring man. The man who had made her get her IUD removed because he worried about her health; the man who had collapsed in laughter over Amanda's frustration with her new diaphragm; the man with whom she had not felt embarrassed when he said he would help her put it in.

The man who had said, very businesslike over the phone to her, "Amanda, it is very important that you talk openly and honestly to Patricia MacMannis about your work. Your relationship with her, as writer and editor, doesn't have, nor will it ever have, anything to do with me. It's time for you to move ahead."

Be careful, be careful . . .

Sigh.

Amanda had never let a married man within four feet of her. She had never been able to get the image of Marco (and that towel) out of her head. It was with abject horror that she had viewed anyone who sought to interfere with a committed relationship. Long ago she had ceased to blame Marco for starting the problems in her marriage; and no longer did she blame Christopher or herself. But what she had *not* understood, not one iota, was how anyone could make love to someone they *knew* would be sleeping side by side with their mate that very night.

And here she was having an affair with a married man. And did she care about Melissa? Frankly, no, she didn't. Granted, the picture she had of her was through Howard's eyes, no doubt distorted slightly in an effort to relieve his guilt (guilt, yes, he did have guilt, now that the initial thrill of derring do was wearing off), but there were too many telltale signs not to know that Melissa was a woman whose heart did not work very well.

"Be careful, Amanda, be careful. . . ."

"Of what?" Amanda had asked. "Because he's married? He was young, very young—almost as young as I was when I married Christopher."

Silence.

"What? *What?*"

A sigh from Dr. Vanderkeaton. "He sounds like a wonderful man who genuinely cares for you, about you. But I would be careful, Amanda. I would be careful to find out what his reasons were for having endured the terms of such a marriage for so long. Particularly when he is as bright and attractive as you say."

"Because, because—he had to see it through."

"Why?"

"Because . . ."

"You say that he never loved her. You say that they have had virtually no sex life, ever. You say that he was reluctant to have a child with her. You say that he has always felt like a prop of hers. You say that he has been terribly lonely for years and years—"

"Yes?"

"And you say they lead a rather fast lifestyle—"

Amanda had vaulted out of her chair, pacing the room. "I will finish it for you," she said, angry. "You are going to tell me that the only reason why Howard is having an affair with me is because I'm wealthy."

No. Dr. Vanderkeaton had not been going to say that. Why had Amanda?

"Of course it has crossed my mind!" she had ranted. "How could it not after Christopher? Eight years and then me? *Me*?" She had burst into tears. "I understand now—you wonder how he could care for me. Why someone who is out there in the world, going places, doing things—how someone like that could care for such a hopeless wretch as myself!"

"No, no, no . . ."

"She goes to his business dinners and parties," Amanda cried, "she travels with him, they have friends—what do I have to offer him, if not money? Sex. Of course, sex! It's all that any of them have ever wanted from me, money or sex, why should he be different?"

Poor Dr. Vanderkeaton had had her hands full. Why she wanted Amanda to be careful—she explained, patting Amanda's back as she sobbed in her lap—was that Amanda was moving too fast, without thinking about the consequences, without thinking of how little she had to fall back on if it should end badly. Amanda had made wonderful progress, the doctor thought, but she wished Amanda could ease forward in her life and not plunge blindly into what might turn out to be an abyss.

It did not help matters that Howard seemed eager to plunge into the abyss holding her hand, Amanda knew. And yet, that was what was happening. Today, at the Wyatts', she had experienced the oddest sensation after Rosanne left them in the bedroom. She had felt as though Howard were drowning in the issue of Melissa and was turning to her to save him; Amanda had felt as though she were drowning in the emotions that Howard evoked from her, and she was turning to him to save her. Together, sitting there, she had thought about the odds of two drowning people saving each other.

Who was she to help him? What did she know about marriage? What did she know about book publishing? And yet he talked and talked and talked to her about his problems, his torture in regard to both, as if he expected her to know what to do. What on earth could she tell him? She whose marriage had been a farce, she who had never had a job in her life, she who had all but dropped out of the world altogether?

For a little while, she had thought she could learn. But then she had embarked on her little adventure of trying to sort out Mrs. Goldblum's affairs and had quickly felt as hopeless as ever.

("IIa-ha-ha," laughed the man at the Social Security office. "You are very funny, Miss Miller."

("I'm glad you are amused, Mr. Onai, but I can hardly pretend my wish in coming here was to entertain you. I really don't know what Social Security is, or what it means, beyond the obvious—that it's something that allegedly reassures society.")

No, about all Amanda could manage—barely manage at that—was to hire people to cope with life's difficulties for her. Even then, as with Mrs. Goldblum's affairs, Amanda had had to turn to her mother for help simply to enlist the aid of Mr. Osborne—Mr. Osborne, her very own estate attorney!

Howard replace Melissa with *her?* Melissa, brilliant and powerful and capable Melissa? Melissa, the woman who had been supporting Howard for eight years in his every endeavor? Strong, dominating, opinionated Melissa?

How could Howard ever be happy with Amanda?

Howard let himself into Amanda's apartment and found her sitting in the living room, drinking a glass of orange juice at the tea table by the window. Her face fell when she noticed his suit. "What has happened?" she asked him, holding the edge of the table.

His answer was to stride over, sweep Amanda up in his arms and bury his face in her neck. "Oh, God, how I've wanted you all day," he whispered.

She allowed herself to be held.

He kissed her, deeply, kissed her neck and ear, and kissed her on the mouth again. He held her tighter.

"What's wrong?" she persisted.

He released her. "Oh, hell," he muttered, turning away. A step later he turned back toward her, running a hand over his jaw. "Melissa turned around and came *back.* She was there waiting for me. We got into a fight and she accused me of wanting to sleep with Cassy Cochran and I told her I'd had it. And I left. And here I am." He grinned suddenly, pulled the Jockey shorts out of his pocket and twirled them around in the air on his finger. "Guess who's got the whole night off?"

"You don't have to go home?"

"Nope. I'm spending the night, 'cooling off.' I could kill for a beer. You want one?" he asked, heading for the kitchen.

"No, thank you," Amanda said, slowly sitting down in the chair.

"I told her I'd check into a hotel," he called from the kitchen. Laughter. "Knowing Melissa, she'll be over at the Cochrans' looking for me."

Amanda was looking out the window. There were amateur firework displays taking place along the New Jersey banks of the river.

"I'll have to call her in an hour or so. Or maybe I should call now and get it over with."

"Why do you have to call her?"

"Said I would," he answered, coming back in. He kissed Amanda's forehead, stroked her hair twice, and then sat down across the table from her. "The only drawback's tomorrow morning. God knows what that's going to be like," he said, taking his glasses off to rub his eyes. He sighed, putting the glasses back in place. "Hey, what's with you? Why so glum?"

"Howard," she said, voice tentative.

"What?" He leaned across the table to take her hand.

Amanda exhaled slowly, thinking. "Howard, maybe it would be better if you did check into a hotel."

He frowned. "Why?"

Amanda sat back in her chair, withdrawing her hand. "I—" She looked at him. "I think you do have some thinking to do about Melissa. Maybe sleeping here with me is not the best preparation for your talk."

"Our talk? Oh, hell, Amanda, Melissa and I don't talk. We yell at each other." Pause. "I want to be here with you. We planned on it, remember?"

Amanda rose from her chair and stood at the window, tracing the sash with her fingers. "Howard. Don't you think the time has arrived that you need to talk to Melissa? About your marriage, about your relationship?"

A long sigh. "There's not much to talk about."

"But don't you owe it to her?" She looked out at the horizon.

"I—" A long silence. Howard rose from his chair and came up behind Amanda, slipping his arms around her waist. He rested his head on her shoulder. "There is only one thing I have to say to Melissa and you're right, now is the time."

Amanda waited.

He gave her a squeeze, briefly kissing the side of her face. "I'm going to go tell her right now." He released Amanda and headed to leave.

Amanda whirled around. "What are you going to tell her?"

He turned, smiling, walking backward. "I'll tell you when I get back."

"Wait, Howard—"

"Let me get it over with, Amanda, and then I'll be back," he called from the hall.

"Howard!" Amanda tore out of the living room. "Howard, wait!"

He was waiting, hand on the front door.

Amanda hung back, struggling to say something. Finally, "What are you going to do?"

He smiled, pushing his glasses. "I'm leaving her," he said.

"Leaving her for where?"

The question hung in the air.

Howard released the doorknob and came toward her. "Amanda darling," he said, reaching for her.

Amanda pulled back from him.

He was surprised. Collecting himself, he said, "It's very simple, really. I love you, Amanda. I loved you the first day I talked to you. I can't pretend Melissa means anything to me now—anything but a reminder of how many years I've wasted."

Amanda folded her arms and looked to the floor.

"Darling, don't be frightened." When she failed to say anything, to look at him, he said, "I can't miss the chance of making a life with you."

"Don't say that, Howard," she said. Pause. "Having sex for a month is not grounds for making a life with someone."

He stepped over to her and wrapped his arms around her. She just stood there, arms still folded. "But I know you," he whispered, "you know I do. And I know that I love you like I've never loved anyone."

"Don't say that, Howard!" Amanda suddenly cried, pushing him away. "It only shows me how little you know about what you're doing!"

"I do know what I'm doing—for the first time in years."

"But you don't, Howard," Amanda said, backing down the hall. "You think you can swing from one vine to another, from Melissa to me. And, Howard, Howard—this vine, *me,* is not attached to anything. There is nothing to support you here. Nothing like what Melissa has given you."

He jerked his head to one side, jamming his hand into his pocket. "Melissa has given me nothing but pain since the day I met her," he said. His eyes came back around to her. "You just don't understand, do you? I love you, Amanda. And I want you, Amanda. It's as simple as that." He sighed. "And I think you want me too."

She was shaking her head, tears starting to fall. "Oh, Howard," she said, slumping into the wall. "Howard. I can't replace Melissa."

"I don't want you to replace Melissa."

"But you do," she said, covering her face. "You think that you can leave her and move in here with me and everything will be all right." She sniffed, wiping her cheek with the back of her hand. "I can't be the reason for you to leave her. You have to leave her because you no longer wish to be married to her."

"I haven't wanted to be married to her for *years!*" he shouted, slamming the wall with the side of his fist.

"Then why have you *stayed* married to her?" Amanda screamed, nearly doubled over.

Silence.

They stared at each other, breathing heavily.

"Christ, Amanda!" Howard exploded, slamming his hand against the wall again. "Why don't you just say it? Go ahead—say it! You don't love me —you don't think I'm good enough for you!"

"No, Howard," Amanda moaned, covering her face again.

He took several deep breaths, pulled himself up and said, "It's money— isn't it? You think I'm replacing Melissa's money with yours. Don't you?"

"No," Amanda said, shaking her head, hands still over her face. She lowered her hands. "It's not money, Howard. What's wrong with you and what's wrong with me is not money."

"What the hell is that supposed to mean? What's *wrong* with—"

"We're like children," she said, backing down the hall another step. "We live like children do, Howard. Both of us. Melissa—my money—it's all the same, Howard. Neither one of us knows what we're doing, and we're just wandering off like children, not thinking, not dealing, not facing any of our problems."

"Jesus, Amanda," he muttered, turning away. "Jesus Christ. Children. That's just terrific. You think I'm a child. That's just terrific." He pointed at her. "You, maybe, but not me, Amanda."

Silence.

He lowered his hand. She was holding herself, shivering, looking down to her feet. He sighed. "I didn't mean that." Pause. "But it makes me angry to hear you talk like that. You know I love you. You know we make each other happy. And I think I know that you love me."

She raised her eyes, slowly. After a long moment she said, "We've done fine in there," gesturing down the hall. Tears were falling from her eyes, but her voice was even, quiet. "But we've failed each other already. Can't you see that? I wanted you to say, 'I'm leaving Melissa, I will live by myself, and I will come back to you when I'm sure I want to get divorced.' And you wanted me to say, 'Move in with me and I will see you through the divorce.' "

Silence.

"Isn't that right? Isn't that what we were both hoping for? Two entirely different things?"

Silence.

"You know I'm right," she said, eyes dropping. "I want you to take care of me, and you want me to take care of you, and neither one of us can take care of ourselves." After a moment she turned away. "You'd better go now."

He fumbled to get the door open and then stood there, looking at her back. "We'll talk tomorrow," he said quietly.

"I cannot talk to you," she said.

"Damn it, Amanda," he muttered. He hesitated and then said, "You want me to just disappear, walk away, as if none of this happened? As if I'm not in love with you? Is that what you want?"

"I want you to leave me alone," she said, back to him still.

Silence.

His eyes narrowed and his jaw tightened. "What goes on around here on Mondays, anyway?" he finally said. "It has something to do with this, doesn't it?"

She whirled around, horror evident. "Oh, leave me alone!" she cried, stumbling against the wall and fleeing down the hall.

He stood at the door for a long time. And then, after taking his glasses off to wipe his eyes, he departed.

22

HOW LONELINESS WAS
AFFECTING CASSY COCHRAN

C assy was not having a fun summer.

It was just as well—she thought, sighing, pushing the WST revised budget forecasts away from her on the desk—that things were so hectic at the station. It kept her too busy to think. Much.

WST's fiscal year had begun on May 1. And now, in late July, after twenty-one years, their transmitter in Weehawken had decided to go on the fritz. At the moment, a thirty-thousand-dollar jerry-rigged job was keeping it going and somehow, somewhere, Cassy needed to find four hundred thousand dollars to really fix it. Soon.

Well, she could always organize another block party. One from here to, say, Philadelphia.

Cassy pushed her glasses on top of her head, closed her eyes and pressed the bridge of her nose.

She longed to call Henry. But she couldn't. He was rafting somewhere on the Colorado River. Besides, she had already called him so much that he had offered to come home.

"Dad called from Chicago."

"Did he?"

"Yeah. He didn't sound very good."

Dad didn't sound very good. Dad didn't feel very well. Dad wasn't in a great mood. All of these expressions meant the same thing: Dad was drunk.

"He hasn't called you yet, has he, Mom?"

Pause. "No, sweetheart, he hasn't."

"Well, I think he wants to find a job first. Then he'll call. I'm sure of it. He said he has a lot of interesting prospects."

Cassy wondered.

She had been amazed last week, when she opened Michael's American Express bill. Los Angeles, San Francisco, Houston, Washington, D.C.—his bills were outrageous.

"Did you separate your accounts?" Sam Wyatt had asked her.

"The credit cards, yes."

"What about your checking accounts, savings—"

"Not yet, Sam."

"Cassy, you've got to do it. Otherwise he might clean you both out."

Silence.

"Cassy?"

"Yes, Sam."

"Whatever you do, don't pay his bills. You've got to let him deal with the consequences of what he's doing."

Sam made the whole thing sound easy. Easy, right. After twenty years, just cut her husband off.

"Twenty-five thousand dollars is a lot of drinking money," Sam had said.

It was closer to thirty, what Michael had access to, but Cassy was not about to tell Sam this. In any event, at the rate Michael was going, it wouldn't matter if it were fifty. His American Express bill alone was over fourteen thousand dollars.

The telephone rang and Cassy reached over to pick it up.

"Hello?"

"Hello!"

"Alexandra, hi."

"Hi. I'm just about to go on the air, but I wanted to check in and see how you're doing."

Cassy smiled into the phone and sat back in her chair. "I'm on automatic pilot."

"But okay?"

"I am okay."

"I'll call you when I get home."

"Great. I'll watch."

"Terrific. I've got to run—"

Cassy hung up the phone.

Life was getting increasingly strange.

Cassy didn't know what she would do without Alexandra. Cassy had often heard about people having friends like Alexandra, but she herself had never come across one before. ("Well," Alexandra had said recently, "if you don't tell anyone what's going on in your life, and if you won't let anyone do anything for you, of course you're not going to feel as though you have many friends.") This friendship had not been Cassy's choice. It was Alexandra's mind-reading ability that had created it. She seemed to know exactly how Cassy was feeling, what she was thinking, and outmaneuvered Cassy in ways that taught her that she could lean on Alexandra without fear of repercussions.

Repercussions, yes.

The night Alexandra said she thought she was falling in love with her, Cassy had handled it with all of the tact and aplomb of the exhausted wreck she had been. She had said she was sorry to hear it, thanked Alexandra for all she had done, and left the apartment with the intention of never coming in contact with her again.

Cassy expected that kind of come-on from men but not from women—not Alexandra. Men almost always said they were in love with Cassy, a declaration that made Cassy want to yawn (unless, of course, it is true that a man's heart is located in his pants), and over the years she had become increasingly adept at handling these hastily offered vows. Classmates, professors, bosses, colleagues, neighbors—Cassy's beauty had been an open invitation for men to try their hand. Or so it seemed. Only a month ago a board member of Rogers, Dale & Company—WST's parent company—had whispered his declaration of love during the dinner for WST advertisers held at the St. Regis. He was sixty, handsome, married and the father of seven children. Three days later a twenty-four-year-old trainee named Henton Ruddenvale had been on the edge of his seat in Cassy's office, swearing that his future happiness lay in Cassy's hands—could she come to love him too?

(Actually, if the men stopped declaring love and started declaring what it was they really wanted, Cassy would pay more attention. The closest she had ever come to cheating on Michael was four years ago, when Morton Gillien, sitting next to her at a movie screening, had whispered in her ear,

"You're married, I'm married, but still, I'd love to fuck you silly tonight." The words "fuck" and "silly" used in the same sentence, in application to her, were intriguing enough on their own merits to warrant Cassy's interest. But she hadn't gone through with it. Morton Gillien, however, to this day commanded a kind of respect from Cassy that the Messrs. I-Love-You never would.)

This was not to say that Cassy had never been approached by women. On the contrary. But their overtures had always been polite, aloof, cautious invitations to get to know each other better—*they* never assumed Cassy would fling herself at them because they said, "I love you."

That night—the night Alexandra had said she thought she was falling in love with Cassy—Cassy had felt vaguely insulted by her. And, more than that, irritated that Alexandra had, in a way, betrayed her own sex with that kind of a come-on.

After a good night's sleep, however, Cassy had changed her mind and felt guilty. It hadn't really been a come-on, she didn't think; Alexandra had been too upset. And who wouldn't be? Of all the people in the whole wide world, anyone who thought she was falling in love with a despairing middle-aged wreck, the wife of her drunken ex-boss . . .

Well, good, bad or indifferent, Cassy had then felt the least she could do for Alexandra was to put her in the hands of a good psychiatrist who could teach her to distinguish between romantic love and infatuation born out of loneliness. Cassy had called Alexandra to make a lunch date, and then she had prepared a little speech.

Poor Alexandra. She had sat there, not touching her food, listening to Cassy go on and on in a manner befitting the Queen Mother. The speech: Alexandra was new in New York, and lonely. She had a huge job to do, a new job, and not even Michael was there anymore to help her, teach her. You see, what Alexandra felt for Cassy was perfectly normal—Cassy was someone Alexandra admired, Cassy knew things Alexandra needed to know and, physically, she reminded Alexandra of her friend Lisa. By transferring her feelings from Michael and Lisa, who were no longer there for her, to Cassy, of course Alexandra thought she was falling in love with her. Didn't Alexandra see that?

"No," Alexandra said, smiling slightly.

Cassy had cleared her throat, taken a sip of water, and said, "Look, Alexandra, I don't want to hurt you—"

"Cassy, let's not make such a big deal out of this, okay?"

Cassy had looked at her. Alexandra's face had been flushed slightly, but her gaze had been steady and she had seemed in fine control.

"I am lonely. I admit it. But," she sighed, smiling, "that night, I was exhausted, and so were you. I think maybe," she began, moving her spoon around with her finger, "I felt as though you and I could be a comfort to each other. As for the love part"—she looked up and smiled—"I do love you, I think, as anyone comes to love a new friend. So," she had concluded, shrugging, "I hope you'll accept my apology for the other night. At the time, my confusion was real, but now I know that my only wish is to be your friend."

So much for Alexandra being in love with Cassy.

Cassy had felt very let down after this luncheon. Without the little ongoing drama with Alexandra, she was left with nothing but the ongoing quiet horrors of her household to focus on—a place she really preferred not to dwell in. At least not twenty-four hours a day. Much as she hated to admit it, the few days before their lunch, with the Alexandra dilemma spinning around in her head, Cassy's day-to-day life with Michael had been bearable. It had actually been almost pleasant, sitting there in front of the TV—with Michael getting drunk beside her—pondering the question of whether bright, beautiful, young Alexandra Waring was really in love with her or not.

And, too, Cassy couldn't deny there had been a vindictive streak in the activity that had seemed to keep her rising anger at Michael in check—that Michael wanted but couldn't have Alexandra, and that Cassy didn't want but could have her, if she wanted.

Cassy packed up the budget reports in her briefcase and went back to the bedroom to undress and take a hot bath.

Alexandra's timing had been perfect. She had called Cassy the night after Michael hit her in the street. When Alexandra asked her how she was, after only a moment Cassy had broken down and cried, telling her bits and pieces of what had happened, about Michael not having come home . . .

Alexandra had been wonderful, saying all of the right things, suggesting all of the right things, reassuring Cassy on all levels.

Alexandra was wonderful. Period.

She had been calling Cassy every day since, asking Cassy how she was holding up, asking if there was anything she could do for her, asking what further news there was. She called at the station in the morning to check if Cassy had eaten anything; she called her at night to check if Cassy was alive. Cassy's reliance on her had grown quickly; only last week she had called Alexandra at three in the morning in the throes of a horrendous anxiety attack. Alexandra had chatted merrily as if it were twelve noon on Sunday.

Cassy wondered if it wasn't the safety of talking to her on the phone and never seeing Alexandra in person that allowed her to open up to her. Well, that wasn't exactly right. Cassy did see Alexandra every weeknight—twice if she wanted to—on television. It was rather like wearing Michael's mirrored sunglasses. She could see Alexandra but Alexandra could not see her. ("Your hair looks marvelous," Cassy said to her on Monday, after the eleven o'clock. "Are you going to someone new?")

Cassy was well aware that Alexandra was on a killing work schedule at WWKK, but she believed Alexandra when she declared that she would lose her mind if she didn't have *some* kind of life outside of the station. And right now Cassy provided the kind of distraction she needed. *(Distraction? Cassy had winced.)* And, too, Cassy knew full well that it was only a matter of time before Alexandra found someone in her life, and then Cassy would be—well, left behind. So she might as well take advantage of Alexandra's kindness while she was still around. . . .

Twenty-eight? Was that really how old Alexandra was?

After her bath, Cassy wrapped herself in Michael's terry-cloth robe. She held the sleeve over her nose and mouth and breathed in. A trace of English Leather. Lime. A trace of Michael.

Oh, Lord, how she missed him at night.

Forty-one years old and Cassy, until now, could have counted the number of nights she had spent alone on one hand.

A robe, an empty bed, an empty house, an empty heart. *No.* It would all work out. Henry would be home in no time—

Five weeks.

Five weeks more of this?

Cassy snuggled down into bed and turned on the new Sony. (The doorman had snickered unmercifully when Cassy had him bring it in from the cab. "Might be less dangerous if you just left it down here," he had said.)

WWKK's newscast was scarcely recognizable from the days of Michael's reign. A new coanchor had been brought in, Peter Bristol, a former Washington correspondent for Associated Press. Alexandra and Peter worked extremely well together, and it was a smooth, sophisticated yet gutsy broadcast, never shying from hard news and yet always working in some brief, warm, local human interest story.

There was talk now about combining the half-hour six and eleven o'clock newscasts into a full-hour show at nine, a change Alexandra was pushing for. Since WWKK was really reporting the news these days, it was virtually impossible to do anything out of the ordinary in thirty minutes. An hour would do the trick, and since management refused to increase the newsroom budget further, it would be a way to give Alexandra and Peter more time to work on feature stories themselves and, at the same time, keep the news-room financially solvent.

On this broadcast they had managed to squeeze in a two-and-a-half-min-ute feature by Alexandra on how Donald Trump was rebuilding the Woll-man ice skating rink in Central Park in record time (a projected four months), for record money. Prior to Trump, the city had spent seven *years* pouring millions into the reconstruction, and had only succeeded in provid-ing a princely living for workers while they were in Florida, where, they claimed, they had been diligently learning about building outdoor ice skat-ing rinks for all these years. (Cassy had burst out laughing.)

True to Alexandra's style, she ended the piece by praising Trump's efforts on behalf of New Yorkers, but also said it would be interesting to see if the public support gained by Trump through his good-will efforts might not be the ace he would need to obtain special concessions from City Hall in regard to some of his commercial endeavors. In particular, Alexandra advised her viewers to keep an eye on Trump's seventy-six-acre development site on Manhattan's West Side, and the response to it from City Hall.

After the newscast was over, Cassy flipped through *Newsweek, The New Yorker* and *The Nation.* At twelve twenty-seven, the phone rang.

"Right on time," Cassy said.

"I've got it down to a science now," Alexandra laughed.

"I loved the Wollman Rink story."

"Thanks." Sigh. "I just wish we had more time."

"You will. One day," Cassy said, putting the magazines on the night table.

"I hope so."

Cassy reached up and turned off the light.

"Cassy, are you going to the Handerville Awards dinner at the end of the month?"

"Probably," Cassy said, sinking down under the covers. "Sy Bolin's nom-inated for best independent documentary and we were executive producer, so . . ."

"I'm going."

"You are? What for?"

"For a story I did at KSCT."

Cassy sat up. "What?"

"As a reporter. On farm foreclosures."

"Alexandra!"

She laughed. "What?"

"What category?"

"Middle market, investigative reporting—"

"Alexandra!"

"What?"

Cassy fell back against the pillows. "You mean to tell me that you haven't always been here?" She laughed. "I keep forgetting—I didn't even know you in February, so when the nominations came out your name didn't mean anything to me."

"Yes," Alexandra murmured, "KSCT seems like a million years ago."

"Yes," Cassy echoed, taking one of Michael's pillows and pulling it close. "Well, then, if you're up for an award, I'll be sure to go."

Pause.

"So how are you feeling?" Alexandra asked her.

"Funny," Cassy sighed. "You know, it's so quiet here. I think that's what's so hard. How quiet it is." A laugh. "I got so lonely tonight I called one of Henry's friends and asked him to come over and make some noise. Skipper makes a lot of noise usually, but even he was leery of coming over to this tomb without Henry around." Another sigh.

"Did you eat dinner?"

"I had some tuna fish."

"That sounds exciting. Tuna fish. For heaven's sake, Cassy, no wonder you feel lonely—if I thought being by myself meant there was no one home worth cooking for, I'd be lonely too."

"Cooking for one, though—"

"I do it."

"Well," Cassy sighed, "your generation is different from mine."

"Oh, forgive me, for a second I forgot I was talking to Grandma Moses."

Cassy laughed. And then yawned. "My mother called today."

"And how is she?"

"Terrible." Cassy laughed again. "I mean she's fine, but she was terrible. She told me to divorce Michael—quick—before he gets home."

"She's not very fond of him, is she?"

"Fond of him? She despises him. According to her, you see, he has ruined my life *and* hers." Sigh. "She forgets, conveniently forgets, all that Michael has done for me over the years. Had it not been for him . . ."

"What?"

"Oh, I don't know," Cassy said, turning on her side and pulling the covers up over her shoulder. "I think I'd probably be living down the block from my mother, with four or five children, waiting for my husband to come home from Thompson Electronics." She laughed. "I'll be damned if that doesn't sound pretty good tonight."

"Really?"

"No, not really. But it sure would be nice if one flesh-and-blood human being lived here. I hate being alone, I always have. . . ."

Silence.

"I'm working on a feature about single mothers," Alexandra said. "I was shocked at the statistics—you city people sure don't stay married much, do you?"

"Many of us don't get married to begin with—"

"That too—but I was struck by how much it costs—how, say, five single mothers are paying for five separate apartments, with five separate children, and they all say it's nearly impossible to keep up, to—"

"Are you preparing me, Alexandra? Are you telling me I'm going to come out of this a single mother?"

"No, silly. I'm trying to tell you about my story."

Cassy rolled onto her back and looked up at the ceiling. It was windy outside; the air whistling in through the window frames was moving the shades, moving the light and shadows on the ceiling.

"I did an interview yesterday with two women who combined households—"

"Are they—"

"No." Pause. "Do you suppose people will think—"

"What would it matter?"

Alexandra chuckled. "It would put a slightly different slant on the story. . . . But you know, now that I think of it . . ."

"What?"

"I never did ask them."

"What, Alexandra? You were going to bring a camera in and ask them if they're lesbian lovers?"

"No."

"Alexandra, stick to your story. How many children do they have?"

"Three." Pause. "One said she moved in, not because of finances, but because of her need for companionship."

"Well," Cassy said, "she's right. Everybody needs companionship. You know, someone to eat with, someone to watch TV with, someone to say good night to." She yawned again. "You know, Alexandra, that's what you've been doing for me. I don't know what I'd do without talking to you."

"You'd talk to someone else."

"I doubt it." Cassy was getting very sleepy. "No, I'd probably just stay right here in bed until Michael came home." She puffed up the pillow. "Do you know I even miss him leaving the toilet seat up? You have no idea how horrible it is to find every toilet seat in the house down—'Everybody's gone, Cassy,' it says to me."

Pause.

"Cassy, are you going to go with Sam to that group?"

"Monday."

"I think that's great."

"Easy for you to say." Sigh. "I didn't mean it the way it sounded. It's just hard for me. I think I'd just rather go on pretending none of this is really happening. That Michael's on a trip for WWKK . . ."

Silence.

"Maybe you should try and get some sleep now," Alexandra said gently. "Do you think you can?"

Cassy nodded. "If I stop thinking about him. I'll think about—I'll think about—"

"Henry," Alexandra finished for her. "On the river. Laughing and having a wonderful time."

"I don't want him to have a good time," Cassy said, mocking herself. "I want him to want to come home—"

"Cassy "

"I know, I know. This is all temporary. 'It shall be revealed,' Sam keeps telling me. I don't know what that's supposed to mean, but it sounds good."

"It means you'll soon know what to do," Alexandra said.

"Yes." Sigh. "Alexandra?"

"Yes?"

"What if he doesn't come back?"

Silence.

"He will," Alexandra finally said. "He will."

"The thought of living in this tomb by myself—"

"Cassy, Cassy, it's all going to turn out all right."

Sigh. "Yes, but in the meantime—"

"In the meantime, invite some people over."

"Who?"

"Me, for starters."

"Would you want to come over?"

"Sure. We could watch a movie or something."

Cassy sat up in bed. "Wait a minute, Alexandra, before I get delirious at the thought of having another human being here, just when would you have the time?"

"Saturday. Sunday. Whenever, we'll figure it out."

Pause. "Really?"

"Sure. It would be fun."

"Fun?" Cassy fell back against the pillows. "Alexandra, you don't know what it's like around here. What I'm like—remember the Bride of Frankenstein? That's me, tottering around the halls of the haunted castle—"

"So I'll chain you to the radiator," Alexandra laughed. "We can still watch a movie."

After hanging up the phone, Cassy curled up on her side around Michael's pillow and thought about Alexandra. Would this be all right? To invite her here—alone? Was this a wise thing to do? Cassy knew what Alexandra had said, about being friends, but still . . . she couldn't help wondering sometimes.

She was being ridiculous. Alexandra was not a threat. She was not manipulative. Alexandra did not prey on people.

She wondered what she should cook for dinner. She wondered what movie they would watch. She wondered if Alexandra liked Cary Grant . . .

Cassy fell asleep.

23

IN WHICH MRS. GOLDBLUM
IS DETERMINED TO LEARN
ABOUT HER AFFAIRS

Three weeks after her hip replacement operation, Mrs. Goldblum informed Amanda that she was as right as rain and would appreciate it if Amanda refrained from hovering about as if she were going to die at any moment.

Amanda was not hovering out of fear, Amanda was hovering about a miracle, warming her heart and her spirit in the glow of Mrs. Goldblum's recovery.

The changes in Emma Goldblum were startling. After a few days of largely Häagen-Dazs coffee ice cream (whose sugar and caffeine, Nurse Sendowski explained to Amanda, had a therapeutic effect on older malnutrition cases), Mrs. Goldblum was on a strict diet of wholesome meals and snacks that were designed to build her up. Build her up? How about rebuilding her altogether? From the fragile, elderly old lady who had been admitted to St. Luke's, there was now a vital, energetic woman of seventy-seven.

Amanda had contacted Daniel Goldblum, Mrs. Goldblum's son, the day after she had been admitted. While Amanda had expected very little, she had not been quite prepared for Daniel's reaction to the news. "What the

hell can I do about it? Mother knows I've got too many obligations here as it
is. I can't go running around the country right now." Controlling her temper, Amanda had said the polite things to Daniel—for him not to worry,
that a phone call to his mother would do great things for her recovery (not
that he had called, the stinker, for four days)—but to herself and to Howard
(when he had still been around), Amanda had vowed to take a contract out
on his life if he did not behave better.

That first week, after an unsuccessful trip to the Social Security office,
Amanda had called her mother to ask her advice; Tinker had called the
family estate attorney, old Mr. Osborne, and within forty-eight hours Mr.
Osborne had arrived in New York. Mr. Osborne (now seventy-eight himself) reviewed what vague information Amanda could offer and then turned
her over to "a very fine attorney, right here in town," a Mr. Thatcher of
Wyndom, Tuttle & LeBlanc, who, according to Mr. Osborne, knew all about
these matters.

Mr. Thatcher sent a paralegal to St. Luke's to interview Mrs. Goldblum
about her personal history and that of Mr. Goldblum. Then Mr. Thatcher
dispatched Amanda to Mrs. Goldblum's apartment with a long list of docu-
ments he wished her to excavate. With Mrs. Goldblum hanging on the
phone, Amanda spent the better part of a day digging and sifting through
Mrs. Goldblum's secretary, closets and boxes under a bed in one of the
bedrooms. (When she came across Mrs. Goldblum's canceled checks, she
was enraged. One after another, year after year, "Daniel Goldblum," ten,
twenty, twenty-five, thirty thousand dollars!)

Two weeks later a night courier delivered to Amanda a pile of forms that,
once signed by Mrs. Goldblum, would not only begin her Social Security
payments but would entitle her to six months of retroactive payments. The
very next morning another package arrived, containing papers for Medicaid
that again, once signed, would cover a good portion of Mrs. Goldblum's
current hospital expenses and provide coverage for the future.

There was something else in that second package as well—a copy of a
letter from Harry N. Thatcher to Mr. Phillip S. Robin of Charger Industries, letting him know that he could look forward to meeting members of
Wyndom, Tuttle & LeBlanc in court one day soon, regarding Charger's
deplorable and damaging treatment of a certain elderly widow named
Emma Goldblum.

Well! Amanda practically flew up to St. Luke's that day. Plunking down
form after form on Mrs. Goldblum's hospital table, Amanda went on and

on about how Mrs. Goldblum's problems were over and how everything was getting straightened out and how all she had to do was—

"Amanda dear," Mrs. Goldblum interrupted, placing a hand on Amanda's arm.

"What?"

"Dear darling heart, I know you mean well, but you must get someone, *someone who knows what they're talking about,* to come here and explain to me what all of these forms mean."

Amanda paused and then jumped back into excited agitation. "Perhaps you misunderstood me. All you have to do is sign here, here, here—"

"I'm serious, Amanda," Mrs. Goldblum said. "I won't sign anything until someone explains to me why I'm suddenly entitled to all of this money."

"Because—"

Mrs. Goldblum pressed on. "Amanda, when it's your life being bandied about by strangers, you would want to make sure you understood exactly what you were signing too." She squeezed Amanda's hand. "That's how this whole dreadful affair began—by my not understanding my own affairs. And now I must."

Mr. Thatcher laughed when Amanda reported this development. "She's absolutely right," he said.

When Amanda asked him to come and see Mrs. Goldblum, Mr. Thatcher laughed again. "No, Ms. Miller, that's not the answer. I think I know what's worrying your friend. She needs to talk to someone from Social Security—someone who can assure her that this money is indeed coming from them and *not* from you."

Amanda called the Social Security office and they told her she would have to come down. She did. She stood in every wrong line, talked to every wrong person, and then finally, after about two hours, was directed to a bright young woman of twenty-three named Sally Goodwin. Sally's eyes lit up when Amanda told her the story about Mrs. Goldblum, and she said she would be delighted to go up and see her. When Amanda looked vaguely surprised, Sally leaned forward and said, "Just how often do you think we get to deliver *good* news in this office? Ms. Miller, I wouldn't miss it for the world. I'll come up one night after work."

Sally and Mrs. Goldblum got on like gangbusters. Sally went over the forms, line by line, explaining what everything meant. Sally pulled out charts from her briefcase; Sally showed Mrs. Goldblum how to use the calculator she had brought, and made her add the figures herself. ("That much money?" Mrs. Goldblum asked, rather overwhelmed. When Sally said yes, Mrs. Goldblum said, "Oh, laws! Now I'll have to learn about taxes!")

Three days later Sally was back, this time lugging a VCR and video tapes. Amanda sat there, smiling in amazement, as Sally hooked the VCR up to the TV and showed both Mrs. Goldblum and Nurse Sendowski how to use it. The four tapes she left with Mrs. Goldblum were from a public affairs program called "Social Security Is for You," an interview and call-in show that ran on cable television each week. The shows Sally had brought discussed issues that pertained to Mrs. Goldblum. She cued one tape up and Mrs. Goldblum was delighted with the hostess of the show ("I do so enjoy seeing young women dressed nicely").

Mrs. Goldblum signed all the papers, became officially registered with Social Security and Medicaid, and called her son Daniel to tell him of her good fortune.

When Amanda returned to the hospital the following afternoon, Nurse Sendowski called to her from the nurses' station, "Better bring a chair with you!" Amanda, not understanding, merely smiled and continued on. Turning into Mrs. Goldblum's room, she found herself blocked at the door.

Mrs. Goldblum, in the company of six other older women (three in chairs and three in wheelchairs), was watching "Social Security Is for You." Amanda waved to Mrs. Goldblum from the door; Mrs. Goldblum waved back and then placed her finger over her mouth, signaling Amanda not to interrupt. When the show was over the women—all in dressing gowns—politely clapped.

Zapping the VCR off with her remote control, Mrs. Goldblum said, "Does anyone have any questions?"

"Emma," a Mrs. Jackson, recovering from a kidney stone operation, said, "do I have to bring the forms to the Social Security office, or can I mail them?"

"I believe the hospital takes care of filing the forms. Amanda dear—"

Amanda was startled into attention. "Yes?"

"Would you be so kind as to ask Nurse Sendowski if she would, when she has a moment, stop in? Adelaide," she said to Mrs. Jackson, "Nurse Sendowski will be able to tell us."

The Grande Dame of St. Luke's Hospital was born that day. When patients weren't mingling in her room, Nurse Sendowski was wheeling Mrs. Goldblum around on visits. And, in a while, it wasn't just patients paying calls on Mrs. Goldblum but *families* of patients as well. And not to talk about Social Security—they were there to tell Mrs. Goldblum their life stories and problems.

When Sally returned to pick up the VCR she extended a rather marvelous invitation to Mrs. Goldblum. When she was back on her feet, would Mrs. Goldblum consider coming on "Social Security Is for You" as a guest? To use her story as a case study to instruct other people? Mrs. Goldblum beamed. Well, yes, Mrs. Goldblum would be very pleased to accept their gracious invitation. (Would Amanda—Mrs. Goldblum whispered—take her shopping before her television appearance?)

Mr. Thatcher himself arrived at St. Luke's one afternoon. Very patiently, very carefully, he explained that Charger Industries wished to settle Mrs. Goldblum's case out of court.

"My case?" Turning to Amanda, she asked, "Amanda dear, is this nice Mr. Thatcher my attorney?"

"Yes," Amanda said.

Mrs. Goldblum looked at Mr. Thatcher and patted her nose with a tissue. Lowering her hand, she said, "Mr. Thatcher, I will expect the accounting of your expenses to be directed to me, not to Amanda."

Mr. Thatcher and Amanda exchanged looks. "Actually—" he began.

"Actually nothing, young man. I pay for the services I receive and that is the end of that. Now tell me," she continued, smiling, "how is my case progressing?"

Mr. Thatcher explained that the daughter-in-law of the late Bernard Horowitz ("Sydelle?" Mrs. Goldblum asked. "I haven't seen her since 1953. How is she?") had produced evidence that Mr. Horowitz *had* set up a pension fund for Mrs. Goldblum's husband ("Well, I know that, dear," Mrs. Goldblum said), and for six other employees as well. It was an informal fund, paid out of pocket by Mr. Horowitz. Mr. Thatcher had also discovered that Bernard Horowitz and Horowitz & Sons Importing were one and the same.

"I don't understand."

"The business was never incorporated. Every business transaction, every asset of Horowitz Importing, was the personal property of Mr. Horowitz. There wasn't a single year that the company's taxes weren't filed as a part of Mr. Horowitz's personal income tax return."

"Is this good news?" Mrs. Goldblum asked.

Was it good news? It meant that Charger was legally responsible to uphold the pension fund, since what they had taken over was not a company per se but Mr. Horowitz's personal assets, liabilities and obligations. ("Of course," Mrs. Goldblum sniffed. "I will be glad to see that Mr. Robin receive his come-uppance.") Mr. Thatcher said that after tracking down the six other employees mentioned in Sydelle's copy of the pension plan—three of whom were still living (ten minutes were spent updating Mrs. Goldblum on the three who were still alive)—Mr. Thatcher had filed suits on their behalf, tacked onto that of Mrs. Goldblum.

"And so what does that awful man have to say now?"

That awful man and Charger Industries wished to settle out of court, to avoid publicity, and Mr. Thatcher had an offer from them. Mrs. Goldblum's pension checks would resume, retroactive payments for the past two years would be made and—

"Good heavens, what more could I want?"

"Two hundred and fifty thousand dollars."

"What?" Mrs. Goldblum and Amanda said at the same time.

"Mrs. Goldblum," Mr. Thatcher said, taking on a courtroom demeanor, "I must point out to you that, if you refuse their offer and take them to court, you stand a very good chance of winning anywhere upward of a million dollars in compensation for what they've put you through."

"That's ridiculous."

"They nearly killed you, Mrs. Goldblum. At the very least, they damaged your health."

"No, no, no," she said, shaking her head.

Mr. Thatcher looked to Amanda.

"No, no, *no,*" Mrs. Goldblum repeated. "Had I taken proper care of my affairs, I would have been on Social Security and would not have run out of money. It's as simple as that."

Mrs. Goldblum refused to entertain any notions of taking Charger Industries to court. When Amanda asked her if she understood, if she really understood what she was giving up—*lifelong* security—Mrs. Goldblum said she was surprised at Amanda. *And* Mr. Thatcher. "Taking that million dollars would be stealing," she said. "My husband worked very hard for many years to provide lifetime security for me. Which he did. And while I'm very grateful to you both for proving that he did, I cannot, will not, consider taking any more than what is rightfully mine. Now, about this offer —what did you call it?"

"Settlement."

"Yes, this settlement. Mr. Thatcher, as an attorney, I would assume you are incapable of lying to your client."

Mr. Thatcher laughed.

"How much do you normally receive in fees on a case like mine?"

Mr. Thatcher looked to Amanda. She shrugged.

"Usually, in a case like this, we receive half of whatever money our client is awarded in excess damages."

"And how much are my excess damages?"

"Roughly one hundred fifty thousand, I'd say."

"So your fee would be seventy-five thousand dollars."

"Well—"

"Well nothing, Mr. Thatcher. You tell that awful man that if he pays me the payments owed to me, my medical bills from the past two years, and pays you seventy-five thousand dollars, I will not take him to court."

"Wait—" Amanda said.

They looked at her.

"Mrs. Goldblum was eligible for Social Security in 1971, was she not?"

"Yes," Mr. Thatcher said, "but the maximum on retroactive claims is six months."

Amanda took Mrs. Goldblum's hand. "You are out fourteen and a half years of Social Security payments. Mrs. Goldblum, I urge you to be compensated for that money in the settlement. Mr. Thatcher is right, you know. Your health was nearly destroyed over this pension business, and you must think about your future, about what needs may arise for money." She paused, watching Mrs. Goldblum's expression. "If for no other reason, you must think of your grandchildren."

After a long moment Mrs. Goldblum said, "I had not thought of it in that light."

And so Mrs. Goldblum agreed to be recompensed for the fourteen and a half years of Social Security payments as well.

After Mr. Thatcher departed, Mrs. Goldblum scratched away with a pencil for some minutes on a pad of paper. "Amanda," she finally said, waving her to her bedside, "I want you to look at this." Hesitating, she pressed the pad to her chest. "This is to go no further."

"Of course," Amanda said.

"Well then," Mrs. Goldblum said, lowering the pad, "this is how much I will be receiving—retro-active-ly—from Social Security. This is how much I will receive from Mr. Goldblum's pension—retro-active-ly. This is how much I will receive in—damages. This is what I receive monthly from Social Security and this is what I receive monthly from Mr. Goldblum's pension." She looked up at Amanda. "So you can see, dear, I'm quite well taken care of." She paused. "I trust we will never have to discuss my financial situation again."

"No," Amanda said, smiling. "I don't think we will."

Two days later Nurse Sendowski caught Amanda on her way to Mrs. Goldblum's room and pulled her into the nurses' station. Nurse Sendowski looked around over her shoulder and then whispered, "Her son's here. He came this morning."

"Daniel?"

She nodded. She looked over her shoulder again. "He tried to get Dr. Renaldi to sign some sort of paper that said Mrs. Goldblum was physically incapable of taking care of herself."

"He didn't sign it, did he?"

"No," Nurse Sendowski whispered, eyes widening, "and he threw a fit."

"Who did?"

Nurse Sendowski broke into a laugh. "They both did."

Amanda thanked Nurse Sendowski, swore her to secrecy, and prepared herself to, at long last, meet the infamous Daniel Goldblum.

"It's very nice to meet you, Daniel, I've heard a great deal about you from your mother," she said, smiling, holding out her hand.

He stood up from his chair on the other side of the bed and briefly shook her hand. His palm was moist. Amanda could see some resemblance between him and his mother, but not much. First of all, he was terribly untidy. He was wearing a suit—an expensive suit—but his shirt and tie looked as though they had been hung up on the floor. He also needed a haircut. His pale face was, at the moment, being mopped with a handkerchief; and the darting eyes behind the wire-rimmed glasses failed to meet Amanda's.

"Yeah," he said, thumbing the waist of his pants with his free hand, making Amanda notice his paunchy middle.

"Wasn't it wonderful for Daniel to come, Amanda? Do sit down, dear, and visit with us."

Daniel looked very annoyed and so Amanda took pleasure in sitting. With a grunt, he reseated himself.

"As I told you, dear, Amanda has been an extraordinary friend to me during this time of trouble."

"Yes," Daniel said, leaning forward to rest his elbows on his knees. "I appreciate your helping Mother in my absence."

Amanda looked directly at him and said, "I would do anything to protect your mother's interests."

Daniel took out his handkerchief to wipe his forehead again. "Yeah, I think that's great." He stuffed his handkerchief in his pants pocket and reached for the box of chocolates on Mrs. Goldblum's table. "I need the number for that lawyer you got my mother," he said, throwing a chocolate in his mouth. It was soon followed by another.

"Daniel wishes to thank Mr. Thatcher," Mrs. Goldblum said.

"Surely," Amanda said, opening her purse. "I have his number right here."

While Amanda was writing the number down, Mrs. Goldblum said to him, "Darling, you should eat something. Why don't you go down to the coffee shop and have a nice lunch?" She held out her hand for the box in such a manner as to suggest that this was not the first time mother and son had discussed the issue of candy.

"Here you go," Amanda said, reaching over the bed to hand Daniel the number.

"Thanks." He scanned the piece of paper and shoved it into his jacket pocket. "I think I will get something to eat, Mother," he said, leaning to kiss Mrs. Goldblum on the cheek. "But I sure wish I could eat your cooking. I really miss it."

Mrs. Goldblum was evidently delighted by this statement.

"I'll be back in a little while. Amanda, nice meeting you." The handkerchief was out again.

"I'll undoubtedly cross paths with you again," Amanda said, a smile pressed into use.

After he walked out, Mrs. Goldblum smoothed her bedclothes. "It was such a wonderful surprise."

"I can imagine," Amanda said.

"Rosanne is coming to visit me again tonight," Mrs. Goldblum said "Did I show you the photograph of Jason she gave me?"

"Yes, I saw it yesterday," Amanda said, pointing to the photo on the bulletin board. "He's absolutely adorable."

Mrs. Goldblum chuckled, reaching for the water pitcher. "When I think of you girls smuggling that child in here . . ."

Amanda laughed, rising out of her chair to assist her. "Did she say when she'll have him back full time?"

"No, she didn't," Mrs. Goldblum said, lying back against her pillow. Amanda handed her the glass. "Thank you, dear. I don't suppose she can until she moves out of that—place." She sighed. "I so hope she can find something close to home."

"I know," Amanda said, easing herself down onto the edge of the bed. "Mrs. Goldblum—"

She smiled pleasantly, swallowing a bit of water.

"You won't be signing any more papers, will you?"

"Are there more papers?" Mrs. Goldblum asked, looking at the nightstand as if there might be some she had missed.

"No, none that I know of," Amanda said. "But if some were to arrive, you wouldn't sign anything. Would you." It was not a question.

"Well, of course not, dear. I've already explained to you—"

"I know, I know," Amanda said hastily, rising from the bed. "It's just, with all the papers flying about, I'd hate to see one escape your watchful eye."

Mrs. Goldblum patted Amanda's hand. "I wouldn't let that happen, dear. Not now."

"No," Amanda smiled, "I didn't think you would."

24

ROSANNE IS PETITIONED

"We're not going to get anywhere if you persist in yelling," the man, Mr. Jones, said from behind his desk. He was tired and upset and flustered. He had already, just moments ago, spilled his coffee and, in the process of cleaning it up, had burned a hole in his desk with a lighted cigarette. Now he was left with a distraught Mrs. DiSantos and a desk blotter that was decomposing into a soggy mess.

"All right, all right," Rosanne said, sitting back down into her chair.

"Okay," he said, reaching for the manila folder. He opened it and a little coffee trickled out of it. "Lanie," he barked into the intercom. A young girl appeared. "Take this and wipe the papers off and Xerox them, will you?"

The girl screwed up her face and took the folder from him.

"Okay, Mrs. DiSantos," he said, "you'll have to appear in family court for the preliminary hearing."

"I don't—"

"Listen to me," he said, leaning forward on his desk. Too late. He looked under the sleeves of his jacket and sighed. He sat back in his chair. "What you say at this hearing is going to be very, very important. You're going to need a lawyer—a good one—and you're going to have to present your side to the judge in a way that discredits every point that has been made in the petition. Or at least prove that what has gone on in the past is no longer true about the present. Or future." He sighed. "You can't let it get to court or—"

"Or what?"

"Or it could take months to settle, maybe as long as a year, and until it's settled, Jason would stay with the Rubinowitzes."

"Oh, God," Rosanne said, dropping her face into her hands. "I just don't understand—he's *my* son."

Mr. Jones sighed again. Then he got up and offered a box of Kleenex to Rosanne.

"Thanks," she managed to say, fumbling for some tissues.

"I know how painful this is, Mrs. DiSantos," Mr. Jones said, moving back to his chair. "But we have to go over the points of the petition. If you want," he said, sitting down and slapping his hands on the arms of it, "I can get a lawyer from Legal Aid to sit in—"

Rosanne blew her nose. "I have to think about it," she said. "Can I have a day at least?"

Mr. Jones cocked his head to consider this. "Yes. But you have to understand, Mrs. DiSantos, you don't have long to prepare. I strongly advise you to consult a lawyer as soon as possible."

"Yes," she sighed, head hanging.

"Look. This is the situation as it now stands. The Rubinowitzes have had the child for almost two and a half years—half of the child's life. And now that you've requested to regain custody of the child, they have petitioned the court, claiming they can provide a better home for the child than the mother —than you can, Mrs. DiSantos."

"But how can they say that?" Rosanne cried, leaping from her chair. "I'm Jason's mother!" she yelled, slamming her hand down on Mr. Jones's desk. "Just because I'm not rich means I can't have my child? Get them another kid! Why do they have to take my child?" She slammed the desk again. "It's not fair!"

Mr. Jones's face expressed sympathetic pain. "I want to try and help you," he said quietly. "Please, please sit down and listen. There's nothing you can do until you understand what you're up against. So please, Mrs. DiSantos . . ."

Rosanne clutched at herself and whirled around. After a moment her shoulders eased slightly, she took a deep breath and then sat down in the chair, still holding herself tightly. "You've got to help me, Mr. Jones," she said in a half whisper. "You know me. You know Jason. You know that he's all I've got." She closed her eyes, tears forcing themselves out and down her face.

There was a brief knock and Lanie came back in with the papers. "Thanks," Mr. Jones said, examining fresh copies in a fresh folder. He cleared his throat, glanced over at Rosanne—whose eyes were still closed—and turned another page. "There are two major points in the petition. The first concerns why you placed Jason in a foster home in the first place, the facts concerning your husband—"

"My husband was sick," Rosanne said, opening her eyes. "Dr. Karrel at St. Luke's Hospital will explain." When Mr. Jones didn't say anything, Rosanne added, "I couldn't leave him when he was sick, Mr. Jones. And I put Jason in a foster home because—because—I'm a good mother, Mr. Jones. Until Frank got well, I didn't want Jason to . . ." She looked to the ceiling for a moment to compose herself. She crossed her legs and began rocking slightly. Finally, "I did everything by the book. I told them the truth, I made sure Jason had a good home, I tried to help my husband get well. He's dead now and everything's different. Jason belongs with me now."

"But you see, Mrs. DiSantos, the Rubinowitzes have come to love the child too—"

"Jason," Rosanne said.

"What?"

"Please stop callin' him 'the child.' "

"Okay." Mr. Jones tried to regroup his thoughts. "Let's get to the actual points of the petition. Okay. One. For the last three years, you and your husband apparently had no means of employment."

"That's not true," Rosanne said, leaning forward. "I've worked almost every day of my life—I make two-fifty a week—"

Mr. Jones frowned. "But, Mrs. DiSantos, there is no record of employment."

"But there—" Rosanne stopped herself. She bit her lip. "What kind of record do you need?"

"Well, let's see. . . . According to this, neither you nor your husband have paid any taxes—federal, state or city—nor have you paid any Social Security for"—he paused, thumbing through the papers—"four years." He looked up. "To all intents and purposes, you've had no means of employment, or any visible means of support. And considering the nature of your husband's illness, as you call it, the court is very likely to assume that you may have engaged in illegal activity—"

"I clean houses, Mr. Jones. I've been cleanin' houses for over three years. I've paid our rent, I've paid for our food, our clothes—I've bought all of Jason's clothes and I gave the Rubinowitzes a hundred and twenty dollars *every* month—and I didn't have to. They got money for being foster parents—"

"But the fact remains, Mrs. DiSantos," he sighed, "you've been earning money under the table."

Rosanne didn't say anything.

"I see." Mr. Jones mulled over this confession. "Well, there's a good side and a bad side to this. On one hand, we can prove that you've been the breadwinner of the family, have diligently and responsibly supported yourself and your husband—do you think you can get character references from your employers?"

She nodded.

"Good. You'll need them." He made a note in his folder. "Now, the problem is, this same information, when revealed, will set you up to be prosecuted for tax evasion." He looked at her. "Your employers as well."

"My employers?"

"They should have been paying Social Security for you out of your salary."

"Oh." Rosanne sighed. She sighed again. "So what can I do?"

He leaned back in his chair, nibbling on his pencil. "I think the best course for you to take is to find out how much you owe in taxes and make arrangements to pay them—*before* the hearing. Then at least you can tell the truth and demonstrate a sense of responsibility."

Rosanne shook her head. "Where am I gonna get the money? I only have about two thousand saved up and I need that money to—"

"Well, that brings us to point two. They claim you cannot provide an adequate home environment for the child—for Jason."

"Well—" Rosanne said, her frustration starting to choke her. "I was lookin' for a new apartment—a nice one-bedroom in Brooklyn—but I won't have deposit money if I have to pay those taxes—and now you say they're gonna take out taxes and Social Security from what I make and so I won't have . . ." Her face caught in silent agony. "Oh, God," she finally sobbed, collapsing into her lap.

"We can file for family housing—"

"I did," was Rosanne's muffled cry. "The waiting list's two to five years."

Mr. Jones didn't know what to say, so he didn't say anything. He tapped the folder against the desk and watched Mrs. DiSantos cry.

25

SAM ASKS FOR HELP

Sam had to do something.

He had known that all along, of course, but now he had no choice. The ZT 5000 mess was creeping into the Wyatts' family life in such a way that Sam knew, if he refused to act much longer, he might lose not only his career, his reputation and his self-respect but Harriet as well. At least her trust—which, in Sam's mind, was as good as losing her altogether.

Sam and Harriet had driven Samantha up to Camp Wyononi in New Hampshire over the weekend. The drive up had been fine; Samantha, in her usual buoyancy, had chattered and sung her head off for the first four hours and then had gone to sleep in the back of the station wagon, nestled in her baggage for a month-long stay. Harriet had spent the quiet time writing marketing plans.

"You know, Sam," Harriet said, "that ZT machine is really wonderful." (Sam had had a working model installed at Gardiner & Grayson, an arrangement he had made long before the trouble started.) "The kids in promotion are having a ball with it. When that review of the Klendon novel appeared in the *Times,* within an hour they were sending out blowups to our major accounts to use for point-of-sales."

Sam missed their exit.

They had made the obligatory tour of the camp ("Honey," Harriet whispered, leaning on Sam's arm by the lake, "I think *we* need to go to camp"); Samantha had only cried for five minutes when they were leaving (as opposed to the year before, when she had to be pried loose from Harriet and forcibly dragged away); and they checked in for the night at an inn a mile down the road.

The Wyatts had eaten a delicious dinner, had strolled down a country lane in the moonlight; they had kissed for a long while by a pond (until the insects got them), and had walked, hand in hand, back to their room. And then, after an hour of trying, Sam had thrown himself out of bed in frustration and self-disgust.

"Sam, come back," Harriet whispered. "Please just come back and hold me."

Sam got dressed and went out for a walk. When he came back, he found Harriet weeping in the bed. He felt as guilty and awful as he had in the old days; it was as if he was returning, still warm, from another woman's bed. There was no other woman—but there was guilt. He had tried to comfort Harriet, but his heart was simply not in it. All he could think about was what Harriet would think if she knew the truth about the mess he was in. Sam Wyatt, executive extraordinaire—business friend to South Africa! *And still he had done nothing.*

The drive home Sunday had been even worse. Harriet was silent and every time Sam looked at her he saw an expression resurrected from the long ago past—an expression of pain, of fear, of helplessness. And it killed Sam to see it.

When they arrived home, Althea reported that Charles Washington had called Sam about the business seminar Sam ran every year for the Urban League. Sam called Charles back—from the bedroom—and said he was terribly sorry but Charles would have to find someone else to run it this year.

When Sam finally succeeded in getting Charles off the phone, he went into the kitchen, only to find Harriet with *that* expression on her face again.

"Why are you looking at me that way?"

Harriet had not answered; she had turned away from him to start fixing dinner. *That,* too, was behavior from years long gone by. The Silent Treatment.

Althea had come into the kitchen at that moment, eating sunflower seeds, one by one, out of the palm of her hand. "So why aren't you doing the seminar, Dad? John signed up this year—at *my* suggestion." Munch, munch. "What am I supposed to tell him?"

"What, are you eavesdropping now, Althea?" Sam said.

"Your voice isn't exactly quiet, you know."

Harriet glanced back at Sam over her shoulder.

"Tell John—whoever the hell that is—that your father's busy," Sam said, walking out.

On Monday night Sam took Cassy Cochran to an alcoholism treatment center on West 59th Street to sit in on a group therapy session for the spouses of alcoholics. Although Harriet had offered to take her, Cassy said that it would be better if Sam did. ("You're too gentle, Harriet," she had said in front of both them the week before. "I'd be sure to cancel. But I wouldn't dare cancel on Sam—I'd be too scared to.") Afterward, they walked all the way home, with Cassy talking the entire way about Michael. When they reached the Cochrans' building, Cassy hugged Sam and said she didn't know how she would ever repay his kindness.

At that moment—whether it was because of the nature of the evening they had spent, or Cassy's vulnerability, he didn't know—Sam heard himself say, "I'm in trouble, Cassy."

Cassy pulled back in surprise. "You're joking."

He gave a sarcastic laugh. "I wish I was."

He walked Cassy across the Drive to sit on a bench by the Soldiers' and Sailors' Monument. Pacing back and forth, he told her the story as best he could: about the ZT 5000 being assembled in Pretoria, about his suspicions that it had been deliberately set up by Canley to increase profits, about Brennan's refusal to do anything about it. He told Cassy that he had to do something—but was at a loss as to how to go about it without completely destroying his career, his reputation and—long sigh—his family. At the last, his voice faltered.

Cassy didn't seem shocked, nor did she seem surprised; she merely sat there, listening, periodically interrupting to ask a question.

"Well," she said when he was finished, "the doing part is easy. WST can find that plant in no time and break the story. As you say, Electronika will move assembly fast enough after that." She paused, thinking. "But what bothers me, Sam, is how Brennan has handled this." She paused again, biting her lower lip.

A breeze blew up from the river, making the trees overhead rustle.

Sam sat down on the bench, sighing. "It doesn't add up, does it? If they were setting me up as the fall guy in case they got caught—"

"Why tell you about it?" Cassy finished for him. "Why give you a chance to prepare yourself?" She shifted around on the bench to face him. "That's what's so strange."

"You know—" Sam started.

"What?"

He shook his head. "It'll sound crazy—"

"Say it."

He leaned toward Cassy, dropping his voice. "I feel like I've been dared. Like Brennan and Canley are daring me to do something. You know? It's as if—'Think you're a tough guy, Wyatt? Prove it.' "

Cassy nodded, staring off in the dark somewhere past Sam. "Yes," she said slowly. "It does sound like a dare. I wonder . . ."

"And this will sound paranoid, for sure," Sam added, watching a Yorkshire terrier being led past them. "I think my office phone is tapped."

Cassy gave a half laugh. "Probably is," she said, looking at him. "Come on." She stood suddenly. "We've got to make a call."

In the study of the Cochrans' apartment, Sam sat on the couch as Cassy called a former colleague of hers in the WST newsroom, Paul Levitz, an investigative reporter for *Conolly's Financial News*. She outlined the situation, naming no names, wondering if Paul had any instincts about it. Cassy listened into the phone for some time, her frown deepening, and then she glanced at Sam. Putting Paul on hold, she asked Sam, "How long has the new president been at Electronika?" When he said eight months, Cassy reported this information to Paul and then her eyebrows shot up. She put him on hold again. "Sam," she said, "Paul just asked me if I was talking about Walter Brennan."

"Oh, man," Sam said, lurching to his feet.

"Look, Sam, I'd trust Paul with my life." She paused. "I think you'd better pick up in the kitchen and talk to him."

Sam sighed, rubbing his forehead. "Okay," he said.

They were on the phone for two hours. After they swore themselves to secrecy—Paul, Cassy and Sam—Paul explained how it was he knew it must have Brennan and Canley Cassy was talking about.

Two years before, Paul had been assigned to write a feature story on Caswell Zander, one of the most illustrious brokerage houses in America. Since a new, younger management team had taken over in 1981, Caswell

Zander had increased its profits by two thousand percent. As Paul's research continued, he found that the increased profits had been largely generated by four key employees—the managing director, the trading chief, an analyst and a stockbroker. The four had an uncanny capacity for "hunches" concerning individual stocks that, again and again, made the house and its major accounts millions. Based only on his preliminary investigations, *Conolly's* reclassified Paul's feature-in-the-making as top secret.

At the time Paul was working on the story, DarkStar Inc. was being slapped with a multimillion-dollar negligence suit by a man who claimed his wife had been electrocuted by a DarkStar food processor—a product that accounted for nearly half of the company's revenues. The publicity was explosive, sales crashed, and DarkStar stock fell eight points on the American Stock Exchange. Two days before the suit was filed, Caswell Zander had sold short three million shares of DarkStar stock (an order to sell the shares it did not yet own) at fifteen dollars. When the stock fell to seven dollars, they bought the three million shares, thus fulfilling their sell order from days before.

"That's—that's," Sam stuttered, "a profit twenty-four million dollars."

But wait. That wasn't all. Caswell Zander then turned the twenty-four million around to buy up DarkStar shares. Ten days later the suit was thrown out of court as a hoax, and DarkStar screamed that it had been set up by its competitors. A PR campaign ensued, the food processors regained their number one share in the market, DarkStar's stock rose five points, and Caswell Zander started unloading their shares at fourteen dollars.

"That's got to be over forty million dollars they made," Sam said.

"Closer to fifty," Paul said.

At the time, Walter Brennan had been president of DarkStar and Chet Canley executive vice-president.

Caswell Zander had an even bigger "hunch" about an automotive stock, and it was that direction Paul had pursued. It was clear—at least to Paul—that Caswell Zander had been fed with inside information from not one but several companies. But how to prove it? Reaching dead end after dead end, he tracked back a few years in Caswell Zander's dealings to look for clues. And there, in 1982, the name DarkStar surfaced again. In February of that year Caswell Zander had bought two million shares of DarkStar stock at four dollars for its clients; in June, ICL Industries filed an official takeover bid for DarkStar and the stock soared; and in August Caswell Zander started unloading their shares at eleven dollars.

Walter Brennan and Chet Canley had *not* been at DarkStar; they had been corporate officers at ICL Industries.

So, as Paul said over the phone, Cassy and Sam could see why Brennan and Canley were two of the forty-eight corporate executives he was keeping an eye on in connection with Caswell Zander. Paul had checked to see if Caswell Zander had benefited from ICL's stock swap to bail out Electronika from the El-San Industries takeover attempt—but no, they hadn't. Paul had interpreted it to mean one of two things: that Brennan and Canley were no longer "playing," or, with DarkStar to run, their parent company had not seen fit to inform them of its pending stock swap with Electronika. But, from what Sam had told him, Paul thought Brennan and Canley might now be playing again for Caswell Zander.

"They're counting on me to leak the Pretoria story, aren't they? To drive the stock down?" Sam said.

"Ten to one," Paul said. "But Electronika's back-page news compared to the story I'm after." He was getting more excited by the second. "Cass, if this pans out, this Electronika angle, I'll go partners with you. *Conolly's* with WST. I get the stands, you get the air. But I need help—now—there's a million loose ends."

Sam sat there, perspiring heavily, as he listened to them bargaining over resources. Manpower, computers, legwork, the Securities and Exchange Commission. On and on Cassy and Paul raced, ending by agreement to meet at 7 A.M. at WST.

By the time they hung up, Sam was a basket case. Cassy came flying into the kitchen, face flushed with excitement. Sam was not to worry. Sam was not to say or do anything until he heard from her. If Sam needed to call her, he should use a pay phone. When she needed to get hold of him, she would send a note to his doorman by messenger. Just talk and walk as usual. Walk? Why did she say that? Did Cassy think they had been followed tonight? No, no, don't worry, but even if they had, look where they had been followed to —they'd hardly think Sam went to an alcoholism center to leak the story. Sam! Sam! Sam! Did he realize the enormity of a story like this? Caswell Zander? Inside trading at one of the most prestigious financial institutions in the world?

Sam got so flustered that he forgot to ask what could happen to him.

It was almost twelve-thirty when Sam walked into the apartment. Harriet was sitting in the living room, still dressed, waiting for him.

"You're alive," she noted, rising from the couch. "I just wanted to make sure."

"I'm sorry," Sam said, "I should have called." He rubbed his face, dropped his hands, and slowly walked toward her. "I was at Cassy's."

Harriet turned away from him, toward the window and crossed her arms, holding herself. "You realize, of course," she said, voice trembling, "that she's very vulnerable right now."

Sam closed his eyes. "Oh, no, Harriet." He opened his eyes and moved behind her. "No, honey," he whispered, sliding his arms around her. He lowered his head to speak softly into her ear. "Honey, you couldn't have thought that."

She turned around, looking up at him. There were tears in her eyes. "Why couldn't I?" she asked him. "She's a very lonely—very beautiful woman." Her head slowly fell forward, forehead sinking against his chest.

Sam pulled her close, pressing his chin down on the top of her head. "Baby, no," he murmured. "Cassy's trying to help me get out of a mess. With Electronika."

Harriet's head flew back. "Electronika?"

He nodded. "Come on," he said, sliding his arm around her shoulders and steering her toward the kitchen. "I've got a lot to explain to you."

26

AMANDA ACKNOWLEDGES
HOW SHE FEELS

Amanda had not heard a word from Howard and it felt as though it was killing her. Every moment that her attention was not demanded elsewhere, her thoughts veered to Howard and the pain reawakened in an instant—a horrible, yawning ache in her chest, accompanied by an unfulfilled longing to cry.

She was seeing Dr. Vanderkeaton twice a week, if for no other reason than to be told she was not going mad. Whatever these feelings were, they were tearing loose all kinds of memories inside Amanda's head and heart. And they hurt. Whether it was the image of Nana lying in her coffin, or of Christopher the night she had left him, Amanda would feel an unfamiliar terror run through her and then, afterward, a rolling tide of despair.

She felt finished. Over. She had played her hand in this life and she had lost. It was all she could do to keep one foot in front of the other to get to the hospital to see Mrs. Goldblum. There, in the light of her older friend's glow, she would feel much better. But then, arriving home, Amanda would collapse on her bed, unable to cry, unable to snap out of it. There was simply no snap left. She wasn't sleeping; she drifted in half-waking dreams of swirling, unseen perils. Eating was difficult. Very difficult.

And her home was haunted. The bed was Howard; the writing room was Howard; Missy the cat was Howard; the river was Howard; the . . .

Could it be, she kept saying to Dr. Vanderkeaton, that one man, in such a brief time, had obtained the power to destroy her? It felt as though that were the case. Even on those days when Amanda woke up with a slender shoot of hope, the hope that she would feel better, she found herself—as if under someone's spell, someone's control—driving a knife through her own heart to kill it. Only yesterday she had been in Shakespeare & Company, buying some Phyllis Whitney novels in large-print editions for Mrs. Goldblum. She had been feeling better, stronger and a bit happy when she thought of how pleased Mrs. Goldblum would be. And so what did she do? Amanda then searched through the recently published titles to find a particular biography, found the book she was looking for and turned to the acknowledgments page: "And my heartfelt thanks to my editor at Gardiner & Grayson, Howard Stewart, whose enthusiasm, guidance and support made this book possible."

The knife had done its work well.

Her mother had been calling Amanda every night at ten, but what Tinker intended as loving reassurance often felt like more baggage to hasten her drowning. "At a time like this, you need to lean on your friends," Tinker would say. (Friends? Amanda would think. [How ghastly it was to realize that her mother had her confused with someone else—someone who had friends to fall back on.]) "Darling, you were right. If this young man cannot stand on his own two feet, you would be repeating the same nightmare you endured with Christopher." (Christopher? Her mother was comparing Howard with Christopher? Didn't she understand that Howard was nothing like Christopher? That there were thousands and thousands of Christophers, and only one Howard Stewart?) "Amanda, Amanda—listen to me! You are not worthless and you are not hopeless!" (Oh, no? Then why had he not come back?)

"Amanda," Tinker had finally said last night, her voice edging toward vexation, "go outside. Take a walk. Go riding. Stand on your head, but, darling, do something!"

And so, this morning, Amanda was trying to pull herself together to go and do something. Dressed in her baggiest jeans and a sweat shirt, she ate five grapes and set out for the great outdoors. She walked out of her building and looked across the Drive to the park. It was a bit too vibrant and lovely for Amanda and so she walked up 90th Street, face to the sidewalk, feeling drained already.

I remember when you first laughed. I remember your hand, exactly what it looked like, when I handed you that glass of wine. I remember looking down at your hair, wondering what it would feel like. I remember your eyes and your lashes and I remember thinking, 'Why is he so kind?'

Stop it, stop it, STOP IT.

At the corner of West End Avenue she turned left, trudging uptown. After only a block, she sat down on the stairs of a Greek Orthodox church and stared blankly ahead.

She had almost called him a hundred times. But every time she picked up the phone, she thought, *To say what?* "I told you I was right. Look at how easily you gave up on me." And then she would grip the phone and her chin would tremble as she could see herself screaming, "I hate you for deceiving me! I hate you!"

She got up and continued walking north on West End Avenue.

I was a fool. I should have taken you when I could. I should have kept you by me night after night, away from Melissa and inside of me. Away from the world, away from hurt, in love with me, and only with me.

How? How could she have done that? How long would it have been before Howard realized his mistake? That he had left the life of his choice for a fantasy that could not exist outside the walls of her home? How long before the charms of her body and their isolation wore off, before Howard yearned for his old life? A month? Six? A year?

"I love you," he had said. How, *how* could he have said that to her? Did love, to him, mean to use her as the excuse to walk out on his wife of eight years? To love her meant to burden her with guilt? To be loved by Howard meant to be left by him?

How many times, she wondered, had he told Melissa he loved her?

Love. No. They had been dying of loneliness and had found comfort in one another's arms. And now—now, the realities behind their loneliness had pulled them apart.

Amanda crossed 95th Street and walked past a large red brick school. Public School 75, it said over the front door. Beneath the door, sitting on a step, was a young girl, perhaps eight or nine. "Hi," she said to Amanda.

"Hello," Amanda said.

"I'm looking for summer school," the girl said. She had curly brown hair and very blue eyes, and was featuring a Madonna T-shirt and red shorts with an elastic waistband.

Amanda glanced at the traffic flying by on West End, and walked over to the girl. "Is it here?"

"I think so, but the door's locked."

"Did you knock?"

"Yep. Nobody came."

"Oh," Amanda said, stepping over to the door. She peered in the window and, with her fist, pounded on the door. After a minute or two a custodian peered back out at her.

"What time does summer school commence?" Amanda asked through the glass.

The custodian frowned and pushed the door open a crack. "What you want?"

"Summer school. When does it start? This young lady—"

"Ain't nothin' here for kids. Not now."

"Are you sure?"

He nodded and closed the door.

Amanda sat down next to the girl. "I'm afraid there is no summer school here."

"Figures," the girl said cheerfully. "Mommy never gets these things right. Wanna play operator?" Without waiting for an answer, the girl leaned over her knees and unlaced one of her red Keds sneakers. With the plastic end of a lace in each hand, she inserted one into a lacing hole. With her free hand she pinched her nose. "Operator," she said. She released her nose. "This is Mr. Green," she said. "I want to talk to Mr. Blue." She pinched her nose again. "One moment, plee-uzzz." The second lace was inserted into another hole. "Go ahead, Mr. Green. Mr. Blue is on the line."

"Ring-ring, ring-ring," Amanda said, reaching to unlace the girl's other sneaker. "Ring-ring."

The girl's face lit up. She brought her sneakers together, picked up the end of a new lace, and inserted it into the sneaker where Mr. Green was already conversing with Mr. Blue. "Operator."

"Yes, Operator, this is Ms. Miller. I wish to speak to—Mr. Stewart."

"One moment, plee-uzzz." The girl put the call through. "Go ahead— sorry, what's your name again?"

"Miller."

"Miss Miller, go ahead, plee-uzzz, your party is on the line."

"Hello?" Amanda said, holding her hand up to her ear. She frowned, reached out, and clicked the receiver. "Operator," she said.

"Operator," the girl said, hand hovering in air, debating whether or not she had to redirect a line on this increasingly complex switchboard in order to take Amanda's call.

"Operator, you gave me Mr. Red and I wished to speak to Mr. Stewart."

"Please hold the line," the girl said, giggling. She reconnected a lace to a new hole. "Hello, is this Mr. Stewart?" She forgot to release her nose and said, "Yes, this is Mr. —" She shrieked in laughter. "Wait!" she cried. She dropped her voice. "Hello?"

"Hello?" Amanda said, hand still at her ear. "Good heavens, I must be on a party line. I'm talking to Mr. Green now!"

The girl whooped with laughter, rolling onto her back, holding her stomach. Amanda was laughing too. Then the girl sat up. "What's your name?"

"Amanda."

"I'm Kiki," the girl said, smiling brightly. "This is a lot more fun than summer school."

"Hmmm," Amanda said. "Well, what are you going to do now?"

Kiki shrugged. "Beats me."

"Do you want me to call your mother?"

"She's at work," Kiki said, bending to survey the remains of her communications empire. "Mrs. Hutter will pick me up in a while, I guess."

"Oh," Amanda said.

In a few minutes a woman came up the front walk toward them.

"Hi," Kiki said.

"Hi," the woman said, pulling keys out of her briefcase.

Kiki scrambled to her feet. "Do you know where summer school is?"

"Better tie those laces before you trip," the woman said. To Amanda, "There's no summer school here. There are only adult reading classes."

"But do you know where summer school is?" Kiki persisted, mashing the toe of one sneaker into the cement with some seriousness.

The woman thought a moment. "I think what you're looking for is over at P.S. 84 on 92nd, but maybe you should call first to make sure. You can use the phone in my office, if you like," she said to Amanda.

Amanda stood up. "Thank you," she said. "Kiki, better tie those laces."

"Okay," Kiki said, bouncing once before getting down to it.

The woman unlocked the door and led them down the "spooky" (Kiki) hall to a small, windowless office. The woman looked up the number and placed the call. "What class is your daughter registered for?" she asked Amanda, covering the phone with her hand.

Kiki cackled. "Yeah, Mommy," she said, yanking on Amanda's hand.

"I'm not her mother," Amanda said, smiling. "I'm but a new acquaintance."

The woman looked to Kiki, arching her eyebrows. "What class?"

"Math," Kiki said, making gagging motions.

"What grade?"

Deep breath. On the exhale, "Thirrrrrrrrrrd."

"Did you hear that? Third." Back to Kiki. "And your name?"

"Kiki McIntyre." She commenced walking about on her tiptoes.

Amanda started to read the papers posted on the woman's bulletin board. They were all variations on one theme: adult reading classes. After the woman got things squared away with Kiki—writing out the address of where Kiki was to report the following morning (she was three weeks late, apparently)—Amanda asked if she was a teacher.

No, she wasn't; she was a program coordinator. And then her expression shifted, eyes widening. "You wouldn't be interested in volunteering, would you?"

"Me?" Amanda said, pointing to herself.

"We're desperate for volunteers," the woman said, coming around her desk. She held out her hand. "Margaret Whelan."

"How do you do? Amanda Miller."

Margaret Whelan wasted no time in explaining that the evening classes were to teach adults to read and write. Most of their students, she went on to explain, for one reason or another, had failed to receive a proper education. She asked Amanda if she happened to know any foreign languages.

"Only a little Old English, I'm afraid."

Margaret Whelan laughed and pressed on. Amanda was a writer? What luck! Amanda had majored in English? At Amherst? Did Amanda know that P.S. 75, this very building, was the Emily Dickinson School?

By the time Amanda took Kiki outside to wait for Mrs. Hutter, Margaret Whelan had outfitted her with a notebook, a paperbound textbook, a lesson plan book and a thick folder that contained all kinds of information about the reading program. She had also secured Amanda's promise to come back at seven to sit in on one of the classes.

Outside, the sun blazing hot, Amanda and Kiki looked up at the very top of the school building. Sure enough, there it was in discreet silver lettering on the brick:

EMILY DICKINSON SCHOOL

"They want me to be a teacher," Amanda said, a bit dazed, to her little companion.

"Maybe you could teach at summer school," Kiki said hopefully.

Mrs. Hutter—Kiki's housekeeper, it turned out—came to fetch her at eleven-thirty. After a short conference concerning Kiki's now infamous summer school, Amanda said farewell. Twisting around to look at Amanda, while crossing 96th Street, Kiki yelled, "If you ever need to talk to Mr. Green . . . !"

Amanda waved and turned to head for home. She slung her books under one arm, on her hip, and smiled. *He would be proud of me.*

Her heart, for a moment, swelled with happiness. And in that moment Amanda knew, without a doubt, how very much in love she was with Howard Stewart.

27

HOW HOWARD WAS FARING

The night Howard left Amanda's, the night of Lady Liberty's birthday, he walked the streets of New York until morning. Partly it was because there wasn't an available hotel room in Manhattan, but mostly because Howard was nearly mad with anger and hurt.

At first he was entirely convinced that the real issue, though Amanda had denied it, was money. He had scared Amanda by coming on too strong, too fast, he thought, and then when he had told her he was leaving Melissa for her, he was positive that Amanda no longer even saw him, Howard, but saw Christopher instead, coming back to live off her.

Live off her? (This thought, while standing on a traffic island in the middle of Broadway, near Lincoln Center, made him lean his head against a light pole, earning murmurs of consolation from the winos sitting on the bench.) Howard did not want to live off Amanda—God, no. Howard wanted to live *with* Amanda, he wanted to—

It was all so screwed up, he thought, striding south on Broadway. Everything. Absolutely everything. He felt sure if he had more money Amanda wouldn't have said a word. But, with his salary, who was he to move in with her without appearing to be another Christopher? But he couldn't make more money than he already was, Howard thought. When he had made the decision to become an editor he had also made the decision that making money would never be a priority—

With Melissa, it didn't have to be a priority, he reminded himself. No, but that hadn't been it. Really. It really hadn't. He had wanted to be an editor in the worst way.

And now you hate it, so what's the excuse?

He didn't hate being an editor; he hated being at Gardiner & Grayson. But was that it, either? He didn't know if he wanted to be an editor anymore. No, that wasn't right. He did want to be an editor, but he wanted to be like Gertrude's vision of an editor—to be out in the field, exploring and discovering and fostering new talent.

A lot of former book editors had become literary agents and Howard had thought about this a lot. These days, the literary agents—the good ones— were out in the field doing all of the discovering. They found the writers and worked closely with them—encouraging them, guiding them, sometimes even preliminarily editing them—and then endeavored to place them with the editor and house that they believed would most likely nurture that writer's career.

Harrison always said the analogy of good book publishing was childbirth. The writer is the expectant mother; the book is the unborn child; and the editor is the midwife. "And the agent?" the gang at G & G would ask. "If they're good, the labor coach; if they're not, a baby broker." Howard liked the image of labor coach—it implied a deep sense of trust, of being "in it" with the writer for the long run.

And there was the money side of being an agent. An agent received anywhere from ten to fifteen percent of a client's earnings. So if an agent did a good job on behalf of good writers, he or she stood a very good chance of making a very good living.

Howard had thought about becoming an agent but then had always dismissed it as a pipe dream. Where to find writers? Why would a good writer choose him as an agent when there were so many established, wonderful agents in town? And what about office space? Telephones? Accountants? Lawyers? Insurance . . .

Over and above the whole idea making him feel exhausted, there was the very real possibility that he could fail. His paycheck, inconsequential as everyone seemed to think it was, was still regular. As was his insurance, his pension plan—

Thirty-three and I'm scared to lose my pension plan?

No, he was scared of going completely bankrupt. Of giving up the identity that his business card gave him. ("Gardiner & Grayson?" people would say, looking up at him with a bright eye. It was extraordinary, the power of that name in America. Howard could go anywhere, call anywhere—the White House even—and people would be very careful to take notice of him.) What would it be like just to be Howard Stewart? Who the hell was that? Without the power of the Gardiner & Grayson name fronting for him, why would anyone give him the time of day?

To be Howard Stewart and only Howard Stewart and to fail and to go bankrupt?

Sigh. It went without saying how Melissa would react to that. And Amanda was even worse—here he was an editor at one of the most prestigious houses in the world, and she already thought he was a failure!

How could she reject him so quickly? Why hadn't she just come out and said, "Please leave Melissa first and then come to me"? But she hadn't and Howard had not known what her reaction would be.

He felt sick.

He had blown it. If he had only kept his mouth shut! If he had only approached the subject of living with Amanda gradually, had given her time to get used to the idea . . . But no, he had to go flying in there, announcing his decision on the assumption that she would be elated by it.

No, no, he later decided, drifting aimlessly in Times Square, ignoring the solicitations of numerous prostitutes—white, black, Asiatic, Hispanic, female, male. No, Howard decided, it was not money, it was not his tactlessness that had made Amanda reject him.

It was because she did not love him.

There. He had admitted it. His worst fear had been acknowledged. Amanda did not love him. If she had, she would have been ecstatic that he was leaving Melissa. Instead, she had panicked at the idea of being stuck with him.

Exhausted, his stomach aching, Howard started trudging uptown, trying to think where he would go from here. The loss of Amanda felt like the loss of his dreams. Without her, he did not much care what happened to him. Would life now be impossible with Melissa? It had *always* been impossible, so what would be new? He had always managed to live a fairly interesting life with her, and there was no reason to think it would stop. In fact, all that had changed was that Howard now knew he was capable of having an affair. So maybe things would be better after all. Would it be so terrible if he had someone for himself in bed once a week? To take the sexual energy that Melissa loathed and discreetly channel it elsewhere, thus taking at least that pressure off their marriage?

Patricia MacMannis instantly came to mind and he followed that thought. She and Tom were rocking and rolling in their affair and, according to Patricia, it was in the throes of ending. She did not love Tom, she said. And she was not in love with Howard anymore than he was in love with her. But Howard really cared for Patricia, they were great friends, they trusted one another, and Howard was almost positive that if he carefully broached the subject with her, outlined what he had in mind, Patricia would—

His thinking was insane and he knew it. Amanda was not even a memory yet and already he was bedding Patricia in his head. And yet, what else could he think about? About Amanda? About the woman he had fallen in love with, and who had *not* fallen in love with him, and who had, the moment he was free, rejected him out of hand?

Yes, he would hurt. For a long, long time. And he doubted he would ever get over her. But what was he supposed to do? Just crumble, give up everything, move to a desert isle? Without Amanda, what would be the point in walking out on Melissa without any attempt at working things out? The worst had already happened—his dreams had been destroyed. And now there were only the realities left. He was married to Melissa. They had been together eight years. They had built a life together, a home together. That's what he had. Right now. In hand. That's what he had to deal with.

Howard arrived home at a little before eight in the morning. By now he was reconciled to the idea that the best plan of action would be to sit down and talk things through with Melissa. Amanda, on that point, had been right. He did owe it to her to at least try to reassess their marriage, their mutual anger and frustrations.

(*Good,* he thought, looking at his face in the hall mirror, *I look like hell. Melissa will be pleased.*)

He went into the kitchen and poured himself a glass of orange juice. Boy, he was tired. He started to make coffee.

The best bet would be to talk to Melissa while driving out to the house. Even with Daddy out there, a swim in the ocean, seeing Melissa's friends, playing some tennis—maybe even a golf game with Daddy—would do a good deal toward setting things right. As a matter of fact, the more he thought about it, the more real Melissa became—sleeping only a few rooms away—the more unreal Amanda became. How would they—he and Amanda—have spent the weekend? Would they have even ventured out from Amanda's apartment? Probably not. Would they have ever played tennis? *Amanda playing tennis?* Would she have ever come to a publishing party with him? ("I know she looks like the Empress of imperial Russia, but she's really my wife," he imagined himself explaining to Harrison.)

Howard closed his eyes, taking a deep breath. He let it out slowly, trying to ease the tightness in his throat.

He was angry. And he was hurt. And he almost felt as though he hated Amanda, making him want to make fun of her, tear her apart, ridicule her until she became so ridiculous in his mind that he could cast her out of it.

God help me. I love her.

But she doesn't love me.

He glanced at the clock. Eight-fifteen. He poured himself a cup of coffee and stood at the window, drinking it.

She does not love me.

As he often did when he felt as though he had had it with Melissa, Howard thought of her the night her mother died. How she had looked, on her knees, sobbing on the bed where Mrs. Collins had been only days before. And he thought about Mrs. Collins and her fears about what would become of her only child. And he thought about those times that Melissa had so freely offered financial assistance to his family.

Melissa. Was it really her fault, the way she was? Was it really irreversible, or had Howard been too scared to stand up to Daddy Collins? To try to break the hold he had over them both? Yes, he had been too scared. But now, now . . . What was there to lose by trying? He and Melissa could talk all they wanted, but their only chance would be if Howard took Daddy Collins on.

Today. Howard could start this very day.

He poured coffee into a fresh cup, stirred in skim milk and a Sweet 'N Low, and carried it to the bedroom. To start with, he would be apologetic to Melissa this morning. Admit he had been wrong by walking out last night. To reassure her that he wanted to talk things out, reassess where they stood. But he would also say that the things that had upset him were very, very real issues—ones he could no longer ignore or put up with. And he would acknowledge the things about himself that upset Melissa, and say they absolutely had to seek outside help—

He froze in the doorway of the bedroom. The bed was made and there was no Melissa. Instead, there were Howard's suitcases, packed, standing at the foot of the bed. There was also a note and he walked over to read it:

You better not be here when Daddy and I come back Monday night. He will probably kill you.

P.S. I should have known it was the rich one.

He had left a note for Melissa to say that she could reach him at the Cambridge House Hotel on 86th Street. It was two weeks and something over nineteen hundred dollars before Howard realized that Melissa was not going to appear, screaming at him and then pleading with him to come home. No, that did not happen. She did not even call.

Rosanne had called him, though, at the office, to tell him of her custody battle with the Rubinowitzes over Jason. After discussing the problems, after Howard declared his financial support to help in any way he could, after Rosanne told him that Amanda had secured a lawyer for her, they got around to the subject of why Howard was not living at home. ("There's a machine," Rosanne told him, "and on it she says, 'Messages for Howard should be left at the Cambridge House Hotel.' ")

Rosanne then found a studio apartment for him on 95th Street between Riverside and West End. That first Saturday of studio apartment living found Howard charging up a storm at Macy's: a pullout couch; a chest of drawers; an easy chair; a color TV; a large butcher block table; a straight-back chair; a brass standing lamp; a brass desk lamp; two window shades; a rug; bath towels; dish towels; bath mat; sheets; blanket; pots; a pan; coffee maker; trash can; dish rack; dishes; glasses; mug; silverware; toolbox; vacuum; clock radio; telephone; hangers—and a spice rack.

Next had come the long list of "essentials" from the grocery store that Rosanne had written out for him, everything from salt to light bulbs to Drano to Campbell's Soup. And then had come the long list Rosanne had written out for the hardware store, everything from a shower curtain rod to light switch plates and extension cords.

All in all, within a week, Howard's apartment had pretty much come together. But, admittedly, no matter how nice the things were that Howard had purchased, he was more than unsettled by his new residence. First of all, it was only after Macy's delivered all of the furniture that it occurred to him that, if he got back with Melissa, all of this stuff would be useless. He blamed Rosanne in this regard; in his confusion and uncertainty, she had railroaded him into taking steps that indicated a permanent separation. And he was not at all certain of that.

And then there was the residence itself. It was a five-floor walk-up, one of ten studios in an old town house. There were two windows that faced north —directly into the back of another apartment house—and there was virtually no sunlight at any time of the day. The plumbing was ancient; the wiring was positively frightening at times (when Howard turned on the kitchen light, the actual event took some sixty seconds of crackling and hissing to take place); and his neighbors were sketchy at best: an old man who showed Howard his loaded shotgun; a woman who was working for an escort service until Hollywood discovered her; and a rather rotund man in a red beret who tried to sell Howard a subscription to the Communist *Daily Worker.*

All this was Howard's for six hundred and fifty dollars a month. "A steal," he was told.

Howard went to work as usual and in the evenings came home to putter. He stayed home one day to have the phone installed and to have cable TV hooked up. (Without it, the only thing Howard could bring in was police radio bands and a flurry of snow.) That night, when everything was in place, Howard fixed himself a steak, watched a movie on HBO, and did the Sunday *Times* crossword puzzle.

Surprising himself, Howard had felt strangely elated. In *his* apartment. Surrounded by *his* things. Doing what *he* wanted to do. And when he had unfolded the couch, had crawled in between his new sheets, his head on his new pillows, he had fallen sound asleep for the first time in months.

It was not long, however, before he started to hurt. He had sent Melissa a card, telling her where she could find him, he had given his new number out to almost everyone he knew and yet his phone had not rung once. (He knew it was working because he had the escort service girl call him.)

And Amanda. Every day he wanted to call her, and every day he decided that he had no right to. Besides, he did not want to be rejected again. *No,* he told himself, *wait.* Some days he felt convinced that his marriage was over, that *he* wanted out of it, and that after he had really learned to live by himself, was really committed to going through with a declaration of independence, then he could call Amanda. But then, other days, Howard missed Melissa terribly. Well, it wasn't as clear as that. When he discovered three cockroaches *inside* his refrigerator one night, for example, it was clear that he missed their apartment, but since Melissa was inseparable in his mind from their apartment, he supposed he missed her too.

Amanda. What would she think of this place? Howard wondered. She would be horrified, no doubt. It made Howard's financial status so blatantly, painfully obvious. He had come to this? Rather, had he always been this? Had not Melissa come into his life, would this not be the way he would have lived?

"Even your precious Harrison couldn't afford to lallygag around as an editor," Melissa had always thought to remind Howard. *"He* had a wife and children to support; *he* was an executive by thirty; *he* edits, Howard—so your excuses fail to impress me."

Would he have done better in his career had he not married Melissa? If he had, say, married Debbie in Columbus?

We live like children do. That was what Amanda had said. Was it true? Had he been living like a child, secure in the knowledge that there were people to care for him?

No.

Yes.

Well, partly—maybe.

One night, around eleven o'clock, the girl from the escort service, Mary Ann, knocked on his door. She had in her hand a bottle of wine, a recent gift, she said. Would Howard like to share it with her? As a kind of house-warming? Touched by her thoughtfulness, and deciding that she was—despite her dubious career—not a bad-looking girl, Howard had invited her in. They sat around and drank the wine, switched to scotch, and she told him all about her life since the day of her birth in Stanley's Crossing, New Jersey. By two, Howard was feeling no pain and was thinking that Mary Ann was actually rather sensational-looking. By two-thirty, he was convinced she was going to be a great actress—an absolute superstar. By three, she was lying across his lap on the couch and Howard was busy exploring her breasts.

That was when Howard received his first telephone call. At twenty after three in the morning. It was a wrong number. No, there was no Lucille here, he told them.

Hanging up, turning back to Mary Ann, all Howard could see was how much makeup she had on, that the blouse he picked up from the floor was polyester, and that the brassiere pushed up over her breasts was red.

Howard gently explained to Mary Ann that he was a married man, confused, yes, but to get involved with her would not be fair to her. He was sorry he had behaved the way he did; he thought Mary Ann was very pretty, very nice, and deserved better than to be used by him.

Mary Ann said she thought it would be fun to be used by him.

They parted amicably, however, and Howard promised to cook dinner for her one night. After she left, Howard sat at the table, held his face in his hands, and cried.

The next day Howard received his first piece of mail. When he saw his home address—his *former* home address—on the envelope, his stomach turned over. Envisioning a long letter inside from Melissa (the envelope was quite thick), one beginning with a tirade and ending with a plea for reconciliation, Howard let it sit on the table for a while. He changed into jeans, poured himself a scotch (he kept forgetting to get ice trays), took the phone off the hook, turned on the floor lamp and then got the letter. He sat down in the easy chair, took a deep swallow of his scotch, and opened it.

There wasn't even a note. All there was inside was a collection of bills, neatly stapled together.

Half of the June bills from the Fishers Island house:	$800
Half of the June apartment maintenance fee:	$450
Half of the June Con Ed bill	$ 47
Half of the June phone bill and calls to Columbus	$ 28
Half of the June garage fees	$ 100
Howard's Racquet Club bill	$575
Howard's dental bill	$240
Howard's optometry bill	$ 60
Howard's Brooks Brothers bill	$539
Howard's June charges on American Express	$325
Howard's June charges on Visa	$ 182

The last piece of paper was an adding machine tape, the total of which Melissa had circled in red.

$3,346

In a panic, Howard dumped all of his charge card receipts from outfitting the apartment. *Oh, no, oh, no,* he said over and over to himself, listing them on a sheet of paper. Next, the charge receipts from Macy's. And, oh, God, the charge slip from the Cambridge House.

He added them.

He checked his math.

He poured himself another scotch and sat down to stare at the piece of paper. Macy's, American Express, Visa for July: $6,600.

Howard got out his checkbook and money market account statement. He had, all told, at this moment, a little over $2,800.

His mind raced. Okay, Melissa plus credit cards equaled $9,946, minus the $2,800 . . . So he needed to pull together about seven thousand dollars. *Seven thousand dollars?* Where the hell was he going to get seven thousand dollars from? And would Melissa charge him for the month of July, too? Could she? He had only lived there for seven days in July. . . .

Of course she can, you fool.

But she had never charged him before for maintenance, the summer house, the garage, Con Ed, or even the phone—Howard had always shared the household expenses and paid his own bills. Own charge account bills, that is.

Howard scribbled more figures until close to midnight. The outcome was not promising. His take-home pay was $820 bimonthly. Okay, monthly income: $1,640 less rent ($650) = $990. Minus Con Ed, phone and cable (around $80) = $910. Minus $100 a week for food, etc. = $510. Subway to work ($40) = $470. And then of course there were laundry and household supplies and, well, it was clear: taxis, tennis, squash, eating out, clothes, all of that stuff had to go.

Well. Sigh. As it was, it would take Howard a month to pay back Melissa, and—oh, God—two *years* to pay back Macy's, American Express and Visa? And that was only on condition that Melissa not charge him for the apartment anymore.

Rosanne. I promised to help Rosanne. Well, that was easy enough, Melissa would have to wait six months.

He tossed the pencil and drank some more scotch.

Now what?

He swept all of the bills into a plastic shopping bag so he didn't have to look at them. And then he took his time, making a list:

—Ask for a raise.

—Close G & G retirement fund. Pull money out.

—Check IRA fund (Melissa).

—Dad. [This was quickly crossed out.]

—Grandfather. [Quickly crossed out as well.]

—Loan? New job? Free-lance?

Boy, he had to hand it to Melissa, if she wanted him back, she sure knew how to do it and keep *her* pride intact. As for himself, just the opposite was true. He knew now he could never go back. Certainly not under these circumstances.

He stood at one of the windows, leaning on the sill, watching the man across the way watch television. Three months . . . In less than three months he had reached for the sky and had fallen flat on his face. And all because of Amanda Miller.

He wondered if she had ever loved him. Even just for a moment.

28

SAM IS ASKED
TO MAKE A CALL

The night Sam explained to Harriet the mess at Electronika, she had reacted much the same way she had when told that two purse snatchers had almost shoved Althea down onto the tracks of the IRT subway two years before. Her face grew taut; her voice dropped in a low, harsh whisper, vowing they wouldn't get away with this; and then she had burst into tears.

The Wyatts had stayed up for almost the rest of the night, talking, wondering, talking, wondering, silent, at times, in their own thoughts.

Lying in bed, with Harriet's head resting on his chest, Sam, gently stroking Harriet's back, had said, "I thought about not doing anything about the Pretoria plant."

"You were thinking of us," she had murmured.

Silence.

"And I was thinking of my career," he said.

At that, Harriet flung herself off his chest to look at him. *"Don't,* Sam— don't try and turn this back on yourself. When you're powerless to fix something, you say, 'I'm powerless.' You can't blame yourself for things over which you had no control."

"But I did have control. I went to Cassy—weeks later, I went to Cassy."

"But—you—went," Harriet said, head jerking forward with each word.

"But I almost didn't," Sam sighed.

"Almost," she said, sounding almost angry, "almost. You *almost* died when you were born. Does that mean you've been dead all these years? You *almost* didn't go to Hazelden—does that mean you've been drunk ever since?"

"But I didn't—"

"Samuel J. Wyatt," she said, giving his stomach a small slap, "guess what? You're human. Yes—human." She curled back down, resting her forehead against the side of his face. "Just like the rest of us mortals."

After a few minutes Sam sighed again. "Althea's tuition is coming up, Samantha's too." Pause. "If worse comes to worst, Althea can probably get some kind of scholarship—and I was thinking . . . we've got the mutual fund, I could sell the—" He turned his head away. "Oh, God, Harriet," he said, slipping his arm out from under her to sit up. He held his face in his hands for a moment and then gave a small laugh. "I was going to say I can sell our Electronika stock." He looked to the ceiling, massaging his throat. "God."

Harriet sat up and ran her hand over her husband's shoulders, back and forth, back and forth. "We'll get through this, Sam. You know we will."

He turned to her. "I never wanted to cause you trouble again."

"You're not causing me trouble," she whispered. "Walter Brennan is causing us trouble. Mack *Sperry* is causing us trouble," she added, smiling slightly. "But not you, Sam. You only make my life better. Always."

He shook his head but didn't say anything.

She slid her arms around him and rested the side of her face against his back. "As long as I have you, and the girls, I have everything." She paused. "I know, because I almost lost you."

"Lost me?"

He felt her head nodding against his back. "Uh-huh. That's why I left you in '73. Because I couldn't bear to slowly lose you."

"Honey," he said, easing her arms from around him. Harriet sat up and Sam fell back on the bed, pulling her down to lie in his arms. "Honey," he whispered, kissing the top of her head, "you'd have to kill me to get rid of me."

* * *

"For Pete's sake," Althea hissed to Sam in the kitchen, "he's a business major. *Business,* Dad—I bring Mr. Right home for you and you can't even remember his name."

Sitting down at the table, Sam lit another cigarette. "Sorry, honey."

"*George,* you called him," Althea said, throwing the dish towel on the counter.

Exhaling a stream of smoke, Sam said, "He should be Mr. Right for you, not me. Mr. Right," he repeated, tapping the ash of the cigarette into the ashtray.

Harriet came in. "John's ready to go," she announced. She looked at Sam's cigarette, frowning slightly.

Althea looked first at her mother, then at her father, and then back to her mother. "Is anyone ever going to tell me what's going on around here?"

After a moment Sam put the cigarette down in the ashtray and got up. "Come here," he said to her.

Althea looked at him, then at her mother, and then back to him.

"Come on," Sam said, holding out his hand.

Althea took a cautious step; Sam reached for her arm and pulled her over to hug her.

"I can't breathe," Althea said over his shoulder, laughing.

Sam released her, stepped back slightly and looked down into his daughter's eyes. "You know how much I love you, don't you?"

"What is *with* you, Daddy?" Althea wanted to know. "You've been acting so weird."

"Yeah," Sam agreed, "I've been acting weird all right. Because I've been feeling plenty weird." He held his daughter's hands, swinging them. He sighed, glancing back at Harriet, and then simply held Althea's hands. "Something's been going on at the office that's not—ethical. And I've been upset, because I haven't known how to deal with them—it."

"The guy who took your files, I bet," Althea said.

He shook his head, laughing a little. "Mind like a steel trap, this girl." He touched Althea's chin. "I will explain everything to you—eventually. But what's important right now is that I apologize to you, for acting so—weird —and to tell you how much I love you."

Althea squinted at him, wary. Sam leaned over and kissed her on the cheek. "You better get going with, uh—" Althea rolled her eyes. "John," Sam finished, moving back to the table to get his cigarette.

Althea watched her father a moment and then looked at her mother. "Well," she said with a little shrug, "thanks for cooking dinner for John."

"I like him," Harriet whispered, moving over to stand next to Sam.

"Only because he knew that Gardiner & Grayson book," Althea laughed, walking toward the door. She paused there, looking back at the two of them —Sam sitting, Harriet standing there, hand on his shoulder. She smiled and came back to them. "I love you, Daddy," she said, bending to kiss him on the cheek. "You too, Mom." Harriet accepted a kiss on the cheek as well and gave Althea's a hand a squeeze. And then Althea went back to the living room.

Harriet sat down, eyes on her husband. Sam smiled and gave her knee a small nudge with his own. Harriet crinkled her nose and waved the smoke out of the air. Sam laughed then, and Harriet did too. "Man," he said under his breath, shaking his head, "it's like old times, isn't it?"

She nodded, watching him put the cigarette out. Her eyes came back up. "Back to the hypnotist when this is over," she said.

"Uh—" said a deep voice at the door. Harriet and Sam turned to look. It was John. "I just wanted to thank you for dinner."

"Oh, George—" Sam said warmly, rising to his feet.

"Dad!" Althea wailed from the living room.

"John!" Sam declared brightly, raising a forefinger into the air.

As they had expected, the doorbell of the Wyatts' apartment rang that night at nine-thirty. Sam and Harriet went to the door together, and when they opened it, they saw Cassy standing there, smiling. "Guess what Lane Smith had in the basement of his house in the country?"

"What?" Sam asked.

Cassy stepped inside, took the door from Sam, closed it, and leaned back against it. "Copies of every piece of paper on the Trinity Electronics deal up to the day he was fired."

Sam whirled back, letting out a whoop.

Cassy laughed, and Harriet laughed too, not quite sure what this really meant.

"We're gonna get 'em—we're gonna get 'em—we're gonna get 'em", Sam chanted like a college cheer. He threw his head back and laughed. "Oh, baby!" he then cried, lifting Harriet off the ground. He put her down and gave her a big kiss on the forehead.

Cassy pushed herself off the door. "There's more, Sam, much more," she said, looking at her watch. "And we've got to hurry."

They went into the kitchen and Harriet made coffee. Cassy started to outline the "part" that related to Sam and Electronika.

Part?

Part.

The story, then, was larger?

The story, then, was much, much larger.

Huh.

The London bureau of *Conolly's* had tracked down Smith and two other dismissed executives of Trinity Electronics. All three were happy to cooperate on condition they be left out of it. *Conolly's* had copies of everything—letters, memos, contracts, telexes—involved with Electronika's buy-out. It was the evidence that proved that, before the arrival of Brennan and Canley, Trinity and Electronika had absolutely no ties with South Africa.

Thank God.

The Pretoria plant was leased from a South American holding company, fronting for a Mexican holding company, fronting for an American company, whose CEO happened to be Brennan's brother-in-law. A stringer for WST managed to get a look inside the plant and, based on what he described, Lane Smith estimated that it could only handle approximately five to ten percent of the assembly for the ZT 5000.

So they never really intended to move full assembly there.

Enough for a scandal, but no, not full assembly.

"Then where *are* the machines being assembled?"

"In Kenya. Right where they were always supposed to have been."

"Huh."

Sam's office phone and the Wyatts' home phone, as they knew, were tapped. There had been no unusual movement on Electronika's stock.

Which meant?

"We think," Cassy said slowly, "that they're waiting for word that the story on the Pretoria plant is about to break." She paused. "And now we're not sure of this, Sam, but it may be you're not the only one at Electronika who has been set up to break the story. We're not sure about that—but we are sure someone's listening on your phones and"—she paused, sighing slightly—"following you. There's a man outside right now—right across the street."

"Althea," Harriet murmured, reaching out to hold Sam's arm.

"No, Harriet," Cassy hastened to add. "He's following Sam." She hesitated and then said, "Besides, there's someone following *him.*"

Sam and Harriet looked at her.

"The FBI."

Sam covered his face with his hands and then let them slowly drop. Reaching for his cigarettes, he said, "I don't believe this."

Cassy went on to explain that *Conolly's* and WST had to go to the Securities and Exchange Commission with what they had—they couldn't sit by and watch what was probably a multimillion-dollar crime-in-progress. But the SEC, they found, was already investigating Caswell Zander in connection with three other transactions that smelled of inside trading. The Electronika connection was new to the SEC, but they quickly saw that it was their chance to observe how the Caswell Zander "syndicate" actually worked. And since it was a federal case, the FBI was brought in. So *Conolly's* and WST were working with them. For them, actually, and in return, of course, they would have the story as it broke.

"So where we are, Sam," Cassy finished, looking at her watch again, "is waiting to see what they do when they think the South Africa story is breaking. Who talks to whom, and who does what, and for whom." She paused, eyes dropping as she touched the edge of the table. She looked up. "We want you to make the call, Sam. Tonight. To Paul. He's at his office now—with company, of course."

Silence.

"We want you to call him and tell him about the Pretoria plant, just as you would have weeks ago."

"And they'll be listening," Sam said.

"Yes." Cassy looked to Harriet and then back to Sam. "I'll be honest with you—with both of you. We'll do our best to protect you, Sam—to keep you clear of all this. But," she sighed, biting her lower lip slightly, "I have to warn you, I can't promise you that whoever is listening on your phone is going to do the same. Rumors can get out. My fears are not about Brennan or Canley—my fears are about the repercussions for you if Electronika thinks you blew the whistle on their chief executive officers. A scandal is a scandal and bad business, as they say."

Silence.

Sam looked down at the table, blinking rapidly. He sighed, and went about lighting a cigarette. He exhaled smoke, rubbed one eye, and looked to Harriet. "What do you think?"

She turned to Cassy. "We've discussed this." She looked back at Sam. "Whatever you decide, honey."

He took a deep breath and looked at Cassy, stretching. "Oh, I'm going to do it, Cassy," he said, dropping his arms. "I'm just trying to think of what I'm going to say."

Cassy beamed. And then she said, "Don't worry about your lines. Paul will ask all the questions, just like a good reporter should." She took out a piece of paper from her purse and handed it to him. "Give me," she said, looking at her watch, "say, twenty minutes, and then call him." She got up from her chair.

"Where are you going?" Harriet asked her.

"Who, me?" Cassy said, checking her watch again. "I've got a date with your elevator man to let me out through the basement."

Sam and Harriet exchanged looks. "Great neighborhood we live in," Sam said, rising from his chair. "I'll see you to the door, Mata Hari."

29

HOWARD IS FACED WITH
THE HORRORS AT WORK

It was still difficult for Howard to believe the board members had been in their right minds when they elected to unseat Harrison Dreiden and name Mack Sperry president and publisher of Gardiner & Grayson. Mack Sperry from the business department? Mack Sperry, formerly a district sales manager for the Jackson Hardware chain? Mack Sperry who disliked reading and thought Lefty Lucerne was the answer to Lee Iacocca?

Yes.

It was true, Howard granted, that Sperry was some kind of wizard with numbers. That was what had got him the job, Howard knew, this magic "numbers" capacity that the G & G board saw as the key to reorganizing the house into a gold mine. But publisher? Why not just make him president so as to spare any pretense that Sperry could see books as anything other than "units"? It was unforgivable, Howard thought, placing the hundred-and-forty-six-year-old name of Gardiner & Grayson in the hands of a man who was quoted in *Publishers Weekly* as saying, "I heard him [another publisher] at ABA and everyone knows that his line—'There's no such thing as a bad book'—is pure crappola. A bad book is one that doesn't sell, and the worst book is one over 312 pages that doesn't sell, and since that's all he seems to publish, I think he should stop yammering about censorship and concentrate on his work."

And this was from whom Howard was to ask for a raise.

He took Harrison's suggestions and prepped himself well (he thought) and met with Sperry, giving him a concise review of his list of books, his contribution to G & G and the reasons why he felt he deserved a raise—and soon.

It was not without difficulty that he got through his presentation. Howard had never cared to look at Sperry up close, but now, sitting here one on one, he had no choice. And it was distracting. First there was the business of Sperry's marine-style haircut, which was enough to throw anyone—including a marine—since few wished to retain the look of boot camp as the mainstay of their personal style. But what was worse—much, much worse—was Sperry's habit, while listening, of lifting his upper lip in a half sneer every five seconds or so. It made Howard feel as though he was trying to talk to a saber-toothed goldfish.

And then there were the guns. All over Sperry's office were replicas of handguns (or maybe they were real, Howard certainly wouldn't have known). Some were mounted on wall plaques; some were on stands in the bookshelves; three were just lying on their sides along the windowsill behind Sperry's desk. After standing up to adjust one of the window blinds, Sperry picked up one of these guns and started spinning the barrel, again and again. Then he stopped spinning it, pulled the barrel out to the side, and held the gun up to look through it. Then, in one motion, he clapped the barrel back into place and took aim out the window, arms outstretched. Suddenly he pivoted and swung his aim at Howard's head.

Click.

"You've talked long enough," Sperry said.

"So I gather," Howard said, touching his glasses.

Sperry put the gun down on his desk and sat down in his chair. "I'll be straight with you, Stewart," he said, frowning, opening a folder and scanning the top sheet. "I hadn't looked at the numbers on you and now that I have . . ." He pushed the file away and looked at Howard. "Frankly, I don't think you're worth keeping at your present salary."

Howard rubbed his chin, feeling oddly like laughing.

"In my opinion, I think your contribution to the company stinks and your attitude sucks."

"I had two bestsellers—"

"And you have the biggest loss leader for the fiscal year with that computer book."

"*I* did?" Howard said, jerking forward. "I didn't even sign it up! As you might recall," he said, settling back, trying to calm down, "the editor was fired and I was assigned to see it through. As a matter of fact," he added, hand tightening, "after the author failed to make the revisions on it, I wrote several memos recommending that the book be canceled."

Sperry's hand was on the gun again, but he didn't pick it up. "What are you saying, Stewart?"

"I'm not saying anything. I'm just reminding you that I wanted that book to be canceled and that your department refused to and"—he took a breath, *oh, what the hell*—"seemed to think all it needed was a snappy title and a hundred thousand first printing to make a go of it." Howard sighed. "Look, Mr. Sperry, I admit it, I've made some errors of judgment on some books, but I can't sit here and be blamed for something I know I am not responsible for."

"You're fired," Sperry said.

Howard blinked.

Sperry closed the folder and threw it over his shoulder, sending papers flying. "Get the fuck out of here."

Howard continued to sit there.

After several moments Sperry narrowed his eyes, leaned back in his chair, and knitted his fingers together on his stomach. "You can learn how to do your job or you can pack up your crap and get out of here. Which is it going to be?"

I could always throw you out the window, Howard thought.

"I'll listen to what you have to say," Howard said carefully, "and then I'll see if I can do the job you want me to do."

"All right then." Sperry stood up. "Pick up your papers and then I'll explain it to you."

"What?"

Sperry moved around his desk and sat in the chair next to Howard. He pointed to where he had been sitting before. "Get your file," he said.

Howard paused and then got up, went around the desk, and picked up the folder and papers. He brought them back and sat down.

Sperry grabbed them, rifled through them to the sheet he wanted, and jammed them into Howard's lap. "Look," he said, mashing his finger on the sheet.

Howard felt ill and loosened his tie.

"Are you paying attention, Stewart?" Sperry demanded.

"Yeah."

"Okay then."

And then Sperry launched into a very complicated explanation of the new "accounting" and "list planning" procedures at Gardiner & Grayson. Howard might not have been a wizard at numbers like Sperry, but he did know enough about math and publishing to know that what Sperry was doing had lots to do with paper and little to do with reality. In fact, the more Sperry ripped apart Howard's list, the more he realized that Sperry was testing him —did Howard understand that a game was being played, and was Howard going to play it?

"Now wait a minute," he said when Sperry started saying how Howard better hope like hell a spy novel was going to be as good as he had said it was. "The sales estimate here says twenty thousand copies." Howard looked at Sperry. "I only signed it up five months ago and the sales estimate, confirmed by your—the business office—was thirty thousand. Who changed it?"

Sperry mumbled something about a "planning" meeting at which enthusiasm for the book had dropped.

"How can enthusiasm drop for a book that hasn't been finished yet? The sales estimate was based on the author's track record of twenty-eight thousand copies on his last book." He looked back down at the paper in front him and ran his finger down the advance sales estimates. "And you've reduced Gertrude's advance sales too—from eighty to—to *fifty-five.*" His head flew up to look at Sperry.

Sperry's mouth started in on the goldfish–sneer maneuver again.

Howard was horrified. Absolutely horrified. Looking down at the "revised" sales estimates on some of his other promising books, he realized that Sperry was using them as insurance to make sure that if he did not actually increase profits in the first two years of his presidency he would at least *appear* to have done so. It was a plan of hocus-pocus paper magic: on the titles most likely to succeed, like the spy novel, cut the sales estimates by one third. The budget would then plan on revenues from a twenty-thousand-copy sale, so when the book came out and sold thirty thousand, there would be windfall income on an "unanticipated" extra sale of ten thousand books.

In other words, feed the G & G board a budget that said the company was holding two pairs, and then miraculously come forth with a full house —Ahhh! Our new president! Miracle worker! The job is his!

Oh, God, what ever happened to the excitement and discovery of book publishing? Howard wondered. What ever happened to writers? To books? All these new games were about computer printouts and MBA mind-masturbation. How was Howard supposed to protect the interests of his authors under a system like this? When time of publication came, what if Sperry *forgot* he had deflated the advance sales figure? The first printing, the promotion budget, everything on the book would be reduced to fit the advance sales projection. What was Howard supposed to do then, say, "Psst—Mack —you rigged the numbers on this one, remember? The first printing should be twenty thousand, not fifteen. Because we know it's probably going to sell thirty—remember?"

"Even though these numbers have been changed," Howard said, "you know I am a profitable editor and deserve a raise, Mr. Sperry."

Sperry grabbed the papers from Howard. "You goddam prima donna editors think you know everything," he said, sifting through the papers. He stopped at a sheet and slammed it down on Howard's leg. "Look at this. Just look at this. Look at the overhead on you. Your office. Your salary. Your department expenses. Your expense account, phone bills, copying— and look at your secretary's salary—"

"Come on," Howard said, "he barely makes fourteen thousand a year—"

"You come on!" Sperry cried, throwing the papers in the air again. "You're the one who came in here asking for a raise. A raise!" He vaulted out of the chair and went around to the other side of the desk. He leaned over it, raising a hand to point a finger at Howard. "Unless your attitude changes, Stewart, unless you join the team around here, I'm gonna kick your ass outta here so fast it's going to make your head spin." He started riffling through papers on his desk. "I am so goddam sick and tired of you fucking shithead editors—" His head jerked up. "Do you need your job, Stewart—or are you the rich kid everyone says you are?"

Howard stood up. He cleared his throat. "I need my job like everyone else," he said. He paused. "Thank you for listening to me, Mr. Sperry, and I appreciate your explaining how things stand." He turned for the door and then stopped. He turned around. "I can't get a raise, right?"

Sperry gave him three goldfish–sneers and then abruptly sat down in his chair. "We'll see," he muttered, pushing his gun to the side of his desk.

Howard sat in his office, looking out the window, refusing to take or make phone calls.

Sigh.

He got up to close the door. He came back to the desk, pulled a sheet of white bond out of a drawer, smoothed it over the blotter and picked up a pen. He thought a moment and then wrote:

> Dear Amanda,
> I need you. Everything is

He ripped it up, threw it away, and started again.

> Dearest Amanda,
> What you said about us was right, I realize now. And I want to change. And I will try to change, but please

He started again.

> Dearest Amanda,
> If there's any hope at all for us, I need to know now.

That got torn up too. Then, after five minutes:

> Amanda,
> You'll be pleased to know that you've destroyed my entire life.

Howard threw that into the trash too.

30

THE UNDOING
OF CASSY COCHRAN

Cassy arrived at WST at five in the morning. On the corner of West 6oth Street and West End Avenue, the windows of her office overlooked the old railroad tracks, a battered section of the West Side Highway, abandoned docking facilities and the beautiful waters of the Hudson River. On normal mornings, at eight, she would swing her chair around to face the windows, sip coffee, scan the *Times,* the Washington *Post* and the *Wall Street Journal,* periodically gazing outside to view the progress of the morning sky. But not today.

It was waiting for her with the security guard downstairs. Carrying *it* up the elevator, she nearly ran to her office. Once there, she threw down her briefcase, ripped open the package and unfolded the copy of *Conolly's.*

CASWELL ZANDER, ELECTRONIKA EXECS ARRESTED
Wall Street Reels in Anticipation of Massive Insider Trading Scandal
by Paul Levitz

"Good, you're here," Sid Freeman said, charging into her office. "I've got our copy for the six o'clock." Cassy tucked *Conolly's* under her arm to accept the script from Sid.

Cassy was holding out the copy, reading, nodding, making her way over to her desk. "This is great," she murmured, going on to the next page. She eased herself down into her chair. "Good, good," she murmured, opening her center drawer, feeling around and extracting her glasses. She put them on and drew the copy closer.

"Chester and Pam are all set downstairs," Sid reported, fidgeting. "They'll start the 6 A.M. and run through the day. Bill's coming in at nine as backup, Lydia at ten."

"Hmmm." Next page. "Anything from Washington yet?"

"Not yet. We should hear around noon."

"How does the tape look?" she asked, still reading.

"Great—I want you to come down now and look at it."

Cassy looked up, thinking. She smiled then, and took off her glasses. She held the copy out to him.

He looked confused. "Take it," she said.

Sid took the copy from her.

"It's terrific. Run with it."

"Cassy, it was your—"

"Uh-uh," she said, shaking her head. "Go on—go!" she said, shooing him out.

He laughed. "Oh, Cass—" He poked his head back in. "I'm not going to be able to make the Handervilles tonight—could you fill in for me?"

She nodded. "I was going anyway."

"Great," he said, slapping the frame of the door.

Sam Wyatt called Cassy from a pay phone at six forty-five.

"We just saw the news," he said. "Man, it's just so hard to believe."

Cassy laughed, turning down her monitor of the broadcast with a remote control, and swung her chair around to look out the window. "Disappointed?"

"Hardly! Ten million dollars of options? It's unbelievable."

"The SEC's frozen trading on Electronika."

"Fifty-three million dollars those guys would have made?" He coughed slightly. "Well, I'm on my way to the office now. There's a board meeting at eight."

"Minus a few, I should think."

Sam laughed. "Did you see Canley take a swing at your reporter?"

They talked for a while longer; Sam promised to let Cassy know how he made out at the office; Cassy reminded him he could give up phone booths as a hobby.

WST was a madhouse all day. Cassy spent most of it on the phone with the independent stations in Washington, Chicago, Los Angeles, San Francisco and London that WST was beaming their "Caswell Zandergate" coverage to by satellite. As the day progressed, so did the scope of the story. Seven other executives at five other New York-based companies were indicted in connection with other Caswell Zander stock and option transactions of the past. And then, at noon, WST was fed live reports from Washington as two congressmen and one senator were indicted concerning government contracts that had been awarded to another Caswell Zander "client"—Linnolare Motors—whose CEO happened to be Walter Brennan's brother-in-law.

The networks of course were on the story now, but WST's head start was serving them well. (That was the thrill; knowing that at CBS, NBC and ABC today they were writing their own bulletins largely from what was being aired on WST.) WST's lead would not last longer than, perhaps, the evening news, but who cared? For today, the story was theirs alone and it felt marvelous.

Cassy left the office at five, feeling a mixture of elation and longing. Perhaps today, more than any other day, she felt the acute loss of having left the newsroom. It made her feel lonely. Left behind.

When she arrived home and saw herself in the front hall mirror, Cassy decided that she definitely qualified for Rent-A-Wreck. Good Lord, what the lack of sleep did to her now. Funny, how she looked in the mirror and could still be surprised by the face that looked back at her. . . .

Oh, well. She supposed being forty-one was better than forty-two.

She poured herself a glass of Perrier and grapefruit juice and carried it back to the bedroom. First, a hot bath, then Operation Face.

Michael.

As soon as she walked in the door, she knew he was there. She smelled him, smelled it, the stench of stale liquor.

He was lying face down across the bed, apparently asleep. Or dead.

No, he was not dead. He was breathing.

Cassy stood there, mind racing. Was he home for good? Was he passed out? Was he here—what was he here for? What should she do? Call Sam? Just talk to him? Pretend everything was all right? Should she go to the dinner? Should she wake him up and ask him if he wanted to go to the dinner?

Oh, Lord, what was she thinking of?

Okay, now, a plan of action. *Just go about my business. Do what I would do if he were not here.*

So Cassy went into the bathroom and started her bath. She came back out to the bedroom. Michael had not moved. She stripped off her clothes, closed the door to the bathroom and got in the bath. She knew, lying there, feeling the heat of the water, that she should be thinking and yet her mind seemed to have closed down. So she closed her eyes and decided that paralysis of the brain was probably a blessing.

She got out of the bath, flipped the drain, and toweled herself dry. She opened the door, went into the bedroom, and stood there, watching Michael. The drain made a ghastly gurgling sound and Michael stirred, turning over onto his back, arm over his face, coughed once, and then started to snore. His face was awful-looking; it was bloated and shades darker. In fact, all of Michael was bloated. She looked at the fingers of his hand and scarcely recognized them as his. His wedding band was gone too, she noticed.

Suddenly Cassy was terrified he would wake up. Fear shot up the back of her spine, into her neck, and then she was trembling. *God, please, God, don't let him wake up while I'm here.*

She crept back to the bathroom and flipped the drain over.

Now what?

She slipped on Michael's robe, quietly opened the medicine cabinet, and stuffed her makeup, cotton swabs and toothbrush in the pockets. She left the medicine cabinet open. She peered out into the bedroom.

He was still snoring.

Her stomach clenched, her breath short and ragged, she tiptoed out. It took nearly ten minutes of agonizing care to get her underwear and stockings out of the dresser drawers, her dress and shoes out of the closet and then—problem. She was running out of hands and pockets. Back to the bathroom she crept for a towel. Spreading it out on the floor, she put her deodorant, hairpins, hair spray, necklace, brooch, bracelets, earrings, brush, comb and slip on it, bundled it all up, and then sneaked out of the bedroom.

Cassy went to the guest room, the last place Michael would go if he woke up. She hurried to get dressed—but her makeup! The eyeliner nearly made her cry with exasperation; her hands were simply shaking too much, making lines that belonged only on maps. She tried to wipe it off with a cotton swab but she was too shaky to do even that correctly.

Just calm down. In five minutes you will be out of here. You will go to dinner. You will come home, prepared to meet him. Just pull yourself together and get out while he's still asleep.

In five minutes Cassy at least looked as if she had made some attempt at dressing for dinner. But a mere attempt it was. She had no foundation on, nor any eye shadow (she didn't dare go back for either), and the earrings had been chosen in haste, not taste. Still, she would pass.

She wrapped everything up in the robe and stuffed it under the bed. She took one last look in the mirror and then she heard Michael—coughing. She stood there, straining to hear—would he go back to sleep? *Please go back to sleep.*

Silence.

She moved toward the door.

"Cassy?"

Cassy's heart pounded. *What to do, what to do?* To get out of the apartment, she would have to go past their bedroom. Her only chance would be if Michael went to the bathroom. That, or hide in the closet until he left. *Oh, God, what if he finds me hiding back here?*

"Cass?" he was calling.

He had been drunk; he was now half drunk.

Cassy heard something. She heard him, she thought, moving around. Toward the bathroom? She longed to move down the hall to hear, but what if he came out? She'd be trapped in the hallway. *Please, God, let him go to the bathroom.*

He did. She heard the all too familiar sound of the toilet seat being hurled up.

Shoes in hand, Cassy was off—down the hall, into the kitchen—*damn, no purse. Don't be a fool, just take your briefcase. Go! Go! Hurry! Keys—never mind! Go! Hurry!*

She slipped out the front door and tried to close it. It was sticking so she left it ajar. She looked at the elevator and in her mind could see Michael coming out of the bathroom, looking for her. Her clothes were only lying out there on the chair . . .

"Cassy?" she heard.

Quick. She put on her shoes and hurried down the hall to the staircase. Her heels clattered on the stairs—*damn*—so she gripped the railing and wobbled down to the next floor. And just in time. She heard their door open and a voice bellow, "Caaaaaassy!"

She pressed for the elevator.

There was noise above. Michael was in the hallway. What was he doing? *God, please let the elevator come.*

The elevator slowly went up past her floor—and stopped. *It's on our floor,* she thought. And then it hit her—*the elevator will stop here next.* She wheeled around and headed for the stairs and was almost on them when she heard the elevator doors open behind her. She didn't turn around, she didn't move. She did not breathe. *If he doesn't hear anything, he'll go down to the lobby.* She heard the elevator doors close and the whine of its descent. *Thank you, God.*

"Please don't run away from me," Michael's voice said from behind her.

Cassy didn't even look back. She let her shoulders slump, dragged herself over to the stairs, and sat down. And cried.

Michael stood in front of her, watching her, and then sat down next to her on the step, careful not to touch her. His voice was low, gentle. "Why did you run away from me?"

When she opened her eyes, she saw that most of her makeup had made the transition to her hands. "I'm tired of being hurt," she finally said, wiping at her eyes. "I don't want to be hurt anymore."

"Oh, Cass," Michael sighed. He pulled a tissue out of the side of her briefcase and handed it to her. She used it. In a moment she looked at him; he was studying his hands.

"Do you think I want to hurt you?" he asked, voice barely audible. "Do you think I ever wanted to hurt you?" He swallowed, still staring at his hands. "I'm sick of failing you, Cass. Over and over again. I can't be what you want me to be. I never could."

A neighbor came out of an apartment down the hall. Neither Cassy nor Michael looked up to see who it was. They remained silent, eyes to the ground, until they heard whoever it was get on the elevator.

"What do you want?" she asked quietly.

He sighed. "I need some money. It's the only time I'll ask."

"He'll be back when he needs money," Sam had warned Cassy. "It's vital that you don't give it to him. All it will do is enable him to keep drinking. And you have to warn Henry, too. Because if he can't get it from you, he'll use Henry to get it."

Next time, Cassy thought to herself. *I don't have the energy to fight him now.* Michael was being nice now, but what would he be like when he didn't get what he wanted?

"Change the locks on your doors," Sam had warned her.

She hadn't, of course. But tomorrow she would.

Cassy opened her briefcase and rummaged for her checkbook. "How much do you need?"

"Whatever you've got on hand."

She opened the checkbook on her knee and looked at the balance, well aware that he was looking over her shoulder. "I have a little over three thousand in my checking account," she said. "Is that enough?"

"More than enough. Thank you."

From the way he said it, Cassy wondered if Michael had expected to get anything from her.

She wrote a check for three thousand dollars and handed it to him, still not meeting his eyes.

He folded the check carefully and put it in his back pocket. "I'm short on cash—"

She looked into the pocket of her checkbook. "I need fifteen for cabs. I have to go to a dinner at the Hilton. Here. Here's forty."

He took the money and put that carefully away as well.

"There are two things you must promise me," she said, putting her checkbook away, "or I'll stop payment on that check." Pause. "One, you see a doctor." She sniffed and glanced over at him. "You look terrible, Michael."

He shrugged, looking down at his shoes.

"And two," Cassy said, rising, "that you're not here when I get back."

"I won't be."

She started down the stairs to the next floor. On the half landing, she looked back up at him through the bars of the banister. "Call me next week. I just can't deal with this right now."

"Me neither," he sighed.

When Cassy arrived at the Hilton, she fled to the ladies' room off the lobby. The attendant, bless her, was fully equipped to deal with broken-down women like herself (this was, after all, New York—where hearts were broken every minute). Cassy had a full selection of repair tools at her disposal, and blush, eye shadow and mascara did much to cover the damage. Only after she was finished did Cassy realize she had no cash to pay the woman, so she wrote her a check for ten dollars—an offering the attendant viewed with a bit of skepticism (this was, after all, New York).

Cassy felt better because she looked better. She felt relieved too, because dealing with Michael had been postponed. *Relieved.* Good Lord, what sense did that make? *Agonizing over him for weeks and then when he shows up—*

She tried to shake her thoughts away and concentrate on the dinner. She took the escalator up to the second floor and followed the people into the ballroom. Taking a deep breath, she moved forward into the people, around the tables, greeting and talking briefly with those she knew. She found WST's table, found her place card, sat down and listened to a young woman from public relations explain that she had heard WST had not won their category.

Cassy ordered a vodka tonic to stop the quaking of her hands. It worked, slowly, and she felt a bit better. She ordered a white wine next. *Oh, great, now the other Cochran will get drunk,* she thought. *They'll all love that.*

Alexandra slid into the empty seat next to Cassy, took one look at her, pressed her hand and asked what had happened. Cassy smiled, weakly, and said, "Michael's back."

"At home?"

Cassy said, looking past Alexandra to Barbara Marioni, to whom she waved, "He's staying elsewhere at the moment." She looked at Alexandra. "Come on," she whispered, "let's forget about him. This is your night. Deal?"

"Deal," Alexandra said, pulling one of her ratings smiles. Her eyes then skipped away to survey the room. "Everyone's talking about WST. You could have at least warned me that you were going to blow up Wall Street while I was in Poughkeepsie today."

Cassy smiled. "It wouldn't have been a coup then, would it?"

Alexandra turned, speaking through a frozen smile, "What the hell is a 'put'? I'll die before I let on I don't know what anyone's talking about."

Cassy patted her hand. "A put, my young colleague, is a bet that a stock will go down a certain amount within a given time. The price of a put, like a call—that's up—depends on the odds. The puts in question cost next to nothing, since the odds of Electronika's—"

"Got it," Alexandra said. "Race track à la Wall Street—they doped the horse and bet he'd lose."

Peter Cannon, WST's financial controller, arrived, and Alexandra vacated his chair and returned to WWKK's table. Dinner was served; Cassy was barely aware of whatever it was she ate (and she did eat—something). Sy Bolin, the producer of the documentary, arrived finally, and Cassy let the PR gal break the news to him that he wouldn't be winning. Peter Cannon was going on and on about something—at first Cassy thought it was the transmitter, but no, it was about the satellite fees they were spending on the Caswell Zander story.

Cassy laughed to herself, sipping on a new glass of white wine. Caswell Zander? Had that really only been today?

The MC cleared his voice at the podium on the dais and the room grew quiet. Waiters weaved in and out, carrying out the debris of dinner. Cassy drank her wine and pretended to listen to the introductory remarks while, in reality, thinking about divorce, Henry, divorce, suicide, the things stuffed under the bed in the guest room, divorce, Sam, God, and what it would be like to be single.

Old and single.

They proceeded with the awards. There were short, wonderful speeches by veteran broadcast journalists and then short, wonderful speeches by veteran and younger broadcast journalists as they accepted their awards. Major Market, Feature Reporting: WCBS in New York won for a story about welfare hotels; WMAQ in Chicago for a story about a controversial community; WBZ in Boston won for a story about Afghanistan. They went on into independent documentaries and poor Sy was mentioned as a nominee but did not get to go to the podium (he left a few minutes later).

Maxwell Faldigrand was supposed to introduce the Middle Market, Feature Reporting category. Last Cassy heard, Maxwell was reminiscing about his days down South, and then Peter turned to look at Cassy. Then Cassy noticed that a couple of people had turned around to look at her. Trying to wake up from wherever she had been, she heard Maxwell say:

". . . and Sid says, 'You want to know who uncovered the story? I'll tell you who. Our station manager, Cassy Cochran, that's who.' "

Faces swung in her direction.

"I know, I know," Maxwell was saying at the podium, "next year will be here soon enough, and the good people at WST will be up here receiving their accolades. But I, for one, can't wait and want to give a round of applause for a job well done. Cassy Cochran, please stand up and take a bow for the WST newsroom."

The applause started in the front and made its way, in waves, to the back. Peter pushed Cassy up on her feet and she smiled, seeing but not registering, quite safe behind the gray veil that had dropped in front of her eyes. And then she saw Alexandra across the room, clapping over her head, face radiant.

Cassy sat down and Peter patted her on the back while she drained her wineglass.

Michael doesn't even know about it.

They got on with the awards and in a few minutes Cassy heard, "KSCT

News, Kansas City, for 'Death of an American Farmer.' To accept the award is reporter Alexandra Waring and KSCT station manager Seth Philby."

Cassy cheered and her table glared at her. (It is not nice to cheer loudly after one of your own has failed to win.) But Cassy couldn't have cared less.

Alexandra glided up onto the dais and everyone's eyes, Cassy noted, were riveted on her. And why not? she thought, eyes returning to Alexandra. With her long, dark dress, a few scattered sequins sparkling under the lights, her hair fanned out in all its glory, and with that face, those eyes . . .

Peter whispered, "Now why don't we ever have anyone looking like that working for us?"

Thanks, Cassy thought.

Alexandra's acceptance speech was quite moving. She talked about the subject of her story—a farmer who had shot himself after losing the farm his family had owned for generations, and the family he left behind. Her message concerned political grandstanding and the economics of greed— "neither of which take into consideration the fundamental needs of human beings. And that when you systematically strip an American of everything that he or she holds dear—their home, their livelihood, their self-respect and their dignity—it should come as no surprise that they will no longer wish to live."

She thanked the individuals who had worked on the story with her, and, on a lighter note, made a special note to thank a Mrs. Kaffundersmelt in Winnopeka for lending Alexandra her fishing waders to go out in the field. People laughed; people loved her.

I love her too, Cassy thought, eyes misting.

And, finally, Alexandra offered heartfelt gratitude to KSCT, the station that had taught her so much. She stepped to the side and Seth Philby ran through his little speech, ending with KSCT being so proud of Alexandra Waring, now of WWKK here in New York.

Alexandra stepped down from the dais, nodding and smiling at the people congratulating her. She said something to a man at the WWKK table and walked on, holding her award, looking directly at Cassy.

Cassy helped herself to a swallow of Peter's wine and then Alexandra was there, looking down at her.

"Come with me for a minute," Alexandra said, touching her shoulder and walking on.

Cassy smiled at Peter, excused herself, and got up. Uh-oh. A little too much wine—but no, it was going to be okay. Throwing her shoulders back, Cassy walked out to the lobby of the ballroom where Alexandra was waiting. "Congratulations," Cassy said, reaching to hug her.

And then she burst into tears, right there on Alexandra's shoulder.

Alexandra stood there, awkwardly trying to hold both Cassy and her award. "Come over here," she said, gently prying Cassy's arms loose and taking her hand. She led her to a couch and sat her down.

Peter came out of the ballroom. "Hey," he said to Cassy, squatting down in front of her. He gave her his handkerchief. "You need some rest, Cassy. You've been working too hard."

Cassy nodded, wiping her eyes. "I'm sorry," she said, looking to Alexandra.

"Don't be ridiculous," Alexandra said.

Cassy started to hand Peter the handkerchief back, but he smiled and said, "That's okay, you might need it. Listen, why don't I take you home? I was thinking of leaving early anyway."

"Thanks, Peter," Cassy began. She hesitated and then turned her eyes to Alexandra.

Alexandra's eyes darted to the ballroom but then quickly over to Peter. "That's all right," she said, offering a quick smile. "I'll see that she gets home."

"No," Cassy said, shaking her head. "You should stay—"

"Peter," Alexandra said, "I would appreciate it if you could get Cassy's things and my purse. It's sitting in my chair at the KK table."

As Peter went off, Alexandra turned back to Cassy. "Don't say a word," she warned her. "I'm taking you home and that's the end of it."

Cassy wiped her eyes, sighed heavily, and fell back against the couch, murmuring, "I think I really am losing it this time."

They heard applause in the ballroom.

"Oh, Alexandra," Cassy said, "tell me it's not the end."

Alexandra looked at her. "It is not the end," she said quietly.

Cassy managed a sad smile, but as she continued to look into Alexandra's eyes her smile faded. Then she looked away, shaking her head. "I don't know what's the matter with me," she said, voice fading too. "I can't believe the thoughts that are running through my head."

Alexandra didn't say anything.

Peter reappeared, holding Cassy's briefcase and Alexandra's purse. They thanked him, Peter told Cassy to take some aspirin before she went to sleep and said good night.

Alexandra steered Cassy to the escalator. Going down, they could see that it was pouring rain outside. "Uh-oh," Alexandra said, "this could be tricky." The line for taxis was miles long; Alexandra finally located an errant bellboy who agreed to run down the street to the parking garage to pick up Alexandra's car.

"KK wouldn't even spring for a limo for you?"

Alexandra laughed, holding Cassy's arm. "Since Martha was filling in for me tonight, I decided to stay longer at the seminar. I drove straight here from Vassar."

They stood outside, under the overhang of the driveway, to wait. It felt good to Cassy; the wind was blowing and the air was damp and the sound of the rain on the Avenue of the Americas was dramatic. In a few minutes they could see the MG slowly maneuvering up to the entrance. They crossed the line of taxis and reached the MG as it pulled in on the other side of the driveway.

The bellboy held the door for Alexandra and a doorman ran across the driveway to usher Cassy in. Alexandra placed her award in Cassy's lap, helped her with her seat belt, and flicked on the radio. It was an all-news station. Cassy reached for the dial and searched for another station.

They pulled out on Avenue of the Americas and the rain came thundering down on the canvas top.

Cassy flipped the radio to FM, found a classical station, turned it up to hear it over the roar above, and sat back in her seat. The car seemed even smaller than it was. A tiny cavern of fogged windows and flailing wipers.

They stopped at a light at the entrance to Central Park South. "I think I'd like to go to your house," Cassy said, watching Alexandra's profile.

Alexandra turned to look at her.

A taxi behind them honked, startling Alexandra, and she put the car into gear. Cassy shifted slightly against the seat belt and continued to watch her.

They drove slowly through the park. There was flooding everywhere. Alexandra periodically glanced over at Cassy, looking vaguely worried. When they reached the East Side exit to Fifth Avenue, they stopped for the light and Alexandra turned to Cassy, hand twisting at the knob of the stick shift. "Are you all right?" she asked—in a way that said she believed Cassy clearly was not.

Cassy nodded.

They drove to Alexandra's building, Cassy humming to the Prokofiev on the radio, eyes still on Alexandra. At Alexandra's direction, she pressed the door opener in the glove compartment; the gates of the garage rose and

Alexandra drove them in and down the concrete tunnelway. Down in the garage, Alexandra pulled around a pillar to park in her corner space. She revved the motor once and cut off the engine.

They sat there waiting for the Prokofiev piece to end, Alexandra staring straight ahead at the wall, Cassy staring at Alexandra. Cassy undid her seat belt and angled her back against her door. When the music was over, Alexandra reached for the dial. "Okay?" she asked.

Cassy only smiled.

Alexandra turned the radio off. She sat back in her seat, looked straight ahead, and swallowed. Her mouth parted to say something, but she didn't. And then, quietly, looking down into her lap, she murmured, "I'm not sure what it is you want."

After a moment Cassy leaned toward her, making the leather of the seat creak. Very slowly, very gently, she placed her hand under Alexandra's chin and pulled it up toward her. "I need you, Alexandra."

And then Cassy kissed her.

Alexandra let Cassy pass in front of her into the apartment. Cassy walked over to the wall of pictures and stood there, briefcase in hand. Holding the door open with her foot, Alexandra reached to put her purse and award on the table and then bent down in the doorway for the newspapers. She closed the door with her foot, glanced at Cassy, put the papers down on the table, glanced at Cassy again, and then turned the lock on the door.

Click.

"You can put your briefcase down there, if you'd like."

Cassy turned away and put it down next to the wall. Straightening up, her back to Alexandra, she looked at the pictures and said, "The biggest night of your life and I made you leave."

She heard the rustle of Alexandra's dress as she came to stand behind her. There was a pause and then, softly, "Are you sure you want to do this?"

After a moment Cassy nodded.

"Cassy." She felt Alexandra's hand on her arm. "Please, look at me." She slowly turned around. It was just Alexandra, she told herself. The same eyes, the same hair, only it was not TV. It was the gentle voice from the telephone, back in the wrappings that had unsettled Cassy from the start. Alexandra took her hands. "I don't want to do anything that you'll later regret."

Cassy closed her eyes, shaking her head. "I don't think you could." She reopened her eyes. "Could you hold me? Please."

She could, and Cassy held onto her, smelling a faint scent of perfume through her hair. Alexandra's hand was moving lightly over her back, up and down, up and down, and Cassy thought, *Are those her breasts against mine? They are.* She wondered at how strange it was to notice it.

She heard Alexandra sigh, quietly, and then Alexandra released her, bringing her hands up to hold Cassy's face between them. The light in her eyes was gentle. "Are you sure?" she whispered.

Cassy nodded.

Alexandra's eyes traveled down to Cassy's mouth then, and in a moment she brought hers over to meet it. The kiss was carefully dry, but different from the one in the car. This, Cassy felt, was a kiss hinting restraint, edging toward somewhere, turning slightly, quite sure in its intent, but not quite sure of how it was being received.

It was so like Alexandra.

Cassy was falling into it, her mind losing the chant—*I am kissing Alexandra. Good Lord, I am kissing Alexandra*—and she started to part her mouth, wanting to know more. But Alexandra's mouth slid away, breezing over the side of her face to her neck, and Cassy found herself being held again, and heard being whispered, just under her ear, "I don't want us to go too quickly." There was a long kiss then, right there under her ear, and it registered with Cassy that she liked it.

When Alexandra let go of her, she felt oddly unbalanced. Alexandra seemed to know this, for as she led Cassy away by the hand, she whispered cautions. "There's a molding here. . . . The counter, on the right . . . The door . . ."

The bedroom was softly lit by an upward cast of citylight through the windows. Alexandra took Cassy over to one and stood there with her, arm around her waist. Across the East River were the thousands and thousands and thousands of lights that made up the nighttime galaxy of Queens.

They stood there for a long while, until Cassy let her head fall on Alexandra's shoulder. "I'm not—" she started to say. She hesitated, swallowing. "Alexandra, I'm not very—" She closed her eyes, unable to follow it through. Alexandra turned toward Cassy and slid her other arm around her waist. Cassy opened her eyes and saw that she was waiting for her to finish. "I don't want to disappoint you," she said.

"Oh, Cassy," Alexandra sighed, pulling her close. "Cassy, Cassy—" Cassy felt her hair against her face, and she felt Alexandra pull her close, and then closer still. "No, no," Alexandra whispered. "You cannot disappoint me. I'm very, very happy. Right now. Just like this." She pulled back slightly to look at Cassy. She kissed her gently on the cheek and then took her hand. "Come over here," she said, leading her over to the bed. "Let's just sit down for a moment. Here."

Cassy sat down and Alexandra sat down beside her, taking both of her hands into her own. "I want you to listen to me carefully." She lowered her head slightly. "Cassy?"

Cassy raised her head to meet Alexandra's eyes.

"I want to make love to you. Very much. But I don't want to scare you, and I don't want to do anything that doesn't feel good to you." She paused, and then brought one hand up to the side of Cassy's face. "There's no agenda here. There's no performance. I only want you to feel how much I care for you, and how much I want to give you pleasure."

Cassy nodded, wondering where, exactly, her breath had gone.

Alexandra was touching her hair now. "You don't have to do anything but trust me." Her voice, in its whisper, was not quite even. Her hand was on the clip in Cassy's hair, and her other hand came up to help undo it. "I want you to tell me when you don't like what I'm doing." The clip was out and Cassy's hair fell. Alexandra put the clip down on the bed and then gently ran her hands through Cassy's hair. "If you can't say it, just touch my hand and I'll know." She let out a quiet sigh, and her hands came down to rest on Cassy's shoulders. "All right?"

Cassy closed her eyes. "Promise not to laugh?"

A gentle kiss was Alexandra's response.

"Could I borrow a nightgown?"

"Of course," Alexandra murmured, kissing her briefly again. She led Cassy over to her dresser, left to turn on the bathroom light and came back. She opened a drawer. "Black, white, blue or gray? Whatever you'd like."

Cassy touched the silk things she was offering. She looked up. "Whatever you'd like."

Alexandra smiled, eyes lingering. "Blue," she finally said, handing it to her and gesturing to the bathroom. As Cassy walked through the doorway, Alexandra said, "Cassy?" She turned. "And what would you like?"

Cassy smiled and felt like crying suddenly. But she didn't. She just said, "Black, I think," and closed the door.

Under the glare of the bathroom light, Cassy squinted into the mirror and thought about what Michael used to say in college when the bar was closing and the terrible white lights would come on: "Hey, *look,* Cass—everybody's Chinese!"

She almost laughed out loud. This simply couldn't be real, she thought. None of this. Not her life, not Alexandra, not Michael's illness—

Michael's illness. As she got out of her dress, she wondered if that was why she was here. Because she knew, finally knew, that her husband—that Michael was lost to her in his illness.

"I felt like every wife and husband in there was talking about Michael," she had said to Sam after a visit to the group.

"It's the disease," Sam had said. "The symptoms of the disease are almost always the same."

"What do you mean?"

"Either everyone in the group is married to someone with the same disease, Cassy, or all of their spouses have exactly the same personality. Which do you think it is?"

It was true. Michael's personality had changed—rather, it had slowly slipped away in recent years. The rages, the insecurities, the craziness—the affairs—she had almost forgotten that he had not always been like this. But then she had not always been like this, either.

Did this count, cheating on him while he was ill? *Was* she cheating on him? Did a woman count? What would Michael think if he knew?

He would love it, she thought, working to clear the mascara from under her eyes. He had even said in recent years, more than once, that he would like to watch Cassy with a woman. "Damn you, Michael," she would say, close to tears, throwing herself out of bed.

It was only now, right now, in fact, that it occurred to her that Michael might not have said it to torture her about her increasing sexual problems. Sexual problems. God, could it have been true that their sex life together had once been a given? That desire had run as free and easily between them as the work they had shared?

So just whose fault had his affairs been, anyway? His? Hers? The bottle's? It was an interesting question.

And now here she was in a strange bathroom, supposedly getting ready to go to bed with a woman.

She sighed, leaning on the sink, looking at herself in the mirror. Forty-one years were looking back at her. Whose line was that? Michael's? Henry's? WST's? And that one? And that one, and that one—

She lowered her head, wondering at how she had supposed she could actually go through with this. It was ridiculous. A twenty-eight-year-old girl from Kansas, sitting out there, waiting for Cassy to come in and make love with her? Cassy, who had felt almost nothing for—good Lord, how long had it been?

Long. It had been a long time.

Well. She couldn't hide in here forever. She looked down at her slip. And then she pulled it over her head. As if on a dare, she stripped down to her naked self and then—then went back to the mirror. *Is there anything here anyone could want?* she demanded of the mirror. It looked at her face, at her hair, at her shoulders and, finally, at her breasts. And then she stepped back from the sink and looked down at her stomach, at her legs and at her feet. And then she went back to the mirror.

I don't know.

She looked at her dress, stockings and underwear lying over the lid of the john. This was really rather funny. She really had gone crazy this time.

There was a quiet knock. "Would you like a glass of wine or something?" Alexandra asked through the door.

Wine? Cassy clapped a hand over her eyes. Leave it to Alexandra to be out there reading her mind, offering something to get her through this. "No, thank you," she said. And then, after a moment, "Alexandra?"

"Yes?"

"If I'm not out of here in five minutes, I think you might have to come in and get me."

There was a low rush of laughter. Cassy smiled in recognition. It was Alexandra's late night telephone laugh. But had it sounded like this before?

She slid the nightgown over her head, loving how it felt against her, and —after seeing what it did for her eyes, for her breasts—she made the declaration that yes, she was completely crazy, and so all of this was perfectly fine because no one could hold her responsible when it was so clear she was so crazy. She reached for the brush on one of the shelves and bent over to brush her hair out. Throwing her head back and looking into the mirror, she thought, *Yes, there might be something here someone could want.*

It took a moment for her eyes to adjust and to see that Alexandra was not in the bedroom. There was one small candle lit, on the windowsill. The bed was turned down. It was not scary.

"Hi." Alexandra was in the doorway, holding a glass and a bottle of Perrier.

Cassy felt something stir in her chest. Alexandra looked so innocently, devastatingly lovely. Innocent were her eyes, her gentle smile from across the room, but devastating was the trick of her hair and the body curving under black. Could this be Alexandra as well? Could everything Alexandra had given her these weeks be an extension of this body? There was nothing frightening about this thought. About this woman across the room. She was familiar, very familiar. It was only Alexandra.

"You are so very beautiful," Alexandra said, putting the things down on the night table.

Cassy lowered her eyes and walked over to the bed. "I wanted—" she started to say, sitting down on the edge. She took a breath and turned to look at Alexandra. "I wanted to say how beautiful you are."

Alexandra watched her for a moment and then eased down onto the other side of the bed. "It's going to be all right," she whispered. Cassy nodded, lowering her head, breath picking up.

"Do you think you can let me hold you?" Alexandra murmured, sliding slowly across the bed. She stopped just next to Cassy, leaning over to look at Cassy's face. She touched her arm, a light, trailing movement that told Cassy she wanted her to move. "Here," she whispered, helping to guide Cassy, "just lie back against the pillows." Cassy did, and Alexandra reached over to pull her legs up as well. "There," she announced, sitting over her, resting her weight on one arm.

Cassy lay there, waiting for what was next, but also half hoping for the nerve to look at Alexandra's breasts. She was curious, having them there in the bottom of her vision, and, besides, she thought it might be nice if she didn't appear to be totally indifferent. But she didn't get the nerve or the niceness to do so. Alexandra brought her hand up to push Cassy's hair away from her face and then gently stroked her cheek. It was sweet and Cassy smiled slightly and turned her head to kiss Alexandra's hand.

She was down next to Cassy in a moment, easing Cassy onto her side and sliding an arm underneath her. Then Alexandra lay on her back, pulled Cassy over snugly against her, and with her free hand brought Cassy's head down between her shoulder and neck and held it there. "Let's just lie here for a while," she murmured.

All Cassy could see was Alexandra's arm. She hesitated, but then reached up to the arm and followed it back to the hand that was in her hair. The hand took Cassy's, and Cassy brought them both down to rest on Alexandra's stomach.

There. Now she could see. The smooth skin of Alexandra's neck and chest—was that a freckle? Perhaps. And then, lower, under the black silk, were her breasts, easing slightly to either side. And there, in the slight shallow of her stomach, were their hands. One young, one not so young. Her eyes moved back up to her chest and Cassy squinted slightly, timing the rhythm of Alexandra's breath against her own. She blinked. She blinked again. And then, timid but determined, Cassy slid the side of her face down. To listen.

Alexandra's heart was pounding.

Cassy's mouth parted and she raised herself up on her elbow to look at her. Alexandra was looking vaguely frightened—or something—and Cassy smiled, touching her cheek. Alexandra took her hand and pressed it against her mouth. And then she pushed Cassy's hand away, reached for the back of her neck, and pulled her down.

Alexandra wanted her. Cassy had no doubts about that now. Alexandra's mouth was searching hers, maneuvering for the best way, careful not to hurry, but careful not to let her go. And then Alexandra had her on her back and was touching the side of her neck, the kiss going on and on, and then Alexandra's mouth hesitated, and Cassy opened her own slightly, wondering if maybe now—

Yes. She felt Alexandra's cautious descent into her mouth. It was Alexandra, yes, and Cassy welcomed her, wondering at her, at them, at what was happening in this marvelously slow experiment. And then Alexandra began easing back, and then her mouth was gone, and Cassy felt it just under her ear, working gently, slowly, down her neck. It felt wonderful and she made a sound to let her know it. It went on for quite some time, with Alexandra's mouth becoming more adventurous, and then the same slow assault that had been made on Cassy's mouth was being made just under her ear, and Cassy could feel the effects starting to travel.

"You are glorious," Alexandra whispered, working slowly down Cassy's neck, and then over, turning Cassy's head slightly to start up the other side. Alexandra's mouth, on this side, was still quiet, but quite there, growing more insistent. And then there was a low roar in Cassy's ear, and there was damp warmth spreading rapidly through it, in it, over it and Cassy's body started to tense and Alexandra's hand was down there, doing something with her nightgown. Drawing it up, yes, that was it, and then she felt Alexandra's knee suggesting something and Cassy sighed, thinking, *Marvelous idea,* and she turned slightly, parting her legs, and she felt Alexandra's leg slide smoothly in to its thigh.

Yes, Cassy thought, bearing down slightly, *marvelous idea.*

Alexandra came sweeping back across her face. There was no hesitation from her mouth now. She was after her—Cassy could feel it—and the deeper she went into Cassy's mouth, the harder Cassy bore down on her thigh. And then there was a sound inside of Cassy's mouth—but it was not hers—and she felt Alexandra lurch slightly against her, down below, and Cassy's mind started to get lost, running from her mouth to down there to Alexandra to—

Alexandra's hand brushed over her breast twice and then lightly settled there, pausing, as she retreated from Cassy's mouth and slid down into her neck again. Cassy felt her hand starting to move, slowly, over and over and around her breast and then, casually, it seemed, slipping under the silk to cover it. Cassy was hanging onto her now, feeling the hand growing stronger on her breast, feeling herself being pulled apart inside, and then suddenly Alexandra's hand was gone—but she was only taking down the straps of the nightgown—but Cassy wished like hell she would hurry it up and she heard herself whispering, "Please, I want you at my breasts."

Alexandra was not getting there fast enough and Cassy thought of simply yanking her head—so slow was that marvelous mouth in making the descent—but then, finally, Alexandra was there, and all was forgiven—quite so, yes, very, very forgiven—as Alexandra started moving tides of gratification through her, pulling the nightgown down farther and farther in the effort to do so, and Cassy said something—anything, God, who knew—and she felt another surge from Alexandra's lower body and Cassy's urgency swung in direction and went plunging. Straight down. God. To there. She fumbled for Alexandra's hand and pushed it down, pushed it over her stomach, pushed it over her hip—come *on,* Alexandra, this is no time to dawdle, God, no.

Alexandra's leg slid away and Cassy shifted back, settled back, wondering whether—

The first touch cut her breath right out of the air.

But then, in a moment, it came back. Through her teeth. And then it caught again, struggled, and Cassy thought, *This is impossible, this cannot be happening.* Alexandra was exploring—no—playing with her, doing what to her oh who the hell cared what it was she was doing as long as she kept doing it—but no, yes, Alexandra was exploring, examining her, seeing which movement evoked a sound from her, and they all were damn it just listen to me can this be me? Alexandra's hand was lingering now, right there, cautious, and then Cassy recognized the same slow style of—slowly, yes—God—Alexandra—was Alexandra really doing this? Was this Alexandra inside of her? Was this—

Everything stopped. "This is wonderful," Alexandra sighed. And then everything gently resumed.

In a few moments she could feel Alexandra sliding out, and then her fingers pulling up slowly, making a wide track as they went. And then the fingers slid down, proving just how easy this track was going to be, and then they pulled back up, and Cassy thought, *No, I cannot be feeling this,* and they moved back down, sliding to there, and they pulled back up, and Cassy said, "Yes, like that," and immediately she thought, *Please don't let me think—please—please—if I start thinking I'm going to start thinking—damn it—no—I'm starting to lose it—damn it, I'm losing it—oh, please don't let me lose it, Alexandra—stay with me, please, just stay with me—Alexandra, this is Alexandra, this is Alexandra doing this to me—God, is it really Alexandra doing this to me?*

And she threw an arm around the back of Alexandra's neck and pulled down on it, deciding she didn't care whether Alexandra could breathe or not because Alexandra knew exactly what she was doing because Alexandra always knew what she was doing and she was doing it to her now and God how Alexandra knew—she knew—oh yes how she knew—God—how could she know so much? *Oh God, Alexandra, are you ever right on it, are you ever on it—*

Cassy couldn't do anything but try and hold herself down when what she wanted to do was what she didn't know what she wanted to do and—*my God, it's coming, oh, my God, it's really going to happen*—God, she could feel it and Alexandra was right with it—*don't stop, Alexandra, just don't stop but of course you won't because you know exactly what's happening to me and you want this too, don't you, and oh, my God, my God*—and then everything was moving and it was pulling, pulling Cassy down and—oh, God—pushing her now, pushing her up, up—*Up—Is it—Is it—Can I—*

Oh, my God, this is it, she thought, *this is it, I'm having an orgasm with Alexandra—God, is this happening? Oh—Oh—Oh—*GOD. GOD. GOD. *But God is this good. God is this good. God is this good. God is it ever.*

God this is unreal.

Oh, yes, yes.

Surely—no wait—

Oh, yes, yes. There. Oh, wait—

Oh, yes, yes.

There. Yes, that was the last.

Yes. For sure.

For sure.

Yes.

Good Lord, I should think so.

She felt a gentle kiss on her chest. Cassy let her arm fall away from around Alexandra's neck, and Alexandra came up to see her.

Look at this wonderful girl.

She slipped a piece of hair from out of the corner of Alexandra's mouth and then used both hands to sweep her hair back off her face—and held it there.

Alexandra was about to cry. No, wait.

And then Cassy smiled, thinking perhaps Alexandra's expression did not indicate this at all—not the anguish in her eyes, not the tension at her mouth. It could be, she thought, it damn well could be that this was the expression of a young woman quite beside herself with desire.

Well, Cassy thought, pushing Alexandra onto her back, she could at least find out if she was right.

She was.

PART III

31

SAM FACES THE MUSIC

It was a long walk to Walter Brennan's old office where the new acting president of Electronika was waiting to see him.

Brennan and Canley had not even spent half a day with the authorities before they were released on bail.

The three ICL executives who sat on Electronika's board were under suspension until the Caswell Zander case came to trial.

Sam's fate had yet to be made known to him.

It was funny how the press reports on Brennan and Canley had affected him. All along, ever since he had found out about the Pretoria plant, Sam had been outraged by their behavior. But then, after seeing and hearing and reading about the life that Walter Brennan had been leading, Sam's outrage had turned to a feeling of sickness. Of feeling sick about what Brennan had nearly done to Sam's family, and about what Brennan had done to his own.

As the president of Electronika, Brennan had made almost half a million dollars a year. It was obscene, Sam thought, that anyone bright enough, anyone who had worked hard enough to achieve a position like that, could sell out simply for—for money. President of Electronika International? A half of a million dollars a year? That wasn't enough?

No. Apparently not. And based on what the press was finding out about the kind of money Brennan had been throwing around in recent years, it looked as though the money he had been "earning" had been up in the millions. But his family hadn't known that. Certainly not. They lived very much like the family of a corporate president: a six-bedroom Tudor house in Westchester County, three nice cars, a summer retreat in Maine, private schools for the kids, an exclusive country club membership, slightly exotic vacations, and a kind of all-around sense of security that families less fortunate could yearn for.

Mrs. Brennan had never known about the Sutton Place apartment in Manhattan or the five-bedroom house in Palm Beach, Florida, much less about the women living in them. And, at first, she told the New York *Post* they were crazy, how could she *own* them if she never even knew they existed? (The *Post* was not crazy, and yes, they were indeed in Mrs. Brennan's name.) And then thirteen-year-old Pete found out *he* owned a condo in Vegas and a yacht in New Jersey. And the trail of bills for jewelery and furs and wild jaunts was growing longer and longer.

As for Canley, it was a mystery where his money was. A cartoon in *Conolly's* suggested that perhaps he had the same investment adviser as former President Marcos.

"Come in, Sam," Matthew Wellman said. "Close the door."

Under the old regime of Clyde Taylor, Wellman had been the financial controller of Electronika. Under Brennan he had been promptly reassigned to run a subsidiary in Peoria, Illinois, in hopes he would resign. He hadn't, and now the board thanked God they still had him to throw in at the helm. If nothing else, they knew Wellman knew the company, and they knew everyone knew that Wellman was clean of this mess. More conservative than they would like, perhaps, but a decent, fiercely loyal company man of the old guard—the old guard that never got into messes like this.

After Sam sat down in the chair that was offered to him, Wellman sat down behind his desk. "Well," he said, "that was some report, Sam. Thank you for sharing it with me."

Sam nodded. Rather than waiting to be grilled by Electronika's board about why Sam had volunteered to bring down its president and senior executive vice-president on his own initiative, Sam had written a report of everything that had happened, Harriet had typed it, and he had hand-delivered it to Wellman the day he became acting president. At least now, Sam had thought at the time, he could live with himself. He was no good at secrets. He was no good at being afraid of what might happen. He just wanted this whole thing over, and he would take it from there.

"I destroyed it," Wellman said. "And if you have a copy of it, I suggest you do the same."

Sam just looked at him.

Wellman sat back in his chair and smoothed the sides of his gray hair with his hands. And then dropped forward, letting his hands fall onto the desk. "Look, as far as I'm concerned, all that matters is that we can go back to being the company we're supposed to be." He plunked himself on his elbows then, hands extending toward Sam. "It was that damn stock swap with ICL that started this trouble. I was against it from the first—" He let out a sigh, shaking his head, lowering his hands to the desk. He looked at Sam. "What's gone on here since Brennan arrived has damn near killed Clyde. I don't think he'll ever forgive himself."

As Wellman slid back into his chair, gripping the arms of it, looking off somewhere, Sam realized that Matthew Wellman was a very angry man and was doing his best to control himself.

"What about the board?" Sam asked.

"If the board knew what it was doing," Wellman said, eyes returning to Sam, "they never would have allowed those thieves from ICL onto it."

Sam started to smile, inside. He was beginning to see the advantages of having a boss who had been kicked around and then exiled by Brennan and Canley.

"So," Wellman said, rising from his chair—Sam rose also— "what's most important to me right now is that the ZT 5000 be launched properly." He walked around the desk. "And I expect you to do it. I want a report from you on my desk Monday morning with your recommendations on how we should handle the PR."

Sam looked at him. "That's it?"

Wellman crossed his arms over his chest and held his chin in one hand, considering this question. Sam had seen him take the same pose in meetings for eighteen years—it meant he was about to say something important. "You should know, Sam, that if it hadn't been for your report it never would have crossed my mind that you were in any way involved."

Sam frowned. "But the authorities, someone must have . . ."

Wellman dropped his arms and slid a hand into his pocket. "Your name hasn't even come up. Not from the SEC, not from the FBI, not from the press—no one."

Sam stepped back, swinging his head around as if he had been hit. Then he came back around to stand as before. He swallowed. "You're kidding."

Wellman slowly shook his head, smiling.

"But Brennan will—"

"Brennan will what? Rot in hell, I hope," Wellman added, jamming his other hand into a pants pocket.

"He'll, he'll—" Sam's hand wavered in the air. He dropped it. "I don't know, but he knows I made that call. His people were listening—"

Wellman withdrew both hands from his pockets and held them up to talk with. "Sam, what Brennan and Canley did in Pretoria is perfectly legal. No crime has been committed at Electronika. Ethics have been violated, yes, but no crime has been committed. The crime is that Brennan and Canley have been on the Caswell Zander payroll—for *years,* Sam, for *years*—supplying them with inside information to defraud the stock market with."

Sam sighed, not quite believing this.

"It has nothing to do with you, Sam. Unless, of course," Wellman said, leading him toward the door, "Brennan wants to add wiretapping and God knows what else to the charges against him." He stopped and turned to face Sam. "You could sue *him,* you know. And you'd win." He paused, glancing down at the floor and then back up. "You could sue *me*—Electronika. For crying out loud, Sam, your report is the best grounds for a class action suit I've ever seen."

"I'm not going to sue anyone," Sam said.

"And I'm going to ask you to help me pull this company back together again," Wellman said. He stuck out his hand.

"Thanks, Matthew," Sam said, shaking his hand. Then he looked up to the ceiling. "And thank You," he added, making Wellman laugh.

32

THE NEIGHBORS STAND
UP TO BE COUNTED

"**K**itty-cats like to be stroked," Rosanne explained to Jason. "You can't pet them like a doggy. Here, like this." She showed him how to stroke Missy, a movement Jason studied with a great degree of seriousness.

Amanda, sitting cross-legged on the kitchen counter, was smiling.

"See how much she likes that? Okay, Jason, you can hold her now." Rosanne gently lowered the cat into his arms.

"Why doesn't he take her into the writing room?" Amanda suggested. "He'll be all right in there, won't he?"

"Oh, sure," Rosanne said, smoothing Jason's hair back off his forehead. "Go on, Jason. Mommy'll be right here, talking to Amanda."

Jason nodded, clutching his new friend. By the time he reached the door, the lower half of Missy was dangling down his front, but she did not seem to mind.

"Mommy?" he said, turning around.

"What, Jason?"

"Can I have this?"

"The cat?"

He nodded, his cheek rubbing the fur on Missy's head.

"She belongs to Mrs. G, sweetie."

"Oh," he said, wandering out.

"Phew," Rosanne said, sitting down at the table. "Am I ever beat. What time's Mrs. W coming? I have to get Jason back to Brooklyn by seven."

"Any minute," Amanda said. "So, Rosanne, we're in agreement now, yes?"

Rosanne did not look happy. "I don't have a choice, do I?"

"Rosanne—you persist in making it sound as though it was your fault. And it wasn't. It was our fault. We were supposed to pay Social Security—"

The doorbell rang. "There she is," Amanda said, jumping down from the counter.

It was Harriet Wyatt, and Cassy Cochran was with her. Amanda led them back to the kitchen, where Harriet kissed Rosanne hello and Cassy dropped her briefcase to hug her, whispering, "Don't you worry. We're not going to let anyone come between you and Jason."

"If I'm still alive," Rosanne said. "You're strangling me."

Cassy and Harriet sat at the table and extracted papers from their briefcases, while Amanda poured them glasses of cold seltzer water.

"We liked Mr. Thatcher a great deal," Harriet said, opening a large folder on the table. "He went through everything with Sam and me and our lawyer—"

"I sat in too," Cassy said, slipping on her glasses.

"And everything seems fine," Harriet finished. "Thank you." She took a sip of seltzer and then thumbed through the papers. "Everything's signed and ready to go—the Social Security papers and our check. And our statement about Rosanne is here too."

"Great," Amanda said, lifting herself back up on the counter. "I signed mine," she said, tapping a manila envelope, "and I've got Mrs. Goldblum's as well."

"And I've got Howard's," Harriet said, opening another folder. "He gave it to me at work this afternoon."

"Howie doesn't have the money for this," Rosanne protested. "Can't we just leave him out of it?"

Amanda visibly paled.

"Rosanne," Harriet said gently, "it's all been taken care of. Howard's as anxious as we are to help."

"I must confess—" Cassy said, handing a folder to Amanda, "this is ours —I was rather relieved that we didn't have to deal with Melissa."

Amanda averted her eyes. "Why didn't we have to deal with Melissa?" she asked matter-of-factly.

Cassy hesitated and then looked over at Rosanne, who was making a frantic motion for her to shut up—which Amanda saw.

"I repeat," Amanda said, looking at Rosanne, "why didn't we have to deal with Melissa?"

Rosanne sighed, sending a now-you've-done-it look at Cassy. "Howie moved out. He doesn't want anyone to know—yet."

"He told—" Harriet started to say, but stopped when she felt Cassy kick her under the table.

"Really," Amanda said faintly, avoiding all of their eyes.

"He's up on 95th Street," Rosanne added.

Silence.

"Amanda," Harriet said, "Howard tells me you're the same Amanda Miller that Patricia MacMannis wants to sign up—a novel about Catherine the Great."

"The one and the same," Rosanne said, grinning.

"They were talking about you in editorial meeting last week," Harriet continued, trying to figure out what it was that Cassy was mouthing to her from across the table. "It sounds wonderful. Patricia and Howard"—Cassy kicked her again and Harriet's eyes grew wider— "were raving about it."

"Good!" Rosanne said.

"Rosanne's my agent," Amanda explained.

"I'm sorry," Harriet said, still squinting at Cassy, "what did you say, Amanda?"

"Rosanne's my agent. She was the one who told Howard about my book."

"But Patricia's going to be the editor," Harriet said, looking slightly confused. DON'T TALK ABOUT HOWARD—oh—that was what Cassy was mouthing across the table.

"Well," Amanda said quietly, "Patricia and I seem to work rather well together."

"That's great," Harriet said, rubbing her shin. "I look forward to reading it."

"I had no idea you were a writer," Cassy said, turning around in her chair to look at Amanda. "And this second vocation of yours, my dear," she said to Rosanne, "is one of the better-kept secrets on the block."

"I get ten percent," Rosanne said.

"Really?" This was from Harriet, who was smiling at Amanda.

Amanda reached down from the counter toward her. "May I have your forms? I'm seeing Mr. Thatcher in the morning."

"Sure." Harriet closed the folders and passed them to Cassy, who in turn handed them to Amanda. "Amanda," Harriet added, "Cassy and I thought it might be helpful if we came to Rosanne's hearing too. Mr. Thatcher said it was a good idea, being mothers ourselves."

Rosanne looked at Harriet. "You'd do that?"

"Honey," Harriet said, leaning across the table to give Rosanne's hand a squeeze, "we want you to get Jason, but we also don't want to lose you."

Cassy murmured her agreement.

Rosanne looked down to the floor.

Cassy took a breath. "And we need to talk about where you're going to live," she said.

"Yes," Amanda said.

Rosanne looked up, eyes glistening slightly.

"Mommy!" came the cry from the other room.

"Coming," Rosanne called, up on her feet in an instant.

After she left the room, Cassy said, "I've thought about having them stay with me temporarily. I've got the guest room—"

"I've thought about it too," Amanda said. "But I don't know what's going to happen with Mrs. Goldblum. She's going to require someone to be with her for a few weeks after she is released from the hospital, and I was rather hoping she would stay here with me."

"I'd like to say she could—" Harriet began. "Well—wait a minute."

Both women looked at her.

"Where is Mrs. Goldblum's apartment?"

"On the corner of 91st Street," Amanda said.

"Well," Harriet said slowly, "if she's not going to be there for a while, would she consider letting Rosanne . . . ?"

Cassy's head whipped around to Amanda. "Would she, Amanda? It would give us some time to find Rosanne an apartment."

"Yes, I think she would," Amanda said. "And you know," she added, pushing her hair back over her shoulder, "you've given me an idea."

A slow smile was emerging on Cassy's face. "Are you thinking the same thing I'm thinking?"

Amanda looked at her, one eyebrow rising.

"What?" Harriet said.

Cassy turned to her. "Amanda and I are thinking that maybe Mrs. Goldblum might want someone to live with her now."

"She has three bedrooms," Amanda said.

Harriet thought a minute. "But would Rosanne—"

"Leave Rosanne to me," Amanda said.

Herself came in at that moment. "The cat's hiding under the couch," Rosanne announced. "A major trauma."

The women laughed.

"I don't know how I'm gonna get him to leave that cat," Rosanne continued, sitting down.

The other three women smiled, exchanging looks with one another.

Rosanne noticed this and frowned slightly. "So what is this—the cat-and-the-canary club or what?"

33

HOWARD MAKES
A PRESENTATION AT
THE EDITORIAL MEETING

On this fine Tuesday morning in August, Howard walked into the conference room for the editorial meeting, touched Patricia MacMannis on the shoulder (a prearranged signal to let her know that Tom wasn't coming this morning—they had finally broken up) and took a seat next to Harriet Wyatt at the far end of the table. Sperry arrived a little after nine-thirty and sat down at the head of the table. Harrison Dreiden, sitting on Sperry's left, was the only one who said good morning to him.

One by one, editors presented the book projects they currently had in on submission. Layton Sinclair talked for ten minutes about a new angle on "The Big Bang Theory" before Sperry threw a pencil at him to shut him up. On to Patricia, who reported that she had won the auction she had been in the day before, and also that she had signed up Amanda Miller for *I, Catherine,* world rights included. ("Now that's the kind of banging we want," Sperry said to Layton, prompting Howard and Harriet to look at each other.)

Carol unwisely got into a fight with Sperry over the new Daniel Rembrois cookbook being over four hundred pages long. He said the length was ridiculous; she said they published cookbooks at G & G, not menus; he said he would cancel the book before publishing it at that length; she said they were combining print runs with Book-of-the-Month and Michael Joseph in England, so if he wanted to get sued, go ahead; and Sperry said he would look into it and, in the meantime, he wished Carol would get him a cup of coffee from the wagon in the corner of the room. "Black, no sugar."

Carol—after throwing her pad and pen down on the table—got it for him.

It was now Howard's turn.

"Actually, the project I want to share with you is not a book project but, rather, a report I have done to show how I am going to make a great deal of money for G & G this year and every year."

"That is not appropriate for this meeting," Sperry said. "Do you have any book projects?"

"No—well, yes, Mr. Sperry, I do. I have one book project for this fall, one for next year, one for 1988, one for 1989—"

"Howard," Harrison Dreiden interrupted, "what are you talking about?"

"I'm talking about how I'm going to make a lot of money for Mr. Sperry. He explained to me how many of my books have lost money, or are going to, and so I have come up with a solution."

Sperry frowned.

"I'm cutting my list back to one book a year."

"Stewart!" Sperry barked.

"I've copied some figures the business department worked up for me," Howard said, pulling papers out of his briefcase, "and also a copy of my editorial plan." He stood up to toss the copies into the middle of the table.

"Anyone who touches those is fired," Sperry said.

Silence. And then Harriet laughed. Then Harrison chuckled. Patricia succumbed next and soon the whole table was laughing.

"Silence!" When Sperry got it, he glared at Howard. "You're fired, Stewart."

"Anyway," Howard continued, leaning forward on the table to address his colleagues, "I'm going to publish one Gertrude Bristol book a year. You see, according to Mr. Sperry's financial plan, the best bet is to stop publishing all books except guaranteed bestsellers. Even so, if we underestimate their sales expectations, not only will we—"

"Get the hell out of here, Stewart!" Sperry yelled, slamming his hand down on the table.

Howard lowered his head to look at Sperry over the top of his glasses. "Excuse me, Mr. Sperry, but I'm afraid you're going to have to make me."

The room was dead silent, and all eyes were on Sperry—whose face was rapidly turning from red to mauve.

"And so," Howard said, adjusting his glasses, "if we underestimate the sales figures from, say, eighty to fifty-five, and then sell eighty to one hundred thousand copies—"

Sperry vaulted out of his chair. "If you don't get the fuck out of here, I'll have you arrested!"

Howard focused his attention on Layton. "According to the business department, I will not only make a huge profit, but I will come in way over budget. In fact, with subsidiary rights income included, according to these numbers, if I publish one title a year, Mr. Sperry could raise my salary to one hundred thousand dollars, and Bob's to forty, and our office will still generate over two hundred thousand dollars a year in profits. But then, who'd need us? Mr. Sperry could edit Gertrude. In fact, Mr. Sperry could fire everybody and edit six books a year. Who knows? Maybe he could fire the sales force and distribute through Jackson Hardware."

"Lunatic," Sperry ranted, storming out.

When the door closed behind Sperry, Harrison Dreiden said, "I think you're a damn fool, Howard, but I can't say this hasn't been fun."

Howard laughed, sitting back down in his chair. "Yeah, well, the show's over for me, I'm afraid."

"We'll make some calls for you," Harriet said. "Won't we, Harry?"

"Can I have Gertrude Bristol?" Layton wanted to know.

"Thanks, Harriet," Howard said, "but I'm thinking about starting a literary agency."

Harrison leaned forward on the table. "I think that's what I would do if I were to start again." Layton was scribbling away in a notebook and Harrison bent sideways to see what it was he was writing. "Oh, Layton," he said, pulling his notebook away from him. "Don't you know it's impolite to play G. Gordon Liddy at the table?"

"I think you'd make a wonderful agent," Patricia said.

There were murmurs of agreement from the other editors.

"You'll keep in touch, won't you, Howard?" Carol asked.

"Of course I will." Howard sighed, looking around the table. "I'm going to miss you guys a lot. Even you, Layton—I think."

"I want one of these," Layton said, ignoring the laughter and reaching for a copy of Howard's report.

"God, will you stop—" Patricia said, yanking it out of his hand and throwing it behind her. "At least act like you're human."

The door crashed open. It was Sperry—with a uniformed custodian.

"Layton touched one of the reports while you were gone," Patricia felt obligated to report.

"Remove that man!" Sperry commanded, pointing to Howard.

The custodian took a few tentative steps and stopped.

"Hi, Ralph," Howard said.

"Sorry," Ralph said, throwing a thumb back in Sperry's direction, "but this guy wants you to leave. He says he's the president."

Everyone was enjoying this scene. Carol got up to replenish her coffee and called up to Harrison, asking him if he wanted a doughnut.

"The receptionist is calling the police," Sperry said, glowering at the end of the table.

Howard stood up. "I'm leaving, Mr. Sperry," he said, gathering his papers together, "but only because you ask me to so nicely."

"That's company property!" Sperry yelled. "Take those papers out of that briefcase!"

Howard glanced up at him, pushing up his glasses. "Yes, sir." He held open his briefcase and turned it upside down, dumping everything from manuscript pages to gum wrappers down onto the table. He rummaged through the mess, picked out a pen and a ten-dollar bill, and stuffed them into his coat pocket. He smiled at Sperry and continued to do so until he had walked all the way around the table and was standing only a foot away, looking down at him.

"Get out of here," Sperry snarled.

Howard continued to stand there, smiling.

Sperry pushed him. Howard fell back a step and laughed. He let go of his briefcase and Sperry, suddenly wary, backed into the table. Howard stepped forward and, in one fluid movement, grabbed Sperry by the arm and under one leg and hurled him onto the table, sending Harrison and Layton diving for cover. Sperry lay on his side a moment and then scrambled to get off, kicking papers all over the place with his feet and leaving black scuff marks on the table.

"Oh, dear," Harriet Wyatt said, suppressing a laugh, "are you all right, Mr. Sperry?"

Howard waited in Mr. Blank's office for his severance check to be drawn up. Mr. Blank had been the head of personnel for thirty years. He was very upset by all of this. Howard fistfighting with the president! The police at Gardiner & Grayson! Mr. Sperry pressing charges! Howard pressing charges! Nothing like this had ever happened before!

Howard just sat there, working on his laundry list of what Gardiner & Grayson owed him.

"But you, Howard, of all our employees," Mr. Blank said yet again, shaking his head in disbelief.

"These figures still aren't right, Mr. Blank," Howard said. "You owe me one month's severance pay for every year I've been here—"

"But you've beaten up the president," Mr. Blank pointed out.

"He started it," Howard said, rising and coming around to Mr. Blank's side of the desk, making Mr. Blank even more nervous. "Look, eleven years —plus twelve days of vacation pay—" He looked at Mr. Blank. "Are you listening?"

Mr. Blank was having a nervous breakdown.

"I've written it all down for you."

"But our company policy has been changed," Mr. Blank pleaded.

"Now, Mr. Blank," Howard said gently, "you know that's not true."

"He'll fire me," Mr. Blank moaned, holding his head.

"No, he won't, Mr. Blank. He'll be grateful to you for getting me out of here. Because, you see," Howard said, going back around the desk and plopping himself down in a chair, "I won't leave until I have what's owed to me. And that will make Mr. Sperry very upset."

"Oh, God!" Mr. Blank said.

It took another hour and forty-five minutes of haggling over how many taxes had to be deducted, how much Social Security had to be deducted and how much interest was due on Howard's retirement fund; and for Howard to make out his final expense account report on his company-issued credit card. But finally, all was a done deed. Howard walked out of the offices for the last time, with a check made out to him for a little over twenty-one thousand dollars.

On Third Avenue, about a block away, Howard looked back at the Gardiner & Grayson building. He counted six floors down from the roof to locate the window of Harrison Dreiden's office. His throat tightened. "Thanks," he said.

34

HENRY SAYS THERE IS SOMETHING DIFFERENT ABOUT HIS MOTHER

When she heard the front door open, Cassy dropped the lid of the pot and ran out to the front hall. Henry put his bags down and grinned. "Hi, Mom."

Was this her Henry? Deeply tan, his hair streaked with blond, and with the stubble of a week's beard, the image of Cassy's own father flashed through her mind. But no, it was Henry. Taller, his shoulders perceptively bigger, this lean and rugged young man was her son.

She threw herself at him and was surprised by the strength, the sheer size of his embrace as he stooped to receive her. "Sweetheart," she said, smelling Ivory Soap in his hair. She stepped back, holding his hands. "Look at you," she murmured, shaking her head. "Just look at you!"

He grinned again, teeth flashing against the brown of his skin.

"Oh, Henry, come on!" Cassy said, pulling him by the hand to the den. She closed the door and pushed him back against it. "I knew it!" she cried, lunging for a pencil on Michael's desk. "You're taller than your father now. Here, stand up straight, sweetheart." She marked off his height and pulled him away from the door to look at it.

"Huh," Henry said, grinning.

Cassy got a ruler out of Michael's desk. "Let's see," she said, holding it up to the door, "if Michael's six one and three quarters, then you're . . . Six foot *three?* Henry—how dare you grow so tall!" she said, hugging him around the waist, pressing the side of her face against his chest. "How can my baby be six foot three?" She leaned back to look up at him. "I'm going to have a hell of a time trying to spank you now."

After Henry took his stuff to his room, he rejoined his mother in the kitchen. "Mom, where did the bench press come from?"

She turned away from the stove. "Is it the right kind?"

"Yeah, but where did it come from?"

She smiled. "Well, I was in Herman's the other day . . ."

Henry sat on a stool and talked to Cassy while she cooked dinner. When, she wondered, had Henry learned to talk so freely? Surely he hadn't talked this much before; her son was suddenly a veritable chatterbox. And such news!

—Henry had saved a thirteen-year-old camper's life. The kid had fallen out of the raft in the rapids and nearly drowned. Henry dove in and dragged him to safety—but not without injury. ("Got it on a rock," he said proudly, showing his mother a horrendous, though fading, slash mark across his chest.) (His *hairy* chest.)

—Henry had saved over one thousand dollars from his salary.

—Henry wanted to try to get into Yale. That was where his boss, Evan Scott, had gone.

—Henry had a girl friend named Jennifer.

(If Cassy was wide-eyed at this announcement, she was even more so when he told her she was a year older than he was.

"She's going to be a freshman at Sarah Lawrence."

"How convenient," Cassy said, wondering if Henry remembered their talk last year about birth control. *[Condoms. Good Lord.]*

"Her parents live in Greenwich. I said I'd call her tonight at eleven."

Saving money, making decisions, needing condoms, calling girls on the telephone at eleven o'clock at night? Whatever happened to trading baseball cards with Skipper?)

He talked straight through dinner, elaborating. Cassy listened to everything but was continually distracted, fascinated by this young man who claimed to be her son. He was so . . . so grown up. And he was so much a Littlefield! She saw her father's forehead, eyebrows and nose; she saw her mother's hair and ears; she saw her own eyes looking back at her, and she saw her own mouth and skin. The only trace of Michael she could see was in Henry's jaw and hands.

In the middle of dessert, savoring his ice cream sundae, Henry gave his mother a very strange look.

"What?" Cassy asked him, eyebrows high.

He swallowed. "You look different."

"I do?"

He nodded, eyes still on her, shoveling another spoonful of ice cream into his mouth. He pointed the spoon at her (a Michael gesture), swallowed, and said, "Did you do something with your hair or something?"

"No." He frowned and Cassy laughed. "Well, do I look better or worse?"

"I don't know—just different. Younger maybe."

Cassy threw her head back and laughed.

Henry grinned. "Yeah, that's it. You look younger."

Cassy laughed again. "Well, I'm hardly going to argue with that opinion. Thank you."

"You're welcome."

Who is this man? Cassy wondered. Well, whoever he was, he was welcome here.

In his room, while he unpacked and Cassy watched from on top of his bed, they got around to the subject of his father.

"He's in Connecticut, at the house," Henry said, pulling clothes out of a duffel bag and throwing them in a pile on the floor.

"I know," Cassy said. "We've talked."

"That's what he said." Henry glanced at his mother. "Are you still going to that place with Mr. Wyatt?"

"Uh-huh," Cassy nodded.

Henry was finished with that bag and tackled another. "Do you think I could go with you one night?"

Cassy was surprised. "Sure," she said. "I'd love it."

"He came out again. To camp, I mean," Henry said without looking at her. "He was in pretty bad shape." He dragged the bag over to his stereo and started transferring cassettes into a storage rack. "Evan talked to me about it afterward. About Dad's drinking, I mean."

Cassy started to say something but didn't.

"Evan's father had a problem too." Pause. "He's dead now."

"Oh, sweetheart," Cassy murmured, "I don't think it's going to come to that."

Long pause. "So, Mom," Henry said, dragging the bag back to the pile,

"what happens now? Dad said he doesn't want to come home right now."
He shook the remaining clothes out of the bag and dropped it, turning
around to look at her. "Or won't you let him?"

"Both," Cassy said. "I want him to get help to stop drinking," she said,
lowering her head, "and he doesn't want to. So . . ."

"But if he does—get help, I mean—he can come home, right?"

Cassy hesitated. Finally she nodded. "If he stops."

"Good," Henry said, walking over to the bench press in the corner,
"that's what I told him." He straddled the bench and lowered himself down
onto it. "This is really great, Mom. Thanks."

Cassy smiled.

Henry sighed, looking up at the ceiling. "Evan said he wished his mother
had thrown his father out. He said that maybe if she had his father might
have stopped." He sat up suddenly, turning to look at Cassy. "You love him,
Mom, don't you?"

"Yes," she said.

He bit his lip and then lay back down. After a moment, "I love him too.
But," he paused, "I almost hated him when he came out to Colorado." He
paused again. "It was awful, Mom. And in front of everyone."

Cassy closed her eyes.

"Evan and I had to carry him into his motel room."

"I'm sorry," Cassy said quietly.

Silence.

"Evan says it's a disease. Do you think that's true?"

Cassy opened her eyes. "Yes," she said. *Whoever you are, Evan,* she
thought, *thank you for helping my son.*

"Mom, it's for you!" Henry called from the kitchen. "It's Alexandra
Waring."

Cassy came in from the living room. She started to say that she'd pick up
in the bedroom, but stopped herself, thinking, *Don't do anything different.*
And so she sat on a stool in the kitchen, picked up the phone, and watched
Henry fix himself a snack.

"Hello?"

"Hi." Alexandra's voice was in that low, rushing tone that Cassy had
recently become so familiar with.

"Hi."

"How's it going?"

"Great."

"Mom—sorry. Do we have any mustard?"

"If there isn't any in the door of the refrigerator, look in the pantry. Second shelf." Back into the phone, "Hi. Sorry."

Alexandra was laughing. "It's so strange to hear you in your mother voice again."

"Again?"

"That's the way you used to talk to me."

"Oh, boy," Cassy sighed, smiling. Henry came back, holding the mustard up.

"You can't talk, can you?"

"That's right," Cassy said, overly cheerful.

Alexandra laughed again. "This is going to be something to get used to."

"Right," Cassy said.

"He sounds great," Alexandra said. "How does he look?"

"He's six foot three now," Cassy said, smiling at Henry. He flexed his muscles for her benefit. "And as strong as an ox."

"Yeah," Henry growled, going back to building his sandwich.

"How was your meeting today?" Cassy asked her.

"Great! We're moving to nine o'clock the week after next."

"Hey, that's terrific," Cassy said, holding the phone under her chin and moving over to Henry.

Alexandra related some details of the meeting while Cassy nibbled on the cold cuts Henry had out on the counter.

"You're gonna get fat," Henry whispered.

"Never," Cassy mouthed, tossing a piece of liverwurst in her mouth with a wink.

"Cassy?"

"Yes?"

"I know this isn't a good time," Alexandra said.

"Well," Cassy said.

"When can I see you?"

Cassy moved away from Henry and slipped back up on the stool. "I'm not sure."

"Friday?"

"Can't."

"Saturday night?"

"Um, I think so. Henry," Cassy said.

"What?"

"I'm invited to a dinner party Saturday night. Would you mind?"

Henry shrugged. "No. Skipper's probably coming over."

"Saturday's fine," Cassy said into the phone.

"Terrific," Alexandra said. "Now I have something to look forward to." Cassy laughed.

"I know you can't say anything," Alexandra said, "so I'll just say it. I love you."

"Yes," Cassy said brightly—shaking her head, no, to Henry, who was holding ham out to her.

"Yes, she says," Alexandra said, laughing. "This *is* going to take some getting used to. All right, I've got to get back to work. I'll talk to you tomorrow."

"Yes."

"Sleep well."

"You too."

"I love you."

"Yes. I'll see you Saturday. Bye-bye." Cassy hung up the phone. "Think you've got enough food there? You won't starve?"

"Yeah." He cut the sandwich in half, no easy feat since it was nearly six inches high. "So you guys are friends now?"

"Who?"

"You and Alexandra."

"Uh, yes," Cassy said, coming over to start clearing the counter.

"I'll do that," Henry said.

"No, sweetheart, I'll do it. It's your first night home."

"Dad really likes her."

"I know," Cassy said.

"She isn't mad at him or anything, is she? I mean, he didn't do any-thing—"

"No, Henry," Cassy said, stretching up to kiss him on the cheek. "Alex-andra thinks a lot of your father."

Henry picked up a half of his sandwich with both hands. "I'll tell him that," he said, taking a bite.

35

A CONVENTION IS HELD
IN THE ROOM OF
MRS. EMMA GOLDBLUM

"**S**he's already got two visitors," the aide said under his breath, "but here." He handed her a pass. "Don't worry, it's Miss Peabody's."

Amanda frowned slightly. "Doesn't Miss Peabody get any visitors?"

The aide looked around and then whispered, "Miss Peabody's the name we use for anything extra we need for someone else." He winked. "Last night we gave Lois Peabody's complimentary puppet to the sister of a kid in pediatrics."

"Oh," Amanda said, smiling. "Well, thank you, Steve. And do thank Miss Peabody for me when you next see her." She walked on toward the elevator bank.

"Hey, Amanda!" a voice called across the lobby. It was Rosanne, waving, on her way to the visitors' station. Steve gave her one of Miss Peabody's passes too. "Hi," Rosanne said, walking past Amanda to slap the elevator button. "Man," she said, wheeling around and collapsing against the wall,

"I'm beat. Althea threw some kind of party last night and I've been vacuuming confetti off the ceilin' all day."

"How are the Wyatts?"

"Good, I guess. Mr. W bought Jason a baseball glove." The elevator arrived and the women stepped into it. "See?" Rosanne said, opening her bag.

Amanda touched it. "It looks like a very good one."

Rosanne snorted. "Like you would know."

They both laughed.

Rosanne shifted her weight from one foot to the other, watching the floor numbers change overhead. "They're all spoony again," Rosanne said, catching the interest of the nurse standing behind them.

"Who?" Amanda said, smiling back at the nurse.

"The W's."

"Rosanne," Amanda scolded.

"Well, you asked how they were. And ya know, they weren't so hot there for a while." She sighed as the elevator doors opened onto Mrs. Goldblum's floor. "I'm real glad, though," she said, stepping out. "I was gettin' kind of worried, what with Mr. W spendin' so much time with Mrs. C and all and Mrs. C actin' so airy-fairy lately—"

"*Rosanne,*" Amanda said, stopping in the middle of the hall.

"What?"

Amanda started to say something and then stopped. "Let us change the subject," she finally said, walking on.

"Okay," Rosanne agreed, walking at her side. She looked at Amanda. "Howie called me." No response on this item. "He's gettin' divorced," she added, watching for her reaction.

"Don't, Rosanne," Amanda said, holding her hand up. And she meant it.

Rosanne frowned but then waved to the nurses' station. "Hi!"

A couple of hi's came back.

Rosanne stopped just outside Mrs. Goldblum's door and sighed. "I wish Mrs. G would hurry up and get outta here so I could stop smilin' when I don't feel like it," she said. She brushed the hair out of her eyes. "This custody thing really's got me bugged, ya know?"

Rosanne's eyes were looking for some reassurance. So that was it, Amanda thought. Whenever Rosanne started talking about everyone else's business it was because something in her own life was bothering her. She was just frightened, today, about Jason. About whether or not she would get him back. Amanda reached out to take her hand. "I promise you," she said gently, "we will do whatever is necessary to bring Jason home."

Rosanne nodded and let go of Amanda's hand. "Wherever the heck that is," she muttered, walking in through the door.

Mrs. Goldblum was aglow. "Hi, girls, join the crowd!"

The crowd was right. Henry Cochran was sitting on the foot of her bed; Daniel was in a chair on the far side; a woman in a dressing gown was in the other chair; a second woman, also in a dressing gown, was in a wheelchair. Everyone but Daniel appeared to be quite happy.

The two younger women said a general hello; Amanda reached over the wheelchair to give Mrs. Goldblum's hand a squeeze; Rosanne swung around to the other side of the bed, leaned past Daniel to kiss Mrs. Goldblum on the cheek, and then retreated to stand at the foot of the bed.

Mrs. Goldblum made introductions: Henry, the nice boy from the book bazaar who brought her some lovely note paper; Mrs. Smith, who was recovering from an operation for a minor health problem that would go unmentioned; Mrs. Vasquez, who—wasn't it a coincidence?—lived on the Upper West Side too; her son, Daniel Goldblum, a business executive here all the way from Chicago; her dear friend Amanda, who was caring for her cat; and Rosanne, Mrs. Goldblum's intimate friend, who had just the most darling little boy.

Well, all this took some time.

Mrs. Smith slowly got up from her chair, saying that she would come back later when Mrs. Goldblum's guests had gone. Mrs. Vasquez echoed her sentiments and Henry hopped to his feet, offering to "drive" Mrs. Vasquez back to her room. She would be delighted—that is, if Henry promised not to drive too fast. All young men drove too fast. No, Henry wouldn't, he promised. Henry said his good-byes to Mrs. Goldblum as well, and the entourage slowly moved out of the room.

Amanda took Mrs. Smith's chair; Rosanne looked at Daniel in his chair, but since he didn't take the hint, she gave up and eased herself onto the corner of the bed.

"You look very tired, dear," Mrs. Goldblum said to Rosanne.

"That's because I am tired."

"You shouldn't get so tired, dear."

"So who's the one in the hospital, *dear?*"

Mrs. Goldblum lofted her eyebrows, turning to Amanda. "Have you ever heard such disrespect in all your life?"

"Yes," Amanda said, laughing, "many times."

"Hey, Mrs. G," Rosanne said, patting her foot. (Mrs. Goldblum had been able to receive pats without any pain at all for a week now.) "I filed those papers like you said and the payments are going to start right away."

"That is wonderful news," Mrs. Goldblum said.

Rosanne looked over at Amanda. "Mrs. G said Jason could get Social Security benefits 'cause of Frank's death." She turned back to Mrs. Goldblum, a warm smile emerging. "I don't know what's happened to you in here, Mrs. G, but it sure is nice. Used to be coupons could throw ya."

Daniel coughed, looking irritated. He started to get up, saying, "While you're gabbing, Mother, I'm going to get a bite to eat."

"Sit down, Daniel," Mrs. Goldblum said, her good humor starting to fade. Once he complied—sighing heavily—she turned and said, "Girls, there's something I wish to discuss with you."

They waited. Daniel concentrated on playing with the edge of the bed sheet.

"As you know, my physician has suggested that I not be alone for my first weeks out of the hospital—"

"Ever, Mother," Daniel said, twisting the sheet. "The doctor said you shouldn't live alone anymore."

"Don't exaggerate, Daniel," Mrs. Goldblum told her son. "He did not say forever, he said for the first few weeks." She paused. "Now then, I wanted to tell you that Daniel has very kindly asked me to live with him in Chicago. Where I can be near my grandchildren."

Amanda and Rosanne looked at each other and then back to Mrs. Goldblum, who, at this moment, was taking a sip of water.

"Maybe you could just go for a visit," Rosanne suggested.

Mrs. Goldblum smiled, shaking her head. "No, dear, it would be my last move."

Silence.

"I don't think you should go," Amanda finally said.

Mrs. Goldblum looked at her.

"Me neither," Rosanne said.

"What do you suggest?" Daniel said, angry. "That Mother spend every cent she has on a nurse? It'd cost a fortune!"

"It's her fortune," Rosanne said, expression hinting that a murder could possibly take place sometime in the near future.

"When you leave the hospital," Amanda said to Mrs. Goldblum, taking her hand, "I think you should come and stay with me."

"But you have your own life, dear," Mrs. Goldblum said softly.

"And so do you," Amanda said, "and I am a part of it—just as you are a part of mine."

Daniel was looking a little panicky. "Mother, you promised."

"No, she didn't," Rosanne said.

"You'll break the children's hearts," Daniel continued, standing up.

"Break the bank, you mean," Rosanne said, jumping to her feet.

"My, my," Mrs. Goldblum was chuckling, shaking her head, "such a fuss."

"Mother, this is crazy!" Daniel cried, leaning over the bed. "You're coming back with me to Chicago and that's that!"

"No, it's not!" Rosanne declared, stamping her foot. She was really angry now.

Nurse Sendowski appeared at the door to inquire if everything was all right. Rosanne used the distraction to launch her offensive. She marched around to Amanda's side of the bed and stood directly across from Daniel. "Mrs. G," she said, plunking her hands down on her hips, "I will not *tolerate* any of this nonsense. How do you think Mr. Goldblum's going to feel about you leaving your home?"

This was a stunner for Mrs. Goldblum, and everyone in the room knew it. Most of all Daniel. "Mother," he sputtered, "you know Father would want—"

"No, he would not," Rosanne said. She turned to Mrs. Goldblum again. "Riverside Drive is your home. It's where you got married, it's where you raised your kids, it's where you've lived for over fifty years." She paused, backing down slightly. "If you move away, Mrs. G, it's gonna be 'cause you don't want to live anymore." Rosanne turned away. "So let's just stop playin' gamon."

Silence.

Mrs. Goldblum was slowly turning her wedding band. "Daniel," she murmured, "I wish you would leave me with the girls for a moment."

"Mother," he started to warn her, "you can't—"

Her look stopped him cold. "I can do what I like." She looked down, smoothing the bedclothes with her palms. "I love you more than anything in the world, Daniel." She paused and then looked up at him. "But Rosanne is right. My place, my life, is here. And I think you know that, darling. And I love you all the more for wanting me to live with you, but . . ."

Daniel glared at his mother for a long moment. When she reached to touch his hand, he spun away, glared at Rosanne, and then stormed out of the room.

Silence.

"He used to do that when he was a little boy," Mrs. Goldblum said with a faint smile.

Rosanne came over to the bed. "I'm sorry, Mrs. G, I didn't mean to yell at him."

"It's all right, dear," Mrs. Goldblum said. "I know you meant well." She drew her hankie out from the sleeve of her dressing gown, patted her nose and lowered her hand into her lap. "Amanda dear," she said, turning toward her, "tell me what you honestly think I should do."

"I think," Amanda said slowly, leaning forward in her chair, "now that you have the money, you should invite your grandchildren for a visit."

Mrs. Goldblum nodded once, without expression.

"And I think"—deep breath— "when you leave the hospital, you should come and stay with me. Nothing would give me greater pleasure than to have you as my house guest."

There was no protest and so Amanda went ahead.

"And, Mrs. Goldblum—Harriet Wyatt and Cassy Cochran and I have been talking, and we all think it would be a most wonderful thing if Rosanne and Jason came to live with you."

Silence.

"Rosanne and Jason who?" Rosanne said.

"I'm serious," Amanda said, pushing on with Mrs. Goldblum. "It would help them out, and Jason adores you—and the cat too, right, Rosanne?"

"Mrs. G living with her cleanin' lady?" Rosanne exclaimed, throwing her hands in the air. "Daniel ol' boy's gonna love this one."

"Rosanne would be working right in the neighborhood," Amanda continued. "And it isn't as if you won't be up and around. Dr. Renaldi says that you will be more fit than ever. Think about it, Mrs. Goldblum, you love children and Rosanne would keep house and do the shopping and—"

"I'm still a pretty good cook," Mrs. Goldblum said, a smile forming.

Rosanne gasped. "Aw no, Mrs. G, you don't know what you're saying. You forget what it's like to have a child in the house—"

"I beg your pardon," Mrs. Goldblum said, highly indignant. "I certainly have not forgotten." Then she smiled at Amanda. "I think it's a splendid idea."

Amanda turned to Rosanne. "And you, Rosanne? Living with Mrs. Goldblum on Riverside Drive? In a nice big apartment? Don't you think the judge will be impressed? Mr. Thatcher seems to think so."

Rosanne thought about this.

"Rosanne dear," Mrs. Goldblum said, "it would make me very happy. I love you, and I love Jason very much." She paused, smiling. "You could have the bedroom next to mine."

"Yeah, right," Rosanne said, dropping her head, "the one with the kitty litter in it."

"And we'll fix up the back room for Jason. It's just right for a boy."

"And if it doesn't work out," Amanda said to both of them, "it doesn't work out. There will always be other options."

"The important thing, dear, is to win that hearing," Mrs. Goldblum said. "Isn't that right, Amanda?"

"Right," Amanda said.

They waited, watching her. Rosanne's mouth twitched to one side and then the other. Then she rolled her tongue inside her cheek. Finally, she nodded.

Mrs. Goldblum smiled. "I believe we've come to an agreement," she said, holding out her hand to Rosanne.

And the ladies shook on it.

36

DADDY COLLINS CALLS
HOWARD A FIDDLE-FADDLER
AND A NEW ENTERPRISE IS BEGUN

Daddy Collins had been the one to break the news to Howard. *"Why?"* Collins had yelled, prompting Howard to hold the phone away from his ear. *"Why?* Why the hell do you think? She doesn't want to be married to you anymore!"

"We haven't even talked since—"

"Talk? Hell, my little girl's been talking to you for eight years until she's blue in the face—and look where it got her. No kids, no—hell, my girl needs a real man, not some highfalutin bookworm who's been fiddle-faddling around the neighborhood."

Silence.

"You understand me, Stewart? I said fiddle-faddling around the neighborhood with that Miller slut. We know all about it, so I'm telling you not to waste your time trying steal any of my little girl's property. Hell, I've got half a mind to kill you, but Lissy just wants out. And she wants out *now,* so she can get on with her life. With a *real* man. So just get your ass down to the lawyer's and get this over with."

Huh.

The next day a messenger had arrived with several papers for Howard concerning the Stewart divorce. There had also been a letter from Melissa— the first communication Howard had received from her:

Dear Howard,

You better look these over before coming to Winston Claridge's office (and *don't* tell Daddy I sent these to you). You'll see that, in terms of money, the only assets you have are in your IRA account (see attached).

I heard about Gardiner & Grayson (a Mr. Blank called here looking for you) and I'm sorry. Strike that—I'm *not* sorry. It will do you the world of good to have to look for a new job.

I should tell you that I found out Amanda Miller was one of your writers—and that you have not been back to see her since I saw you go there. Don't take Daddy's threats seriously. He wants to blame you, when in fact it is me that wants out.

Are you surprised, Howard? I don't think you should be. Things have never been right between us—and I could only see that after you left. I know what I want now, and I want to start again while I'm still young enough to start a family.

Perhaps one day, when all of this is over, we can see our way to being friends. But, for now, let us just wipe the slate clean so we can both start again.

Melissa

And who, had Howard presumed, did Melissa want to start again with? Howard had no trouble guessing. In fact, he could envision the whole scenario:

Melissa calling Daddy, telling him she had followed Howard to Amanda's; Daddy telling Melissa to throw Howard out; Melissa packing his stuff and writing the note; Melissa fleeing to Fishers Island, crying on the ferry, pulling up in the driveway, Daddy running out of the house, screaming, "I'll kill him for hurting my little girl!"; Melissa calling Stephen Manischell; Stephen running up the road . . . No, that part was wrong. Stephen would have been *waiting* for Melissa with Daddy Collins.

God, this hurt.

Howard had sorted through the papers until he came to the IRA. There had been little yellow stick-um things stuck up and down the margin, with notes in Melissa's handwriting that, put together, read:

Howard—

Legally, the money in the IRA is yours. However, you may re-

member that all of it is not. I'll trust you to do what you feel is
right. If you choose to pay me back, I suggest you *not* take the
money out of the IRA (you will pay heavy penalties), but take out
a loan from the bank, using the IRA as collateral. You can probably get a loan at 7%, and your IRA is locked in at 13% for four
more months.

HOWARD'S IRA ACCOUNT [it said]

Year	Howard	Melissa
1982	500	1,500
1983	500	1,500
1984	1,250	750
1985	1,500	500
1986	2,000	
Total	5,750	4,250

It had hurt. It had hurt a lot.

Amanda, Melissa and Gardiner & Grayson. Well, Howard thought, he
might as well call his parents and see if they were going to fire him too.

"How do you feel about Melissa, Howard?" his mother quietly asked on
the bedroom extension.

"I'm not sure, Mom. Shocked, I think, more than anything else."

The crackle of long distance.

A sigh from his father on the extension in the kitchen. "Howard, I'm just
going to go ahead and say it. I think this is the best damn thing that could
happen to you. That girl—"

"Ray—" Allyson said.

"No, go on, Dad," Howard said.

"Look, Howard," Ray said, "I don't want to sound like your wise-ass old
man, but when you're really in love with a woman, she brings out the best in
you. Right, Al?"

Allyson laughed. "On some days, dear."

"You know what I mean," he said. "Howard, it isn't any of my business—"

"But you just have to say it," Howard finished for him.

"You only get one shot in this life," Ray said, "and if it's not working out,
you have to do something different. Else—what's the point?"

Crackle, crackle went the connection.

"We haven't felt you've been happy for a long time," his mother said
gently.

Howard sighed, regripping the phone. "No, I haven't been. Not for a long time." He hesitated and then said, "Mom, do you think I could just talk to Dad for a minute?" Of course he could. Did Howard know how much she loved him? How much they all did? And how they would love it if he came home for a visit? Debbie had got divorced, did Howard know that? Finally, Allyson did indeed get off the phone, and Howard told his father about Gardiner & Grayson and about what he was thinking of doing, the literary agency, and what a literary agency was, and how he could fail—

"Hold it, hold it," his father said. "Tell me about what happens if you succeed."

And so Howard started talking about the discoveries of new talent, about fostering the careers of writers for years, every book getting better, every day bringing new ideas, new directions, new possibilities in publishing—

"Okay, okay," Ray said, "I've heard about Disneyland before. Now what I want to know is, how much do I get to invest in it?"

Invest?

"Dad, I—"

"I know what you're going to say," Ray interrupted. "But just remember that I let you and Melissa invest in my business—"

"And got a twenty percent return on our—"

"But the point, Howard, is that I *let* you." Pause. "Remember that, Howard. I needed help, and I knew it was your mother's doing, but I took your help because I needed it. And because from you I could take it. No point in the Stewarts losing the farm again, so to speak. That's how the family lost it, you know. They wouldn't ask anyone for help. Brains, Howard, let me tell you, the Stewarts have always had brains—and none of us have ever been scared of hard work. But pride . . ." He sighed. "Pride. That's the one that will always bring us down."

Crackle, crackle.

"Five thousand," Howard said.

Well, there it was. His desk. His telephone. His lamp. His Rolodex. His battered copy of *Literary Market Place,* filched from G & G, courtesy of Bob. His clock that said 2:30 P.M.

Howard Stewart Literary Agency, Inc.

Now if he could just keep his clients from seeing his actual office, Howard thought it would be fine. Maybe he'd get a little stir crazy—it was one room, after all. But, it was his. His company.

He grinned, kicking his feet up on the table, looking out the window at the woman ironing across the way.

Howard Stewart Literary Agency, Inc.

On the desk lay Howard's business checkbook from Chemical Bank. It was funny, that. He had just walked off Broadway one afternoon into the branch office on the corner of 91st Street. Melissa would have sneered at the office; Amanda, Howard was sure, would have described it as "utterly charming."

It was a little village bank in the middle of New York City. With villagers. Just neighborhood folks, sashaying on in and on out each day, hailing the tellers and bank officers by their first names. A mom with a stroller; a grandfather buying a savings bond for his grandson; a Puerto Rican couple conversing in Spanish with a teller; an elderly Hungarian woman watching a bank officer figure out her estate papers; a Fordham Law student, taking out a loan; a seven-year-old depositing $4.35 from his bottle collection business; a doorman cashing his paycheck; a nurse asking for her balance . . .

Howard had walked in and was watching all this activity (he didn't think he had ever been in a bank this small), when an attractive young woman asked him if she could be of assistance. Howard had been startled. (At First Steel Citizen, Melissa's bank, the goal was to see how long employees could avoid contact with their customers—visually, verbally and certainly in terms of service.)

Howard had ended up sitting down with this nice woman and telling her more than he had probably ever told anyone about his financial life. And within an hour Howard had said he wanted his money transferred out of First Steel Citizen and into Chemical. Yes, he would like a personal checking account. Yes, a money market sounded good too. And yes, God, yes, a checking account in the name of Howard Stewart Literary Agency, Inc. And yes, Howard would like it if they transferred his IRA account to Chemical too, in four months, and yes, he would appreciate it if they loaned him the money to pay back Melissa. Yes, he promised, he would see an accountant to set up the finances of his company. And yes, he promised, he would take her card and call her if he needed any help or questions answered.

Yes, Howard liked his new little neighborhood bank very much.

The buzzer of the apartment startled him. He got up from his desk, went over to the intercom by the door and pushed TALK. "Yes?" He released the button. Nothing. He pushed TALK again. "Hello?" Nothing. He hit the intercom and then pushed the OPEN button, hoping the visitor was not another kindly soul pushing the *Watchtower* like yesterday. He walked out on the landing and peered down the five floors of ancient wooden stairwell. "Hello?"

There was a grunt and Howard could see a body dragging a very large box in through the door.

"Hi," he called again. "Are you from Golden's?"

A young guy looked up the stairwell at Howard. "Man, you expect me to go mountain climbing or what? This thing's *heavy.*"

"I'm coming," Howard called, loping down the stairs. Carrying the box between them, they managed to get it up to Howard's apartment. Howard gave him two dollars, thinking, *Don't forget to write it down. This is a business expense.*

After the delivery guy left, Howard opened a Coke and circled the box. This was it. His *office.* And then he dove into it, searching for, finding and lifting out the stationery. He opened the smaller and his heart skipped a beat. On wonderfully white rag paper, there, in elegant black type, it said THE HOWARD STEWART LITERARY AGENCY across the top. Along the bottom, in discreet small type: 319 West 95th Street Suite 5A New York, New York 10025.

Suite 5A. (Snicker.)

There were legal envelopes and smaller, printed note paper and envelopes; printed announcements of the agency's opening; and manila envelopes and printed labels and notebooks and accounting books and ribbons for his printer and file folders and paper clips and a stapler and a ruler and a pencil holder and a blotter and glue sticks and accordion files and index cards and legal pads and nifty pens that flowed black ink in smooth streaks.

Oh, and there was other stuff too, and Howard spent the better part of the afternoon and night unpacking and organizing it all. At the bottom of the box, tucked in the corner, was the smallest box containing the biggest news Howard's business cards.

It was fun, this setting up shop. Setting up *his* shop.

The day Howard was to appear at Melissa's lawyer's was the day that Howard worked hardest on his new enterprise. He was up at five, at his word processor at six, and by eleven had completed nine very important letters. The first was to Gertrude Bristol, Howard's former bestselling author. His letter, like the others he had written, said in part:

> My years spent as an editor, combined with my newness to the agenting profession, have placed me in a rather unique and exciting position. While I have no desire to try to steal established

writers away from the agents who have served them so well over the years, I do, however, want to have a chance at representing some of the writers coming up in the generation behind them.

In short, Gertrude, send me your unpublished protégés. As an editor, I will help them write their very best; as a new agent, I will kill myself to see that they get published.

"Kill myself to see . . ." Hmmm. Howard decided to leave the letters out overnight and see how they looked in the morning.

His phone rang at eleven-thirty. It was Shaye Areheart, a marvelous editor at Doubleday. "I just called to see how you were doing," she said, her voice exuding genuine warmth and cheerfulness—two precious commodities Howard was in dire need of, of late.

"Oh, pretty good," Howard said, putting his feet up on his new desk. "Did you get my announcement?"

"Yes, it looks terrific. Actually, that's the real reason I'm calling," she said. "Howard, you are going to find me the most wonderful new novelist of the decade, aren't you?"

Howard laughed. "Well, I'd sure like to. And if I find him or her, you know it's going to be you I'll call first."

"Oh, Howard, you are always so nice," she laughed. "So when can I take you to lunch? I hope your new celebrity status doesn't mean you're going to be difficult to pin down."

"What celebrity status?"

"Well, what other—and I quote—'devilishly handsome young editor threw a certain powerful publishing exec across the table during an editorial meeting'?"

"What? What are you reading from?"

An intake of breath. "Oh," Shaye said quietly, "then you haven't seen it."

"Seen what?"

"Leonore Fleischer's column in *PW* this week."

Howard asked Shaye to read him the piece, which she did. It was very, very funny. Someone—Patricia? Harriet maybe?—had given her a blow-by-blow description, plus a copy of his proposition to publish one book a year. They talked a bit longer, about Sperry in particular, when Howard was struck by an idea.

When he got off the phone with Shaye, Howard searched through his Rolodex, found the number he was looking for, and placed a call. He was on the phone for over an hour, his smile expanding with the excited discussion taking place on both ends of the line. When he got off, he looked at his watch. He had a half hour before he had to leave for Melissa's lawyer's office. And so he placed another call. To *Publishers Weekly.*

"Yes, hello, is Leonore there, please? Tell her it's Howard Stewart, the editor who throws powerful publishing execs across tables."

Howard hummed, tapping a pencil, as he waited. She took his call. "Hi, I wanted to thank you for your piece." He scanned the notes he had made on a legal pad. "Yes, yes. Ha! Right. It was right down to the last detail." He laughed. "Yeah, well, that's why I'm calling. There's actually a sequel to the story." Tap, tap, tap with his pencil. "If I were you, I'd leave his name out of it. He'd probably shoot you." A laugh. "Oh, so you know about the guns. Yes. No, it's true. More like twenty of them." They finished that little item and Howard moved on.

"Well, I've started a literary agency. Oh, good, you got it." He leaned back in his chair, smiling. "Today is my first day of business, and I have a project I thought would interest you. As I said, it's sort of a sequel to your story." Pause. "Right. It was Sperry himself who gave me the idea."

He sat up and pulled his chair up to his desk. "The working title is: *How to Get Ahead When Your Boss Doesn't Have One.*"

Howard nodded, smiling broadly. "Subtitle: 'The Psychology of Corporate Oppression. . . .' That's right, anyone who's interested can contact me here. William Trent, at Wharton. He did a book with me two years ago, you might recall. . . ."

Winston Claridge's secretary showed Howard right in.

Daddy looked like he always looked. And being in an attorney's office did not faze him at all—a cigar was stuffed in one cheek, and a glass of bourbon was in one hand, and Howard was quite sure the swizzle stick in it had come from his pocket.

"I'm sorry to see you under such painful circumstances," Howard murmured.

"Painful?" Collins said, dropping into the chair with a loud wooshing noise from the cushion. "Hell, I'm celebrating."

Melissa looked wonderful. Howard had no doubt that she had carefully planned and orchestrated her appearance for his benefit. She said, "Hello, Howard," extending her hand to him as though she expected him to kiss it. He did not. But he did see that her engagement and wedding ring were gone.

She saw that he saw and she smiled.

Winston got right to it, summarizing the content of the stack of papers before him that Howard assumed was his divorce.

"Drink, Stewart?" Collins asked, getting up to reveal a small bar in one of Winston's cabinets.

"No—wait, yes," he said.

"Mr. Collins gave you and Melissa, on your wedding day, a joint gift of two hundred shares of IBM stock—" Winston was saying.

"It all goes to Melissa," Howard interrupted.

Winston looked to Melissa, who nodded, and he read on. Apartment, car, furnishings, bank accounts . . . all to Melissa.

Collins gave Howard warm bourbon, which Howard drank down in two gulps.

"I'm glad you're being a man about this," Collins said, puffing smoke in his face.

The grounds for divorce were irreconcilable differences. Right, Howard nodded, experiencing some difficulty in breathing—and not because of Daddy's smoke.

Winston pushed an envelope across his desk toward Howard, mumbling something about "rings."

"What?" Howard asked, trying to snap to attention.

"You may have the engagement and wedding ring."

Howard looked to Melissa.

"Take them, Howard," she said.

Howard, blinking rapidly, folded his arms and stared at Winston.

And then they came to Howard's great-grandmother Mills's diamond watch, which Winston said Melissa would return to him.

"No," Howard said, jumping up from his chair. He spun around, his back to the three, and shoved his hands in his pockets. After a moment he turned around, sighed, and said, "I gave it to her because I wanted her to have it. Just because we—" He looked at Melissa. "I want you to have something from me. It wasn't all bad, you know."

Melissa thought a minute and then turned to Winston. "Take out the Rolex then. I'd like Howard to keep it."

She had been going to take his watch?

Winston fussed with a ruler for so long that Melissa finally got up, snapped the pen out of his hand, and slashed the line out of the agreement herself. She threw the pen down. "Neatness is not the issue here," she said, going back to her seat.

Howard bit his lip to keep from laughing.

Melissa's eye caught his and she almost laughed too. She gave a little sigh then, still looking at Howard, and smiled—smiled in a way Howard hadn't seen in a long, long time.

Please don't be nice, he thought.

They got through everything else. Winston said he would send a copy of the papers to Howard's lawyer—

"No, I'll sign them now," Howard said, walking up to his desk.

"Howard," Winston said, taking off his glasses, "you can't just—"

"No alimony, right?"

"Correct."

"No alimony to me, right?"

"Correct."

"We've settled the property, right?"

Winston nodded.

"So when I sign this, everything's settled, right?"

"You still should at least—"

Howard went ahead and signed the papers. While he was signing the last one, Collins let out a belly laugh.

"What?" Howard asked him, handing Winston his pen back.

"Look for yourself," Collins said.

Howard turned to Melissa. She smiled. And she raised her hand. "I'm glad I could put it back on before Stephen got here. He would be very angry if he saw I wasn't wearing it."

A diamond. The size of . . .

Collins threw his head back and roared.

Howard's throat caught. He coughed. He swallowed. "Congratulations, Melissa," he said, making for the door.

"Howard," Winston called out. He waved the envelope containing the rings. Howard walked back and took it from him. Turning, he glanced down at Melissa. She was not smiling now.

Howard went to the door and as he opened it Collins said, "Don't, little girl. He was always a bum, that guy."

Howard carefully closed the door behind him.

37

CASSY'S SATURDAY NIGHT

Cassy tossed her keys into the silver bowl, dropped her purse on the front hall chair, and looked at herself in the mirror.

There was no denying it, she thought, touching the corner of her mouth. She *was* looking younger these days.

She went into the kitchen, poured herself a glass of water from the refrigerator, and leaned against the counter, drinking it. Ten minutes after two. She smiled. It was late, very late, and she was tired.

But what a nice kind of tired.

If people had told her that she was capable of having an affair with a woman, she would have told them they were out of their minds. If people had told her that she was capable of having an affair—period—she would have told them they were out of their minds. All right, so Cassy was out of her mind, but why wasn't she feeling guilty?

Well, maybe she did, with Henry—but did she really?

No.

Perhaps it was because it felt so safe, that Alexandra felt so safe. To Alexandra, secrecy was everything. And too, she made so few demands on

Cassy—mainly because she herself was in no position to fulfill any more than those which she had already demonstrated she could. But shouldn't Cassy be feeling guilty toward Alexandra? Surely this affair couldn't be good for her, not with all that was attached to it.

But then, Cassy thought, who else *could* Alexandra have an affair with? Alexandra didn't have time for a real lover. Her commitment to her work discounted any chance of a full-time relationship—at least Cassy's concept of one.

That was what had come between Alexandra and her "friend" Lisa, Alexandra had told Cassy. And before Lisa, her fiancé Tyler, and before Tyler, Gordon. That all of them had ultimately declared that they would have been better off falling in love with the Invisible Woman—then at least they would have known, from the beginning, that she *was* invisible, and would have been spared the hours, weeks and months of waiting for somebody who never materialized.

Cassy went back to Henry's room and peeked in the door. Skipper was snoring away in the far bed. He too, over the summer, had grown so much. (He snored like a man now.) Henry was sleeping peacefully, curled up on his side, his long arms wrapped around a pillow. She leaned over to kiss him but didn't. His breath was slow, even, and she hung there a moment, listening, trying to regulate her breathing to his. No, too slow. She touched his hair and he stirred slightly; she retreated from the bedroom and closed the door.

She went into the guest room and, after a moment, pulled the subway poster of Alexandra out from behind the dresser and leaned it against the wall. She sat down on the edge of the bed and looked at it.

It was still so hard to believe.

What did all this mean? Was she falling in love with this girl? A mere girl who knew nothing about commitment, about marriage, about stretch marks and staying up all night to watch over a sick child? Alexandra knew nothing of pain, Cassy was pretty sure. She kept searching for it in Alexandra—the damaged part, the area beaten and dented and frayed from living—but Cassy couldn't find it.

No. Cassy did not think she could fall in love with someone like that. Man or woman.

But she could fall and had fallen in love with this idea of someone being in love with her. Someone who could look at the wreck and see something worth reaching for, salvaging . . . Saving. That was what Alexandra had done. Saved whatever small pockets of joy Cassy had managed to hold onto over the years.

Tonight, when she arrived, Alexandra had been in the middle of cooking dinner. That in itself seemed slightly wondrous to Cassy. When had anyone *ever* cooked dinner to please her? *(No wonder men like wives,* she had thought, eating the piece of veal Alexandra held up to her mouth.) Cassy had been rather wound up and, over dinner, had found herself talking about anything and everything that was in her head (Henry, Michael and WST) and Alexandra had listened, nodded, smiled, laughed and murmured reassurances. And at one point—stopping talking long enough to eat—Cassy had looked at Alexandra and had had the most remarkable thought. *I am happy. I am so very happy right now.*

After dinner they had changed. (That was another wonder to Cassy. Going to the closet and pulling out a nightgown and negligee that she would have chosen for herself had she bought them. But Alexandra had bought them. For her.) And then they had gone into the living room, put in a video cassette—what had it been? Carole Lombard had been in it—and they had turned out the lights.

Was that the best part of the evening, the movie? Close, she thought, smiling, but no. Alexandra had sat up against the end of the couch and Cassy had nestled back in between her legs to receive what had felt like the world's most wonderful massage ever. Her shoulders. Her arms. Her back. Her neck —ohhh, her neck was always so stiff these days. Her head. Her temples. Under her eyes. Even her hands. An hour. One full hour Alexandra had given her of this.

No wonder she couldn't remember what the movie had been.

And then, after the movie was over, they had gone to bed. Cassy smiled again to herself, thinking of this. The thoughts vaguely triggered off other things as well. She could feel them. Inside.

What surprised Cassy more than anything else about this whole affair was just how much she enjoyed making love to Alexandra. She almost liked it more than when Alexandra touched her. (Almost.) Looking at the subway poster in front of her, she shook her head. Alexandra's composure, her confidence, her poise—everything about her was in such control. And from that first night they had been together, Cassy had wondered at the power she possessed that could so obviously, completely undo Alexandra. God, it was thrilling, stripping Alexandra of that control, slowly taking it away from her and then using it as her own. Over her.

It was wondrous. All of it. The laughter and the warmth and the comfort and—*yes, admit it, Cassy, admit it, the sex is a miracle; Alexandra probably invented sex; okay, I admit it, the sex is great, so can we move on now?*—the trust and the closeness and . . .

Cassy sighed and moved Alexandra back behind the dresser. She was talking herself into something she knew she didn't want to talk herself into.

In her room, on her pillow, was a note from Henry:

> Mom,
> Dad called around 12:30. He didn't sound very good. He's in 212 at the Hotel Wynne and wants you to call him. I told him you'd be out very late and he said he didn't care what time it was—call him when you get in. No matter how late.

"But, Daddy," Cassy whispered in the dark, standing on the porch stairs, "Mommy said she'll never speak to you again."

Henry Littlefield laughed. "Don't worry, Princess," he said, rubbing the top of her head. "Your mother will forgive your old man."

"I'm not mad at you," Cassy said, hugging her father around the waist.

"Because you know how much I love you," he said, picking her up. "Don't you, Cassy? Know how much I love you?"

Cassy dialed the Hotel Wynne and asked for Room 212. Was she imagining it, or did the hotel operator hesitate before putting her through?

The phone rang seven times before it was picked up—and dropped. At last a voice—Michael's voice?—said, "Yeah."

"Michael? Michael, it's Cassy."

"Yeah." Vague, confused. And then, "Cassy? Cassy?"

"Yes, Michael. It's Cassy."

A low whimper. "Cass, I'm sick. I'm so sick."

"Michael?"

He started to cry. "I need you. I'm so sick." A second whimper. "I need . . ."

"Do you want me to come get you?"

"Help me. I'm so sick. Cassy? Cassy?"

"I'm here, Michael."

"I thought you hung up."

"I'm still here, Michael." She looked at the clock. "Michael, stay there, in your room—I'll be there in a few minutes."

"Cassy? Cassy?"

"Michael, I'm coming."

"Will you come?"

"Michael, I'm coming! I have to get off now so I can get there. It'll only be a few minutes."

"Will you come?"

"Michael, I'll be there in a few minutes. Just stay in bed until I get there."

She went to the kitchen and scribbled a note to Henry in case he awakened. She grabbed her purse, picked up her keys, opened the front door and stopped—

Don't go alone. They said not to go alone.

Who the hell am I going to call at three in the morning?

Alexandra? No.

Henry—no, no, no.

Sam.

He'll be sound asleep.

She started through the door again, and stopped again. She rubbed her eyes. She sighed and closed her eyes a moment. And then she went back to the kitchen and called Sam.

No, he was glad she called—what was up? He did? The Wynne? No, she had done the right thing. Yes. He'd dress and pick her up in the lobby of her building in fifteen minutes.

Cassy sat in the lobby, listening to the tock of the grandfather clock, watching the front door. The doorman was sitting in a chair across the lobby, listening to his Walkman and reading a copy of the *Racing Form,* occasionally glancing up at Cassy.

"I've got a child in the house!" Catherine Littlefield screamed into the telephone. "I can't go running all over town after him."

Cassy stood by the kitchen door, listening, shivering in her nightgown.

"Then go ahead and lock him up!" She slammed the phone down and buried her head in her hands.

"Is Daddy all right?" Cassy asked.

Catherine's head jerked up. "That's right—go ahead—be concerned about your father! You don't give a damn about me, do you? Do you, Cassy?" She jumped up from the chair, sending it crashing back onto the floor. "Answer me! You love your father more than me, don't you?"

"I love you, Mommy."

"No one loves me!" Catherine wailed, throwing herself against the wall.

Sam arrived and the two of them walked up to West End Avenue to find a cab. The driver they got insisted on expounding his views about Fidel Castro and Cuba, and Sam conversed with him while Cassy stared out the window. When she pressed her forehead against the glass, Sam took her hand.

Dr. and Mrs. Daley drove them from the church to the cemetery in their big blue Cadillac.

"He looked so good," Mrs. Daley said to Catherine, looking back at her from the front seat.

"Just like when I first met him," Catherine said, adjusting her hat. "Oh, Cassy, look at the front of your dress." Catherine pulled a handkerchief from her purse and started wiping at it.

Cassy, with a low moan, turned away from her mother, pressing her forehead against the glass. "Daddy," she screamed in her mind, "you can't leave me here!"

"The child's upset, Catherine," Mrs. Daley said.

"And I'm not? Here I am, left all alone, with a child to support . . ."

The lights of Lincoln Center flew by Cassy's eyes and then the cab slowed to a stop. Sam paid the driver, reached over Cassy to open her door, and held her elbow from behind as she got out. Out on the sidewalk, he took her arm. "You okay?" She nodded and they went into the lobby of the hotel.

Sam looked around and then asked the bellboy how to get to Room 212. The bellboy exchanged looks with the desk clerk. "He wants to know about 212," he said.

The clerk asked Sam to step over to the desk for a word in private. Sam left Cassy there and walked over to the desk. They talked for a minute and then Sam came back, with a key. "This way," he said, steering her to the elevator. "He's been here for four days. They've been worried about him, but didn't know who to call."

The elevator stopped at 2 and they got out.

"Whatever happens," Sam said to her, "just remember that this could be the start of the road back."

Cassy nodded, swallowing, looking at room numbers.

They found Room 212. Sam knocked. No answer. He knocked again. There was a sound—a voice—something.

"Michael?" Cassy called. "Michael, it's me. It's Cassy."

Silence.

Sam inserted the key and opened the door a crack. The smell of vomit hit their nostrils. Sam poked his head in. "Okay," he said under his breath, opening the door.

Cassy covered her mouth with her hand.

Michael was lying across one of the twin beds, his clothes and the bed-clothes stained with . . .

The bedside lamp was on its side; there were trays and dishes with half-eaten food on the dresser and floor. Empty bottles, dirty glasses, a newspaper torn to shreds . . .

Michael's eyes opened a crack. And then they flew open. He struggled to sit up, struggled to see. "I told him I didn't have to sit in the press box," he mumbled, head rolling back. He started to slip over the side of the bed and Sam lunged to catch him.

"It's okay, Cochran," he said, pulling him upright. "Cassy, clear that stuff off the other bed."

Cassy let go of the door and did as she was told.

"I forgot the way," Michael slurred to Sam, trying to keep his eyes open. "I thought it was on the other side."

"Okay, here we go, we're going to move over here," Sam said, pulling Michael up on his feet and half carrying him to the other bed. "Just lie back. That's it." Over his shoulder to Cassy, "Get a wet washcloth."

There was broken glass all over the bathroom floor. Cassy tried to step over it, reaching up for a washcloth.

Oh.

Her stomach lurched dangerously at the sight in the sink. She wet the washcloth at the bathtub faucet, wrung it out, and went back out.

"Put it on his forehead," Sam said, covering the phone with his hand. He was talking to the hospital, Cassy realized.

She leaned over Michael. He was so old, so wretchedly ill. She wiped his face and hands and went back to rinse out the washcloth in the bathroom. She came back, folding the washcloth, and placed it on his forehead. After a moment she went over to the closet.

"Okay," Sam said, hanging up the phone, "an ambulance is coming. I need to let the front desk know."

Cassy walked back to the bed, holding a shirt.

"No," Sam said, shaking his head.

Cassy stood there.

"Don't—wait. Hold on a minute, will you?" he said into the phone. "No, Cassy. We want him to see the clothes he wore to the hospital."

"But—"

He shook his head again.

Cassy pressed the shirt to her face.

Sam explained the situation to the front desk.

Michael started muttering, rocking his head from side to side.

Cassy sat down next to him and began to weep.

"They can't!" Michael suddenly yelled, sitting bolt upright.

Cassy grabbed his shoulders. "It's all right, Michael. It's only me."

His eyes closed and he began to sag. Cassy gently pushed him back down on the pillow and put the washcloth back on his forehead.

Sam hung up the phone and sat down on the edge of the bed. He reached over Michael to touch Cassy's arm. "It's going to be all right," he murmured.

"Over there," Michael said, trying to point to somewhere.

38

THE HEARING

"There's Cassy," Harriet said to Amanda.

Cassy was struggling with one of the glass doors. She stopped pushing and starting pulling and succeeded in getting it open. "Thank heavens I've found you," she said, coming in. "I'm with them," she explained to the receptionist, pointing to Harriet and Amanda across the room on the couch. She walked over to them, heels resounding on the linoleum floor. "You wouldn't believe where I've been. I wrote down 6 Lafayette instead of 60."

Harriet moved her briefcase so Cassy could sit down. "It's all right," she said, "we've just been sitting here, waiting."

"Mr. Thatcher and a social worker—a Mr. Jones—took Rosanne to the judge's chambers," Amanda said, "and then they came out for Mrs. Gold-blum." She looked at her pendant watch. "That was almost an hour ago."

Cassy slowly blew out a breath and used both hands to push back the loose strands of hair from her face. "So are we going to the hearing?"

"I would assume so," Harriet said, settling back against the couch, checking her watch. She looked over at Cassy and said, in a low voice, "How are you?"

Cassy looked at her for a moment and then shrugged. "To tell you the truth, I'm not really sure." She fell back against the couch, crossing her legs. She glanced at Amanda, looked down at her skirt, and smoothed it with her hand. "My husband's in the hospital," she explained. Then she looked up at Harriet. "Sam's been wonderful—I don't know what I would do without him." She dropped her eyes back into her lap, slowly shaking her head. "Poor Henry . . ." She bit her lower lip and then shook her head again. "There's so much to sort out."

Harriet was nodding. "Just try and take it a day at a time," she said gently.

Cassy brought her hands up to press the bridge of her nose. Closing her eyes, she took a deep breath, nodding. "I know," she said into her hands. "I know."

The three women sat there, each with her own thoughts.

Harriet checked her watch again. "I've got to call in to the office," she said, getting up. She walked over to the receptionist and asked where a pay phone was. "I'll be out in the hall—around to the right," she told them.

"Okay," Cassy said. She shifted slightly, recrossing her legs toward Amanda. She pulled down on her skirt. "So how are you?"

Amanda turned her head, drawing a slow, sad smile. "Do you prefer courtesy or the truth?"

Cassy gave a small laugh, touching at her earring. "Well, I'm about to have a nervous breakdown, does that help?"

Amanda nodded. "I am not very happy," she finally said. "I mean that I am, about some things, but about others, I . . ." Her voice trailed off and so did her eyes.

"Howard," Cassy said

Amanda looked at her.

Cassy smiled slightly. "Rosanne."

"Ah, yes, Rosanne," Amanda sighed, sliding down in the couch to rest her head back against it, looking to the ceiling. She crossed one arm over her chest and brought her elbow up to rest on it, holding her pendant in her hand. "It was the block party," she murmured. "When it happened." She turned her head to look at Cassy. "Do you remember that day? When I met you?"

"Yes." Cassy looked back down at her skirt, thinking. "I remember that day very well," she said quietly. After a moment she turned to face Amanda, bringing her arm up along the back of the couch.

Amanda looked at her, waiting.

"Don't walk away from it," Cassy said.

Amanda blinked.

"It's none of my business, I know," Cassy said, her eyes moving away. But a second later they came sweeping back. "Amanda—" She reached over to lightly touch her arm, hesitating. "Time passes so quickly—and you're young, now, and so you don't know yet what—what—" Her voice was barely a whisper. She took a breath and tried again. "What I'm trying to say is that things are never right, that"—she shook her head slightly— "that, no matter who you love, it's not going to be easy." She paused, biting her lip. "Amanda—you might never be young enough to try again." She closed her eyes, sighing. "I'm sorry," she said, withdrawing her hand. "I have no right—"

"It's all right," Amanda said quietly, watching Cassy fighting back tears. "I think you are very kind for talking to me." Cassy wiped at one eye. "Rosanne is so right to love you so much."

Cassy let out a little laugh, blinking rapidly.

Amanda smiled. "I always wondered if she talked about me."

"Oh, no," Cassy said, opening her purse for a tissue. "She never did— before. It's only been recently." She dabbed at her eyes and put the tissue back in her purse, snapping it closed. Her eyes came up to Amanda's. "Last Friday she said she thought Howard was scared to see you."

A flicker—of something—passed over Amanda's face.

"And she said," Cassy continued, sniffing once, smiling now, " 'Ya know, Mrs. C, for a smart guy he sure is stupid—how could anyone be scared of Amanda?' "

With this statement, Amanda's head fell forward.

"And you know what I said, Amanda?" Pause. "Amanda?"

Amanda brought her head back up, swallowing.

"I said," Cassy said softly, "you only get scared of someone when you're scared they don't love you."

Amanda closed her eyes and turned her head away.

When Harriet returned, she stood there, looking down at the two of them. At one end of the couch, Amanda was lying with her head back, her eyes closed. At the other, Cassy was leaning forward, crouched over her lap, pressing a tissue against her mouth. Harriet sighed, silently, and eased down between them, sliding an arm around Cassy. In a moment Cassy turned and started to cry, quietly, on her shoulder, and Harriet started to gently rock her.

This was how Mr. Thatcher found them.

Harriet looked up at him.

Amanda looked up at him.

Cassy, releasing Harriet—sniffing, wiping at her eyes with the tissue— looked up at him.

"It's over," he said, smiling. "Rosanne gets Jason back at the end of the month."

The reaction was spontaneous. All three women laughed and cheered and starting talking at him at once. They didn't have to go to a hearing? It was all done, all decided? Where was Rosanne? This was official, wasn't it? Did Jason know?

Rosanne came slowly walking out with Mrs. Goldblum on her arm. When the three women turned, the ladies stopped.

"By gosh, we did it," Mrs. Goldblum declared, eyes shining brightly.

39

AMANDA HAS A
VISITOR AT THE
EMILY DICKINSON SCHOOL

Featuring a trailing blue cotton dress, a long lavender scarf and a tinker's delight of necklaces and bracelets, Amanda waltzed into the classroom promptly at seven. Her attire evidently met with her students' approval, for they applauded.

The class was in full attendance: Mrs. Mansolo, formerly of Naples and now of New York; Mrs. Lopez, formerly of Newark and now of New York; Mr. Krotzski, formerly of Warsaw and now of New York; and Mr. Williams, formerly of Riker's Island and now of Manhattan.

It was their fifth class together and they were already on page 70 of the workbook, which, according to Margaret Whelan, was extraordinary. ("How," she asked Amanda, "are you moving them along so quickly?" "It's their doing," Amanda explained. "I tell them what page the other classes are on and they simply refuse to leave until they are ahead of them. My students are fiercely competitive," she added, not without a touch of pride.)

But it was Amanda who was learning so much! Amanda spent the first half hour of every class discussing some document or form that one of the students had been handed from the outside world. At the very first class Mr.

Krotzski, with a deeply furrowed brow, had handed her a New York State driver's manual. Since then, Amanda had been spending time with him outside of class deciphering it. Now, prior to this, the closest Amanda had ever got to learning how to drive had been learning the difference between broughams and carriages in Victorian novels. As a result, Amanda found the driver's manual perhaps even more wondrous and enlightening than Mr. Krotzski did.

What else was she learning about? Green cards, American citizenship, vaccinations, the Iron Curtain, small business loans, parole regulations, transatlantic postage and on and on and on. And then, this evening, it was Mrs. Lopez' turn and guess what her forms were? Social Security! *Hooray!* Amanda dazzled the class with her wealth of knowledge, and not only did Mrs. Lopez fill out her forms, but the entire class now knew how this magnificent system worked in ways most Americans did not! (More applause.) (They clapped a great deal in this class.)

And then they got down to the nitty-gritty, and Amanda was explaining the difference between "there," "their" and "they're" when the door to the classroom opened.

It was Howard.

"Sorry," he said, his face coloring. "Uh, Mrs. Whelan said I could sit in on your class. I'll be teaching too." His eyes were pleading with Amanda.

After a moment she smiled. Broadly. "We would be very pleased to have you join us. Class," she said, turning to them, "this is Howard Stewart. He is going to be a teacher too and would like to observe the brightest class in the school."

They clapped (for Howard or for themselves, it wasn't quite clear).

Howard took a seat in the back of the room. Mrs. Mansolo turned around in her chair. "You must telll the werrrld you ahre imporrrtant," she said, waving him forward.

Howard laughed, his face turning an even darker shade of red. He went up and sat to Mrs. Mansolo's left.

"Goot," she said, bowing her head.

Amanda was nervous for about ten minutes, but then her attention slipped away from Howard and back to the students and soon she was thoroughly wrapped up in the lesson, forgetting his presence entirely. Howard sat there, mesmerized. Amanda's color was high; her body was in high gear as well. When she wasn't making sweeping gestures with her arms, she was wildly dashing off examples across the blackboard—slashing and underscoring left and right. She praised her students constantly; when they were reading out loud, she would walk behind them, pull their shoulders back, lift their books off their desks, and make them hold them up in their hands, whispering, "Be proud of how much you know!" And then, between points in the workbook, she would whirl around—dress billowing up and around after her—and deliver a quick lecture:

"To know how to read is to have the world open to you! If you can read, you can learn anything and everything you ever wanted to know. What does a lawyer do? Go to the library and find out! How do you fix a radio? Go to the library and find out! Is Clint Eastwood married?"

"Go to the library and find out!" the class chorused, Howard included.

"Yes!" Amanda cried, shooting her fist up in the air.

(They clapped.)

The class didn't end until close to nine-thirty. They all walked out of the classroom together and at the front doors of the school the students said goodnight to Amanda and to Howard. "I just have to write a note to Margaret," she said to him. He watched what she scribbled:

> Dear Margaret,
> Page 96!
> Sincerely,
> Amanda

She slipped the note under Margaret's office door and let the custodian know they were leaving.

"Are you really teaching a class?" she asked him, walking down the hall.

"Yes." Pause. "Rosanne told me—"

"Rosanne has been very busy, I must say," Amanda said. Howard reached ahead to hold the door open for her. "Cassy Cochran appears to know more about you and me than you and I do."

Howard followed her outside. "I don't mind. I like Cassy."

Amanda smiled slightly, glancing back at him. "I do too." She waited for him to catch up and then they turned right onto the sidewalk. "Her husband is in the hospital."

"I heard." They walked another step and then Howard stopped. "Why do you think she's stayed with him?"

Amanda shifted her books, bringing them up to hold against her chest. She sighed, raising her eyebrows. "Rosanne says no one who hasn't been there can ever really understand."

Howard frowned slightly. "What, like her and Frank?"

"Like her and Frank," Amanda said. They walked on. "And there's their son."

"I don't know"—Howard shrugged— "it just seems strange, a woman like Cassy . . ."

Amanda stopped dead, her mouth falling open.

Howard whirled around. "What?"

"Some people thought your marriage was a little strange, you know."

"Okay, okay," Howard said, raising his hands as if to defend himself.

"Oh, Howard," Amanda sighed, "I'm sorry, that was a very unkind thing for me to say."

"No, really, it's okay." He looked around and then up at the street sign: 95th Street. "I, uh"—he gestured down the street— "I live here now." He ran his hand over his jaw. "You wouldn't want to come up, would you? To see—hey, did you know? I'm an agent now."

"I heard," she said, smiling.

"Well—would you? Like to come up?" And then, more quietly, "It's not too soon, is it?"

Amanda held out a hand to him. "It's not too soon."

Howard grinned, took her hand, and started pulling her down the block. He apologized the entire way. It wasn't much, wasn't anything at all, Amanda would hate it, find it creepy and awful and . . .

"If it's yours, how could I not like it?" she said.

While they walked up the stairs, Howard gave a running commentary (in whispers) about the various inhabitants of the building, pausing only to ask Amanda if she wished to stop and catch her breath. She didn't and they soon reached the fifth-floor landing, where Howard groaned at Amanda's inquiry about who was next door in 5B. "Later, I promise, later," Howard said, unlocking his door.

She liked it, Howard could tell, and as he grew more certain of it, he grew more excited about showing her things in it and she, in turn, seemed to get more excited about seeing them. The bookshelves? She did? He had built them himself. Build some for her? Sure. . . . The curtains? That was Rosanne's doing. . . . "I love the desk too." "Look, see, my files. My stationery. You do? Sure, you can have all the cards you want. . . . Yeah, I do get distracted—it's kind of hard not to watch. No, he's scooping ice cream. He always eats ice cream during the news. Over there? Some lady. She irons a lot. I washed them—hung upside down to do the outside. No wonder Rosanne would never do the windows. What? She washes *your* windows?"

He poured her a glass of white wine while Amanda tried out the chair at his desk.

He had made his first sale. Yes! His commission would be twenty-five hundred dollars. Had Amanda received a contract yet? Yes? Good, Amanda would need Mr. Thatcher. Explain it to her? Sure, he'd love to.

Howard came back in and handed her the glass of wine. Sipping his beer, he sat down on the edge of the desk, watching her. She was holding the glass in her lap, tracing the rim with her finger. Howard lowered his glass to rest it on his leg, took a breath, and said, "I love you, Amanda."

She didn't move for a moment. And then she murmured, "I know," rose from her chair, and moved over to the window. Looking out, she took a sip of wine and put the glass down on the sill. "There were men before you, Howard," she said quietly.

Silence.

Howard took a swig of his beer and put the glass down on the desk.

"I didn't love any of them," she finally said, bringing a hand up to rest at the base of her neck. "But then, I wouldn't have seen them if I had." She sighed slightly, lowering her hand. "I never wanted to fall in love again."

After a moment Howard said, "I can understand why."

"It's funny," Amanda said, nodding slightly, "but I think you probably do." She picked up her glass, turned around, leaned back against the sill, held the glass to her mouth, and then sipped. Lowering it, "Whoever it was at the time would come every other Monday—"

"Amanda—don't," Howard said gently. "Look, you don't have to explain anything about—"

"But I do." She pressed her lips together for a moment, eyes moving away. "I do. Because I love you too, you see." She looked at him. "And I'm so scared, Howard," she murmured, closing her eyes, "I'm just so scared."

He was over there in a moment, taking the glass out of her hand and putting it on the sill, and then taking her into his arms. "Amanda, don't," he whispered as she started to cry.

"I can't help it, Howard. I'm just such a mess. You don't know, you just don't know," she sobbed into his shoulder.

"No, Amanda, no," he said, holding her tighter. "Darling, you don't know what the world is like. We're all a mess, we're all just pretending to know what it is we're doing, and the rest of the time . . ." He sighed. "The rest of the time, Amanda"—he kissed the side of her head—"we spend fantasizing about people we think can fix everything. And they never do. But we keep waiting for them to do it for us anyway. You know that—God,

Amanda, in my book, you're way ahead of the rest of us." He kissed the side of her head again. "You're writing a book—teaching—taking care of Mrs. Goldblum, of Rosanne. Amanda, you are not a mess. The world's a mess, not you." He stepped back to bring her head up. Her face was stained with tears, and he smiled, kissing her on the forehead. Then he reached back into his pocket and pulled out a handkerchief. "Here," he said, wiping her face. And then he held it to her nose.

"Oh, Howard," Amanda groaned, swiping the handkerchief out of his hand. "I'm not that much of a child." He laughed as she turned away to blow her nose.

Then he went over, took her arm, and pulled her to the couch. He sat them both down. "Listen," he said, taking the handkerchief out of her hands and throwing it on the table. "I have something I need to tell you."

She looked at him, a touch of fear returning to her eyes.

He took her hands. "I didn't leave Melissa," he said. "She threw me out. She was also the one who filed for divorce."

No reaction. And then, "Did you want the divorce?"

"Yes," he said. "Yes, I did. But I didn't want you to think I was able to come to that decision right away. It was made for me. And I'm glad, only . . ." He sighed. "I wish I could tell you I had been the one—"

"I know, darling," she said, bringing up a hand to his face. They looked at one another, a bit sad, and then Amanda's face came alive. "Try as you might, Mr. Stewart," she said, sweeping her hand out to gesture to the apartment, "it will be very hard for you to minimize all that you are doing."

Howard smiled, threw his arm around Amanda and pulled her in against his side. "Bet you never saw the Taj Mahal before," he said, looking at the room.

"No, I haven't."

"Good," he pronounced, "so now you know this is it. This is what all the hoopla's about."

She smiled and suddenly dropped her head to his chest. "I do so love you," she sighed, holding onto him.

"I know," he said, stroking her hair.

Her head jerked up. "Do you suppose I'll ever be able to make love with you on Mondays—ever?"

He threw his head back and laughed. "God, Amanda!"

"Wait, wait!" she cried, scrambling to her knees, going up to hold his head between her hands. "Darling, Howard, you don't know how hard it was for me to keep you away on Mondays! And for what? Ghosts!"

He closed his eyes, starting to laugh again.

She gave his head a little shake. "Don't you know how I longed to be with you?" she scolded. "Whenever I could be?" She stopped shaking his head and simply held it, staring down into his eyes.

Howard reached up to take her hands. He kissed one and then the other. "I'm laughing because I thought you were seeing someone else while you were seeing me," he said.

Her expression turned to utter amazement. She sat back down on her heels. "After you?" she finally said. She went back up onto her knees. "After you?" she repeated, slipping off his glasses and tossing them behind her. "Golly," she said, holding his head, "you're really quite as mad as I am." And then she brought her head down to kiss him.

His arms slid around her and Amanda, still holding him, still kissing him, moved her leg over to straddle his lap. Once there, she raised her head from his mouth, looked in his eyes—smiling a mysterious smile—and slowly moved her hips down around him. He managed to move them both farther out on the couch and Amanda really smiled then, settling in and sliding her legs all the way around him.

She sighed, smiling, and touched his hair. "The only problem is," she murmured, "I can't tell if that's you or the material of my dress caught between my legs."

He squirmed slightly. "Both," he said, stretching his neck to kiss her.

And then they went wreckless with each other, not caring at all for the welfare of their clothes. Amanda's dress was off before her scarf, Howard's pants before his shirt, and this went here and that went there and Amanda's bracelets were rolling about on the floor and she was reaching down into his shorts and he was ready to rip her brassiere apart out of impatience and Amanda was laughing and he was laughing and then Amanda sat up and said, "I don't have my diaphragm."

They sat there. She hit him on the chest. "The diaphragm *you* made me get, thank you very much."

And Howard said not to worry, he had something, and went off to the bathroom and came back and found Amanda completely naked, standing about the pillows she had pulled off the couch. "How does one operate such a thing?" she wanted to know.

They did not get right to it. First Howard had to hold Amanda naked against him. And then he had to remember her breasts. And then Amanda had to do something about his Jockey shorts and certainly, certainly, offer a warm greeting to all that had been carried in them and that seemed so eager for her to do so. But they finally did pull the couch out into a bed and they did carry on about the condom Howard had brought from the bathroom— "What do you mean you never used one, Howard, don't tell me this is left over from high school." "Yikes, it's cold, Amanda." "Don't be silly, it will be more than sufficiently warm in a moment"—and their sex was a great, urgent, noisy affair, and both came very quickly and quite happily so, and within a half hour Howard was padding back to the bathroom again for another condom and they started in all over again, all over each other, and this time there was no fuss over the condom but instead over who might expire first, Amanda or Howard, in this splendid game of trying not to come, of trying to hold back—teetering, edging back, edging forward but-oh-not-quite, edging back—and then Amanda said, "I am going to die if I don't come," and so she did—very loudly so—and then Howard didn't stand a chance, not with the kinds of things that Amanda was saying, and so he came too, making a great masculine-moaning event out of it, and it was only when he was still that Amanda started laughing into his neck, quite unable to stop, and Howard said, "What is it?" and she whispered in his ear and then he sat bolt upright and looked to the window.

They had not gone unobserved.

Howard dove back down and hid his face in her hair, asking now what was he supposed to do—"some literary agency, this is"—and Amanda couldn't stop laughing, but when she did she wanted to know how on earth were they ever going to get up with all those people there.

40

SAM'S AFTERNOON

S am and Cassy finished talking with the doctor and walked back into the detox ward. It was not a cheery place. In every bed lay a man rendered helpless by drug withdrawal. Alcohol, barbiturates, amphetamines, tranquilizers, heroin, crack . . . legal and illegal addicts alike, each was struggling against the horrors left by the chemicals listed on his chart.

Michael Cochran, with five days behind him, was the best of the lot. He knew where he was; he had not had a seizure for three days; he could eat something this morning and it had stayed down. Sitting at his bedside was his son Henry. Henry was pale beneath his tan, thoroughly shaken by the sights the ward had to offer. Next to him, on Michael's bedside table, was an enormous vase of flowers Cassy had brought two days before.

Following his father's eyes, Henry turned around. His face eased slightly. "Here comes Mom," he said.

Michael, fingering the neck of his hospital gown, did not say anything. His eyes followed Cassy as Sam steered her to his bedside. Cassy sat down opposite Henry; Michael raised his hand slightly and Cassy reached to take it. Hold it.

Sam, standing next to Cassy, cleared his throat. Michael continued to look at Cassy; Cassy was trying to offer Henry a smile of reassurance.

Cassy turned to Michael. "Michael—"

"I love you," he said.

Cassy was near tears. She rose from her chair and leaned over the bed to hold her husband for a moment. "Don't be frightened, sweetheart," she whispered.

Sam cleared his throat again. Cassy released Michael—he held onto her arm as she sat down—and she looked up at Sam briefly. She coughed. "Michael," she said softly, leaning toward him, "you have to do it."

"But I'm fine, Cass," he said. "In a few days—"

"You're not fine, Michael." Pause. "You're very ill and you have to get well." She sighed, looking down, taking his hand in both of hers. "I want you to do what the doctor says." She brought her eyes up to meet his. "And it's not just the drinking. It's the pills too."

Michael shook his head. "Come on, Cass."

Sam nudged Cassy's leg with his foot.

"You're addicted to alcohol, Michael, and you're addicted to pills. I've just been with Dr. Warren—Michael, he *knows,* he knows what he's talking about. And he says if you don't go for treatment, you might—"

Michael pulled his hand away from her and crossed his arms. "What?"

Pause. "I don't want you to die, Michael," Cassy said, starting to cry. "Please—Michael, you've got to get some help."

Sam handed her his handkerchief.

"I'm not going to drink anymore, Cass," Michael finally said. "I learned my lesson."

"There's no lesson left to learn," Sam said quietly. "There's only a choice. Whether or not you want your life back."

"Christ, Wyatt," Michael muttered.

Cassy raised her head. "If you don't go for treatment—"

Michael's eyes narrowed.

"—you can't come home," she finished. After a moment, "I mean it, Michael. You leave here and you're on your own."

Michael turned to Henry. "What do you think about that? Your mom's throwing me out of my own house."

Henry looked to Sam.

"Stop looking at him and answer me, Henry. Do you think this is fair?"

Michael paused and then went on. "You heard what I told her—I told your mother I'm not going to drink anymore. You believe me, don't you? You know I won't."

Henry turned away.

"Henry." He looked back at his father. "Do you think she's being fair?" Michael asked him. "She isn't, is she? No, she's not." A sob from Cassy made Michael's head swivel in her direction. "For Pete's sake, Cassy, what the hell are you bawling about? I'm the one whose family's walking out."

"Dad—"

"Even that bitch of a mother of yours didn't walk out on your father—"

"And he's dead!" Cassy screamed, standing up. "God damn you, Michael!" she cried, pounding the bed. "Don't you get it? You're *dying,* Michael. You're going to die just like he did!" She recoiled suddenly, covering her mouth. She spun around, blindly pushed Sam out of the way, and ran out of the ward, heels echoing down the hall.

A nurse hovered nearby, watching.

Sam sighed and dropped down in Cassy's chair.

Across from him, Henry was crying. Silently.

Michael covered his face with his hands. "Leave me alone," he said, bowing his head.

Sam's eyes shifted to Henry. Henry wiped his eyes with the sleeve of his shirt. "Dad," he said, touching his father's shoulder.

"No," Michael said, jerking away. "I don't want you to see me like this. Go away."

Henry looked at Sam, wiped the side of his face again, and tried again. "We want you to come home. More than anything. But you have to go to that place first. It won't be for long." Pause. Sniff. "Dad, Mr. Wyatt went there. And he's okay now."

Silence.

"Henry," Sam said gently, "why don't you go see if your mother's okay? I'd like to talk to your father for a while."

Harriet heard the front door close. "Althea?"

"Guess again!"

"Sam?" she called. "I'm here. In the bedroom."

In a minute Sam appeared in the doorway, carrying a quart bottle of spring water. "What are you doing home?" he asked, tired, leaning heavily against the door frame, twisting the cap off the bottle.

Harriet was still in her work clothes, lying on top of their bed, a copy of

Publishers Weekly resting on her stomach. "I'm on strike," she announced. "What about you?"

He raised the bottle and chug-a-lugged several mouthfuls. "Ahhh," he said, lowering the bottle and moving into the bedroom. He loosened his tie, looking out the window. "I went to see Cochran with Cassy." He put the bottle down to take off his jacket.

"How did it go?" Harriet asked, propping her head up with another pillow.

Sam slid his tie off and unbuttoned the top button of his shirt. He tossed the tie on the chair, picked up the bottle, and moved over to the bed. "Cassy's flying him out to Hazelden."

"Oh, thank God. That's wonderful, Sam."

Sam sighed, sitting down by Harriet's feet. He took another slug of water. "Man, it wasn't easy," he said. He bent over to untie his shoes.

"It's wonderful, Sam. You should feel very good."

"Yeah, right," he said, slipping his shoes off. He held the bottle in one hand and scooted up on his side next to Harriet, propping himself up on one elbow. He kissed her on the mouth.

"Hi, handsome," she said, smoothing his eyebrow.

He rested the bottom of the bottle on her forehead for a moment, leaving a ring of moisture on her skin. He smiled, took another swig, and reached over her to put the bottle on the night table. "So you're on strike, huh?"

Harriet closed her eyes, smiling. "Sperry went crazy today in preliminary sales conference and I walked out."

Sam curled up next to her, resting the side of his face on her chest. "You did?"

"I sure did," she said, stroking his hair.

"Do you want to quit?"

"I don't know," she said. She laughed.

Sam chuckled too. "What?"

"He knocked Layton over backward in his chair."

"Why?"

"I don't know. We were just sitting there, listening to Patricia doing her presentations, and—"

"Patricia?"

"MacMannis."

"Oh, right."

They lay there for several moments, all quiet but for their breathing.

Sam propped himself back up on his elbow to look at her. "Do you want to go to Kenya?"

Harriet's eyes opened. "Kenya?"

"Uh-huh. We were talking about it this morning. Paul thought it might be a good idea if I could see the machines coming off the assembly line with my own eyes." He traced her mouth, lightly, with his forefinger. "What do you think?"

"Well, I don't know."

He laughed, bending to kiss her neck. "You're a big help. Do you want to quit?" he said, nuzzling her ear. " 'I don't know.' Do you want to go to Kenya? 'I don't know.' "

Harriet squirmed, ticklish. "But I don't know."

Sam raised his head. "I think we should go. You've got a hundred and ten years of vacation coming . . ."

"But everything is such a mess at work right now—"

"It's always a mess—"

"What about the girls?"

"We'll get your parents to come up. It'll just be for three weeks."

"Three weeks!"

"I thought we might take two weeks and travel around . . ."

Harriet pulled him down on top of her, slipping her arms around him. "I'm scared to think about it, it sounds so wonderful."

"Good. Then we're going. I'll tell Paul tomorrow."

"Sperry will hit the roof—"

"Let him," Sam said, gently pressing himself against her.

"It will have to be after sales conference—"

"Right, right . . ."

"Sam—"

"Mmm?"

"Honey, close the door. Althea might—"

Sam groaned, rolling off her. "Kids," he growled, getting up and closing the door. He turned around.

Harriet waved. "Hi."

He took a running leap and Harriet shrieked.

41

SUNDAY
PART I: BREAKFAST AT AMANDA'S

"Hi, we're here!" Rosanne called, taking her keys out of Amanda's door. "Hey, hold on a minute," she said, nabbing Jason by the collar of his baseball jacket. "Come on, sweetie, let's take off your jacket and hang it up."

"Hi," Amanda said, sailing into the hall, cotton caftan trailing in behind her. "We've only just sat down to breakfast." She bent over to kiss Jason. "Hi."

"Hi."

"Would you like some waffles?"

He nodded. "Is Missy here?"

"She's been waiting all week to see you."

Rosanne was hanging his jacket up in the closet. "Say hello to Mrs. G first, Jason."

" 'Kay." He was off.

"Man, this cat," Rosanne sighed, closing the closet door. "He'll probably want to sleep with the thing."

Amanda smiled. "How are you holding up?"

"Okay, I guess," Rosanne sighed. "But I'll sure feel better after we move in. The Rubinowitzes . . ."

"Fortuitously," Amanda said, ushering Rosanne ahead by the elbow, "we must only wait for a few more days."

The women walked into the kitchen where they were just in time to see Mrs. Goldblum give Jason a bite of her waffle. "Isn't that good, dear?"

Jason nodded, chewing, looking around.

It took another second for it to register on Rosanne that there was someone else present. The chef at the waffle iron.

"Howie," Rosanne said, eyes wide.

"Good morning, Mrs. DiSantos." He bowed, fork in hand. "You better take your seat. Your waffle's coming up next."

"Hello, dear," Mrs. Goldblum called, patting Jason's mouth with her napkin.

Eyes on Howard, Rosanne edged over to the table, felt for the chair, and sat down.

Amanda opened a cabinet, reached for a plate, and placed it on the counter next to Howard. She kissed him on the back of the neck and then came back to the table, Rosanne's eyes following her. When she sat down, Rosanne leaned forward to get her attention, her head practically on Amanda's place mat.

"It's not polite to stare, Rosanne," Amanda said, smiling, reaching for the pitcher of orange juice.

Rosanne's head swung to Mrs. Goldblum. She was busy discussing with Jason the probability of Missy's whereabouts at the moment.

Rosanne's head swung to Amanda, who was pouring her a glass of orange juice.

Rosanne's head swung back to Mrs. Goldblum; Jason ran off in search of the cat and Mrs. Goldblum resumed eating her breakfast.

"Am I going crazy," Rosanne finally asked, "or doesn't anyone else notice that somebody's livin' in the wrong house? You know, like—what's wrong with this picture?"

"What, dear?" Mrs. Goldblum said, sipping her tea.

Rosanne leaned toward Mrs. Goldblum, hands resting against the edge of the table. "Was that guy here when you got here?"

Amanda gave a low chuckle.

Mrs. Goldblum lofted her eyebrows. "Do you mean Howard?"

"Howard," Rosanne repeated, "yeah."

Mrs. Goldblum patted her mouth with her napkin and leaned forward slightly too. "Amanda and Howard have an arrangement," she said confidentially.

Rosanne fell back in her chair, looking to Amanda. "Oh, well, that explains everything."

"One perfect waffle, coming up!" Howard said, walking over and swooping a plate down in front of Rosanne. "Will Jason eat now, do you think?"

"He should eat his fruit first," Mrs. Goldblum said.

Rosanne clapped her hands over her eyes and then peeked out between them. "I thought I recognized this scene—it's the Waltons."

"Who are the Waltons?" Amanda said, rising from her chair.

"I so enjoyed that program," Mrs. Goldblum said.

Howard placed a small bowl of fresh fruit on the place setting next to Rosanne. "I'm John Boy."

"Jason," Amanda called at the door to the writing room, "your breakfast is ready."

"So what's this arrangement?" Rosanne said. "Mrs. G? Come on, somebody . . ."

"Well," Mrs. Goldblum began, refolding her napkin, "Howard stays with us on Wednesday and Friday and Saturday nights, and when my visit is over here, Amanda will stay with Howard on Friday nights." She lowered her voice and added, "It makes Amanda very happy, otherwise I might not approve."

Jason came thundering into the kitchen, Missy bundled in his arms. "Found her," he said, jumping to a stop.

"Put the cat down, sweetie, and eat your fruit," Rosanne said, patting the chair beside her.

Amanda took the cat out of his arms and Jason climbed up into the chair. Amanda kissed the top of the cat's head and rubbed it against her cheek, looking across the room at Howard.

"Somebody ate the canary and it wasn't the cat," Rosanne observed, shaking the napkin open and tucking it in under Jason's chin.

"Rosanne," Howard said, bending to check the progress of his work from a side angle, "when do you want to move—Friday, Saturday or Sunday?"

"Like this, sweetie," Rosanne said, adjusting the spoon in Jason's hand. "I get Jason on Sunday."

"I'm returning home on Saturday," Mrs. Goldblum said.

"Do you think you could bring Jason home on Saturday?" This was from Amanda.

"Maybe."

Amanda put the cat down on the floor and returned to her seat.

"Watch what you're doing, Jason," Rosanne said. "The cat will still be here after breakfast."

"It would be nice if you all could move in at the same time," Amanda said.

"That would be very nice," Mrs. Goldblum said.

Rosanne ate a piece of her waffle. "I'll try for Saturday."

"I'll help you pack," Howard said. "And the Wyatts said we could borrow their station wagon to move your things."

"And Jason can stay here, and then we'll meet you over at the apartment," Amanda said.

Rosanne frowned slightly. "Hey—Mrs. G."

"Yes, dear?"

"There's somethin' funny going on around here. Or as Miss Spoony over here would say, 'A plot is afoot, methinks.' "

"I don't think so, dear," Mrs. Goldblum said brightly.

Rosanne's eyes shifted to Amanda.

"Not a thing," Amanda said, sipping her juice. She put the glass down. "What time do you have to be at Cassy's?"

Rosanne shrugged. "Any time. I don't think she's back yet—why?"

"Would you tell her something for me? If you see her?"

"Sure. What?"

"Tell her I took her advice."

Rosanne's eyes narrowed, suspicious. "So what's Mrs. C been givin' you advice about?"

Amanda smiled and looked across the room at Howard.

"No kiddin'," Rosanne said, falling back in her chair. "Mrs. C talked to you?"

Amanda nodded.

"Huh," Rosanne said, straightening up, smoothing her napkin and picking up her fork with great ceremony, "and I wasn't even sure if she was listenin'."

42

SUNDAY
PART II: CASSY COMES BACK
FROM MINNESOTA

Alexandra was waiting at the gate at Kennedy. In sunglasses. And a scarf. Until she took Cassy's arm, Cassy wasn't even aware that it was she. "Don't be angry," Alexandra said, taking Cassy's overnight bag from her. "I've got a car waiting. I needed to see you," she added, pulling Cassy along.

"Alexandra—"

She stopped and the sunglasses swung in Cassy's direction. "I needed to see you," she repeated quietly.

Cassy sighed, looking somewhere over Alexandra's shoulder. "Of course you do," she finally said, looking back at the sunglasses. She offered a sad smile, lowered her head, and then slung her arm through Alexandra's. "Let's go." They walked through the rest of the airport without speaking.

Alexandra had a limo waiting. After the driver closed their doors Alexandra took off her glasses and untied her scarf. Shaking out her hair, she said, "He can't see us. He can't hear us." Cassy's expression was blank. "The driver," Alexandra explained.

"Oh," Cassy said.

"I'm sorry to surprise you like this," Alexandra said, "but I knew it would be the only time I could see you." She reached for Cassy's hand. It was given, reluctantly, and after a moment Alexandra released it. "So he's in," she said.

"He's in," Cassy said, nodding, looking at the dark glass between them and the driver.

"Is it—was it a nice place?"

"Oh, yes," Cassy said, still looking ahead. "Very. And they were very nice." Pause. "He was so frightened. It's very strange, you know—seeing him so frightened. Crying, sober. I've never seen him cry when he wasn't drinking."

Silence.

The car pulled out onto the expressway.

"Cassy," Alexandra said softly.

After a moment Cassy turned to look at her.

"I want to help you," Alexandra whispered, reaching for her hand again.

Cassy swallowed and turned away. "I'm afraid you can't." She sighed. "Not this time."

Silence.

"I don't want to lose you."

Cassy dropped her head, closing her eyes.

"I know we can't—" Alexandra stopped, her lower lip starting to give way. "I need you. As a friend. I'm willing to just be—"

"We've gone too far, Alexandra."

It was said in scarcely a whisper, but Alexandra heard it. She turned to her door, jammed her elbow down on the rest, and looked out the window. In a few moments she started to cry.

Cassy slumped back in her seat and looked up at the roof, blinking back tears.

Alexandra's crying eventually subsided and she tried to pull herself together. "I always knew he'd come back," she said, wiping her eyes with a tissue, looking at herself in a compact mirror. She snapped it shut and slid it back into her purse. "I feel rather stupid carrying on like this."

Cassy rolled her head to the side, looking at her. "Come here," she said gently, holding out an arm. After a moment Alexandra moved over to be held. She started to cry again. Cassy, resting her chin on top of Alexandra's head, stroking her hair, started to talk. "I don't think I'm stupid for caring for you," she murmured, looking ahead. "You're one of the most wonderful things that has ever happened to me. The timing . . ." She sighed and was quiet for a while.

"I love Michael, I've never lied to you about that. But, sometimes, I wonder if I even know what love is. Or what kind of love it is I have for Michael—or if I even know who he is anymore. Or who I am, for that matter." She absently kissed the top of Alexandra's head. "I'm not even sure how you happened to me."

A low moan came from somewhere inside of Alexandra.

Cassy swallowed. "I'm a mother, Alexandra, and that . . . You know I have to see this through, see my family through. Twenty years . . ." A sigh. "I've got to see what this will mean—if things will—oh, Lord, I don't know, it may be too late. I just don't know. But I've got to find out." She shifted suddenly. "But—Alexandra—" Cassy brought her face up with her hand to look at her. "You mustn't wait for me. Hope that we can—really, it's so very important that you don't. That you go on with your life— because I have to go on with mine." She swallowed and whispered, "You so badly need someone who can give you what you need, what you want."

Alexandra closed her eyes and resettled her head under Cassy's chin. A long sigh. "I need you."

"No, Alexandra, you don't," Cassy said. "You need someone nearer your own age, for starters. You're just coming into—into"—sigh—"into what I'm leaving."

"Age isn't the issue and you know it."

Pause. "It is an issue. An important one. One day you'll know it. Feel it."

"God," Alexandra said, "I wish you'd give that up."

"What?"

"Your obsession with age." She reached to touch the diamond of Cassy's engagement ring. "If I married a forty-one year old man, no one—not even you—would say a word. You'd think it was great."

Cassy shifted slightly, moving Alexandra's head a bit. "It's very different with men."

"Tell me about it."

Cassy gently laughed. "No, that's not what I meant."

"I know what you meant."

"I know you do," she said, patting her back.

Silence.

"I really fell in love with you, you know," Alexandra said.

Silence.

Alexandra sat up to look at her. "When I was in college I thought I was

in love with Gordon. Later I thought I wanted to marry Tyler, but then Lisa
—" She let out a slow breath, eyes drifting away. "When Lisa happened, all
I knew was that getting married to Tyler was not such a great idea. Not
until I figured out what it was I was looking for." Her eyes came back to
Cassy's. "I didn't want to fall in love with you, Cassy. I wanted you to be
like Lisa. But you weren't." Her eyes started to fill. "Where I want to go,
the world I want to work in—Cassy, you are the biggest handicap I could
choose. But I haven't had a choice since I met you. It's you I want. With
me."

In the course of this, Cassy had closed her eyes. A single tear was now
working its way out from under one lid.

"I'm not trying to talk you out of what I know you have to do," she
continued, sniffing, wiping at one eye. She dropped her hand back down
onto Cassy's shoulder. "I just wanted to tell you this, so you would know—
because I'll never bring it up again." She paused. "I want us to stay
friends."

Cassy opened her eyes. After a moment she pushed Alexandra's hair back
off her face. "We need to give it time," she said.

Alexandra let out a breath. "I can handle it."

Cassy sighed, a faint smile on her lips, twisting a strand of Alexandra's
hair between her fingers. She let go of it and eased Alexandra away from
her. "It's not you I'm worried about," she said. "You don't know it, but
you'll get over me a lot quicker than I'll get—" She clamped her eyes shut
and covered them with her hands, sucking her breath in through her teeth.
"Damn it," she said, dropping forward into her lap.

The rest of the ride was no less difficult.

By the time the limo pulled up to 162 Riverside Drive, neither was able to
talk. The driver opened Cassy's door and she simply gave Alexandra's hand
a squeeze and got out. The driver handed her bag to the doorman and he
took it into the lobby. As the driver was walking back around the car to get
inside, Cassy ran back to the door and opened it.

Alexandra just looked up at her, eyes a wreck.

Cassy hesitated, mouth trembling, and then leaned down. "I did love you,
Alexandra," she said, kissing her on the mouth. "Don't think I didn't." She
pulled back—hitting her head on the roof—but cared about nothing except
getting the door closed between them. And then she stood there, looking
down at her own reflection in the window.

The car pulled away.

Cassy held her face in her hand for a moment, composing herself. And then she turned around and saw Rosanne. Standing there. Looking at her. Her expression was one of shock, and one of concern, and Cassy did not want to see it. She walked past Rosanne into the building. "Are you coming or going?"

"Coming," Rosanne said, following her in.

Cassy did not meet Rosanne's eyes once. Walking into the elevator, she said hello to the elevator man, turned around, watched him close the gate, and said, "Mr. C will be home in six weeks."

"Great," Rosanne said. And then, "I'm sorry I had to switch Friday on you. With Jason and the move and everything—"

"It's quite all right," Cassy said, watching the floors go by. "In fact, it's better." She transferred her bag from one hand to the other. "Henry's girl friend is coming for dinner tonight."

"Oh," Rosanne said.

Cassy got off the elevator first and led the way to the apartment. "I thought you might bring Jason," she said, turning the key in the door and opening it.

"He's at Amanda's."

"Henry?" Cassy called, throwing her keys in the bowl and walking on.

Rosanne closed the door and stood there a moment, thinking. When she walked into the kitchen, Cassy turned from the counter. "He went to Connecticut to pick the girl up," she said, tossing the note in the trash. She shook her head. "Can you imagine? Our little Henry?"

"He's not so little anymore," Rosanne said, putting her bag down and going to the pantry.

"No, he sure isn't," Cassy said, walking on with her bag to the back hall.

Rosanne took out the bucket of cleaning supplies and a fresh cloth and headed for the living room. She put the bucket down and started picking up magazines and neatly stacking them, throwing out newspapers and fluffing the pillows of the couch and easy chairs. She was in the process of taking everything off the tables to dust when Cassy came in.

"Rosanne," she said, folding her arms and leaning against the side of the bookcase.

"Yeah?" Rosanne glanced back at her; her expression was innocent.

Cassy sighed and held the bridge of her nose for a moment. Releasing it, she said, "Tell me what you're thinking."

Rosanne's eyes slid away and she bent over to take a can of Pledge out of the bucket. "What do ya mean?"

Cassy pushed off the bookcase and took a step forward. "I mean I don't want you to—" She couldn't finish.

Rosanne looked at her. "I saw," she said. And then she proceeded to spray Pledge on the coffee table. "And I'm glad it was me and not Henry."

Cassy rubbed her face. Dropping her hands, she walked over and threw herself down in a chair. Rosanne was polishing the table. "It's over," Cassy said. When there was no response (except a very well polished table) she said, "I can't pretend I have a good explanation for why or how—"

"Look, Mrs. C," Rosanne said, suddenly straightening up. She paused and then turned around. "I'm on your side—always was, always will be. I just don't want to see the kid get hurt. Or you," she added. She tossed the cloth into the bucket, sighing. "I knew there was somebody, ya know. I just didn't figure it to be—" She gave a little laugh, yanking on her bandanna. "You know who I thought it was—for a while?"

Cassy was not up to answering.

"Mr. W. Yeah."

"Oh, Rosanne," Cassy said, holding her forehead in her hand.

Rosanne looked at her for a moment and then came over to stand in front of Cassy's chair. "Look, Mrs. C," she said, kneeling down and resting the can of Pledge on the floor.

Cassy was shaking her head.

Rosanne thought a moment and then spoke. "If she likes you, then I like her." No reaction. Mouth cinched up to the side, thinking. And then, "It happened 'cause of Mr. C, didn't it?"

"I don't know," Cassy said honestly.

"And it's over 'cause of Mr. C, isn't it?"

"I don't know," Cassy said honestly.

Rosanne shrugged, playing with the can of Pledge.

"How did you know?"

"What?"

Cassy wiped at her eye with the back of her hand. "How did you know?"

"The new underwear," Rosanne said.

"Good God," Cassy sighed, looking to the window.

The two women sat there for a while longer. But they did not speak of it again.

Ever.

43

THE HOMECOMING

Late Saturday afternoon found Rosanne and Howard still hard at work at the Krandell Arms Hotel. It was very hot work; the wind that blew through the open doors and windows of the seventh floor was humid and—for some reason making it seem even hotter—someone had decided to cook cabbage in the communal kitchen. Howard's hair and shirt were soaked with perspiration; Rosanne's bangs were slick against her forehead.

After Rosanne taught Howard the basics of packing ("Some smart guy you are—so what do ya *think's* gonna happen to those cups under the plates?"), the two did not talk much. By now, as they were nearing the end, Howard could interpret Rosanne's instructions in sign language:

A nod: Okay, pack it.

A wipe of the forehead: Oh, man, I've got to think about that stuff. Go on to something else.

A shake of the head, in combination with a shrug: Chuck it—I don't care.

A thoughtful smile: No, put it on the pile of things to give away.

Howard was, at first, quite amazed at the atmosphere of the Krandell

Arms. Spanish music was blaring from one room next door, while the Beatles were playing from the other side. People wandered the halls, visiting, smoking pot, eating potato chips—some fully dressed, others not nearly —and there was very serious discussion taking place (in many different languages and combinations thereof) about what was going down tonight, Saturday night. But by now Howard was used to it, so when a fight broke out in the hall he—like Rosanne—was barely conscious of it. Howard did not even blink when Ceily came in (outfitted in black leather) around four o'clock and said to Rosanne, "I like his ass but *fine.*"

It was unsettling, packing Rosanne's things, seeing the remnants of her life with Frank pass through his hands. He packed the flatware and was startled to discover, in a small leather box tucked back in the top of the closet, sterling silver place settings for four, with a lovely "D" monogrammed on the handles. Howard looked at Rosanne, wondering about her earlier life. Other thoughts passed through his mind, too. Like the first fight between Melissa and Rosanne.

During a dinner party celebrating Daddy's birthday, Melissa sat there, scowling at the end of the table, bitching about the rattle in the handle of one of the knives. "That damn Rosanne did it," she declared across to the table to Howard. "I'm sure of it. We had no rattles before she started cleaning the silver."

By the time Melissa confronted Rosanne, the case against her had grown alarmingly tremendous. Melissa ranted and raved for five minutes—about the rattle in the handle of the knife that was making life such torture for Melissa; the rattle that had caused her such humiliation at the birthday party for Daddy; the rattle that was sure to bring rack and ruin down upon the the heads of the Stewarts . . .

Rosanne, when Melissa paused to take a breath, said, "Okay, okay, I admit it. Howie and I were throwin' knives at each other. We were gonna run away and join the circus."

Melissa glowered, speechless with rage. "Howard!" she finally screamed. "Tell her she's fired if she does not pay for the repair of that knife!"

Howard succeeded in calming Melissa down, but then when Melissa demanded to know of Rosanne if she was grateful to them for paying for the repairs of the tragic knife handle themselves, Rosanne turned to Howard and said, "If I were you, I'd forget the knife and get the rattle in her head fixed."

It had never occurred to Howard that Rosanne might have silver of her own.

Howard packed the Christmas presents from the Stewarts: the clock radio the first year ("With gratitude and affection, The Stewarts"; the electric blanket from the second year ("With Love, Howard and Melissa"); the food processor from the third year ("Love, Howie and Melissa"); and the microwave oven from last Christmas ("Love, from Howie and the Bitch"). The presents had not been difficult to select; Rosanne had always told Howard exactly what it was she wanted. But buying the presents and hiding them from Melissa had been difficult. (Melissa would have freaked—buying presents for the *cleaning woman?* Didn't Melissa give Rosanne ten dollars at Christmas?)

Howard tried to think about Amanda. About what she would be doing, about what she was wearing. What she looked like. When she smiled. When she first woke up. (This morning, snuggling up behind Howard, she had whispered, "Who left this marvelous man here in my bed? Am I dreaming?")

The day was very painful for Rosanne. It was so much, going through all of their things, hers and Frank's, making decisions about what would go, what would go into storage, what would be . . . given away. Howie was a big help. He seemed to know when to come over to her and take something of Frank's out of her hands—a shirt, a pair of pants, a jacket—and get her moving again.

Rosanne had bought a footlocker to store special things of Frank's for Jason. When she would ever have the courage to open it again she didn't know, but she packed it with agonizing care. Frank's high school yearbook; Frank's high school varsity jacket; Frank's sports trophies; Frank's high school diploma; Frank's army pictures; Frank's medals; Frank's uniform; Frank's honorable discharge papers; their wedding pictures; Jason's baby book, a framed photograph of Frank the day the car dealership opened; and, sigh, Frank's leather jacket.

Howard politely ignored the fact that Rosanne sobbed all the way through the ordeal of the footlocker.

Rosanne kept out one photograph album for herself. To take to Mrs. G's, to keep by her own bedside.

At five, they were finished. Rosanne went to find Creature, Buzzy and Zigs to help take stuff down to the Wyatts' station wagon. She found them drinking beer in Buzzy's room, watching a Mets game on a fuzzy black and white set (whose antenna was an elaborate structure consisting of coat hangers and aluminum foil). Anticipating that they would have second thoughts about their offer to help, Rosanne was touched when they jumped to their feet and turned the game off without a word of protest or excuse. They followed her back upstairs to Rosanne's room and shook hands with Howard (another surprise). Howard went down to bring the station wagon around to the front of the hotel.

"Okay, guys," Rosanne said, "everything goes but those boxes over there." All eyes went to those boxes "over there." "There's a lot of good stuff in them. Frank's clothes, mostly," she added, in a softer voice. She cleared her throat. "Don't go through them till I'm gone, okay?"

Creature, Buzzy and Zigs agreed.

"I don't care how you divvy up that stuff," she said, going to the closet, "but I wanted to give each of you something of Frank's. And you can't hock it, all right?" She narrowed her eyes at them.

"Wouldn't do that," Creature mumbled.

"Yeah, right," Rosanne said. "Okay," she said, pulling out Frank's black winter overcoat. It was from the old days, the days when they had gone to church. It was a good coat and Rosanne showed them the satin lining. "It's for you, Creature. Frank would want you to wear it when you visit your mother."

Next was a charcoal-gray suit. "Zigs, this is for you. Now look, here's a receipt from Barrows around the corner. You just take it in and get the suit altered. It's all arranged." A sniff. "Frank would want you to wear this on a job interview."

Last, but not least, three of Frank's leather hats. For Zigs. "You'll look pretty sharp," was all she said.

It was teary time for all, and they all hated it and tried to pretend it wasn't.

God, this was hard.

They made three trips down and up the stairs (the elevator was out again) and Howard called Amanda to say they would be leaving soon. When the last of the boxes and suitcases had been taken out, Rosanne was left by herself in the room. She sat down on the corner of the stripped bed (it was staying), propped her head up on her hands and studied the walls, tears gently flowing from her eyes.

There was a lot to say good-bye to.

After a long sigh, she got up. She unplugged the phone to carry it with her, slung her bag over her shoulder, tucked the photo album under her arm and took one last look. And then she closed the door and locked it.

Out on the street, the station wagon and its cargo had drawn quite a crowd on the sidewalk, and Creature and Buzzy and Zigs had formed a protective line alongside it. Howard was sitting in the driver's seat, elbow hanging out the window, listening to the radio.

Rosanne came down the stairs and people in the crowd said good-byes. Howard started the car. Rosanne kissed Creature and pressed the keys to the room in his hand. "After you find the things you want, give the keys to Ernesto, okay? He knows you have them," she added, moving on to Buzzy. She gave him a hug.

"Gonna miss ya," Buzzy said.

"Yeah," Creature echoed.

Rosanne hugged Zigs.

"Fine-lookin' fox, that one," Zigs said as Rosanne went around to the other side of the car.

"Bye-bye!" Ceily called, coming outside and waving.

"Geez," Rosanne said, jerking the door open. "You'd think I was movin' to Miami—I'm moving four blocks, for cryin' out loud!" She gave one more wave and got in the car.

"Ready?" Howard said, putting the car into drive.

"Yeah." She leaned forward to wave through Howard's window. "Bye!" she called.

Everyone waved good-bye and the station wagon pulled out. The guys—Creature, Buzzy and Zigs—stood there, in the street, watching the car wait at the West End Avenue light, right signal flashing.

"When I was a kid," Buzzy said, "we had a car sorta like that."

"I can't believe you don't have the keys," Rosanne said, swinging her crossed leg back and forth in agitation.

"I told you, I forgot them," Howard said.

They were sitting in the lobby of 184 Riverside Drive. The boxes and suitcases were all upstairs, stacked in a tidy heap by the apartment door.

Rosanne sighed. "What are they doing—walkin' on their hands? I thought you said they'd meet us here."

"They are, Rosanne," Howard said. "Relax, they'll be here in a minute."

"Relax, the man says," Rosanne muttered, getting up. She walked across the lobby to look out on the Drive.

"It be good to have Mrs. Goldblum home," Boris, the doorman, said to her. "She nice lady, yes?"

"Yeah," Rosanne said, "she nice lady."

Boris nudged Rosanne's arm. "Did you see?" he asked, nodding toward the building directory.

"See what?"

"Come—I show you. Come," he repeated, waving her over to the directory on the wall. "Look," he said, pointing with his finger.

GOLDBLUM, E—DISANTOS, M   5-C

"Huh," Rosanne said.

"Mailbox too. Up today."

Howard walked over.

Rosanne turned. "They've got my name up."

"Great. You're official then."

"Probably raised her rent sixty million dollars," Rosanne said.

"I don't think so," Howard said. "Mr. Thatcher said—"

A wild burst of honking made them both turn to look out at the street. A yellow Checker cab was pulling up in front of the building. In the front seat, Amanda was waving like a maniac, while, in the back seat, Mrs. Goldblum was demurely adjusting the angle of her hat.

Howard dashed out and opened Amanda's door. She got out, whispered something to him; he smiled and kissed her on the temple. Then he hopped around to open Mrs. Goldblum's door. Howard helped her out and Jason came scrambling out behind her.

"Hi, Mommy! We're late!"

"Yeah," Rosanne said, picking him up and hugging him. She growled into his neck, sending him into gales of laughter. Rosanne shifted Jason to one arm and turned to Mrs. Goldblum. "Hi."

"Hello, dear." Mrs. Goldblum looked up at the building. She smiled. "My, but it's nice to be home." She touched Rosanne's arm. "I'm very happy."

"I'm sorry we're late," Amanda said to Rosanne, "but I couldn't find the keys."

"Must be catchin'," Rosanne observed.

Amanda took Mrs. Goldblum's arm. "Come, let's go in."

Mrs. Goldblum took a step toward the door and then stopped. "Where is Missy?" she asked, looking around.

"Oh, the cat!" Amanda said. "Howard, don't forget the cat. She's on the floor in the back."

"I'll get her!" Jason cried, struggling to get down out of his mother's arms.

"I don't think Jason can carry the box by himself," Mrs. Goldblum said, continuing on inside.

Rosanne and Jason got the box with the cat inside it. The taxi driver and Howard unloaded Mrs. Goldblum's suitcases, and Howard paid the driver.

The caravan proceeded to the elevator, where Amanda held the door for Howard and the suitcases. He squeezed in, the doors closed and the elevator started to climb. "Mommy," Jason whispered, "I'm all squished." Everyone laughed.

"Okay," Howard announced, "we're here." Amanda held the door while everyone filed out.

"My goodness," Mrs. Goldblum said when she saw Rosanne's things in the hallway.

"Don't tell me you're changing your mind," Rosanne said.

"Never," Mrs. Goldblum said on an intake of breath.

"So where are the keys?" Rosanne wanted to know.

"I've got them—" Amanda said, inserting one into the door.

"But where are *my* keys?" Rosanne persisted.

"I think they're inside," Howard said.

Amanda pushed the door open and stepped back for Mrs. Goldblum to walk in. Then she waved Rosanne and Jason in. She looked at Howard and they exchanged smiles.

"Home again, home again, jiggity-jig," Mrs. Goldblum said, turning on the foyer light.

"SURPRISE!" a group of voices cried.

Mrs. Goldblum blinked twice and Rosanne said, "Geez, look at what these guys did."

The guys—Harriet, Sam, Cassy, Henry, Althea and Samantha—were laughing their heads off, standing under a banner that stretched across the living room: WELCOME HOME MRS. G, ROSANNE & JASON. ("Missy too!" someone had hastily scribbled in the corner.)

"Look," Rosanne whispered to Mrs. Goldblum, "somebody wallpapered."

Mrs. Goldblum touched the wall. "It's beautiful," she said.

Everybody started talking at once and poor Mrs. Goldblum was quite overcome by it all, looking first this way and then that, her eyes filling with tears.

"We only just this minute finished," Cassy said, pointing to the paint-splattered white overalls she was wearing. "I nearly died, Amanda, when you said you were leaving—"

"I tried to give you time—I lost the keys," Amanda laughed.

"Me too," Howard said.

"Look at you, Mr. W!" Rosanne said, pointing at him, in hysterics.

He screwed up his face. White paint was all over his face and hair, save for his eyes. "Kitchen ceiling," he said.

"Do let Missy out, dear," Mrs. Goldblum reminded Jason as Amanda led her away.

"You better like it!" Samantha Wyatt cried, doing a little dance. She too, like her father, had white paint all over her.

"A week," Althea said to Rosanne, "we've been coming over here."

"Come see," Cassy said, pulling Rosanne by the hand.

The tour was a success. In addition to the wallpaper, the living-room windows had new, white, gauzy floor-length curtains. The kitchen was a cheerful yellow and the ceiling, replastered in places, was spangly white. Mrs. Goldblum's room had been wallpapered in a pale rose pattern; Rosanne's room in a pale blue; and Jason's room was off-white, with blue trim, blue curtains and twelve major-league baseball pennants adorning one wall. In Jason's room there was also a large wooden toy chest that had belonged to Henry.

"Picture time!" Althea ran around announcing. "Before we eat, we've got to take pictures!"

All of the other Wyatts groaned at this, apparently knowing something about Althea's picture-taking methods the others did not. But it sounded like a splendid idea to Cassy and she quickly corralled everyone into the living room, where Althea was setting up some very imposing equipment on a tripod.

"Let me just check it," Althea said, pushing this, twisting that, and then pressing something and running out from behind the camera.

"Here she goes," Harriet groaned, leaning into her husband.

"What is she doing?" Cassy asked, swinging Rosanne's hand.

"Watch," Sam said.

They did. Althea turned around in front of the camera, struck a very serious, very sexy pose (as sexy as splattered overalls allowed), held it and— FLASH-CLICK. The camera took a picture of her.

"When Althea said she wanted to be a photographer," Harriet sighed, "we had no idea she meant of herself."

Sam chuckled, pushing Harriet to the area Althea wanted them in. "We should be grateful, Harriet. She hasn't taken a picture of us for two years."

"Oh, Dad," Althea said, fussing with her equipment. "I took pictures last Easter."

"Two of us and two hundred of herself," Harriet laughed. "Come on, Samantha."

Althea lined everyone up into position. Back row: Howard, Henry and Sam. Second row: Amanda, Rosanne, Cassy and Harriet. Sitting in the front, in a chair, Mrs. Goldblum, with Samantha and Jason and Missy sitting at her feet.

"Where are you going to go, Althea?" Howard asked.

"Watch—she'll hang from the ceiling," Sam said.

"Next to you," Althea said, looking through the viewfinder. "Okay, flash, check, film, check . . ."

"Oh, Sam, she doesn't have that thing on it, does she?"

Althea straightened up and addressed her subjects. "Okay, listen up! I want everyone to look right at the camera and say cheese."

"Cheee—" everyone started, laughing.

"No, not yet! Wait a minute."

"Jason, don't lick the cat. You'll get rabies," Rosanne said.

"I think not, dear," Mrs. Goldblum said.

"Howard," Amanda whispered, feeling a hand sneaking around in the vicinity of her derriere.

"Mom, you don't have to bend," Henry said. "I can see over you by a mile."

Cassy straightened up, smoothing back her hair.

"Okay, listen up!" Althea said again. "When I get over there, then you say cheese. Wait! Listen! The camera's going to take more than one picture—"

"I knew it, Sam."

"Oh, boy," Samantha said eagerly.

"All right, everybody. Ready?"

"READY!" they chorused.

Althea touched something and the camera started to hum and she ran around and pushed herself in next to Howard.

"Cheeeeeeeeeee," the group laughed, terrifying the cat and making Jason's job of holding her very difficult.

FLASH-CLICK went the camera.

WHIRL.

"eeeeeeezzzzzzzeeeeeeeee—"

FLASH CLICK.

Laughter.

WHIRL.

Laughter.
FLASH-CLICK.
"Althea?"
WHIRL.
"What, Dad?"
FLASH-CLICK.
"Pull that strap up!"
WHIRL.
"Oh, Sam, she's not—"
FLASH-CLICK.
"Missy!"
WHIRL.
"Wait, sweetie . . ."
FLASH-CLICK.
"Till *Star Wars* is over."
WHIRL.
"Henry—"
FLASH-CLICK.
"What, Mom?"
WHIRL.
"Stop with the devil's horns."
FLASH-CLICK.
Laughter.
WHIRL.
"Really, Althea."
FLASH-CLICK.
"Wait a sec, Mom—"
WHIRL.
Nothing.
Nothing.
Nothing.
Silence.
"Do you suppose that's it, dear?"
"Beats me, Mrs. G."

44

CONCLUSION

The family life of the Goldblum-DiSantoses is not a particularly quiet one, nor should it be assumed that the household is without its minor disagreements and crossed wires of communication. And, too, there are always little ongoing problems, such as why it is the darn cat persists in only wanting to sleep with Rosanne, and where, exactly, it is that Mrs. Goldblum is getting off when she tells Jason that he doesn't have to eat his spinach if he doesn't want to. But, in all honesty, one would be hard pressed to find a happier family on Riverside Drive than that of the Goldblum-DiSantoses.

Mrs. Goldblum, incidentally, landed a job. Her appearance on "Social Security Is for You" prompted so many viewers to write and call in, the Social Security office hired her to cohost the program every other week. She has taken her new celebrity status with great ladylike aplomb, succumbing to vanity only in the form of having her hair done once a week and purchasing five new dresses from Bergdorf Goodman. She weighs eleven pounds more than when the DiSantoses moved in, and her arthritis is much better since Rosanne started giving her massages and applying hot packs on a regular basis.

Mrs. Goldblum's grandchildren—Daniel's two children—come to visit their grandmother for two weeks each summer. And since Mrs. Goldblum has not given her son a dime, she is both startled and elated that Daniel has at long last settled into a job selling real estate.

Jason is attending P.S. 75, the Emily Dickinson School on West End Avenue, where he is doing very well in his studies. He is also a star player in both the Pee-Wee Baseball and Football Leagues.

Rosanne is still working for the Cochrans, the Wyatts, Amanda Miller and—every other week—for Howard Stewart. She recently received her high school equivalency diploma and has been accepted into the School of Nursing at Hunter College. At this writing, Rosanne is dating Carl Rendoza, Jason's baseball coach, who is a police officer with the 24th Precinct.

Sam Wyatt is still at Electronika International, only now as corporate vice-president, public affairs, which means he spends a great deal of time flying between New York and Washington, keeping an eye on domestic and international politics as they relate to Electronika's operations. But his new job also means that Sam oversees all of Electronika's corporate donations— political, social and cultural—a responsibility that Sam is, quite frankly, reveling in. From the Urban League to the League of Women Voters, from college scholarships to public television, from Junior Achievement to the National Council on Alcoholism, Electronika's dollars as spent by Sam Wyatt can be most readily and effectively seen. Sam himself can be seen many mornings jogging in Riverside Park; it can also be seen that Harriet is behind him, prodding him on with a small stick.

Walter Brennan and Chet Canley were found guilty of five violations of securities laws, paid fines in excess of one million dollars each, and served a six-month sentence in a county jail. They now run a consulting firm that maintains offices in both New York City and Albany.

Electronika International successfully negotiated a buy-back of their stock from ICL Industries, and Matthew Wellman has been officially named president. The ZT 5000, as everyone knows, is a resounding success.

Harriet's corporate life took a dramatic turnaround when Gardiner & Grayson was sold to a communications conglomerate. Mack Sperry was fired and carried out with his gun collection, and a new publisher was brought in whom Harriet loves working with. The feeling is mutual and Harriet is now a division vice-president. Harrison Dreiden, Carol Roundtree, Tom West and Patricia MacMannis are all still there, and happily so. Patricia is soon to be married to a writer at *Newsweek,* a gentleman introduced to her by Howard Stewart. Layton Sinclair was kicked out of Gardiner & Grayson with great enthusiasm, and he has since risen to new dubious heights as the founder and publisher of Sinclair Dynamics, a vanity press for business executives.

Althea Wyatt's major at Columbia University has changed from history to premed to English, but since she has begun talking nonstop about Oprah Winfrey, her parents are anticipating a change to journalism. She is currently living on 115th Street in an apartment she shares with two other girls (and John—a fact she has neglected to mention to her parents).

Samantha is currently enjoying good grades and immense popularity at the Findlay School.

Amanda Miller's novel, *I, Catherine,* did indeed get finished and was recently published by Gardiner & Grayson to a most agreeable critical and financial reception. It is a major book club selection here in the States, has been sold to publishers in four other countries, and has been optioned for a television mini-series. Rosanne's ten percent interest in the book, as Amanda's "agent," has netted her something over thirty-three thousand dollars thus far. Amanda's royalties are being donated to local and national literacy programs. She still teaches adult reading classes and, although she is hard at work on a new novel (about Isadora Duncan traveling back in time to lure Emily Dickinson on a trip to Europe), Amanda maintains a voluminous correspondence with many of her former students.

The Howard Stewart Literary Agency is flourishing and although its president still lives in his fifth-floor walk-up apartment, the company now shares office space with another agency in the Flatiron Building in downtown Manhattan. By the way, Howard did such a good job representing one of Gertrude Bristol's protégés, the great lady herself is now one of his clients.

Although Amanda and Howard technically aren't living together—they spend alternate nights at each other's apartments (and yes, they do make love on Mondays—quite enthusiastically so—and yes, they always remember to close the curtains in Howard's apartment)—there are strong hints of pending matrimony, though neither will confirm it. Amanda is wearing a lovely diamond ring from Cartier's which Howard bought for her; plans have been seen concerning the restoration of the South Tower of Amanda's apartment; and many happy trips and phone calls are jointly made to the cities of Columbus and Syracuse.

The marriage of Melissa Collins Stewart and Stephen Manischell ended in a very long, very messy divorce trial. Melissa sued on the grounds of embezzlement and adultery, and Stephen countersued on the grounds of severe mental cruelty and claims that the marriage was never consummated. Melissa now lives in Connecticut with Daddy Collins and makes a hundred and ninety thousand dollars a year at First Steel Citizen Bank.

Michael Cochran came home from the rehabilitation hospital and has not taken a drink since. He refuses, however, to attend the after-care group therapy sessions his doctors strongly advised, and Cassy has given up trying to get him to go. Michael is on the road most of the time now, successfully executing a variety of free-lance producing assignments. His health, energy, talent and good looks have been restored, and his reputation in the industry is slowly emerging as one of a "new man."

Henry Cochran is at Yale in New Haven and comes home almost every weekend, as his romance with the fetching young Sarah Lawrence student, Jennifer, is still going strong. Skipper Marshall is at Middlebury College in Vermont and has a girl friend named Sadie who is doing much to brighten his life.

When her contract with WWKK expired in early 1987, Alexandra Waring moved to Washington, D.C., as a network correspondent, where her fame and popularity are expanding to national proportions. She was the first of Michael's contacts to come through for him with free-lance work. Though Alexandra and Cassy have not seen each other since 1986, the women correspond regularly in newsy, cheerful letters that are read by the entire Cochran family.

In the beginning, when he first returned home, Cassy and Michael acted like two comrades at the end of a great war, beaten and dazed, instinctively taking their places at each other's sides until the fatigue of battle left them. It left Michael first. And it was not long after he was out on the road that Cassy came to suspect that there was someone out on the road with him. But she did not ignore it. She asked him about it. And he told her the truth. Yes, there was.

The Cochrans have decided to let some time pass, to go on as a family, to see where life is taking them—together or separately. They do make love on occasion, still, and they both call 162 Riverside Drive home, still, and they will always, always, share the joys of their son.

Cassy is in therapy with a psychiatrist she likes very much, sorting and sifting through the years of her life, trying to arrive at answers in the places where only questions have existed. She still runs WST (yes, they got their transmitter fixed, and yes, Cassy did take a film crew up to see Sister Mary at the Children's Clinic, and yes, WST did win several awards for the Caswell Zander story), but Cassy is delegating more and more responsibility to department heads, with her sights moving closer and closer toward news. But she is not sure yet, not sure at all, about how or when to try to make the transition. But just the fact that it seems possible to her makes her realize just how much she has changed. With the first half of her life behind her, no one is more surprised than Cassy at the growing sense of freedom she feels about how she might wish to live the second.

Cassy can be seen most mornings walking to work along the promenade that borders Riverside Park. And she can be seen most evenings sitting by the living-room window, work papers in her lap, her eyes looking out to the river.

ABOUT THE AUTHOR

Laura Van Wormer grew up in Fairfield County, Connecticut, and graduated from the Newhouse School at Syracuse University. A former book editor and media writer, she has lived in the Riverside Drive neighborhood for ten years. This is her first novel.